SWORD OF LIGHTNING

He raised the sword on high, moved body, thought, and will in a certain way that pierced the Overworld, then swung down again—and tore the sky asunder.

"Zeff of the Ninth Face," Avall roared, through the wind and lightning he had summoned and was about to release, "your fate is mine, and it starts for you tomorrow!"

And with that he aimed the sword at the top of a distant mountain. And once again he clove the sky asunder. Fire blazed up on the horizon as a tree he could not see yet knew existed exploded into fire.

A firm pressure curled around his sword arm, and fingers pried at his palm. "No, brother," Merryn whispered. "It's a joy and a temptation. But never forget that first and foremost it's a weapon."

Rann reached up to unbuckle the chinstrap. "It's rained for three days," he chuckled. "I hope that'll be sufficient to forestall any fires your...impulse may have ignited."

"Not for Zeff," Avall snapped. "Not ever."

WARAUTUMN

A TALE OF ERON

TOM DEITZ

BANTAM BOOKS

New York Toronto London Sydney Auckland

WARAUTUMN

A Bantam Spectra Book / August 2002

SPECTRA and the portrayal of a boxed "s" are trademarks of Bantam Books,
a division of Random House, Inc.

Copyright © 2002 by Tom Deitz
Cover art copyright © 2002 by Gary Ruddell
Map by James Sinclair

ISBN 0-553-38071-0

Published simultaneously in the United States and Canada

Bantam Books are published by Bantam Books, a division of Random House, Inc.
Its trademark, consisting of the words "Bantam Books" and the portrayal of a
rooster, is Registered in U.S. Patent and Trademark Office and in other countries.
Marca Registrada. Bantam Books, 1540 Broadway, New York, New York 10036.

PRINTED IN THE UNITED STATES OF AMERICA

OPM   10 9 8 7 6 5 4 3 2 1

for
the past, present, and future members of the
Delta Gamma Drama Society
at
Young Harris College
Proof that one *old dog can learn new tricks*

Acknowledgments

Phil Albert
Sharon Albert
Anne Lesley Groell
Linda Jean Jeffery
Tom Jeffery
Betty Marchinton
Buck Marchinton
Larry Marchinton
Deena McKinney
Howard Morhaim
Lindsay Sagnette
Juliet Ulman

and especially John Butler and T. J. Cochran,
who just ambled in and made themselves at home

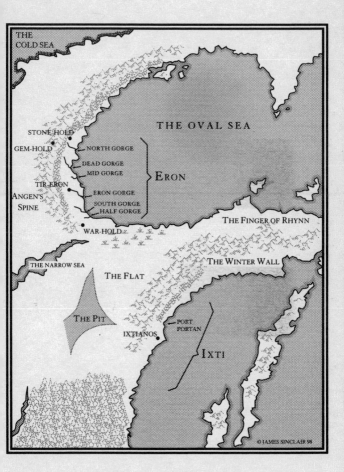

THE COLD SEA

THE OVAL SEA

STONE-HOLD

GEM-HOLD

NORTH GORGE

DEAD GORGE

MID GORGE

ERON

TIR-ERON

ERON GORGE

SOUTH GORGE

HALF GORGE

ANGEN'S SPINE

WAR-HOLD

THE FINGER OF RHYNN

THE NARROW SEA

THE WINTER WALL

THE FLAT

THE PIT

IXTIANOS

PORT FORTAN

IXTI

© JAMES SINCLAIR 98

PART I

CHAPTER I:

BRIEFINGS

*...fire and war and a forest and a valley—and a fabulous hold
hewn into a mountainside...*

Torchlight gleamed on the smooth copper alloy that surfaced the eleven siege towers ranged in a shot-long file at the
foot of what had once been a long, grassy slope—a slope now
studded with neat rows of alert, though seated, warriors, each
with a naked sword laid crossways across his or her mail-clad
knees. That same light showed on the dozen trebuchets atop
that slope, and on the dozen more of each device secreted in
the woods a quarter shot behind the ridge that rimmed half
that incipient battleground.

Lesser fires flared in the field before the towers, their
furtive, shielded flames fixed at precise intervals along a palisade of carefully cut posts twice as tall as a man. The adver-
sary waited behind that barrier, vigilant in the twilight—yet
token resistance at best, in view of the massive hold looming at
its back. Their presence there was a feint: a calculated show
made solely to enforce the illusion of overwhelming opposition.

Flames smaller yet dotted the massive arcades that spangled

the upper third of the hold—Gem-Hold-Winter, to be precise—from end to end, north to south: more torches, with the odd glow-globe thrown in. The effect was to wash the upper reaches of that edifice with vertical stains of crimson, as though it burned already. Its roots were white, however: white as ashes—or white as a too-hot forge—save where a span-wide crack six spans high showed like the shadow of a blasted tree just south of its center, its edges softened by the soot of recent conflagration.

Only the mountains beyond the hold were not firelit. Yet even there the last rays of a setting sun limned scarlet edges along the snowcapped peaks of Angen's Spine, whose bulk was already one vast black cutout against a sky purpling into night.

War could be beautiful, thought Vorinn syn Ferr-een, as more torchlight touched that which crowned his head: the high-domed helm of the War Commander of the Kingdom of Eron, which he had worn since this campaign had begun—though without that which now encumbered its lower rim: the narrow band of the Regent's circlet, which he had worn for less than a hand. Light glanced off Vorinn's mail, too, and off the embroidery bordering his surcoat of Warcraft crimson that soaked up firelight like water soaked up salt.

For perhaps a dozen breaths, he studied the vista before him, then turned smartly and strode back into the forest that cloaked the heights opposite the besieged hold.

It was a forest that also cloaked an army—the Royal Army of Eron, in fact, come here to Megon Vale to quell an...impropriety wrought by an increasingly powerful and rebellious sect within a powerful and long-established clan.

Had it only been half an eighth? Vorinn wondered, as long, strong strides carried him through a gate in his own palisade and thence past forges, armories, and clusters of four-man tents, interspersed with supply caravans and corrals well stocked with horses. There were mess tents, too, and bathing tents, and larger tents that marked the headquarters of clans, crafts, and officers of state.

In the center of the whole vast, sprawling array stood a tent only slightly larger than the rest, its canvas dyed the maroon of Clan Argen. Argen was not Vorinn's clan, however, but that of another, less martially inclined, man who also happened, though imprisoned, to be Vorinn's brother-in-law—and King. A cluster of smaller tents nestled against the larger one, these the province of what had been that Sovereign's household.

—Which were now Vorinn's to do with as he would, though he had not spent even one night there, having come to the Regency a scant four fingers past.

Which was why he had demanded—and been granted by his anxious Council—half a hand alone. He was ready now. Ready to confront the future.

They were waiting for him when he ducked inside the tent: a dozen anxious warriors, half of whom were kin. He sought the latter from reflex, notably his vigorous, middle-aged uncle, Tryffon syn Ferr, Craft-Chief of Warcraft; and the Chief of Clan Ferr itself: his aged two-father, Preedor. Lady Veen was there as well: Shift-Chief of the Royal Guard; along with a few more clan- and craft-kin—mostly cousins. For the rest, there was a scatter of men and women drawn from other clans and crafts than Ferr and War—notably Nyll of Gem and Eekkar of Myrk—for it would be unwise to make what now looked to be a long-term siege seem but a single clan's endeavor.

Four of them were new anyway, because four of the faces Vorinn was accustomed to seeing around this table were moving—and *not* in a way that betokened a quick return. He tallied the absentees grimly: Rann syn Eemon-arr, the captive King's bond-brother, who had been Regent as recently as that afternoon; the half brothers Lykkon and Bingg syn Argen-a; Myx syn Eemon-ine; and Riff syn Ioray. He did not name them what some already did, however, which was either rebel or traitor. A decision on that awaited more information.

For now, he had to confront not one but two all-but-impossible occurrences.

"Chiefs and Commanders," he murmured in general

acknowledgment, as he claimed his accustomed place to the left of the vacant King's Seat, pointedly ignoring the chair to its right, which had belonged to the King's chief adviser: that same absent Rann.

"Lord Regent," a few voices murmured back, given force by the solid rumble of Tryffon, who was an island of stability amid a sea of chaos and rumor.

Vorinn glanced around in search of a squire, expecting the ever-attentive Bingg to appear with wine and food unasked. But it wasn't that smart, sprightly thirteen-year-old who served them, but an unfamiliar young woman in Woodcraft's brown and orange. Still, wine was wine, and Vorinn accepted the well-cooled mug with courtesy, took two sips, then addressed the assembly at last.

"Have we found someone to give a clear account?" he asked with so much force to his voice that what he had intended to be a casual query came close to being a demand—a tendency he would have to watch. His gaze fixed first on Veen, then on Tryffon.

Those two exchanged glances in turn.

"I would know what happened at the hold first," Vorinn added, to break what seemed an impasse of decision.

Tryffon puffed his cheeks, looking relieved, then motioned to a solidly built man of about thirty who had been waiting patiently in a corner. He wore Lore's bronze, quartered with Argen's maroon, beneath a cloak of Warcraft crimson. "Levvin, if you would?"

The soldier rose promptly, looking competent and dour—though much of a mold with his countrymen, with black hair; clean, angular features; smooth skin; and dark blue eyes. And if that hair was shorter than the norm, well this was war, and long hair both a hindrance and a risk, especially to one unhelmed in battle.

"Lord Regent," Levvin acknowledged formally, with a tiny nod. "And Council Lords. I am here to serve you."

"Your clansmen are known for accurate observations and

unprejudiced reporting," Vorinn replied in turn, with somewhat forced formality. "Therefore, please tell us what you saw transpire on Gem-Hold's lowest arcade a finger before today's sunset, more or less. Omit nothing, no matter how unlikely or difficult to believe."

Levvin took a deep breath and nodded again, this time with conviction. Typical of his clan-kin under such circumstances, he also closed his eyes, the better to confirm the images called forth by a well-trained memory.

"It was as you said," he began: "A finger before sunset, more or less, and the side of the hold facing our forces was graying into shadow. I was watching through distance lenses, as was my duty. I had been assigned the center of the lowest arcade to survey, which happened to be the one on which those in control of the hold had exposed High King Avall."

He paused. "Shall I describe that as well? I was watching when they lowered him over the side."

Vorinn glanced sideways to where a scribe in Lore's livery was taking down the account. "Briefly, for the record."

"Very well," Levvin continued promptly. "Just past sunrise of this same day, the Regent, Rann syn Eemon-arr, demanded that the usurper-Chief of Gem-Hold-Winter, Zeff of the Ninth Face, surrender himself, his armies, and the hold to the cause of Law and Justice in Eron. Rann gave him until noon to respond, and at noon Rann and many of you here—I could list them if need be—received Zeff's reply. Zeff, who had absented himself after Rann's ultimatum, appeared on the lowest arcade in full war gear appropriate to his clan and station, but also bearing the replicas of the so-called magic regalia, which he had captured when he captured the King, including, in particular, the replica of what has come to be called the Lightning Sword. Instead of relinquishing the hold, however, he motioned eight men forward, and together they lowered a circular tabletop a little more than a span in diameter over the balustrade, fixing it to the rail from behind by a means we could not determine. This disk was draped in white fabric that appeared to be a Ninth Face winter-cloak, which was then re-moved. Beneath it was the King, Avall syn Argen-a, with his arms, legs, and torso clamped spread-eagled to the wood, and with his feet set on a platform so that he might not suffocate. He was naked—I assume to prove that he had not been muti-lated and thereby rendered unfit to reign. Zeff then proceeded to mock our demand, and countered with a demand of his own—that we had until dawn tomorrow to withdraw our forces. In punctuation of that threat, he raised his sword—which, though it appears exactly *like* the sword called the Lightning Sword in form and substance, lacks that one's magi-cal properties, so we supposed—and slashed it down in an arc from sky to earth. An explosion ensued—not quite lightning, though that is the only word that seems even vaguely appropri-ate—and the siege tower to the immediate right of the Regent's tower was destroyed and several soldiers killed. At that time the Regent's party withdrew."

"All of which we knew," one of the younger subchiefs noted from the far end of the table.

"It is needed for the record," Tryffon snapped. "Be silent."

Levvin nodded appreciation, took another sip of wine, and continued. "Zeff withdrew as well, but nothing else changed as the day waned. Avall remained where he was: exposed below the arcade. Three soldiers guarded him at all times, one of whom was changed every hand. A finger before sunset, three more guards returned, this time escorting a man in a plain white robe whom we identified as Kylin syn Omyrr, late the High King's harpist, and more lately prisoner in Gem-Hold by his own actions, for reasons that are still unclear. In any case, Kylin was seated and a harp set beside him, but he was not at that time asked to play. A moment later, Zeff returned, in the company of two more guards, whereupon those who had es-corted Kylin departed. Kylin then played for Zeff—four songs, we think—and then Zeff appeared to offer him wine and filled a goblet for him with his own hands. The account now becomes…difficult. From what I could discern—for it was growing dark and no torches had yet been lit on the arcade—Kylin reached for the goblet. Instead of taking it, however, he reached *past* it and seized the sword Zeff had worn earlier when he called the lightning. Kylin then moved *very* quickly—more quickly than I would say a man *could* move, and certainly a blind one like Kylin—and unsheathed the sword at the same time that he reached around the side of the tabletop and grabbed Avall's wrist with his other hand. And—"

He broke off, gnawing his lip, as though he were at a loss for words. "And then," he went on at last, "he—it seemed the two of them disappeared. There was no smoke, no light, simply an *absence*. One moment Avall was on full display, the next, he was gone. The clamps that had held him remained, and they appeared to be closed and locked, but he was no longer in them."

"And Zeff?" From Vorinn.

"Zeff acted like a man who had been stunned—but only for a moment. He slapped at his side as though the sword were still present, then leapt forward as though to check on Avall—he had to race his guardsmen to do this—and, when he was satisfied that Avall was indeed...gone, stood up very straight, shivered twice, turned on his heel, and returned inside."

"I'd give a lot to hear what he said then," Tryffon chuckled, as Levvin opened his eyes again. "It's easy to maintain dignity for a dozen breaths; two dozen is four times as hard."

"I'll remember that," Vorinn observed dryly. Then, to the assembly at large: "This account is entirely consistent with what we first heard reported. Does anyone have anything to add? Or any questions?"

"Not I, at the moment," Tryffon replied. "If I think of any, I know where to find Levvin."

Vorinn waited three breaths longer, then glanced at Levvin, who still stood at full report. "You have done your duty and more. Go with our thanks and good will, off duty for the rest of the night, save as we may find need to summon you."

Once Levvin had departed, Vorinn nodded to Veen, who motioned another soldier to rise from the same bench where Levvin had been seated. "Forima," she said, to the slim, dark young woman in Glasscraft livery, "you were closest to Lykkon's tent when this transpired. Would you please tell us what you witnessed there?"

Forima looked distinctly uncomfortable, even frightened, yet when she spoke her voice was calm. "I wish I had more to report, Lady," she began, "and a clearer memory of what I *did* see. If any of you have questions, please feel free to ask, as I don't know what details might be important to you. In any case, what I witnessed—experienced might be a better term—was this.

"It was almost exactly sunset, and I had just left my tent to begin the trek to the front, where I was to replace my bond-sister, who was already stationed there. I was in full armor, but had not yet donned my helm. For whatever reason, my route took me directly past Lykkon's tent—I would have been no more than a span away from it, at closest. I heard voices within, but thought little of it, though I knew of the...disagreement within the Council that had occurred earlier in the day. Then, suddenly, I heard a noise—not so much a boom or an actual explosion, as a cracking sound, as though someone had snapped a whip or shaken a sheet of leather. At one with this, I saw the tent...light up from within, as though someone had dropped a glow-globe. The tent's sides bulged as well, and I heard the sounds of items falling or being thrown about. This alarmed me, and I flinched away and fell. By the time I had found my feet again, I heard more voices, but the only words I could make out clearly were someone crying 'Avall' and another calling out, 'Kylin'—both as if surprised. Fearing that something terrible had transpired, I returned to Lykkon's tent. Perhaps I called out, I don't remember. I do recall debating whether to enter without permission, for by that time I was certain that I heard His Majesty's voice. And then I heard more sounds—it sounded like men wrestling—and then I heard metal hitting metal—and was immediately struck...not so much by any force, as by a wave of cold that was— It was like a giant fist had thrust out of that tent, reached into me, and grabbed all the heat from my body. I couldn't breathe, and I think I fell again. When I revived—it was no more than a few breaths later—I was shivering, and others were emerging from nearby tents, also shivering. I called out to Lykkon, but got no reply. I then shouted that I was coming in, but when I looked inside, the place was in complete disarray—which is when I went in search of you. The rest you know."

"And you are certain you saw no one leave?" Preedor inquired carefully.

Forima shook her head. "Not on the side on which I stood, on which lay the only proper exit. I am told there was no sign of anyone cutting a way out elsewhere."

"They space-jumped," Veen concluded flatly. "Simple enough. Zeff would have had to use the master gem in order to wield the sword as he did. We know he had it, because Avall was wearing it when he was captured. Kylin must have sensed its presence as well, and taken a very large risk that he could use it to jump away."

"But the thing's mad!" one of the younger Warcraft chiefs protested.

"Apparently that madness is variable and subjective," Vorinn retorted. "I gather that Avall had regained some control over it. And we already know that the gems seem to act to Avall's benefit, since he's the one who found the first one. Even mad, it might act—or incite one to act—in Avall's favor if given the chance. Maybe. I know it's a stretch, but it's the only one we have."

"And what about what happened in Lykkon's tent?"

Vorinn shrugged. "It would make sense for Kylin and Avall to jump back here when they disappeared from Gem-Hold. I would have thought they would reappear in Avall's quarters, but perhaps they wound up in Lykkon's because that was where the largest concentration of their comrades was.

Or—more likely—because that's where Rann was—we all know how close he and Avall are. In any case, whatever happened there happened *very* quickly and may well have involved some degree of impulse—even madness, given that the mad gem was a factor."

"And what *did* happen?" From a confused-looking Stonecraft subchief named Dessann, who had been asked to join the Council at the same time Vorinn had taken the Regency—mostly to represent Stone, which had lost Rann and Myx.

Vorinn leaned back in his chair, fingers laced across his chest. "It appears that Avall—and Kylin, Rann, Lykkon, Bingg, Myx, and Riff—and about half the furnishings in that tent—jumped away. We have no idea where they went, but it doesn't seem to be nearby." He paused. "No, actually, I *do* have an idea, but it's only that. We know that the gems often act on pure instinct and will, and I can easily imagine that Avall—if he was in control of the gem, which makes most sense—wanted nothing more at the moment he found himself free than to join his sister, or else his wife. In either case, he's shots away by now."

Tryffon tugged his short gray beard. "But if they went to where Merryn is, and she has the real regalia, they could be back here anytime."

Dessann looked even more confused. "Forgive my ignorance, fellow Councilors, but I appear to have missed some crucial information—"

Vorinn glanced at Tryffon. "No one told him? I tend to forget who knows how much about what."

"Apparently not everything," Tryffon replied, scowling at Dessann. "Where did we lose you?" he asked tolerantly.

Dessann shook his head. "I know about the gems—all subchiefs do, at least those who came from Tir-Eron. That is, I know their history, and I know that they power the regalia. But this talk of replica regalia and space-jumping, and—"

Vorinn lifted a brow at Tryffon. "It appears we keep secrets better than we thought." A pause, then: "Very well, to catch you up *very* briefly, with a promise of details filled in later, the situation is this:

"Not long after Avall became King, he began to feel that the regalia—the magic regalia, I mean—constituted a threat, both from people who might want to steal it and to himself or any successor who might use it too eagerly or capriciously so that it came to be regarded as a crutch. For this reason, Avall had duplicate regalia made—very *fine* duplicates, I might add—and had false gems inserted into the various items, since he reasoned—rightly, I think—that a great deal of the regalia's power came from people's *idea* of it—power their fears and beliefs *subsumed* upon it, as it were—which has nothing to do with the effects produced by its actual use. Once the duplicates were completed, he dispatched the only person he could truly entrust with such a mission—his sister, Merryn—to conceal the real regalia in a place only she would know. With her, he sent all the other gems, except the mad one—the master gem, we sometimes call it."

"The one he was wearing when Zeff captured him?" Dessann ventured.

"Correct. And of course he was also wearing the duplicate regalia then, though very few outside this Council knew that at the time—either that he was wearing it, or that it was 'false'—"

"Not false enough, apparently," Dessann muttered.

Vorinn glared at him. "Suffice it to say that far too soon after Merryn was dispatched to hide the regalia, we received word that Gem-Hold had fallen, and that the regalia was required—one way or another—to ransom it. Obviously we needed to retrieve it, and before anyone could stop her, Avall's Consort-apparent, Strynn, took that task upon herself—she and a woodswoman named Div. The fact that neither she nor Merryn has reappeared with it tells us that she has not yet succeeded."

"And this 'jumping'?"

"Simply stated: the ability to disappear in one place and reappear more or less instantly in another, using the power of the gems—which suck heat from anything alive nearby when they are used thusly. It actually happened a few times at the Battle of Storms, but most people missed it."

"And that's all?"

"That's enough for now."

"Indeed," Tryffon echoed. "Which brings us back to Merryn."

Vorinn nodded. "So I was thinking. And that, in turn, presents two scenarios. Either Merryn has not yet hidden the regalia, in which case—should Avall have jumped to where she is—they should indeed be back here very soon; or else she *has* hidden it, and they will have to retrieve it. And in the *latter* case, they could either jump to the hiding place quickly— which I doubt, because of the number of people involved, but which could have them back here by sunrise, since Avall will know about the ultimatum—or else they will have to proceed afoot—which will take who-knows-how-long."

Tryffon looked troubled indeed. "So we basically have to contrive three plans: one in case Avall returns before dawn with the regalia, one in case he returns without it, and one in which he does *not* return."

Vorinn regarded him solemnly. "Correct."

"At least the balance has shifted," Veen offered. "Two hands ago Zeff had two major bargaining points: He had the King, and he had the master gem. Now he has neither. If we move in the morning, we could very well force his hand, even without the regalia. Why, if Avall can do all this jumping, there's nothing to keep him from jumping into the hold itself and settling matters there without us even being involved."

Tryffon looked startled. "That's true. It would also be just like him."

"Two good points," Vorinn conceded. "Which I think mean we've decided that the least we do at dawn is remain where we are."

Tryffon grinned through his whiskers. "A siege is still a siege, eh, boy? And even without magic on our side, we're stronger."

"But they've got blackmail on their side," Veen warned. "Avall was the King, but he was only one man. There are still a thousand innocent people in that hold. Who's to say who Zeff will serve up on a tabletop next?"

"The subchiefs of War and Ferr, I'd be willing to bet," Tryffon growled. "Or Crim herself."

"Or all the chiefs," Preedor suggested. "That's what I'd do, if I was ruthless."

"Maybe even Rrath," Tryffon took up again. "To show they would even sacrifice their own."

Vorinn snorted. "*Rrath?* Well, they probably do consider him a traitor, so he'd be expendable in that regard. On the other hand, he was unconscious the last we heard of him. Besides which, they don't dare kill him, because—conscious—he knows more about the gems than anyone else they've got to hand."

Veen cleared her throat. "Speaking of Rrath, has anyone told Esshill about all this? He'll have heard anyway, by now; but I think we owe it to him."

Vorinn scratched his chin. "No, and I suppose we ought to." He glanced up at the squire. "Do you know where—?"

The girl nodded and darted out—only to return an instant later with a spare, tired-looking young man of twenty, dressed in plain Argen-a livery, for all he was not Argen-a. His eyes were grim, his mouth a thin, hard line.

"He was on his way here," the squire explained. "We met in transit."

"And I can imagine why," Vorinn murmured, motioning Esshill to one of the spare seats they always kept open in the Council Tent. "You are Rrath syn Garnill's bond-brother, is that correct?"

Esshill nodded glumly. "I am," he added after a breath, for courtesy.

"And you are no doubt aware that affairs have changed, as far as the King's captivity is concerned?"

Esshill looked uncomfortable. "I know that Avall disappeared from the arcade at Gem-Hold, that Kylin might have been involved, and that they may have returned here, and vanished again, with half the Regency Council."

Vorinn nodded in turn. "And what you want to know is whether this in any way involved Rrath?"

Esshill tensed, but would not look at anyone. "I'm grateful anyone remembered him," he said harshly—"and surprised."

"He's a prisoner the same as everyone else in the hold," Vorinn replied with forced calm. "We've as much concern for him as for anyone—except the King, of course—and you have to understand that."

"I do—in theory. That is, my head does. My heart doesn't. My *heart* says that Rrath has been used over and over—and I've had to suffer through it at least as badly as Rann has suffered because of Avall."

"Agreed," Tryffon rumbled. "But you must in turn concede that Rrath is very smart, for all he might also be a fool. But in either case, it was his choice to cast his lot with the Ninth Face—of which decision, so I am aware, you were not informed."

"I wasn't," Esshill retorted. "And believe me, I *will* have an accounting of him for that if he ever regains consciousness. Until then"—he looked down again, eyes bright with tears—"it would— Forgive me, Lords, but I must say this— It would be nice if I had any sense at all that even one of you cared a broken stone about my bond-mate's fate."

"If you have strong words to say," Tryffon broke in, "you would be wise to say them now. I'd rather we knew where we stood with you than have you suddenly go rogue and betray us."

Esshill looked up sharply. "I'm no traitor," he snapped. "Never to my Kingdom, and only to my clan when they moved without me. For his part, I have no choice but to respect

Avall for doing everything he could for my bond-brother. But you must be aware that Rrath's in danger in there. He knows as much about the gems as anyone, and that information is valuable. Unconscious, he's safe. But they'll want to revive him, and since he's already betrayed them, they'll have no reason to go easy on him. Which is why I pray every moment that he doesn't revive."

"So do we," Vorinn agreed.

"Is there—I don't suppose there's any chance that he got out when Avall did, or as part of that?"

Vorinn shook his head, grateful that he didn't have to explain about jumping—and that Esshill seemed to have kept silent about it as well; they didn't want the whole army knowing. "Not that we're aware of. From what little we've been able to piece together, when one jumps with the master gem, one generally takes any human one is touching along with one, together with whatever clothes and accoutrements he or she is wearing. Depending on circumstances—and this would seem to involve two people jumping together—it also appears to take whatever easily portable objects are in the vicinity: a rug one might be standing on, for instance; but not something otherwise fixed, like the tabletop to which Avall was clamped. That's the only way we can explain how Avall and Rrath jumped away with all that gear that was in Rrath's caravan when we were back at the Face's citadel on the day they both got captured: because both of them were in the bond, and those two minds were strong enough to...attract their immediate environment."

He broke off, because Esshill's face had gone cold again. "Damn him for that, too."

"I think it took them both by surprise," Vorinn responded. "I can't imagine that Avall would have tried to jump into the Ninth Face's citadel, and certainly not with Rrath. We're all but certain that he was seeking information and the whole affair went out of control."

"Bond-brother as exploitable resource," Esshill growled.

"That's another one Avall and I will have to work out between ourselves."

"As is your right," Vorinn conceded. "But that assumes much and in any case is for later. For now, we wanted you to know that we *are* aware of your situation and that we're doing as much as we can—but that there are a great many variables at work here which *no one* has ever faced before. In the meantime, consider yourself at liberty. You can fight if you want; you can be a squire if you want; you can sleep all day if you want. The only constraint is that you must remain in camp. We don't dare risk your doing something brave and foolish like Kylin did. It appears they underrated him. They won't repeat that error, especially now that matters have shifted in our favor."

Esshill looked up again, his face not one whit warmer. "I appreciate the intent," he said formally. "Now, if you have no further need of me—"

"Not now," Vorinn replied. "You may let yourself out."

"Lord," Esshill acknowledged stiffly—and with that he rose and departed.

"We'll have to watch that one," Tryffon opined, when a hand of breaths had expired. "He's balanced on the knife edge between loyalty to Priest-Clan and to us. More importantly, he's balanced between love of his bond-brother and anyone who can ensure that brother's survival, and hatred of anyone who threatens him—either of which, depending on circumstances, could be us."

Vorinn nodded grimly. "Trust me, Uncle, that watch him I shall."

CHAPTER II:

SHELTERING

"Finally!" Div groaned shamelessly, pointing through curtains of cold gray rain toward a deeper darkness in the canyon wall to their left that *might* indicate a cave in which she, Strynn, one birkit, and two horses could shelter for the night. They had been toiling up this barren, rocky defile for what seemed like days (though it was barely an eighth of one), all the while keeping close watch on the quick mountain stream beside them, lest it rise far enough to constitute a threat. The parent threat—the rain—had caught them out three hands past noon, but the stream—blessedly—still frothed and rumbled half a span below the level stretch of bank that comprised what passed for a path in this particular part of the Wild. The Eight knew there were no actual trails here, three days southwest of War-Hold-Winter, because nobody in their right mind came here; one way was therefore as good as another.

Which was fine, if one were wandering aimlessly about on holiday, but not if one were trying to track someone—*two* someones, actually, since the previous evening. And *that* extra body complicated things, too, because most of their initial progress had come from Strynn knowing Merryn so well she could second-guess her. But that had been before Merryn had acquired a companion—probably her war-shocked former comrade-in-arms, Krynneth syn Mozz-een, if a few scanty, and somewhat disturbing, clues were any indication.

Now they had to rely mostly on the birkit, because the finding stone Strynn wore on a chain around her neck merely indicated the direction in which Merryn's matching stone lay, not the distance between them. Unfortunately, even that sketchy information was often rendered useless by cliffs too sheer to climb or rivers too wide to ford, which obliged them to take detour after detour, and required them to recheck their route a dozen times a day, which further slowed their progress.

Nor was Div's woodcraft of much help, since the ground was too rocky to show prints—though she had spotted scrapes upon the stones that could have been made by horseshoes. The birkit—which mostly tracked by scent—agreed. Indeed, it was that semisapient, bear-sized carnivore that had insisted they turn from the wide alpine meadow they had been traversing, and into this darksome declivity between two fire mountains, one of which was still alive and rumbling. Never had Div been so close to one, nor wanted to be so far away. They would be totally at the beast's mercy after today, too, because this downpour would erase any other tracks that might be present. That it would also wash away a great deal of scent did not brook contemplation.

Then again, most of what she wanted to contemplate right now centered on being warm, dry, and asleep—for that day's trek, as no other, had worn both her and Strynn down to the nubs of their endurance, with the result that they were panting heavily, stumbling often, yawning frequently, and having trouble thinking at more than an instinctive level.

"Finally," Div said again—because she wanted to hear a human voice and Strynn had not responded.

"Finally indeed," Strynn muttered behind her, sounding tired, miserable, and grouchy, not all of which, Div suspected, could be blamed on fatigue and rain. *Eight deliver her from pregnant women!* Slogging through the Wild with one seemed to be her lot of late—though whether that was to remind her of the discomfort she no longer had to worry about, barren as she was, or to rub that fact in her face, she had no idea.

They were both walking at present because the horses—Div's stallion, White Sky; and Strynn's mare, File—had borne them steadily all afternoon and were overdue for a rest, and the footing thereabouts was problematical anyway. She only hoped there was room for their mounts in the cave, for all that the horses were born to weather storms like this and worse. Misery was misery, regardless of one's shape or skin.

"Another finger, I think," Div called back. Her voice rang loud off the rocks, only to be muffled by the rain. It was an odd effect and somewhat eerie. Div shuddered from more than mountain chill.

"I hope," Strynn retorted. "All that's keeping me awake is walking." Without breaking stride, she shrugged her sodden, stone-colored cloak higher on her shoulders so as to shift the edge of her hood farther beyond her face. Div did the same, further blurring the distinctions of class, age, and build that would have marked them as coming from different worlds a year ago, but now made no difference at all, and certainly not in how they got along, which was famously.

For another shot they trudged onward, their minds thick with thoughts of rest, while their bodies continued to pick their way across a mixture of mud and slippery rocks, on one of which White Star would have fallen had Div not offered a steadying hand. Only the birkit padding ahead seemed unperturbed. Then again, it was a creature of the Wild, with a double coat to ward off weather. With its low-slung stance and thick, steel-gray summer fur, it was almost invisible against the rocks—especially when both were veiled by rain.

Indeed, it finally disappeared entirely, only to attract their attention by yowling directly above their heads—from a ledge they hadn't seen, but which, a few spans farther on, proved easier to reach than the cave that had been their goal, and which subsequently revealed a larger cave than the one she'd first spotted had been: easily four spans across the front and half that high, with a dry floor; the whole sufficiently capacious that the horses would not have to share much of their mistresses' space.

Nor did it take more than a breath to realize that someone had camped there before them: Merryn and Krynneth, in fact, to judge by the distinctive prints of Merryn's horse's shoes. Which was pretty much what they had expected.

What they *hadn't* expected was that a great many other hoofmarks showed there as well—two with Ixtian shoes—along with the spoor of a number of men, who, by their boots' characteristic heels, were also Ixtian. Div's heart gave a little double-thump at that, though they both knew that bands of renegade Ixtians who would not accept the fact that their side had lost the recent war still harried the fringes of the southland like mosquitoes harried the marshfolk. But what filled her with a sense of alarm even her fatigue could not dispel was the fact that the Ixtians' tracks were the same age as Merryn's and Krynneth's. Which meant that two of their closest friends had somehow fallen in with their country's recently defeated foes.

At least that was the assessment Div made all in a flash, even as she heard Strynn gasp, and knew that her companion had made precisely the same judgment. "Tell me those aren't what I think they are," Strynn choked, her voice gone low and shaky with what Div feared was very close kin to the resigned hysteria of someone at the end of endurance suddenly confronted with one more trial to bear.

"If we can guess from here, I don't think we'll change our minds when we get closer," Div heard herself saying, even as she dismounted.

Strynn hit the ground almost as fast as she did. And groaned. "You're right," she said numbly, through what Div only hoped was shiver born of cold.

Div regarded her levelly—someone had to remain calm after all, and, in light of what present circumstances indicated, hat someone was unlikely to be Strynn. "Let me stress this as trongly as I can right now," Div began, wishing she had more aith in what she was about to say. "We don't know *what* this neans. It could mean a lot or it could mean nothing. It—"

"*Nothing!*" Strynn all but shrieked, pointing to the nearest roup of prints. "You call those nothing? There's no way Merryn would have taken up with a group of Ixtians of her wn free will. Think, Div! She was carrying the regalia! The *uagic* regalia. There's no way on Angen she would have let nything that powerful anywhere near Ixtian hands."

Div's eyes went huge, even as her will to do anything but leep receded. She shook her head to clear it. "Yes, I know— trynn, I'm sorry. I'm tired and I'm sleepy, and my brain urned off for just a moment. But—"

"But what?" Strynn raged. "My bond-sister has almost cerainly been taken captive; that seems to be a fact. Those captors ow have the most powerful weapon on Angen, and we have o idea what they plan to do with it. Or—"

"If they plan to do anything!" Div snapped. "You're assuming a lot of things, Strynn— You're—" She broke off and lumped down in place, suddenly shaking. "We—We *have* to e rational, Strynn." She slapped the stone cave floor for emhasis, then folded her arms around herself and remained vhere she was, staring at the rain.

The birkit was staring too—first at Div, then at Strynn. Div elt as much as heard what she had come to know as its warnng growl begin deep within the creature's throat. Her already nuddled mind clogged even further as the beast thrust its houghts among them curiously—probably seeking to learn vhat had her so upset.

"Rational!" Strynn spat, through a scowl that spoke of more ersonal discomfort. But something about the way she stood roved that she had regained a modicum of control. Or peraps that had been the birkit, too: damping down strong emoions, as it was wont to do when tempers threatened to get out f hand. "No, you're right," she managed at last. "We've seen small evidence and used it to reach big conclusions. We're assuming that because Merry and Kryn are outnumbered they're not in control. But both of them are Night Guard; these other are probably Ixtian regulars at best; it would be no problem for the two of them together to get the upper hand, if it even came to that."

"Assuming that Merryn and Kryn are still allies, which, let me remind you, is not a given."

Strynn glared at her. "Thank you for the optimism."

Div found her feet again and motioned toward the rain "We have to be practical, Strynn. It's raining and night's coming on. Much as I know we'd both like to start out thi very moment to find out what's happened to Merry, we can't— not and risk what might now be even more important than i was before, if this bunch of phantom Ixtians really have captured Merry and Kryn *and,* in a worst-case scenario, found an recognized the regalia. But think: If we can't continue, th odds are good that they can't either, given that this rainstorm looks pretty wide-ranging. In any case there's no way they car know we're following them, so whatever pace they've been making is the pace they'll continue to make. Therefore, if w stop here, we can rebuild our strength, contrive a course of action that's based on logic, not emotion—and scour this plac from top to bottom for more clues without wasting too muc time."

"You're right—of course," Strynn conceded. "Best we mak camp, then decide. Anything we do now is likely to get u killed, tired as we are. But I hate it."

"And the horses," Div reminded her. "They're worn-out a well—and we have to have them—to carry supplies, if nothing else. A rest now could result in us making better time tomor row."

You need to sleep, the birkit told them flatly, speaking—i that was the term—directly from mind to mind. *You g straight,* it continued helpfully. *Those-You-Seek go around.*

How do You know this? Strynn demanded.

*She dreams: You dream. When water falls like this . . . sometimes
we see those dreams and . . . know.*

Strynn fished the ring that bore the finding stone from the
neck of her tunic and stared at it speculatively, where it glittered like frozen fire on a chain, barely above the palm of her
other hand. "And there's always this. We'll never lose track of
them entirely."

Div didn't want to add that Strynn's assertion only held true
if Merryn still retained possession of her matching ring, but
didn't want to smother what was a barely waxing flame of rationality—in both of them, for she cared for Merryn almost as
much as Strynn did. "I think the Ixtians must be career soldiers," she said, instead. "Look how they've cleaned up after
themselves when they didn't have to."

Strynn nodded wearily. "Which also suggests that they
don't plan to return, which could be good or bad."

"I think," Div retorted, "it simply means that they're taking
matters as they come, just like we are. Now," she continued,
more loudly, "we have to put this behind us for a while.
There's nothing we can do at present but plan; we therefore
tend to business as usual. 'There is strength in routine,' my
one-mother used to say. We can think while we work, and the
work itself will help us think more clearly."

"'And one can endure anything as long as one knows how
long that enduring will last'—as *my* one-mother used to say,"
Strynn added, with a yawn. And with that she started toward
what had clearly been the previous tenants' fire pit.

Per their usual arrangement, Div, who had Beast-Hold con-
nections, attended the unpacking and care of the horses, while
Strynn made fire and saw to the rest of camp. It was good
they'd arrived when they had, too, because the rain was falling
harder than ever. There was also enough wind to whip those
crops about, though the steep sides of the ravine kept all but
the worst gusts at bay, even if enough still managed to find
their way in to irritate the quasi-feline birkit. Div thought that
odd, given that the beast had seemed untroubled when actually

out in the weather. Suddenly it seemed very human: willing to suffer stoically when there was no choice, but anxious to choose comfort when that was an alternative.

"Big fire or small?" Strynn asked, seeking solace in routine as she wandered over to help Div unharness their mounts. "It's not all that cold, but a big one would help us dry out. On the other hand, there's not enough firewood to see us through the night."

Div nodded toward the saddlebags she had just hoisted down. "We've dry clothes if we're lucky, and tomorrow might be sunny enough to dry these, if we make ourselves take the time. So I'd say we should change, then make a cook fire, eat dry what we can, and get a good night's sleep. The... previous tenants have left sleeping hollows, so we should avail ourselves of them."

Strynn stifled a yawn, then snared a saddlebag and padded off—barefoot—to lay out their bed pads and find dry clothes. When Div saw her again, she was naked and drying off with her towel. Her hair hung in damp black tendrils around her face, and even thus disarrayed she was beautiful. Taller and more full-figured than Div, whose body displayed a hard wiriness born of years in the Wild, Strynn's true distinction in a nation of beautiful people was the absolute symmetry of her face and—now Div saw it revealed—figure. The rest wasn't that different from other High Clan Eronese women—not even that different from Div, who had the same black hair (though shorter, for convenience), the same dark blue eyes, the same sharp cast of cheekbones and jaw.

Avall is luckier than he knows, Div thought, with a mental sigh. Twice lucky, actually, to have both Strynn *and* Rann as lovers—lovers who were not only beautiful, but brilliant and loyal as well. Either would die for him. She wondered if Rann would do as much for her.

No! she told herself. Better not to think of that now. Rann was far away with the army. Perhaps he was even now recov-

ering from a day of battle, for the army had certainly had time
to reach Gem-Hold-Winter. Perhaps—

No! she told herself again, and forced her mind into more
practical—and imminent—channels, all of which, not unexpectedly, wound up back at Merryn.

Strynn had found a dry undershift by then, and pulled it on.
Div located another amidst her jumble of garments and accepted Strynn's towel when her own proved damp from a bath
in a river that morning—a bath she had naïvely assumed
would be her sole wetting of the day.

Soon enough they were dry, the horses fed and tended, and
the birkit become less restless. Strynn got a small fire going,
then yawned again. "I'm sorry," she murmured, shaking out
her blankets in another homage to mindless routine, "but I
have *got* to get a nap. If you'll stand watch for a hand, I'll cook
when I wake up. Don't let me oversleep."

Silence. Then, from Div: "You don't think I'm crass for not
suggesting we go after Merry now?"

"No more than I am," Strynn replied seriously.

"Merry can take care of herself," Div continued through a
yawn of her own. "We need to remember that."

You need to sleep, the birkit told them again. *I will keep
watch.*

Div stared at the beast keenly, wondering if the sudden increase in fatigue she had felt wash over her with its "words"
was coincidence or something more purposeful, for she knew
that the beasts were more than casually tuned to human emotions and desires—and could sometimes link their own emotions to minds they had shared. A second yawn ambushed her,
then another. She finally gave up thinking and stretched out on
what, by its size and shape, might have been Krynneth's sleeping place.

Strynn lay down beside her, close enough to touch hands
but not to crowd. Thunder rumbled. The sky grew darker as
night advanced. Rain fell harder but never reached them. At

some point, the birkit inserted its firm, warm bulk between them. Still fighting it all the way, Div slept.

She awoke to find herself still lying on sandy stone beneath an overhang of harder rock, with someone close beside her. Yet when she sat up and looked around, it was to find the rain gone and the sun shining in what was obviously a glorious morning.

But...she had only meant to nap until dinner! Had she in fact slept through the night? A glance at Strynn beside her made her start. *Her floor-mate wasn't Strynn at all!* Rather, the face that blinked bleary eyes at her through a fringe of long black hair belonged to...*Rann.*

Chills raced over her—at which point something told her this was a dream, even as something else urged her not to fight it, that she was entitled to this much peace and joy, however ephemeral.

Rann smiled sleepily at her, then rolled back over, turning bare shoulders to her—shoulders that she saw to her surprise were tanned where by rights they should be white as marble.

Unable to confront such a novelty, yet strangely unconcerned, she rose and moved—walking was too ordinary to note in a dream—toward the light of day. It came, she discovered, from beyond a brow of rock not unlike that under which she and Strynn had sheltered, save that neither horses nor birkits were present. Filled with a joy she could not source, she drifted toward full daylight—and gasped.

She looked out at a perfect bowl of blue: blue water beneath a sky of that same hue, save that it shone where the water glittered. A conical island of dark stone spangled with lush vegetation rose maybe two shots beyond the invisible shore, close to the center of the lake. Cliffs surrounded it, of the same stone, and much of a height. They were steep, too, nearly vertical, but ringed with terraces and shelves, and pocked with caves. None of which was to say that the area was bereft of life. Trees cloaked the island and crowned the cliff tops, while patches of vegetation clung languidly among the rocks, as though they were leafy visitors from the Wild come to lie in open sunlight for a season. It was the most beautiful place Div had ever seen, and the most peaceful, the most serene, the most...restful. She was as happy as she had ever been.

She had to tell Rann! Breathless with joy, she turned and dashed back into the chamber. But it wasn't Rann who rose from his bed to meet her, it was a hollow-eyed Strynn rising from where she had obviously been busy reviving the cooking fire; and this wasn't the bright and wonderful place, it was the darksome cave in which they had sheltered from the storm. Div's heart sank, even as she felt the remembered joy like an ember of warmth in her soul. The birkit was happy, too, she saw. Why it was almost smiling—as much as a birkit could—in its sleep and, barely audibly, purring. Strynn, however, looked more troubled and nervous than ever. "What?" she demanded, as she saw Div's grin.

The grin wilted. "I dreamed...a good dream—though I suppose that's all it was. I'll tell you later. What's wrong? Besides the obvious, I mean."

Strynn shook her head; then, to Div's surprise, stumbled forward and hugged her: not as a friend, but as a child would clutch its mother. "Oh, Div," she sobbed wretchedly. "I...I dreamed I was the birkit, and then I dreamed about Merry. I don't know where she was, because it was dark. But I know she's in terrible danger."

CHAPTER III:

SUNSET AWAKENING

(SOUTHWEST OF ERON—HIGH SUMMER: DAY LXXIV—EVENING)

"*Where are we?*"
"*How did we get here?*"
"*What about the war?*"
"*What about the gem?*"
"*What about Avall?*"
"*What about Kylin?*"
"*I'm cold.*"
"*You're shivering.*"
"*So am I.*"

The words were a litany of shock, surprise, amazement, and alarm as they echoed around what was not quite a cave yet more than a cove inset in solid rock.

Six voices. Six young men who were conscious, and a seventh who was not. Four clad mostly in bright silver mail and the maroon velvet livery of Eron's Royal Guard, one in the similar garb of a royal page, one in a stark white prisoner's robe, one nude. Two half brothers, two sets of bond-mates, one legally linked to no one at all. The youngest: thirteen; none older than twenty-three. Three smiths, two stonemasons, a musician, and a shipwright-warrior.

All shouting their confusion in a place human voices had never stirred.

And then, from the most coherent of the lot, orders:

"Riff: firewood."

"Bingg: fire. Then find some wine; we need it."

"Myx, see to Kylin."

"Lykkon, check the sky and see if you can find out where we are."

"But Lord Regent—"

"We're alive; we're apparently well, and we all have some idea what's happened. Anything else can wait a finger. Now, Avall, if you would, come with me."

And with those commands, chaos sank back to order and seven lives began to progress again—untold shots from where they had been a scant fifty breaths before.

"It's the place in my visions," Avall murmured after a pause so protracted Rann feared that his friend and Sovereign had once more lapsed into unconsciousness, though he had walked to the ledge unassisted and now stood with his bare feet on solid stone, staring out at a place neither he nor the others had ever seen—with their physical eyes. Rann stood beside him, one arm around his bond-brother's shoulders, as much for his own sake as for Avall's, though chills still wracked both of them from when the gem had sucked life-warmth away during that insane, desperate act that had brought them here.

Wherever *here* was.

Here was...

It was away from the war, for one thing.

Away from anyone who wanted things from Rann he was not prepared to give.

Away from decisions, duties, and responsibilities.

Away from anything he did not want to do beyond seeing to his friends and himself.

Here was also a sheltered slot in the face of a cliff: a slot ten spans wide, four deep, and two high; set—apparently—halfway up a mountainside, which in turn overlooked a lake that disappeared from view to either hand. Treetops showed below, and vines crept in at intervals, while the far shore—which looked to be two shots away—was a curving file of cliffs, pocked with caves and fissures similar to the one in which they were ensconced.

"My vision," Avall repeated softly, like a man in a dream. His eyes were dilated, Rann noted. Probably his own were, too—from shock. Night wind ruffled Rann's hair and flipped the cloak that Avall had wrapped around himself against Rann's legs. Avall shivered again.

"What vision?" Rann dared finally, though he wasn't sure he wanted to know, because anything Avall said was bound to be strange past knowing, and he faced too much strangeness already: six grown men and a well-grown boy jumped from a soldier's tent near Gem-Hold-Winter to a place none of them had ever seen before, all in the blink of an eye.

Avall took a deep, shuddering breath. "I...saw it in Fate's Well when I drank from it back in Tir-Eron before we embarked on this escapade. And I've seen it a few times since: an island in a clear blue ring of lake. But I didn't think it was real." Then, even more softly: "And even if it is...how can we *be* here, Rann, when none of us have ever seen it—and the gems only take us to places we've already been or—apparently—to people we know?"

"But they give us what we want, too, sometimes," Rann murmured. "And if I had to guess, I'd say someone—probably you—wanted this place very, very badly indeed."

"A place *like* this, perhaps," Avall conceded, clutching the cloak more tightly. "A place where everything is new and we're free to start all over."

"Some of us," Rann muttered. "But we'll have to go back, you know. Too much depends—"

"I didn't *expect* this to happen, Rann," Avall flared. "I only wanted to destroy the gem so it would never ever hurt anyone

I love again. The rest— No, never mind: you're right: We have to get back. That is I do—if I can."

"If you can," Rann echoed. "But can you? With the gem destroyed?"

Avall frowned, which segued into yet another shiver. "I don't know," he whispered through his teeth. "We've all undergone so much; maybe we *need* to anchor ourselves in familiarity before we venture away from it again. It's too late to do more than police our quarters tonight. But tomorrow— Tomorrow— Well, I suspect I've taken care of that, right and proper, by smashing the gem. But I have no choice but to try—if there's anything left—"

Rann regarded him keenly. "That's a perilously big 'if'— and I frankly don't think you're up for it, brother. Your skin's as cold as ice, in case you haven't noticed."

Avall shook his head, but otherwise didn't move. Then, slowly, like a man in a dream: "Maybe you're right, Rann. And maybe my heart's telling me what my conscience wants to deny."

"What's that?"

"That if I did anything else even marginally magical tonight, it might... kill me."

Rann nodded bleakly—but made no move to rejoin their companions. "Food, fire, and shelter. That's all we really need—for now."

Avall reached out to seize his hand. "Food, fire, shelter—and *friends*," he corrected fiercely. "Always and forever, friends."

A cough from behind startled Rann.

"There's plenty of firewood," sturdy blond Riff announced, padding up in his hose feet to stand beside them. He had also shed his surcoat and mail hauberk, Rann noted, less by sight than the relative silence when he moved. Which was a good sign, he supposed, for it meant that at least one of their number was already acclimating to what was clearly the heat of more southern climes than they were dressed for. And to suddenly being... somewhere else.

As for the others—young Bingg was building a fire in the wide sweep of stone floor behind them, letting new flames replace the old flames of the fading sun. Slim, narrow-faced Myx was sorting through the odd array of material that had come with them when Avall had jumped them here, and Avall's look-alike kinsman, Lykkon, was standing on a precipice to the right, staring at the sky and scowling.

Which accounted for the more functional members of their band. The little blind harper, Kylin, was still asleep—or unconscious—though now covered to his chin with Lykkon's spare cloak. And dreaming who knew what, save that it was surely strange past knowing—for he had lapsed into a kind of babbling madness instants before they had all come here: a madness, Rann suspected, that was a function of contact with the death that had lain hidden within the gem he had used to jump himself and Avall away from the place they had both been captive. Maybe Avall had been right to smash it.

Yet still Rann remained where he was, as emotions warred within him. He ought to be sick with fear, he knew, for he had no idea where they were beyond the obvious. *Ought to be,* but for some odd reason wasn't. Eight! He ought to be in *shock*— they all should be. But—

Heat washed up his back, and with it came ruddy, flickering light, exactly as the sun's light faded. A few stars already spangled the sky.

"Let's go face it," Rann sighed, and steered Avall back to the fire Bingg had lit, using an abandoned raptor's nest for tinder and lamp oil to get it started. He was already adding larger twigs from the small pile Riff had brought, courtesy of a dead tree that had fallen athwart the overhang's southwest corner. Myx checked one last time to see that Kylin was comfortable, and scooted over to join them. Avall hugged his cloak closer about his body but made no move to seek more clothing. There were chafed red bands around his wrists and ankles, Rann noted for the first time, legacy of his being manacled to a tabletop for most of the day. He still looked dazed, too. Or more preoccupied than anyone had a right to be. Or both.

By unspoken consent, they ranged themselves around the fire. Bingg had indeed found a bottle of wine, which he opened and extended solemnly to Avall. "Your Majesty..."

"No King, I," Avall murmured, though he accepted it, "save maybe King of the Mountains, the Lake, and the Woods."

"And what better to be King of?" Rann challenged, then glanced at Lykkon, who had just rejoined them.

"What happened?" Riff dared at last. "I *think* I know but... did the gem?"

Avall nodded solemnly. "Apparently when I struck it with the hammer, it... jumped us somewhere I've never heard of except in visions, never mind visited. Why here... I have no idea."

"The war? How far are we, do you think?" Myx inquired casually, but his usually merry eyes were hard as stone.

A tired shrug. "Far away, I suspect—and hope, right now. How far depends on what Lyk's been able to determine about where we are."

Lykkon took a long draught of wine and passed it on. "If I were to guess," he said carefully, "I'd say we were west of Gem-Hold, not only because we can't see the Spine from here, but because the sun wasn't as close to setting when we awakened as it was back in the camp. Of course some of that depends on how long we were unconscious."

"If we even were," Rann countered. "I know I was, but jumping doesn't usually knock one out. And in any case, it only felt like a hand of breaths."

Lykkon cleared his throat. "I'd also say we're farther south, based on where the stars are. You can see several southern stars you shouldn't be able to see this early back at Gem."

"Across the Spine and south, then," Myx summarized. "Where no one lives that we're aware of."

"Which is both good and bad," Avall observed. "At least we have some supplies," he added, after an expectant pause.

Riff glanced at him in mild confusion. "So we're not going back?"

"If you mean *jumping* back, we probably can't," Avall told him frankly. "I smashed the gem, remember?"

"And why *did* you do that?" Myx demanded testily, legacy, perhaps, of earlier intoxication, though jumping seemed to have burned most of it away.

Avall glared at him—not because he disliked him, but because the man was already awakening old angers when he wanted everything new again. "Because, by using it when it was mad, it drove Kylin mad in turn, and I didn't want that to happen to anyone I care about again—ever."

"I've kept the fragments," Lykkon confessed, looking a trifle sheepish. "Just in case."

"As you should," Avall conceded sourly. "We'll still need to study the thing."

"Things," Rann corrected with unexpected bitterness. "Now that it's been smashed."

"Which makes me wonder whether the fragments have the same properties as the whole," Avall mused. "Not only madness, but the other, more useful things. If we're stranded here—well, it pains me to say it, but they could very well save our lives."

"Which brings us back to *here*," Myx growled. "Can someone be more specific than 'southwest of Gem-Hold-Winter'?"

Avall took a deep breath, steeling himself for contention, should it appear. "If this is indeed the place in my visions, then we're on an island in the middle of a lake with a file of cliffs encircling it."

"Let's hope it's an island with food," Bingg muttered. "Lyk's stash of delicacies won't last long."

"Fish in the lake, at minimum," Myx offered matter-of-factly. "Probably small game and birds here. But for anything that would really fill us or support us long-term, we'd need to reach the mainland."

"Which I assume we will," Rann gave back, shifting his gaze to Riff, whose clan—Ioray—ruled shipcraft. "In the meantime, we need to look at this logically. Food, we have some of and can eventually get more. Shelter—we seem to have found that as well, though I'd hope for something cozier for cold weather. Ideally, something we can close off."

"For winter," Myx echoed darkly.

"Which leaves clothing," Lykkon finished. "We basically have what we had on, which is fairly sturdy—all but Vall and Kylin, I mean. Fortunately, we're all much of a size, except Bingg, and my clothes chest was one of the things that made the jump."

"Point me to it," Avall sighed. "I'm tired of sitting around in just a cloak."

Ever dutiful, Bingg hopped to his feet and showed Avall a middle-sized oak chest that had fallen over but otherwise sustained no damage. A quick inspection produced three sets of indoor clothing, all in Argen maroon. Avall claimed the most worn set and started dressing. "It would be helpful," he observed as he pulled on Lykkon's third-best pair of house-hose, "if someone briefed me on what's happened since I was captured. About the war, I mean."

"And if you briefed us on what happened while *you* were captured," Rann countered. "Like what's going on with Zeff and the master gem."

Avall shrugged. "I don't know all of that. I was imprisoned every moment I was in the hold, and they plied me with imphor to get me to talk, but I've learned how to talk around the truth somewhat, and I listened carefully to how they phrased their questions. But to answer *your* question: One night Zeff came storming into my cell with the master gem, demanding to know how to work the regalia. I don't remember the specifics of the confrontation, but he was as angry as I've ever seen him—and he's not a man who angers easily. Basically, he beat me and when he saw that he'd bloodied my face, forced the gem into the blood, so that we wound up...linking—I won't say 'bonding.' Luckily for me, I was able to draw some force from the Overworld while we were joined and managed to use that to fling him away. He left, but beyond that, I don't know anything until they came to my room, stripped me, and clamped me to that tabletop. That, and the fact that I was able to contact Kylin while he was harping—probably because the gem was so close—along with the fact that Kyl's a very strong thinker. The rest you know."

Lykkon scowled. "So you think Zeff learned how to link the gem to the sword from you?"

Avall shrugged in turn. "He might have, but I have no way to know what he found in my brain while we were...together. Though of course I'd have shown him *nothing* by choice."

"What about other gems?" Rann inquired. "Have they reached the mines yet?"

Avall tugged on an overtunic and rejoined them. "If they have, I haven't heard about it. But that doesn't mean much; information is hard to come by in there. What I've told you really is all I know, honestly. Oh, I could add a few details, but I'd as soon save them for later, since something tells me we're going to have plenty of time to talk. In any case, we've got more important things to discuss right now—like what's been going on in the camp and elsewhere."

Rann and Lykkon exchanged troubled glances. "You don't know about the coup in Tir-Eron, do you?"

Avall looked up sharply. "What coup?"

"Simply stated," Rann replied, "Priest-Clan staged a coup. It was Mask Day, and they used the chaos that's so pervasive then as a cover to contrive the assassination of most of the existing chiefs—including some of their own, apparently. They've taken over the Citadel, and, as far as I can tell, it's martial law in Eron George—Priest Law, better say. We've been busy with the siege and couldn't help—either way we'd have had an enemy at our backs and we were closer to Gem when we got the news."

"And to me," Avall gritted. "You should've gone back to retake the Gorge, not forged ahead to retake me."

"It's over and done," Rann flared. "And I did nothing against the advice of my Council. In any case, Tyrill *is* alive—or was—but she wasn't in a position to regain her chieftainship, never mind the stewardship you gave her when you left. We've had a few messages from her, however—she's a survivor, that one. As to whether the problem has spread to the other gorges, we don't know. It makes a certain amount of sense for the same thing to have happened everywhere, but it makes as much sense for some of the other Gorge-Chiefs to act unilaterally and try to oust Priest themselves. Granted, the cream of your army is at Gem, but there are still able men and women elsewhere. Remember that Vorinn's as good as you have right now, and he missed the last war entirely. He's also got a brother who's martially inclined—*and* is somewhere in the north."

"So to cut to the core," Avall concluded, "the army can do as much good where it is as back in Tir-Eron, and the heart of the realm is at present a theocracy with two surrogate governments thrown in: one in Tir-Eron under Tyrill, who's my legal representative there, and one at the front—probably under Vorinn, if I know anything."

"Vorinn in fact," Myx confirmed. "It was announced in camp shortly after Rann abdicated."

Avall rounded on Rann fiercely. "You *abdicated*?"

Rann looked him straight in the eye. "The choice was how and when I saw you die. That wasn't a choice I could make."

"Oh, Rann, Rann," Avall groaned, burying his face in his hands. "I'm not worth that. I'm not worth you ruining your life over."

"It's done," Rann whispered. "And you're still King."

Myx exhaled listlessly and stood. "Not that this isn't

interesting or important, but...shouldn't we take better stock of our situation? Avall said he's seen this place in a vision, but that's the only proof we have that we really are on an island in the uninhabited west. There could be a twenty-towered palace right above us and we wouldn't know it from here."

"True enough," Rann agreed. "But from what we saw in what little daylight was left, there were no signs of habitation anywhere out there. No lights, no roads. Which is not to say they don't exist, but any exploration should probably wait until daylight. At that time...we should split up. Someone will have to stay here with Kylin, I suppose, but one group of us should go down to the lake, another group should see what's above us, and we also need to explore laterally. I'd say we do the first two in the morning—with an eye to finding fresh water that isn't lake water—and if we have time, check out the other in the afternoon. That should keep us busy. We also need to see what we have in the way of bows, as they'll probably be our most effective hunting weapons."

"And tomorrow night"—Avall looked troubled but went on—"tomorrow night, much as I despise the notion, I'll try to bond with what's left of the gems. I don't think I have it in me to try that before then, and I refuse to let any of you try."

"And tonight?"

"Tonight," Avall said through a yawn, "we set watches, while the rest try to get some sleep. I don't know about anyone else, but I'm exhausted." He looked around expectantly. "What do we have for bedding?"

"My camp bed didn't make it," Lykkon sighed, "but we all have our cloaks. There's the rug itself, and a couple of cushions I had scattered around."

"More than enough to keep us warm," Avall said through another yawn. "Now then, who's taking first watch?"

"I will," Riff volunteered. "Seeing how I was most sober before all this began, and seem to be least...affected now."

"Very well," Avall agreed. "Now, what say the rest of us take inventory, and when anyone gets too tired to work, that person can go to sleep. The fire won't last all night anyway, unless we work at it. Fortunately, we won't need it for warmth."

"No," Myx said softly. "But what will we do when winter really does arrive?"

CHAPTER IV:

DEAD OF NIGHT

~~~~~~~~~

Tyrill san Argen-yr took a deep breath and shuffled toward the bridge. It was one of two bridges that stretched from the Isle of The Eight to the banks of the Ri-Eron, in which the Isle was centered. This was the southern bridge, however: the one Tyrill had rarely used for most of her eighty-odd years, simply because she'd had no reason to use it. South Bank—by convention, not Law—was largely the province of what passed in Eron as a middle-class (there was effectively no lower), and was therefore the haunt of assorted businesses and small holdings belonging, in most cases, to Common Clan or clanless. A few High Clans had holds there as well, notably Lore, and some of what were known as the Earth Clans—like Beast, Grain, and Tanning—but they were the exceptions.

Some of those holds were in ruins, too, courtesy of rebellion run rampant on Mask Night, thirteen nights before. Fortunately for their owners, most were sufficiently extensive that even fire could not claim all of them. And fortunately for Tyrill, ruins made excellent shelter.

The Eight knew she had sheltered long enough in the lee of what had been the kitchen of one of Beast-Hold's septs: shel-

tered there and waited, clad in the darkest, most nondescript
hooded cloak her squire, Lynee, could find, while she watched
the night progress and traffic on the South River Walk grow
thin. And if anyone had chanced to note her there—why, they
would have seen nothing more than a thin, white-haired crone
sleeping off too much drink—as evidenced by the empty beer
pot beside her, and the smell of the stuff lavishly splashed
across her tattered clothing.

She was, however, as sober as the neatly laid flagstones beneath her, when she steered her way into the moonlight. Two
moons shone bright on the Ri-Eron to her right, as she angled
toward the waist-high wall that marked the edge of the River
Walk. She made a point of wobbling and occasionally flailing
for balance, too—this in spite of the cane that was far too necessary, and joints that hurt far too much. Once, she even let
herself stagger into the wall itself. She would have to be careful
about that, though; too much motion would draw unwanted
attention to what needed as few witnesses as possible. Still, she
made it a point to stop and cough loudly several times, each
time raising her hand to her lips.

She wondered if it was wise to attempt what she was planning. A quarter ago she would have said no, but a quarter ago
her Kingdom had not been in chaos, her loved ones lured
away, imprisoned, or dead, and she herself unhomed. Why, if
not for the bravery and largesse of her Common Clan squire,
Lynee, she might well be dead herself.

But if things went as they ought tonight, someone else
would die instead.

She had never killed anyone outright. But she now possessed a tool with which she could kill at some distance while
remaining relatively undetected, and it would be a shame not
to use it for the greater good of Eron.

She wondered about that, too: who that half-seen figure had
been, that had left those objects on the floor of her favorite
two-son's shrine. She did *not* wonder what they were, however, nor how to use them; and their use had, indeed, become

almost second nature in the few days since she had acquired them.

And there was her target now!

The bridge terminated in a guard station staffed by Priests of The Eight. Or, more properly, by Priests of the Ninth Face, since that radical sept now governed its parent clan. The guards changed shifts eight times a day, generally at cross-eighths, so that the portentous times—midnight, dawn, sunset, and sunrise—were always policed by the same person. That guard would have come on duty almost two hands ago, and if he was true to his habits would step outside precisely at midnight, take a turn around the station, perhaps piss over the parapet if he thought no one was looking, then return to duty.

When he did, Tyrill would be ready.

Another breath and she staggered farther up the way, but not far—never far—from the wall. She also coughed into her fist again, but when she lowered it, fingers still deft from eighty years of smithing snared something from the folds of her clothing—something a quarter of whose length she could conceal in her hand, while the bulk ran up her sleeve. Something she had previously loaded with a small glass dart tipped with one of the most potent poisons in existence.

And there was the guard: right on time! He had sauntered out of the back of the station and disappeared around the farther, western, side. Tyrill quickened her pace in his absence. Range could be crucial with this particular weapon. He turned the corner obligingly; she slowed again as he started past the station's front wall and toward her.

It was now or never.

But he wasn't turning! He was coming toward her! Had she drawn more attention than she thought?

"Lady," the man called with polite authority. "It's late, and there *is* a curfew. I must ask—"

He never got a chance to frame his question, because Tyrill chose that moment to cough again. Only she didn't really cough. The hand she raised contained a blowgun of Ixtian origin, and that blowgun housed a dart tipped with scorpion poison. The cough was a puff of wind carefully applied. And such was Tyrill's luck—or skill—that her first attempt struck home. She couldn't see the dart, of course, but she did see the man swat his neck where bare skin showed above his blue surcoat. Nevertheless, she betrayed nothing, merely reeled to the rail again and used it to brace herself (with the blowgun still in her hand in case she had to drop it into the river hastily), while the man continued forward. He managed three more steps before his eyes went very wide and he stumbled. Turning clumsily, he fled back to the guard station—perhaps to summon help—except that he could not cry out, for that poison froze the voice early on. Then the breath. Then the heart. Tyrill didn't even have to dispose of the body, for the man—frantic in his haste—struck the wall as he tried to turn the corner onto the bridge, slipped on something she couldn't see—and tumbled over. She heard the splash as he struck the water a span below her feet.

One less whisker on the Ninth Face, she chuckled to herself, then continued drunkenly on. And Fate was not merely with her tonight, He was courting her, it seemed. For not only had the guard disposed of his own body, he had also knocked the poison dart free. It glittered on the stones where he had stood, visible courtesy of particularly cooperative moonlight. Tyrill ground it to dust beneath her heel, wondering why she felt so little remorse about killing that man; wondering, more to the point, who should be next to taste the scorpion's sting.

Tyrill was not the only person haunting the smoky shadows of Tir-Eron that night. Her senior squire, Lynee, was also busy, but much farther down the River Walk, where the private estates of the less prosperous members of High Clan septs began to give way to those of rising status in Common Clan. Granted, a third of the buildings facing the pavement were still businesses or small holds, and a third were state-run apartments given over mostly to clanless folk—and now, refugees from South Gorge and Half. But a third were also the holds of private citizens or families; most walled, and far enough from the heart of the city that the turmoil that had marred Mask Night had reached there but sporadically. Only one had been torched, and that in error. And while the Ninth Face had dutifully made their sweeps in search of High Clan chiefs they could disempower, they had found no one home—in large part because those chiefs were already sheltering in disguise with trusted, but less politically visible, neighbors.

Lynee's family owned a candle shop farther west, but one of their primary customers had long been an increasingly affluent Common Clan family, and it was that estate she was approaching now—like Tyrill, in the guise of an unsteady drunk.

She was not drunk, however, when she knocked a certain cadence on a certain gate and was summarily admitted—not to the estate itself, at this time of night; but into the gate-warden's quarters, where waited another member of the former Council of Chiefs.

It was hard not to bow to the man who rose to meet her from where he'd been reading in the gate-warden's common hall. One *usually* bowed to Clan- and Craft-Chiefs, and certainly to ones as renowned as this one, for Lynee had come to meet Ilfon syn Kanai, former Craft-Chief of Lore, who—happily for him—had been absent from Tir-Eron during the uprising: a fact about which Priest-Clan was known to be deeply concerned, since Lore, with Smith, War, and Stone, was among the most powerful clans.

In any case, Ilfon was not one to stand on more than minimal ceremony, and merely grinned wryly at Lynee's amazement—which made her blush furiously, to her chagrin. *But how could she not?* Even in a nation of handsome men and beautiful women, Ilfon surpassed the norm. Though not as tall as many, his features—like Strynn's—were absolutely symmetrical in a way that had been studied, in particular, by Paint, but by the sculptors in Smith and Stone as well. Like Strynn, too, no one feature tipped the balance toward perfection, but again like her, the consensus was that Ilfon's face achieved some "finer synthesis" of all elements deemed, by the beauty-obsessed Eronese, to be desirable.

That had been...before. Now, he was dirty by design, had dyed his hair a nondescript brown, and cut it roughly. Finally, he'd managed to convince one of his squires that it was in the best interest of all involved to break his nose—which indeed served as a very admirable disguise—especially as the swelling and bruising had not entirely abated.

But it was not Ilfon's looks that concerned Lynee now; it was what he might have to tell her.

"I've little time," Ilfon said, motioning Lynee to the other seat, then glancing up to see if their nominal host had departed.

"Nor have I," Lynee replied, though she accepted his offer. "Tyrill's abroad tonight, doing who-knows-what, though I suspect."

"What?"

"I will only say that if any of the Face are found dead under mysterious causes, they might be less mysterious to Tyrill. Beyond that—"

Ilfon grinned again. "I'm used to wait-and-see."

Lynee shifted restlessly. "Lord...have you learned—?"

Ilfon nodded in turn. "Most of what Tyrill desired. Unless things have changed in the last two hands, the King's heir is, indeed, safe, as is the heir's foster-one-mother."

"You found Evvion?"

"It wasn't hard. You know how she hates ceremony? Well, she hates revelry more. She therefore tries to find some reason to absent herself from Tir-Eron on Mask Night. And frankly—and to her benefit now—she's been so unobtrusive for so long that people tend to forget she exists. She's like a shadow. You don't think of her as real—not since her husband died—Avall and Merryn's father. Before that, you should've seen her. Then again, you should've seen him. You know he and I were bond-brothers?"

"I did not," Lynee confessed. "It never occurred to me to wonder, much less ask. In any case, Evvion is...where?"

"With what remains of Eemon's elite in one of Stone's summer holds down near the coast."

"I thought Evvion was Criff."

"There *is* no Criff anymore, not really. Certainly not since almost fifty of them were poisoned on Mask Night, including the top ten chiefs at one sitting. But long before that Criff—Clay—was part of Stone, and Stone had already effectively reabsorbed it through necessity after the plague. In any case, Evvion has Averryn and between them and these wretched usurpers lies what is supposed to be the most unassailable clanhold in the Kingdom, save those that belong to War. Oh, Priest can dig them out—or starve them out in time. But it will *take* time. Right now, they're counting on chaos in Tir-Eron and the absence of the royal levies to cement them into power. That and Common Clan support, which, as you can see, is not universally in favor of the Face—and clanless, which is mostly concentrated here and south of here, where the war did the most damage.

"The problem is," Ilfon went on, "those people are used to appealing to Priest-Clan when times get hard, and Priest has suddenly found its resources at a low ebb when demand is at its highest."

"So you think they may fall?"

Ilfon shrugged. "I have no idea. The Kingdom has at least four aspects right now. There's the army, to start with, and whatever they're up to at Gem. They might return soon and they might not, and if they do, I wouldn't want to be Priest-Clan.

"Then there are the northern two gorges, in which, so we are told, affairs are much as they were before the war, since they couldn't get involved in it because of the weather. Their best soldiers are off with the King, of course. But their leadership is, we believe, mostly intact, so it's quite possible that Avall might start a government-in-exile in, say, Mid-Gorge, then work south to retake Tir-Eron."

"Which leaves the south," Lynee said.

Ilfon nodded. "Which leaves the south. It has its own problems, because most of the war was fought there. A lot of the High Clansmen there were in Tir-Eron for the summer, coordinating rebuilding with their Chiefs, or else sourcing supplies. A lot of *them* bore the brunt of Mask Night, so there are whole clan-septs down south with no one in charge—which means that the crafty among Common Clan are moving into the positions they've vacated, which makes them Royalists by default because they won't want to lose what they've so lately acquired. But there are a lot of homeless people down there as well, and Priest is having to send its more traditional, least political, and most altruistic folks there to try to placate more hungry people than we've ever had, while trying to shift the blame away from themselves. It's a neat little dance—to watch, but not, I imagine, to be involved in."

"And Tir-Eron?" Lynee dared.

"It all meets here," Ilfon sighed. "And now I must depart. You have what you came for and more. Tell Tyrill I appreciate her efforts, but to be careful. But tell her also that Avall's heir still lives."

"He's Eddyn's child," Lynee corrected automatically.

"Avall's heir," Ilfon repeated.

And on that small note of tension, Lynee withdrew.

Dawn found both Lynee and Tyrill in bed, and Ilfon a dozen shots downriver.

CHAPTER V:

What Dawn Brings

(NORTHWESTERN ERON: MEGON VALE—HIGH SUMMER: DAY LXXV—BEFORE DAWN)

~~~~~~

"Lord Regent?"

Vorinn was awake by the time the second word began and alert before it concluded. He prided himself on that trait, though it had been born into him, not ingrained through training, and was therefore not so much an achievement as it otherwise might have been.

In spite of the formal address, one hand sought the dagger beneath his bed pad even as he squinted into the gloom of his tent. The voice belonged to one of Avall's former Guardsmen, a man named Ravian, whom he did not know well. He wore full war gear, however, which meant that he was fresh from the front, where the army kept watch in shifts, day and night. He also carried a small lantern, the light of which obscured a lean and fine-boned face.

"Lower that so I can see you," Vorinn yawned, rising up on an elbow and scraping the hair out of his face one-handed. "You have a message, I assume?"

Ravian nodded. "The Ninth Face is moving. We can't tell much in the dark, sir, but there's activity on the galleries *and* behind their palisade."

"Activity?"

"As I said, we can't see much in the dark—unfortunately. And the enemy isn't using torches."

Vorinn was already reaching for his clothes as he slid upright. "Has Tryffon been informed?"

"We came to you first, as is proper. But word should be reaching him and the rest of your Council even now."

Another yawn. "What time is it?"

"A hand before sunrise, more or less."

"So Zeff does intend to enforce the deadline," Vorinn muttered, mostly to himself.

"He intends to do something," Ravian agreed. "We should know what very quickly."

"Not soon enough, probably," Vorinn snorted. Scowling, he snared his leather war-trews from the stand beside his cot and began to draw them on. "Send in my squire and tell the Council I'll meet them behind our palisade in half a hand. Faster, if they can manage."

Ravian sketched a bow, then backed toward the entrance flap. "You have but to say, Lord Regent." And with that he ducked out. Vorinn heard the squire fumbling around in the outer room, but didn't wait on him to continue dressing. He preferred to manage that on his own, anyway; but squires *were* useful for things like adjustments and buckles.

One finger later, fully armed down to war-cloak and helm, with a sleepy-eyed squire and a pair of anxious-faced guards in tow, he was striding uphill toward the palisade that ringed his own camp, angling toward the gate that would admit them to the corral in which their warhorses were lodged, ever at ready—in case.

Tryffon bustled up to join him, along with two other subchiefs from War. "Preedor's coming," Tryffon grumbled. "He moves slowly in the morning, but he's moving."

"As is Zeff," Vorinn replied tersely. "Is there any more news?"

"Movement and more movement is all I know," Tryffon replied through an unsuppressed yawn.

"I guess we'll know by dawn," Vorinn retorted, gazing east, to where the sky was quickly brightening. The peaks of the Spine were crowned with red fire where the ice on their summits caught the first light, but pink was spreading down their slopes, dispersing midnight blue and purple and banishing black to the shadows where it belonged.

Someone had possessed the foresight to get their horses ready, and Vorinn mounted handsome black Iron with the same casual ease with which he donned his boots. It was mostly for effect, he conceded; he couldn't imagine that Zeff would press for battle now, given that he had lost two major bargaining points. But Zeff was wily, and the game of feint and parry barely begun. Vorinn would have preferred to fight—perhaps single combat. But he also knew that combat was not—yet—an option.

The gate swung open before them as they exited the camp and entered the slope that ringed the vale. Fires burned everywhere, if small ones: one to every eight soldiers, two of which number changed every hand. They waited there in the predawn gloom: good soldiers from all the clans and crafts, their heraldry like springtime flowers, though Warcraft's red predominated—entire or quartered with the colors of other clans and crafts.

Nor had discipline lapsed even slightly since the events of the previous day, though speculation and unease had surely increased, as it would have had to among soldiers. But the army, Vorinn sensed, was still strong and perfectly controlled.

They rose as they saw him, saluting him as he and his party advanced toward the centermost siege tower.

Which, he supposed, was marginally safer now that Zeff had lost his principal weapon. No lightning would blast this tower today. But even as he advanced, Vorinn's gaze scanned the second palisade that draped the vale: the one before him, a quarter shot beyond the first wall of royal shields. There was indeed movement there, but he could not tell more, save that people seemed to be flooding out into the field between Zeff's palisade and the hold proper, but under cover of dark blankets or other fabric, so that it was impossible to make out what they were doing with any degree of certainty.

And the arcades—movement there, too, but likewise masked by fabric and furtiveness. The galleries would be getting true mornlight soon, and wouldn't need torches anyway. He hated that: that the foe in Gem-Hold could almost certainly see him better than he could see them.

Wordlessly, he dismounted and climbed the steps that kinked up the center of the tower. Only when he had reached the level below the top did he step out onto a platform. Pausing only to settle his cloak and set his Regent's circlet on his hair, he strode to the rail and waited. Tryffon joined him on the right, Preedor—with some difficulty—on the left. Veen held his helm, her face hard with determined pride. He wondered how she felt about Avall's disappearance, given that her star seemed linked with the King's far more than it was with his own.

Time passed.

Slowly, it seemed, though those who waited below probably felt that it moved far too quickly, if it was battle at dawn they faced. Vorinn didn't blame them. In spite of the recent war with Ixti, very few Eronese under the age of sixty had seen more than mock training battles hand to hand. He hadn't either—but he was different. Battle was born into him.

The sun's rays were moving faster, too, their earlier creep down the mountains now become a precipitous slide. In a moment, a ray would touch the golden ball atop the Hold's centermost tower, and dawn would officially arrive.

Zeff had demanded that the King's forces be withdrawn at dawn. But that had been yesterday. This was now.

Where was Zeff, anyway? Would he even bother to appear? *Could* he even appear? Had his failure yesterday weakened his position past enduring? Vorinn had no way of knowing.

But then it didn't matter, for gold suddenly gleamed like fire atop the hold, and morning swept down its whitewashed walls.

—To reveal Zeff standing where Vorinn had last seen him: on the lowest of the pillared arcades. Even the tabletop on which he had displayed Avall remained in place, token, it would seem, of arrogance as much as anything.

Zeff wore white, but he did not wear the helm and shield he had captured when he had taken Avall: the ones that were precise replicas of the magic regalia. And the matching sword was gone, of course, as was—presumably—the master gem.

But it did not seem to matter. Zeff looked as composed and arrogant as ever. And he raised his speaking horn to his lips and called out one lone word.

"Behold!"

The sound belled around the gallery and assailed the vale below like brazen thunder.

And was clearly a signal to begin the next stage of the confrontation.

It was as fine a show of coordinated action as Vorinn had ever witnessed, for all it was effected with what looked like draperies, blankets, and ropes. Whatever the mechanism, the darkness fell away from the backs of the galleries to reveal line on line of people roped one to another and likewise tied to the hold's balustrades—men and women, without distinction, excepting the very old and the very young. Most wore clan or craft colors—probably Zeff's idea, since it made them easy to identify. Nor was the move unexpected; Tryffon had suggested the possibility in yesterday's Council.

What was different was the magnitude.

"Unfathered," Tryffon breathed beside him, voicing Eron's most virulent curse.

"Indeed," Vorinn agreed.

"Regent," Ravian murmured at his back, having rejoined them at the base of the tower. "Look at the ground."

Vorinn did—and could not suppress a chill at what he saw.

The shroudings they had seen being put in place earlier had been removed there as well, so that the entire area between the palisade and the hold was now revealed to be carpeted with what had to be most of the hold's remaining population, staked out spread-eagled at intervals along the ground. Not dead or tortured, merely as a taunt. Most were grim-faced and stoic, but a few looked as though they would have cried out had they not been thoroughly gagged. "Eight damn them!" Vorinn spat.

"Damn them indeed," Tryffon echoed. "That's a pretty scene."

"Not one they can maintain, however," Vorinn replied at once. "That has to be virtually the entire complement of the hold. I'm sure the idea is to forestall attack, since any missiles we hurl will be bound to impact our own, and any attack on foot will probably be a signal to start cutting throats."

Tryffon nodded sagely. "Which means there's no one but Ninth Face folk to maintain the hold—which means they can't soldier. It also means there's no one to work the mines."

"Or," Veen spat, where she stood behind them, "that they no longer have to."

Vorinn nodded grim agreement, then looked around at his assembled Council. "Tell everyone on the field to move back exactly one span, but that's all. It won't mean anything in strategic terms, but it *will* be a reply—which Zeff, if we're lucky, will take as a sign of weakness. It'll also puzzle the cold out of him. And that's what we need right now: puzzlement and confusion." He paused, gnawing his lip, then motioned to his squire to bring his own speaking horn, which he raised.

"Zeff the traitor," he called. "You seem to have odd notions about the proper treatment of Gem-Hold personnel—a lapse in your upbringing which I am sure the Council of Chiefs will address in their good time. In the meantime, I will report what I have seen to His Majesty, Avall."

And with that, he turned and started back down the siege tower's stair.

"You won't be able to maintain that deception much longer," Tryffon grumbled, behind him.

"No," Vorinn agreed. "But if things go as I hope, we won't have to."

"And if they don't?"

"I'll do what all soldiers do. I'll fight as long as I can—and then I'll either win or die trying."

CHAPTER VI:

EXPLORING

(SOUTHWEST OF ERON—HIGH SUMMER: DAY LXXV—DAWN)

～～～～～

For a moment—that cold, still moment before true awakening—Avall was utterly lost.

Not that he'd had any real home for quite a while—not for more than a few nights at a time, anyway. The dungeons at Gem-Hold certainly didn't count, and for most of two eights before his incarceration there, home had been a camp tent, around which the landscape changed every sunrise. Before that, he'd divided his time between the royal suite in the Citadel in Tir-Eron and his own youthful quarters in Argen-Hall. And before *that,* it had been the war with Ixti, which meant camp tents again.

And prior to the war? Why, home then had been the Wild, and bedrooms had been ruined way stations, birkit dens, or the Ri-Eron itself—but it was wisest not to think about that timeless interval when he had floated beneath the ice, sustained only by the gem's determination to keep him alive. Just as he preferred not to think about his earlier tenure in Gem-Hold-Winter, when he had *thought* that the only aberration in the life his culture had laid out for him was an early marriage to someone he liked but did not love, and who was carrying a child he had not begotten.

Now, home was to all intents a cave. But at least it was a cave he shared with the people he loved best in the world. The *men* he loved best, he amended, for the tally of his beloved had always included his twin sister, Merryn; and lately had expanded to include Strynn and Div as well. It was odd, he reckoned, how so many of the people who presently filled his days were people he hadn't known half a year gone by. Myx, Riff— even Zeff: all were new daubs on the canvas of his life. Veen, he had known but barely, and the same for Vorinn and Kylin.

Well, he conceded, as he rolled over on the section of rug he and Rann had claimed, he supposed he would know some of those people much better before very long. As for the landscape: It was the new thing now, the same as yesterday to the casual eye, but full of mysteries unseen. Mysteries they would begin unraveling with the rising of the sun, which was still a few hands away.

Movement beside him was Rann turning over as well. Avall let him nestle against his back, took the hand that snaked around his body and held it to his chest as he hadn't done since they'd camped in the snow the previous winter. He'd had the gem, then, to draw strength from Rann, all unknowing. Now they had to draw strength solely from what they had to hand.

As for the war— *That* was a damned hard call. Everything he had been taught cried out to him that he should not have rested even this one night; that he should have grabbed that handful of gem shards at once, and tried as hard as he'd ever tried anything in his life to jump back to Megon Vale. People were getting ready to *die* there, for Eight's sakes—and, more to the point, die for him—for what he symbolized, at any rate. For good or ill he was King, and that meant doing what was best for the people no matter what the personal cost.

But for one crucial, half-mad moment, that cost had been too high, and all the anguish of the last few eights had caught up with him and crystallized in the horrible injustice of the madness that Kylin had caught from his oh-so-brief encounter with the afflicted stone. And in that awful moment, he had done the unthinkable: destroyed—tried to—the most power-ful object in Eron. All for his own selfish reasons. True, he had been genuinely concerned that it had driven Kylin insane; but a dark, selfish part of his soul-of-souls suspected with too much certainty for close inspection that what he had really been do-ing was removing the gem from any future equations that might involve their mutual interaction.

He was saner now, however, and knew that his fate lay back at Gem-Hold-Winter.

Or did it? Fate surely had a hand in this preposterously ex-travagant leap through space. So perhaps this *was* where he was supposed to be. Ultimately, he supposed, the best way to determine whether Fate wanted him to jump back was to *try* to jump back. And if he couldn't, why, then he would still try to get back as quickly as he could by conventional means, for Strynn's and Merryn's sakes, if not his own. But in order to ac-complish even that, he first had to get off the island. And the first step toward that had already been planned for shortly af-ter sunrise.

That notion made him feel oddly content—tired, sleepy, and apprehensive, but content.

For a short while longer, he watched the fire die through slitted lids, and woke again to the sound of Bingg boiling wa-ter for cauf.

Half a hand later, full of cauf, camp-sausage, and way-bread, all except Myx, who knew more than the rest of them together about healing and would therefore need to remain with the still-comatose Kylin, were splitting up for the first round of explorations. Avall and Rann would scout the shore, while Riff, Bingg, and Lykkon would investigate the heights. They would meet back at the cave at noon to share informa-tion and plot their afternoon session.

"Are you sure you're up for this?" Rann asked, as he and Avall paused at their shelter's northern edge. The roof came down to the floor there, like the corner of a pair of lips, but the floor extended farther out than the ceiling, to form a kind of ledge. Runoff from rain had made a channel beyond, going down. Riff, Lykkon, and Bingg were already a dozen strides along it, scanning the undergrowth for some place to turn right and begin their trek upslope. There was growth aplenty, for vegetation covered every surface that was not too steep to support it, while the view above was masked by limbs, save at one point where they could see exactly enough to determine that their shelter was set three-fourths of the way down a massive escarpment of porous gray stone.

"They fed me enough to get by; they clothed me—until yesterday," Avall retorted. "The Eight know I've had enough rest, and, however I may look, I'm not fragile, and certainly not broken—no thanks to Zeff in the case of the latter. I've got a bit of a headache, granted, but that could be the result of anything from gem residue to sleeping without a pillow last night. In any case, I'll be much better when I know more precisely what our situation is." And with that, Avall led the way down the trail.

Actually, it wasn't a trail in the sense that anything living had made it. Mostly their route consisted simply of a fairly steep slope leading off to the right, following a depression between two low ridges, so that water kept it swept free of debris. Avall wondered how often it rained here. Or snowed. The sky had been clear so far, but half a day was no indication.

They could see little of the lake or the ring of cliffs beyond, courtesy of the intervening trees, but Rann was watching the landscape keenly. They heard birdcalls and the murmur of the wind among branches, but no other sounds save the occasional rustle of small animals—probably squirrels. What bare rock showed was still gray and porous. "I'll wager this was once a fire mountain," Rann mused. "I'd say it exploded ages ago, and the top came down in the middle. There's one like that up past North Gorge, though I've never seen it."

Avall shuddered. "Do you think this one will?"

Rann shrugged. "Not so soon that we wouldn't have warning. It looks pretty benign around here."

Avall indicated a nearby stand of evergreens. "Plenty of wood for whatever we need wood for."

Rann nodded again. "More wood than we've got appropriate tools to work, I'd say. Something tells me we're going to have dull swords before this is over."

"You sound like you think we'll be here for a while."

"We may be—unless you can get the gem working, which I frankly doubt, given that it's in pieces."

"I intend to try."

"I know you do," Rann growled. "But we have to be realistic. If this is an island—"

"It is."

Rann stopped again, and this time he sank down on a knee-high, moss-covered rock that protruded from a froth of bracken to the left of the trail. They'd covered almost two shots by then, and looked to be roughly halfway to their goal, though the lake was only visible as an occasional flash of blue ahead or to the left. "But how do you *know* that, Avall?" he asked wearily. "I truly don't understand your talk of having seen it before."

Avall flopped up against a tree, and began stripping leaves from a waist-level twig. "I saw it in a Well once," he—almost—snapped. "As I've already told you. Beyond that"—he shook his head—"all I can think of is what *you've* already suggested: that the gems give you what you want—if you want it badly enough. And I wanted a place away from everything."

Rann gestured expansively. "But here? How? Not that it isn't beautiful."

Avall let got the twig. "I had a lot of time to think about that while I was imprisoned, actually. And I think it comes down to water—or liquid, anyway."

Rann raised a brow.

"No, think, Rann," Avall went on quickly. "We know the gems need blood in order to activate. I'm not sure how or why they do, but they do. We also know that they display some of the characteristics of the Wells. Blood is liquid; so—obviously—is water. The water in the Wells has to come from somewhere, and it's not unreasonable to suppose that all water is connected at some level deep underground. So even if I haven't been here, maybe the gems—augmented by the Well water, or something—could tell where there was a watery place that fit my notion of what I wanted. I'm sorry, Rann, I know it sounds crazy."

"It sounds like you think the gems are sentient."

Avall's face went absolutely serious. "I believe that more than ever. But even if they're not, they seem to be—mostly—benevolent."

"Mostly."

Avall sighed, thrust himself away from his tree, and started down the trail again, talking over his shoulder. "In any case we have more imminent problems—the main one being that we really can't stay here. I'm not sure how big this place is, but seven young men could exhaust its resources rather quickly, I'm afraid. We'll need to burn a lot of wood if we're to stay warm this winter, for one thing. And we haven't seen any sign of animals large enough to keep us really well fed; which means that Myx is probably right in that regard, too: The place is too small to support a population of, say, deer. I assume there are fish in the lake, but we'll get tired of fish soon enough, and *really* tired of smoked fish if that's all we have to eat this winter. And we'll run out of sugar, bread, salt, and cauf long before that. We have to find some kind of tuber or such like—I'm hoping Lyk can help there, as I've never been much good with plants or farming."

"Or we could get off this place—which would at least expand our options."

Avall nodded again. "We'll have to. We've already seen that there are more caves in the cliffs opposite ours, and the landscape looks pretty ragged there—so I think we can reach the top fairly easily. The trick is going to be getting there."

"I assume you've ruled out swimming?"

"Well, we all *can* swim except Kylin, and even he can manage if someone helps him—when he's conscious, which he isn't. But it looks to be almost two shots from here to there, which is a fair distance, especially if we want to take anything else across. We could use logs as floats, of course, but unless we can jump there by gem power, it seems to me we're looking at building rafts. Which brings us back to Kylin. Obviously we can't leave him here, but, unless he comes around in some manageable way, some kind of raft appears to be our only choice."

"You're forgetting something," Rann said through a grin.

"What?"

"Riff. He's a shipwright by clan. We tend to forget that, because we've always known him as a soldier and as Myx's bondmate. But he's Ioray by birth, which is incredible luck, if you ask me. If it even is luck. I—"

He broke off. Straight ahead rose a screen of laurel twice as high as their heads and maybe two spans deep, splitting the trail neatly. "Left," Avall decided. "It looks like the growth is thinner that way."

"Slope's not as steep, either."

"Lead the way."

Rann did. And while the land was rockier thereabouts, the undergrowth was commensurately less dense. So it was that before long they found themselves following the bottom of a defile where rocks rose higher than their heads—until they ended in the merest scrap of stony beach. It was no more than a span wide, and stretched south but not north, with boulders taking over again in the latter direction. Even so, it was enough to provide the clearest view yet of the strange place in which they were now marooned.

"Beautiful," Rann said, sinking down on a convenient boulder.

And so it was.

Ahead and to the left, the island tapered inward to a cone at least a shot above their heads. It was a fairly steep taper, too, but not so much it could not support a good growth of trees, mostly conifers, but also some tall broad-leafed trees neither Avall nor Rann could identify. The ground—what they could see of it—sported a lavish cover of ferns and moss, ornamented with a fine selection of wildflowers. Avall was glad to see the latter, as many wildflowers had medicinal properties. The summit was forested as well, though the trees there didn't look to be as tall as those lower down. But there were also at least three places where naked stone showed, notably the cave where they'd sheltered, which was clearly visible. Avall sniffed the air appreciatively, only then aware that it was utterly devoid of the scent of smoke and horseflesh that had haunted his nose for days.

"Coastline curves around out of sight," Rann observed, pointing straight ahead. "That fits with my fire-mountain theory, as does the fact there also seem to be a fair number of declivities running down from the peak. I'll bet if we were to look down on this place from above, we'd see a many-pointed star."

"We would," Avall agreed dreamily. "I *have* seen it from above..."

"Later," Rann grunted, rising to hop lightly atop a higher boulder to Avall's right. Small waves lapped against the shore. Avall scooped up a handful of water and drank it absently. It tasted good, though with what he could only describe as a slightly "dark" flavor, with a hint of salt that made him wonder if there might not be some kind of connection to the western sea. He had started to let his gaze drift toward the curve of cliffs, when he caught a flash of movement to the left, where the island's nearer shoreline bent around out of sight. Birds, it turned out: a considerable flock of good-sized ones wheeling and swooping, but never venturing far from land. Even as he watched, one arced down, skimmed the lake's surface, and rose again, with what had to be a fish flipping in its talons. Which relieved some of his concern about food.

They were noisy, too, their raucous cries enough to draw Rann's attention that way. "Rocks look steep there," Rann observed, "which I bet means they nest there, like in the sea cliffs up past North Gorge. There'll be eggs, if we're brave enough to get 'em. Those lads look big enough to give a fellow a solid peck."

"We'll wear armor," Avall shot back with a grin. "That may be all it's good for down here."

"Down here," Rann echoed. "I—Oh, Eight, *look*!" he cried, pointing at the juncture of land and lake.

Something had risen from the offshore waters: something serpentine and senuous, and as long as a man was tall. It appeared to have a head at the end, and that head looked to be snapping at the birds. All at once the beast heaved itself upward in a leap that took its forequarters clear of the water, which revealed a thicker torso and what might be either forelegs or fins. It was too far away, at half a shot, to tell for certain.

Avall scooted back from the shore reflexively, scanning the nearer wavelets anxiously. "Looks half like a geen, half like a serpent."

"One of those big serpents like they have in southern Ixti, maybe," Rann offered.

Avall scrambled up on the rock beside him, and found even that not as far above the water as he would have liked. "Puts a few restrictions on swimming, I'd say," he gasped.

Rann nodded ominously. "And let's hope there aren't many of them, that they're exclusively aquatic, and that, if they're not, they den on the mainland, not here."

"We'll have to explore the entire coast to confirm that last," Avall observed. "All of us. With arms. In armor."

"Tomorrow at the soonest," Rann gave back, "given what we've still got on our plate today." Without comment he scrambled to a higher rock. Avall followed. This one—hopefully—was higher than the water-beast's head could reach.

In any event, it gave them a better vantage on the opposite

shore, which bent somewhat closer there. Even so, it was hard to tell much beyond the already established fact that the lake seemed ringed with what was effectively a wall of cliffs, though swaths of vegetation showed as well, as did the darker slashes of caves. "Doesn't look like we can make landfall just anywhere over there," Avall opined. "We'll have to target someplace where we can actually get *up*shore as well as *on*-shore. Optimally someplace we can make it over the ledge at the top."

"Agreed," Rann said, wiping his brow. "Want to explore that other branch?"

Avall checked the sun, which still had a fair way to go until noon. "We've got time."

The other fork skirted the merest thread of beach for only a dozen spans before it was interrupted by a waterfall that slid down rocks thrice as high as either of their heads, beside which a fallen tree trunk made a convenient ladder up to the rocky rim of a small pool four spans across, which ultimately proved to be the lowest of four, all connected by cataracts. There were fish, too, but none longer than a forearm. "If nothing else, we'll be clean," Rann sighed, rising from where he'd been sampling the water from the last one. "And look: The feeder stream turns back toward our cave."

And so it did. It was a much less precipitous slope, too, running a quarter shot above the route by which they had departed, though the stream kinked sharp left half a shot from the cave, so that they had to scramble through raw woods the last part of the way, and jump down a bank at the end, which put them back on the trail from which they had commenced.

Myx handed them mugs of what looked and smelled like cauf once they returned to the fire pit. He looked smug. Avall wondered why, even as he sampled the brew. It tasted odd, but not bad.

Rann scowled at his uncertainty.

Myx motioned to a clump of dried ferns spread across his cloak. "Found these just around the corner when I went out to piss," he explained. "Clanless folks use it to extend cauf, when they can't afford as much of the real thing as they'd like. It won't hurt us, and it even has some of the same energizing effect if you don't mind your cauf having a bitter edge."

"One problem solved," Avall chuckled, as he sank down and tugged off his boots.

"Here come the others," Rann prompted, even as a noise drew Avall's attention that way.

The first thing they noticed was that every single member of the returning party was even wetter and muddier than Avall and Rann had managed to get themselves. Bingg looked like he was trying not to grin. Lykkon looked by turns almost giddily happy and pensive—which was becoming typical for him.

Myx passed them cauf as well, which evoked the same commentary as before. "You lads look like you have a lot to tell," Avall observed, noting that Bingg was divesting himself of his muddy boots and sodden tunic. "Why don't you go first, then we'll brief you?"

Lykkon and Riff exchanged glances, as though trying to determine who should take precedence. Riff was older, but Lykkon was kin to the King.

Finally, Lykkon cleared his throat. "Do you want the good part first, the bad part first, or—?"

"Start with the bad," Avall advised, leaning back against a cushion with his arms folded across his chest. "We also saw something troubling."

Lykkon nodded. "I have to start with a good thing, though. We made it to the top with no problem, and you can see pretty well up there, since the trees are no more than a fringe around a lake that fills the top, about which more anon. In any case, there's a finger of stone up there that wasn't hard for someone light and nimble like Bingg to climb, which he did. He could see the whole place, and you're right: This is an island, almost round, and almost exactly in the center of the lake. The cliffs that ring it are much of a height, too, though I think they're less steep to the east."

"Nothing bad so far," Avall murmured, surprised to find himself getting drowsy.

"No," Lykkon agreed. "Not here—not that we saw. But on the opposite shore—well, it's a good thing I had a distance lens with my gear, and that I took it. I used it to survey the other side pretty thoroughly, and I saw something moving over there. I was hoping for deer or mountain goats. What I saw, unfortunately, was geens. Not a lot, but there's what looks like a trail over there going from one of the caves up to the top of the cliffs, and I saw several going up and down it. In other words, they have a nest over there. Which means—"

"Which means," Avall finished for him, "that we don't have free license to make landfall just anywhere—assuming we can even get there."

"Which assumes we can't get somewhere else entirely with the gem," Myx added from where he was tending Kylin, who had evidently soiled himself, to judge by a sudden whiff of foul odor.

"I may try that sooner rather than later," Avall sighed through a sip of cauf. "Probably right after lunch, which I'd hope would be right after we finish these reports."

"Sounds good," Lykkon agreed, which prompted Riff to start sorting through a pile of large wet leaves he had brought with him—which in turn produced a handsome fish as long as his forearm. He had already beheaded and gutted it.

"Part of the good news," Riff offered dryly. "Actually, there's quite a lot of that. As we said, the top of this place is a large pond or a small lake. More to the point, it's warm—even steaming in places—so we've got a nice place to bathe. Even better, the water precipitates salt there, so we've got a source of that as well."

"And the fish?" Rann inquired.

Bingg looked smug. "Twig spear, and luck. Of course I had to go in after it, which explains me being wet, and then I wound up having to scramble up a muddy bank, which explains the rest."

"We found another stream not far off," Avall informed them. "We won't lack for fresh water."

"And what else did you fellows learn?" Lykkon inquired, after the fish had been spitted and set to roast above the fire.

"Like you lads," Avall began, "good news and bad." And with that, he told them about the long-necked creatures in the lake.

"Don't think I want to do this," Avall grumbled a hand and half later when, full of fish and well-watered wine, he wiped his knife on the hem of his shirte and scooted back from the fire pit, around which he and his companions had lunched. It was midday now, and getting remarkably warm—so much so that they'd all shed their tunics and boots, and Myx and Riff had doffed their shirtes as well. Without clan colors to differentiate them, the lot of them looked more like brothers than ever, save for Riff's fair hair and stockier build.

"What did you do with the fragments?" Avall continued, looking pointedly at Rann.

Rann reached into his pouch and produced a smaller one, made from a scrap of bandage sylk. "I gathered up the obvious bits as soon as I could. When I get time—which should probably be soon—I need to give the rug a thorough going over in case anything got left there that might cause trouble later. What kind of trouble," he added, "I don't know. But it strikes me that even small shards of the gem might cause problems if one got in the wrong place."

And with that, he passed the pouch to Avall.

Avall weighed it in his hand, then scowled and undid the twist of string that was the bag's only closure. He did not tumble the contents into his hand, however, but set the sylk on a flat stone between his legs and peered down at what he had just revealed.

The gem had been the size of the first joint of his thumb— the size of an eyeball cut in half. Almost a perfect oval, it had also been red with a bluish cast in certain lights, and its depths had held sparks like frozen flame, somewhat like an opal but more brilliant. The surface had been smooth, like a polished river rock.

Now it had been shattered—yet even the fragments displayed symmetry. Though struck with a jeweler's hammer almost in the center, the stone had not dispersed into random fragments as glass would do, and certainly not in a way that suggested the impact they had suffered. Rather, it had shattered into a series of smaller ovals as though one had taken the master gem and sliced across its width to produce disks of varying thickness, all of them oval in cross section. There were five major ones, plus three slivers so thin they were almost transparent, one of which had broken.

"The question is: Where do I begin?" Avall mused.

"I'd say start with the smallest that still looks viable," Lykkon suggested. "The very thin ones might be too thin. The others...we have some evidence that the strength the gems display depends on their size."

"We also have evidence that some are better at some things, some at others," Avall gave back. "In any case, I suppose your idea is as good as any. Though with my luck, it probably contains memories of Kylin's madness now—as well as Barrax's and Rrath's."

"Are you going to blood yourself?" Bingg asked anxiously. "And do you want some of us to...bond with you, just in case?"

Avall shook his head. "Yes, to the former, since so many variables have changed. As for the latter: No. But if anything happens, you know what to do."

And with that, he took a knife he had borrowed from Lykkon and made a tiny incision in the heel of his left hand. Blood oozed forth, though very little, for Avall was being careful. Nor was he letting anyone know how frightened he was. It did no good—unless one had actually experienced firsthand the madness that dwelt in the gem.

He had. And Zeff had, when he'd tried to force Avall to reveal the gem's secrets all those days ago. That had been terrible, but at least he'd been able to divert some of his horror to a
productive end—if wreaking violence on the body, mind, and
soul of another human being was productive. In any case, he'd
thought even then that the gem might not have been quite so
eager to drag him down to death as heretofore. Or maybe it
was simply that he had been distracted.

A deep breath, and he selected the smallest viable fragment—it was roughly one quarter the thickness of his little
finger—and gingerly picked it up, then dropped it into his
other palm and closed his bleeding fist around it.

Reality shifted, as it always did. Time slowed, but not as
suddenly as once it would have done. And there was, indeed,
the expected eager surge of energy, hard on the heels of which
came the expected warning, and the expected awareness of
lurking death. That death was reaching for him, too, but it was
as though it had lost some of its force. *No!* It was more as
though something now lay *between* him and it, like a layer of
ice between a skater and deep water. He let his mind touch
that layer experimentally. It felt—if that word could properly
be used—like Kylin. Or perhaps it sounded like Kylin or
looked like him. It was as if a tiny layer of Kylin's most essen-
tial self had been frozen, then shaved off and inserted between.
He pushed at it with his mind—and heard on another level entirely, Kylin groan and call out something unintelligible.

That shocked Avall so much he almost withdrew himself
from the gem. Instead, he tried to focus on what he was supposed to be doing: seeing if the thing could jump him—them,
rather—away from wherever they were and back to the war it
was their responsibility to rejoin.

With that in mind, he tried to relax, to center his awareness
on two things alone: the lay of the land as he perceived it and
the need to return to the war.

And felt nothing unusual whatever.

He tried harder—and achieved no more.

Harder, trying with all his considerable mental might to picture the camp as he had left it, with the Council Lords gathered in conclave on what must now be noon on the day Zeff's ultimatum had been supposed to expire.

Nothing.

Nothing.

Either the gem was not strong enough; he simply did not want to return badly enough; or he was too fearful that he might return and strand his truest friends here. In any case, nothing occurred.

"Give me another," he demanded, opening his hand but not his eyes, and sensing as much as anything Rann removing one bloody gem and replacing it with the next larger.

As soon as Avall closed his fist around this one, he knew it was different. Oh, it still contained the same "things" and the effects were the same, but the proportions were clearly altered. And it contained less of Kylin's presence than the previous one had, but more of a new presence he thought might be Rrath.

And so it was with the next larger stone, and the next.

Which only left the largest.

Barrax was waiting in that one—without any protective insulation. Or much warning.

What little remained of Barrax, anyway. And while death still lurked there with Ixti's former king, that death was not so all-encompassing. Or maybe it was simply that Avall had now learned what to expect. Or that he, himself, was stronger.

Which was not to say that the invisible combat that ensued was either pleasant or devoid of risk. Far from it. It was only that Avall was able to free himself this time—or *flee* himself. And, for the first time ever, able to break that contact without also breaking contact with the gem.

He was shivering when he opened his eyes, and more when he opened his fist, inverted his hand, and let the fragment fall to the sylk.

"I couldn't," he breathed through his shudder. "I didn't. I can't—not yet."

"Barrax?" Rann murmured, his face tense with concern.

Avall nodded, shuddered again, then paused, as he recalled something he hadn't noted before. "But maybe not as much of him. And below him—or beyond him, or however you want to say it, is—I *think*—still a fair bit of that old familiar power."

"And the next step?" Bingg asked bravely.

"To try *combining* the fragments," Avall replied. "But not now. And maybe not tomorrow. Not if I'm going to be able to do anything else useful."

"And the rest of today?" From Rann.

Avall looked troubled. "I'm—for some reason, that left me more drained than it ought. In fact, much as I hate to suggest it, I think I'd better stay here with Kylin while the rest of you explore mid-level. My advice in that would be to head north along the trails we know and try to maintain a roughly equal distance between the shore and the peak. Proceed until the afternoon's half-over, bring back anything you find that might be eatable, and try to get back here by dark. I'll make small forays and try to get through to Kylin."

"Not with the gems you won't!" Rann snapped.

"Not unless I have to," Avall agreed with a yawn. "But he's still my subject, damaged in my service, and I am—still, by Law—his King."

"Law," Rann echoed softly. "I wonder if there *is* any real Law left in Eron at all."

CHAPTER VII:

FREEDOM—AT A PRICE

(SOUTHWEST OF ERON—HIGH SUMMER: DAY LXXV—LATE AFTERNOON)

~~~~~~

...the soft, desperate snuffle of thirsty horses, now alarmed...

...the clatter of nervous hooves on dusty stones scoured with steel horseshoes made in an alien land...

...the thud of anxious flanks against unyielding oak...

...the glint of waning sunlight filtered through broken glass to mirror itself in dulling equine eyes...

...the scent of hot tile, hot stone, hot wood, and hot, sweating bodies that could ill afford to render up more moisture...

...and another scent entirely...

...well-fed, reptilian—and free...

...another snuffle...

...another stomp...

And then, like a whip crack in thunder-heavy air, a scream.

And then another...

Merryn woke to the sound of horses screaming.

Almost, she ignored it. The Eight knew this wasn't the first time the beasts imprisoned in the adjacent suite of stalls had indulged themselves in a round of noise. Panic did that—or fear. Or raw animal need—like thirst.

She didn't blame them, either: penned up like that in expectation of care and feeding that was unlikely to occur unless Merryn herself provided it—and her plight was the same as the horses', the same as Krynneth's, with whom she shared what had been built as a tack storage room adjoining a stable, but which had proved as sturdy, and impervious to escape, as any prison cell.

The only difference was that she had known early on that their sole chance of survival depended on husbanding their resources. The horses didn't. They had drunk all the water their Ixtian masters had given them; there was no more; and now—amidst stifling desert heat—they were dying.

At least they didn't know that.

At least they continued to live in *now*.

Unlike herself and Krynneth, who had no choice but to lie on the floor (because it was cooler) and try *not* to think about starvation, desperation, and their own mortality.

Merryn therefore ignored the horses—and might have returned to slumber, had Krynneth not chosen that moment to flop over in his sleep and utter a loud and forceful "no!"

It was nightmares again, she assumed—probably about the Ixtian army, which Krynneth chose to call "the burners." The Eight knew she'd had plenty of bad dreams about them herself during the ten days of captivity by a renegade band of that number that had culminated in their present incarceration. She stared at Krynneth idly. Dirty, smelly, unkempt, and stubbly, he didn't look like much—like a rangy, dirty scarecrow, if truth were known—but Merryn knew that properly cleaned and dressed, and with his pale blue eyes free of fear, he was one of the handsomest men in Eron.

And one of the tastiest, if they didn't get out of here soon, and he died before she did.

But she didn't want to think about that now, and so she

remained as she was: resigned to lying on the flagstone floor, staring at the seam where whitewashed limestone walls a quarter span thick butted against a vaulted roof of that same stone, above which tiles lay athwart oak boards that would have dulled any knife by now, presuming that she'd had one.

As the door—oak, well made, and leading to an exercise run before the stalls—would likewise have resisted such assault.

There was light because there were two windows no wider than her outstretched fingers and thrice that high—too narrow to crawl through unless one went a bone at a time—which seemed increasingly likely.

There was heat because it was summer and the cooling effect of yesterday's freak late-evening shower had long since dissipated, along with most of the surface water.

There was clothing because they'd been imprisoned in the clothes they had worn when that same cadre of Ixtians who terrified Krynneth had captured them—minus armor, weapons, and jewelry, unless one counted manacles at wrists and ankles among the latter.

And there was water, because the stable's pump was in their room and—blessedly—still functioned, if only at a trickle, recent rain notwithstanding.

There might be food, if they could catch a rat, or stall-snake. Or if straw could be chewed long enough to coax forth some nutrition.

But mostly there was despair—and weariness—and sleep.

. . . dust drifted within golden shafts between window wall and floor . . .

. . . and the horses abruptly screamed louder.

Merryn blinked to full alertness, cursing herself for letting complacency rule her. For hiding within the sounds of panicked horses were others, from the courtyard beyond the stable: sounds which had not been present before: mostly a kind of sporadic grinding crunch, coupled with heavy, thudding footsteps and an occasional raspy hiss. She blinked again, waiting for the dizziness that had ambushed her upon waking to disperse.

Fine, then: She knew.

Geens: man-sized lizard-things that generally hunted in packs of four, and which she was more convinced than ever might be intelligent.

But now that she had identified their low-pitched vocalics, she was both cheered and alarmed. Cheered because anything alive moving around beyond their prison was likely to change *something,* which might result in them *not* being stuck there for good; and alarmed because geens, though they were perfectly willing to scavenge, as these were clearly doing, preferred live prey when they could get it.

All of which took Merryn maybe five breaths to assess before she was on her feet and staggering, somewhat unsteadily because of the manacles, toward the wall in which the windows were set. The nearest showed nothing, but the other was quite a different matter.

Framed by limestone walls as thick as her forearm, she gazed out upon a sand-paved courtyard maybe twenty spans square, with the bulk of a collapsing hold-house barely visible to the right. It was late in the day, and the westering sun was painting the far wall an attractive shade between purple and red, and the snowcapped mountains beyond a nicer shade of pink. It was edging the leaves of the fruit trees along that wall with red, too, but more to the point, it was casting its light upon four healthy-looking, full-grown geens, three of which were tearing vigorously at the corpses of the five dead Ixtians—who, as recently as yester eve, had been full of dreams of conquest and extravagant passions. The last time she had seen those men alive, they had been relaxing around what had once been a campfire, recently bathed after days on the non-existent road, and getting happily drunk while they plotted how they would take the magical royal regalia Merryn was supposed to be in the process of concealing and use it to depose Ixti's new king, Kraxxi, after which it would serve to spearhead a march north into Eron on the second war of conquest in half a year, only this time they would be victorious.

They hadn't. In the manner of disaffected soldiers, they had quarreled, and then one of them had killed all the others—the ones who were being eaten now. Whereupon the sole survivor—a man named Orkeen, who had been fool enough to don the entire achievement of regalia in a moment of drunken, vain, madness—had blithely doffed that regalia and, still under its influence for whatever reason, strolled casually into the campfire. His blackened corpse lay athwart the ashes now, where even the geens seemed disinclined to touch it.

They were proving to be picky eaters, too. Most carnivores went first for the organ meat; these seemed to favor the big muscles of hip, leg, and lower back. Even as she watched, one planted a three-toed foot on the torso of the man named Inon (who had been nominal leader of the crew), bit into his thigh, gave a savage wrench, and gained not only the chosen morsel, but the entire leg, which it transferred to its short forelimbs. Looking oddly human, it proceeded to gnaw the meat to the bone. It had been a bare leg, Merryn noted. They were having little truck with meat that had been clothed.

"Merry?"

Krynneth's voice startled her so much that she yipped in alarm and jerked back from the window, rattling her chains in the process.

Nor was she the only one who heard that noise. Geens could hear better than most reptiles, and before she could steady herself, the nearest one squatted down on its haunches, then leapt with blinding speed toward the window behind which she had been crouching. Its lizardlike head filled the narrow slot, yellow eyes distorted by the wavy glass set behind the heavy bars. Claws drew streaks on the pane. And then, with another oddly human gesture, it drew back a claw and flicked the pane—hard. Cracks starred out from that impact, and Merryn was more than glad that the opening was too narrow for any part of a geen to insert itself far enough to do damage.

Not that it didn't try. Another flick sent glass rattling against the stone sill, and brought a hint of breeze, atop which rode the musky scent of reptile. It also brought the scent of sun-ripened carrion. Merryn was grateful that the glass had been intact ere now.

The commotion further roused Krynneth, who blinked once, saw what was transpiring, and retreated to the opposite wall, where he recited his entire vocabulary, which consisted of *yes, no, shit, piss, damn, key,* and *Merry.*

"Stay calm, Kryn," Merryn hissed. "They can't get in this way. And there's a wall and a door between them and our door."

"Damn," Krynneth repeated, which seemed to be more than sufficient.

Somehow Merryn managed to hold her ground, though it took all the willpower she possessed to make no sudden moves that might rouse the geen to greater exertions.

Abruptly, it was gone, bounding away out of sight to Merryn's right. Scarcely daring to breathe, she returned to the window and gazed out, fearing every instant to find herself facing the claws of a very cunning beast that had lain in wait outside.

In that, however, she was fortunate. More to the point, she got close enough to renew her investigation, and that revealed two things. One was that the beast *had* moved on, to judge by the way the others had ceased their munchings and were gazing toward something out of sight to their left. The other was that the already fractious horses, which had been housed in the other end of the stable, had now gained confirmation of the fact that four of their primary predators were not only skipping about three spans and a wall away from their stalls, but were also now cognizant of *their* existence—with the result that the poor, trapped beasts had redoubled their already cacophonous—and probably suicidal—ruckus.

Which only served to fix the geens' attention squarely upon them.

Horses whinnied and screamed. Even six spans away, Merryn heard thumps of bodies against stone and hooves kicking sun-hardened wood.

The geens were a fury of movement as they hopped, leapt, and scurried toward the source of that noise, which clearly proclaimed fresh meat. A terrible scrabbling sound ensued, coupled, incredibly, with the heavy smack of one leaping atop the roof. Tiles shattered; wood groaned and splintered. Dust shifted down from the ceiling.

But the geens, for the nonce, were thwarted. Certainly three of them came stomping back into view.

And then Merryn saw something that froze her heart indeed. The geens were stalking around the courtyard, peering intently about, as though in quest of something particular. One picked up a limb that had fallen from one of the fruit trees, shook it experimentally, then smacked it against the wall, as though to test its strength. It shattered—but the more supple limb that same geen wrested from the tree did not.

Another followed its example, while the third one—the one that by the pattern of spots mottling its hide was the one which had tried to get at her and Krynneth—prowled through the human detritus around the fire, reached down, fumbled for something on the ground—and to Merryn's abject horror, rose again with the Lightning Sword clutched in a scaly, black-clawed fist!

"Damn," Merryn muttered, only then aware that Krynneth had crept over to stand beside her. "Damn, oh damn, oh damn," as she clutched his arm for comfort that would have shamed her any other time. Krynneth was sweating profusely, but saying nothing.

As for the geen...

Something was clearly occurring within its narrow, scaly skull, because it was standing absolutely frozen, with a startled expression—if something with so little flexible flesh on its bones could be said to *have* an expression—on its face.

Thought roared out at her so strongly that she flinched.

Geen thought.

It *was* thought, too.

Not the raw ravening instinct she would have expected from a beast.

Except, perhaps, from a birkit—if what Avall, Div, and Rann had told her about their sentience was true.

As to what the geen thought: *That* was hard to determine, if for no other reason than because it proclaimed itself so loudly. Mostly she sensed surprise, overlying an endless pit of hunger like froth upon a sea. But there were images along with it, the bulk having to do with eating horses—which made Merryn cringe in revulsion.

Yet along with those baser impressions came a keen curiosity about the world at large, and especially about these other two-legged predators that were so strong and weak by turns.

"You want free."

The thought was a jolt in Merryn's mind. *Had the geen "thought" that at her? More to the point, if it had learned that from her, what else had it learned? Maybe how to get in to where she and Krynneth were trapped? How to secure a free meal of humans at its leisure?*

"The long claw will not let me," came the unexpected answer.

And that was all. The contact shattered as though it had been smashed with a hammer. Merryn uttered a cry, and reality came whirling back, only to vanish once more as what sounded like lightning slammed into the stable to the right. Light flared through every chink in the doorjamb; the walls shook and trembled, and another healthy cascade of dust poured down from the ceiling. One arch cracked but held. The rattle of sliding tiles filled the yard.

There followed the worst sounds Merryn had ever heard: the screams, wails, and cries of seven horses having their throats torn out and their bellies opened.

Or maybe not, for there was another sound as well: one full of anger and fear combined, as at least one doughty equine proved unwilling to surrender its life without cost. Hooves sounded loud on stone floors as the beast lurched from side to side. And hard on those noises came the dull thud of something large being kicked, followed at once by the clear crack of bone breaking and the long shivering screech of a geen in pain. Wood ripped and splintered.

But then—miraculously—hooves clattered in the yard. Forgetting the geens, Merryn dashed to the window—to see that one bleeding horse had indeed broken free—her own faithful Boot, in fact—and was careening around the courtyard. Once, twice, the mare made that circuit, but on the third, Boot found sense and charged through the gate that the geens had conveniently left open.

As for her fellows, they were surely all dead now, or at least they had all stopped screaming. But that wasn't the worst sound anyway. Indeed, for a fair long while, Merryn had to put her hands over her ears as she waited for the slurps, grunts, and tearings of the geens' grisly feast to cease.

Yet even that was not the worst of the waiting; for every moment, she feared to hear the slapping tread of heavy reptiles approaching. Forbidden, she and Krynneth might be—to one geen; she doubted the others would care, if they were still unsated.

But to her surprise, they seemed to have eaten their fill. Or at least they left the now-silent stable and, one by one, stalked back into the yard to disappear through the open gate to the right.

All save one.

Merryn's heart skipped a beat when she saw that one. It still had the sword, she realized with a chill that had nothing to do with temperature. And it grasped that sword very much as a man would grip one.

Twice, that geen stalked about the yard as though searching for something—and Merryn had a terrible feeling she knew what. Indeed, it paused the second time it passed what remained of her window into the courtyard. A yellow eye peered

n at her. Somehow, Merryn met that gaze clearly—until it
blinked and continued on.

She lost sight of the geen after that, and did not locate it
again until it had reached the ruined gate. It turned there,
raised the sword once more, and slashed it down.

Lightning followed it straight into the stable. And Merryn
knew no more.

CHAPTER VIII:

SCAVENGING

(SOUTHWEST OF ERON—HIGH SUMMER: DAY LXXV—LATE AFTERNOON)

~~~~~~~~~

Merryn had gone blind.

That was her initial assessment, anyway, of eyes that did not seem to want to open properly. Certainly *something* was keeping them restrained, something crusty, she determined, as awareness increased a level. And perhaps that something was connected to the throbbing in the back of her head, or else to the sharper pain between her brows. She raised a hand without thinking, felt something slide off her shoulder to clink noisily to the floor. A stir of her legs produced the sound of stone grating against itself.

Her fingers found her head at roughly the same moment that she got one eyelid open, from which she concluded that she had been struck by something that had fallen from the ceiling, or else she had struck something *when* she had fallen, and that the crusty matter in her other eye was blood old enough to have dried. Groaning, she tried to push up on an elbow, heard more stone shift and grind, and then had to halt abruptly, as pain throbbed through her head with sufficient force to make her want to vomit.

Concussion, she told herself. Nothing that couldn't be survived ...

Survived...

What had *she survived, anyway?*

And what about Krynneth?

Oblivious to the pain it cost her, she sat up in truth, clawing at the recalcitrant eye. The lid moved a little—enough that she could see more, if not better. Enough, in any case, to confirm that she lay on the floor of the stable, and that a good chunk of the front wall had collapsed, bringing down a fair bit of the roof along with it, much of which now spilled down around them, revealing an opening into the courtyard beyond.

It took Merryn a moment to realize what that meant. "Free," she muttered. "We're free." Then hard on its heels: "Danger."

There were geens about, after all.

Geens, in fact, had done this.

No, *one* geen had: a geen with a magic sword. *Her* magic sword.

As to why it had done that: called the lightning down on the very place Merryn and Krynneth had been imprisoned, she did not want to contemplate. Instinct perhaps? Or impulse? Or—just possibly—altruism? She had no idea. *Eight! Had the beast actually acted on her desire for escape, which it had admitted knowing?* Or had she been controlling it, all unknown? Or had the sword?

No! She wouldn't think about that now. Not when death had receded the smallest increment. Not when she still had to see to Krynneth.

It wasn't hard to find him, for all he was covered with a skim of stone dust like a fish floured up for frying. He sat hunched up by the wall with his arms clasped around his knees. His eyes were wide-open, his jaws clinched, and he was repeating over and over, "Don't eat, don't eat, don't eat." By which Merryn assumed he meant that he was not to be eaten. She didn't blame him, either. At least *she* was marginally rational. But Krynneth? Who knew what lurked in his poor tattered mind? Perhaps it had snapped entirely and she would never again enjoy even those brief periods of lucidity that had passed between them before their captivity.

In any case, this was no place to linger. The walls of their prison had been shattered, but she and Kryn still wore manacles and chains that could easily spell their doom in the world at large. But the keys...

She swallowed hard. *Where* were *the keys, anyway?* She remembered keys mostly from a ring Inon had worn. And Inon was not only dead, he had been...sampled by an inquisitive hungry geen.

Still, this was no time for delicacy or squeamishness. Leaving Krynneth where he sat, Merryn made her way to her feet and began clumsily picking her way toward the rift in the stable's wall. It was close to sunset out there, and the shadows were long already. She would have to hurry if she wanted to accomplish anything. There was reason to think that Inon had not had the particular keys she sought; but in that case, who would? Ivk had locked her and Krynneth away, then gone bathing. But it had been Tahlone who had observed a shade too loudly that they only had one lock suitable for securing the tack room door, and since Tahlone was older, it made more sense for him to control its key than the boy. On the other hand, Inon had been the Ixtians' leader, so *he* was likeliest to retain the keys to the manacles. Surely not Shaul, who was not a pleasant person, or Orkeen, who had dared don the regalia, gone mad for his pains, and stepped—or been driven—into the fire.

Did it really matter? All the bodies would have to be searched eventually. Setting her jaw against what was already an unpleasant stench of burned meat, freshly exposed viscera, and excrement, Merryn made her way to where Inon lay sprawled upon the earth. She remembered how he had wound up there, too. He had rushed Orkeen in a rage, slammed into the "magic" shield, and the shield had done as it was designed to do: absorbed the force Inon had hurled into it and returned that force tenfold, while stripping away the top several fingers f Inon's flesh to finance the effort. Which was why she could ee the gleam of ribs, cheekbones, and pelvic crests, along with fair expanse of the poor man's guts. He was also missing a eg, courtesy of a rapacious geen. Fortunately, he had been hirtless when he died, which meant that there was that much ess to search. And the shield didn't act as efficiently on metal s on flesh, so perhaps the keys—if he'd had them—were still ntact. In any case, Inon's leather gear-belt was gone in front, ut the buckle—albeit somewhat abraded—was still present. And while there was indeed a key ring, she saw at a glance that one of the keys worked the manacles.

Ivk had fallen into the fire upon his death, and had only vorn trousers in any case, so she postponed inspecting him. Which left Tahlone as next most likely guardian. Tahlone had een killed by a single sweeping blast of the Lightning Sword, nd had crumpled where he stood. A mug of brandy had ig-ited in his hand and consumed his baggy sleeve to the shoul-ler, but his body was largely intact, if rather scorched in ppearance and missing its hair. He also had the keys: a large ing of them, in fact, among which Merryn quickly identified he ones she wanted. A bit of deft finger work freed first one vrist, then the other, before turning to her ankles. The ring till in her hand, she stretched luxuriously, letting her limbs ex-lore limits that had been denied them for days.

But only for a moment. A deep breath, a quick check for urking geens, and she returned to her erstwhile prison, intent pon releasing Krynneth. But even as she sank down beside im, fumbling for the most likely key, she wondered if she was vise to release him, given that a scant ten days ago he had been ble to overpower her rather handily, thereby beginning the irst of two captivities. More to the point, he had been half-razy even then, which fact she had seriously underrated until fter she had dropped her guard long enough for him to clout er on the side of the head with the hilt of a knife—thereby precipitating a period of unconsciousness from which she had wakened to find herself neatly and thoroughly bound. He

had feared "the burners" then—and had completely misrea
her motives in possessing the regalia. Which were the only rea
sons that even vaguely supported such an otherwise preposter
ous action.

But would any of those reasons have altered?

Could she risk such an untrustworthy ally now?

Could she afford not to? At least he had stopped the litany o
"don't eat...don't eat...don't eat."

"Come on, Kryn," she muttered, helping him to his feet, bu
leaving his manacles in place for the nonce. "There are bette
places to be than here." Somehow she steered him through th
shattered wall and into the clearer ground of the courtyar
trying as hard as she could to keep him from seeing the car
nage that lay there. It was time to continue the search, she sup
posed—but first, she snared a bottle of unopened wine fror
the several that were strewn about, the contents of which ha
provoked the drunkenness that had precipitated the Ixtian
disastrous bout of fratricide. Popping the cork, she raised th
bottle to her lips and treated herself to a long draught, even a
she acknowledged the foolishness of that act. Still, it warme
her and gave her strength. She passed the rest to Krynneth t
do with as he would.

For herself...

The answer to that question was easy enough; after all, sh
still had a duty to perform.

Steeling herself for whichever of fear or disappointmen
found her first, she trotted toward the gate through which th
geens had departed. Every nerve she possessed tingled as sh
approached, and she wished she had thought to bring a swor
lest the beasts still be lurking about. Fortunately, logic caugh
up with impulse in time to remind her that ducking belo
wall level might be a good idea, and she was, in fact, almo.
scooting along on hands and knees when she finally reache
the gate proper and, very cautiously, peered beyond it.

She saw nothing. Nothing that hadn't been there befor
anyway. Nothing, that is, except geen tracks everywhere, a

heading out into the sere grass and sand that surrounded the hold. She followed them a dozen paces—far enough to see them turn north, paralleling the river. More to the point, she remained there long enough to determine that the geens themselves were nowhere in sight. Not that she expected them to be; at a run, geens could cover ground in a hurry, and these were sated and would want to go to ground for the night to sleep off their loathsome feast.

She almost followed them anyway—the lure of the sword was that strong, and stronger still was the onus of responsibility she had taken on herself when she had begun her quest to conceal it. But there was still Krynneth to consider, not to mention the fact that she was tired past moving and so hungry that the sun-dried grass was starting to look tasty.

Besides, it would be dark soon, and the geens would have the advantage. *Besides,* geens had dens, so if she was patient and followed their spoor, she would still come upon them in good time. Granted there was still the problem of the sword, but she suspected the sword would do more harm to the geen that carried it than the geen would do to the sword, and with all those arguments pointing her toward rest and recovery in lieu of immediate—and probably foolhardy—action, she turned smartly and marched back toward the hold.

The dead men hadn't moved, of course, and Krynneth was still sitting obediently where she had left him. Setting her jaw, she strode past him—straight to where the remaining pieces of regalia still lay where Orkeen had shed them before wading into the fire. To her surprise, however, she was strangely reluctant to touch those marvels of metalwork—and wound up using a fold of Tahlone's cloak as insulation between her skin and the actual metal until she could secure them more properly. Helm first, then shield, she shifted them to the shadows beyond the hold's empty back door.

A dozen anxious breaths were all it took to confirm that the horses were indeed thoroughly and messily dead (which fact further supported her decision to remain where she was for the night), and she turned her attention to the dead men in earnest. The Eight knew she didn't want to leave them strewn about like that: burned, sword-blasted, and half-eaten—yet she had no inclination whatever to bury them, even if there had been time, which there wasn't, what with night drawing on and the sword now a rogue element in the world. To postpone decision, she stripped the intact Ixtians of valuables—mostly finger rings or ear studs—and weapons, which included a number of daggers.

But not, she discovered to her dismay, the cache of loose gems she had demanded that Avall, Strynn, and Rann surrender upon her departure on this errand. Those, she had sewn into her pouch, but that had been discovered long since and claimed by Inon, along with the ring that contained the finding stone. The pouch had *not* been on Inon's body, however—unless it had been blasted away to the Overworld by the shield, which did not seem likely. Nor did Tahlone have it—or Shaul, or poor young Ivk—as a quick search proved. Which left Orkeen.

She tried not to think about him. Though not a pleasant man, and clearly rougher and more volatile than the rest of Inon's crew, no one deserved to die as he had: controlled, as it seemed, from without; his body forced to step into the flames of the cook fire and remain there until his clothing ignited and he died.

But if *he'd* had the gems...

Who knew what effect flames would have on them? Especially if they were, as Avall suspected, partially sapient.

She debated checking the packs first, thereby saving the worst for last, but finally concluded that a cursory inspection of Orkeen's body was in order. The pouch had been leather, after all; perhaps it would not have been consumed entirely. If she saw it, she would inspect it. If she did not, she would check the packs.

Even so, she almost missed it. Blackened as it was, it was hard to tell from a section of viscera that had erupted from

Orkeen's abdomen when intestinal gases had thrust those organs through charred muscle and skin. But that had to be it; she could even see the embossed sigil of her clan through all that ruin. Holding her hand across her mouth in anticipation of a stench that would surely make her gag, she reached forward with Shaul's eating dagger and snared the remains of the pouch's ties. She had to rake it through cold ashes to avoid touching Orkeen's body directly, but she managed, cursing herself for squeamishness all the while.

Wrapping it, like the shield and helm, in a fold of cloak, she rose and bore it away, sparing a glance to confirm that Krynneth wasn't up to mischief.

He wasn't. Indeed, he didn't seem to have moved from where she had left him, like a particularly obedient—or dispirited—child.

Slumping down against the stable's most intact wall, she opened the fire-hardened leather and tumbled the gems into her hand.

They were still red, and still bore sparkling motes in their depths, but it was obvious that something about them had altered—luster, perhaps, or brightness. And not only their physical appearance had changed; it was—there was no other word for it—as if they were asleep. Or perhaps, like Krynneth, they had been driven so deep within themselves they could no longer respond to her presence.

Krynneth stared at them with absent interest. "Jump," he said, increasing his vocabulary again.

Merryn raised a brow. "You keep that up, we'll be able to talk like real people before long."

"Jump," Krynneth repeated tonelessly.

The brow lowered as quickly as it had lifted. "Maybe, but not now."

"No?"

"No," she echoed patting his hand. "They were in the fire, Kryn," she went on, speaking aloud partly for his benefit, but equally as much for her own: to hear a human voice that was not giving orders or sounding afraid. And because talking helped clarify her thoughts. "They don't look the same, and given their capricious nature, we've no guarantee they would act the same, either. If they're like Avall thinks: somehow alive, the fire could have killed them. If not... well, jumping isn't the first thing that would occur to me to do with them, anyway."

She scowled at that, wondering what the first thing *was*. "I suppose the right thing to do would be to see if I can bond with one of them—probably Strynn's. Then try to bond with you. That way"—she gnawed her lip. "That way, maybe I could... fix you."

She broke off abruptly, wondering whether she had said too much, given that she was still not certain whether Krynneth should be considered an ally or a foe. In either case, she would have to keep an eye on him. Prove himself he might—eventually; but until then, she would have to watch every move he made—which would make even simple acts a drudgery.

As for jumping—well, the gems could certainly jump one to a person or place. But she could think of only one place to which it would be useful to jump, and that was to wherever the geen with the sword was.

Which might, in fact, be possible—if she took the remaining two pieces of regalia with her. But which could also get her killed in a heartbeat if the sword wound up amid a nest of geens. Granted, she seemed to have achieved some rudimentary rapport with one of the creatures, but that was nothing to rely on. Besides which, there was Krynneth. If she jumped away, she would be stranding him on his own, and the Night Guard code of honor would not let her do that. Yet if she took him with her, it might be to his doom.

Of course he might die anyway—they both might. But she was still on a royal quest, and if she so chose, she could look on the last few days as a merely an unplanned diversion. She had intended to go west, anyway. And this *was* west. Beyond that, the only real criteria she had established as far as a viable hiding place for the regalia was concerned were that it be as far from human habitation as possible—even deserted habitation, which ruled out anywhere nearby, since there was no reason this hold could not be resettled—and that there be some kind of identifying landmark sufficiently near at hand that it could be recovered at need in future years.

In any case, her course of action was set for her: Whether she liked it or not, she had to retrieve the sword. If she was lucky, the geen had dropped it close by— What earthly need did it have for a weapon, after all?

But suppose the beast was as mad as Rrath had been. Human minds could only endure the full power of the gems under certain circumstances, so what would one do to a geen?

Well, for one thing any aberrant conduct could easily result in the thing getting itself killed by its fellows—especially if it turned on them. Even better, the blade itself could have turned on the beast with fatal results, in which case she was lucky again, and might not have to travel far to find out for sure.

Now *that* was a comforting notion—but even so, it was not one she was prepared to address at the moment, what with night coming on and neither she nor Krynneth having been fed in over a day. She helped herself to another quaff of wine and rose, turning to yank Krynneth up with her. He rose easily. *Too* easily, perhaps. *Had he lost that much weight? And how much had she lost lately, on a diet of camp fare and water?* Fortunately, food wasn't a problem in the short term, what with the hold, the Ixtians' supplies, and an ample cache of freshly dead horse. And while the latter notion held little appeal, she had eaten horse before, and the alternative was to waste a ready supply of meat.

Whichever alternative she chose, she had to build a cook fire—one well away from sight or scent of the bodies. She also needed to investigate the house in search of a place to sleep for the night. There were geens thereabouts, after all; and with the stables now in ruins— Well, there was absolutely no way she was going to sleep outside tonight.

As for tomorrow...

Food, first, in large quantities. Then...

Tracking she supposed.

Or—

A bath? It would consume a hand at most, if they hurried, and make up for that in comfort. Besides which, there was the small matter of Krynneth, who hadn't bathed since sometime before she had met him, and that had been over an eight ago. Yes, tomorrow morning, like it or not, and quest be damned, she was going to get him into the river, then into some clean clothes, if she had to pillage the Ixtian dead to do it.

In the meantime—

"Eat?" Krynneth queried hopefully.

"Yes," she sighed. "That's a good idea. Do you think you could find some firewood? I'll go see if there's anywhere to cook inside, though I don't think it's very likely, else these lads wouldn't have set up out here."

"Yes," Krynneth repeated. Which settled a great many things for the nonce.

CHAPTER IX:

LATE-NIGHT DISCOVERY

(NORTHWESTERN ERON: GEM-HOLD-WINTER—HIGH SUMMER: DAY LXXV NIGHT)

'But what *I* want to know," Zeff said emphatically, and not for the first time that evening, never mind that day, "is where in three worlds was Avall?"

"Not on the siege tower; that's all we know," Ahfinn replied wearily, dodging deftly aside as Zeff swept by on his latest round of pacings. Those took him by a small table on which bread, wine, and cheese were always arrayed. He paused there to refill a goblet he had already refilled twice—then turned in place to glare at his adjutant, eyes blue as his Ninth Face tabard, but far, far colder.

"I knew *that* much a finger past sunrise," Zeff snapped. "I've spent the rest of the day scanning their camp from our top gallery with the best distance lenses I have, and learned nothing—and curse them, too, for not cutting down more trees. I could see the top of what might be the Royal Pavilion but nothing at all of who goes in and out there." He took a long draught of wine for emphasis.

Ahfinn availed himself of that opportunity to refill his own goblet, though he was drinking more slowly than his Chief. He hated it when Zeff got like this; then again, whatever else he was, Zeff was also human—and it was human to vent one's frustrations. He only hoped Zeff didn't realize how much he was revealing about himself in the process. Information was power, after all, and Ahfinn had acquired quite a lot of information about his Chief of late—if not a clear notion of the extent of that Chief's hold on sanity.

Something had certainly changed since Zeff had tried to wrest the secret of the gems from Avall. And changed again since yesterday, when he had called the lightning, then snatched defeat from victory's jaws.

"Think, Chief," Ahfinn ventured finally, trying to look as serious as his youth allowed. "Avall had minimal food once we brought him here. He was also plied with imphor wood and—forgive me—physically abused. Any of those things alone could have worn his stamina to a nubbin even without what happened."

Zeff rounded on him, his lean face dark as thunder. "And what *did* happen?"

"You were there as well as I was," Ahfinn retorted. "Avall was clamped to the tabletop; there was that...confusion with the sword; then Kylin grabbed Avall's hand, whereupon he simply...*wasn't*—nor was Kylin. We've chosen to call it magic because that's how we're conditioned to term such things; but it could just as well have been anything from a very clever conjurer's trick to intercession by The Nine."

"If The Nine could free him," Zeff sniffed coldly, "it would mean he has Their favor absolute, in which case we wouldn't be sitting here now."

Ahfinn shrugged beneath his own blue surcoat—wool, where Zeff's was velvet. "They're capricious. They don't always agree. Perhaps it's a test."

"It *is* a test!" Zeff flared, claiming a seat on the padded bench built into one wall. "A test of patience. The fact is, Avall vanished yesterday, hasn't been seen since then, and hadn't obviously returned this morning. That tells me a number of things. Rationality dictates that he and Kylin somehow returned to their camp, since that would be their nearest place of refuge, as well as being where their friends are. It also tells me that Avall could have been injured in...transit or became sick thereafter. He could even have been killed—what Kylin did certainly looked to *me* like the work of a desperate man, and such things often go awry. For that matter, they could simply have vanished completely. We could have witnessed a very spectacular suicide-regicide, for all we know. And that's the problem, Ahfinn: We know nothing."

"We know that Avall didn't reappear this morning," Ahfinn replied with a carefully contrived calm he hoped would be contagious. "Even that fact, tenuous as it is, gives you more time in which to find new gems. We also know that Rann didn't reappear, which I find interesting."

"Rann is Avall's bond-brother," Zeff spat. "If Avall *was* injured, it would be perfectly consistent with Rann's character to abandon everything else to nurse him."

"Which would also explain Vorinn's presence on the tower."

"And Tryffon's and Preedor's and Veen's. But the rest—I don't know, Ahfinn; those two particular absences just seem odd."

"There's still an army," Ahfinn offered, "one that's only going to get bigger while ours can only remain the same."

Zeff scowled. "Conceded. But then we may ask another question. When Avall and Kylin vanished, Kylin had the Lightning Sword—without its proper gem, apparently, but which still worked after a fashion even with the 'wrong' one. Why, therefore, hasn't anyone been out there wielding it against us? That's why I had most of the hold folk out on display today: to prevent anyone using the Lightning Sword on us. Fortunately, as far as we can tell, it's the only actual weapon among the three."

"Agreed," Ahfinn sighed. "So where are we, then?"

"Waiting," Zeff replied sourly. "Exactly like our foes."

"We could always try to revive Rrath again."

Zeff glared at him. "Another exercise in frustration? Are you trying to drive me mad?"

Ahfinn chose not to answer. "I'll check on him if you like."

The glare did not diminish. "Suit yourself—only get out of my sight."

Ahfinn sketched a bow and withdrew. He did not, however, exit Zeff's quarters; rather, he opened a door to his left that let onto an empty corridor lined with identical round-topped doors. He walked straight to the third one on the right, fumbled briefly with a large bronze ring at his waist, chose one from the dozen keys clustered there, and thrust it into the lock. A pause to compose himself before entering, and he slipped into the chamber beyond: one of a series of small, austere rooms that permeated this part of the hold—rooms that had been built as a matter of course but had not yet had any particular function assigned to them, thus their sparseness. Which made them perfect as cells—or sickrooms—in which capacity this one presently served.

Rrath—Rrath syn Garnill, to use the full name of the young man who lay faceup on a plain white cot against the opposite wall—had not moved in any obvious fashion since Ahfinn had last looked in on him two days earlier, nor had he changed for the better. Never large, even by Eronese standards, Rrath seemed to have shrunk in all dimensions since he had been brought here by the same band of Ninth Face soldiers that had captured Avall back at the Face's primary citadel. That was odd, too, Ahfinn considered. Usually when one wasted away one simply got thinner and thinner until no meat remained on one's bones for the soul to consume, whereupon one died. Rrath, however, merely seemed to be...diminishing. He was almost certainly shorter than when he had first arrived.

Ahfinn shuddered as he stared down at the man. *Nine, but it was cold in here!* Maybe he should talk to Zeff about installing a brazier to knock the chill off the room. Maybe that would aid Rrath's recovery.

Somehow he doubted it.

Rrath was victim of....of himself, he supposed. Why, he hadn't even been a Fellow of the Face for a year yet; only since the previous autumn, when old Nyllol had recruited him. But he *had* been a remarkably fast riser—perhaps too fast. Certainly if he had behaved with more circumspection they might have retrieved Avall's magic gems long since. As it was, Rrath had fallen in with Avall's brilliant but fatally flawed cousin, Eddyn, and everyone in the Face knew how that had ended: with Eddyn dead, with the gems out of reach in the regalia, with Avall on the Throne, and with Rrath having—briefly—worn the regalia—which had promptly driven him mad, then forced him so far into himself that not even the Royal Healers—not even Avall, with intercession from one or the other of the gems, so he had heard—could recall him.

Perhaps Zeff could have—if he had dared use the gem.

But Zeff had *not* dared: not since the episode with Avall—and if Zeff dared not, there was no doubt whatever about whether Ahfinn dared.

Maybe if they found more gems...

Sparing one final glance at Rrath—a glance marked by the rare privilege of actually seeing the man breathe—Ahfinn shook his head sadly, returned to the corridor outside, and re-locked the door.

As he approached Zeff's chambers, the sound of voices reached him. He paused at the portal, listening. A messenger had just arrived, so it sounded: one of the Fellows newly returned from Tir-Eron, if he heard right—and that was a neat trick, too, given that Gem-Hold was effectively surrounded. Still, the Face knew of entrances that the Royalists did not, and that knowledge had served them well so far. The question was, did he announce himself or simply remain in place, listening?

The former, he decided.

Straightening his tabard, Ahfinn rapped a courtesy cadence on the door and reentered his Chief's chambers.

Instead of glaring, Zeff ignored him, intent as he was on a dark, slightly built young woman clad in the tight black garb of those whose duty it was to come and go from the hold unseen. By the ritual cup of greeting still clasped in her hand, she had only just arrived. She looked tired but alert. Ahfinn doubted that he had missed much more than ritual.

"And now," Zeff addressed the woman, motioning her to a seat and claiming one himself, as did Ahfinn, "how fare things in Tir-Eron?"

The woman's face was sober. "Things could...fare better."

Zeff raised a brow. "How so?"

The woman took a deep breath. "On the surface, affairs proceed decently if not well. That is, people—the low clans—go about their lives much as before. Rather, I should say those from Eron Gorge and north go as before, as much as they can without the implicit leadership provided to them by the Chiefs. What we had not reckoned on was the extent of displacement in the south, nor on the number of refugees who must be fed, housed, and the pains in their souls attended to. Our stores, already stretched thin, are now, I fear—"

"—Overtaxed," Zeff finished for her. "The question is, has there been direct dissent?"

"Not to say, though we have observed meetings of Common Clan and clanless—and dispersed them quickly with appropriate arrests. But there also seems to be at least one covert effort afoot to systematically assassinate our guards, generally those in remote locations. Mostly they just turn up dead with no mark on their bodies we can find—if we can find those bodies before the fish or the flames do, which seems never to be the case."

"And the Chiefs?"

"Which Chiefs? Ours, or the others?"

"Both."

The woman shifted position, staring at her drink. "As far as the other Chiefs are concerned, after Mask Night, we have had little success in...accounting for those we have not accounted for already. Nor, unfortunately, have we identified where those survivors might be gathering, though surely they must be doing so—all of which means that we must be on guard at all times."

Zeff steepled his fingers before him. "And why do you suppose this is? This problem with the rank and file?"

The messenger looked up at him. "May I be frank?"

"You may."

"Because we reckoned on the people being angry at the High Clans for withholding access to The Eight, but in fact what seems to have affected them far more strongly is this rumor that Avall has proven that the soul and the body are not bound together. That alone—proof that the soul exists—seems of greater import to them than any sort of access to The Eight we can provide."

"In other words," Ahfinn broke in, "the fact that they have more reason to suppose there is something to life...hereafter gives them less reason to question the facts of their life in the here and now."

"That, in essence, would seem to be the case," the messenger conceded carefully.

"Not what we wanted to hear," Zeff growled. "I—" He froze abruptly, cocked his head, and glanced toward the door. "Someone's coming—in a hurry, by the tread."

Ahfinn followed his Chief's gaze, but by then a knock had sounded in urgent cadence. "Come!" Zeff called at once, his face dark as thunder. Ahfinn pitied anyone who used that cadence frivolously.

The door opened immediately, to admit a short, wiry young man whose clean novice robe did not mask a dirty and sweaty body. "Forgive me, Chief," the lad began, glancing around quickly, his gaze pausing briefly on the messenger. "Forgive me, I say—but you wanted to be told at once, no matter what."

Ahfinn's heart double beat, both from the news and the light he saw waken in Zeff's eyes. "You've reached the mines!"

The novice nodded, barely suppressing a grin. "We have. And, sir—the news is even better than that. We have—we think we have—discovered a few more magic gems!"

Zeff was on his feet at once, all anger and apprehension fled from his face. "Ahfinn, go with this lad immediately. Tell them I will be down as soon as I can make myself ready. Fate seems to have rolled the dice again; it remains to see how much of our fate that higher Fate has altered."

CHAPTER X:

REAWAKENING

(SOUTHWEST OF ERON–HIGH SUMMER: DAY LXXVI–EARLY MORNING)

Avall was running.

He did not recall beginning, only that he was doing so now. Effortlessly.

His legs marked out impossibly long strides across an endless plain of sand—sand laced ever more frequently with hard earth and short, sturdy grass that turned yellow or tan a hand above the earth, but which still evinced a comforting green about its roots, even in what seemed to be the silver-blue of moonlight. Small animals dived here and there among those shadowed shoots, and for some reason they made Avall hungry enough to reach down now and then and scoop one up. If he ate them, he did not recall.

There were birds, too: a few, that rose from among that low growth. And every so often there were snakes and lizards: moving shadows among the still. Never mind the insects that rose chirring in his wake as he rushed along.

Tirelessly.

Never pausing.

Running.

Running at the head of the pack.

The light of a single moon beat down on him, and the stars whispered that it was not yet morning. He wondered why he wasn't sweating. The wind whipped along his sides, touching more of him than it ought.

Something glittered in one hand, flickering in and out of sight.

He turned minutely, aware that others ran behind him and altered their courses to suit.

His shadow slid around and ran before him, long across the plain in the silver light.

But it was not *his* shadow.

Not the shadow of a middle-sized, neatly built young man.

This shadow was longer and taller. It had thick-thighed legs with three-toed claws for feet and a torso that was heaviest toward the hips. The arms were roughly the same size as his own, though the head was longer.

And there was a tail, tapering from a thick base to a sharp whip that stuck out straight behind as he ran. His back was a zigzag ridge of hand-sized plates.

He was hungry.

But it was a craving for more than food. Something had awakened in his brain that had not been present before: something profound and bright—something that filled spaces, where before there had been nothing but base desire.

He wanted, he realized, to *know* things.

And that desire flowed into him from a strange new place, from the shiny thing in his hand, in fact. And that hand hurt, he noticed, yet it was a pain he would never relinquish. It was like the exquisite pain when one's mate bit one during copulation. Or the pain in the base of one's teeth when they clamped down on a rival's neck and sent him down to doom.

The sword did all that.

The *sword* . . .

He paused, looked at the long shadow that extended from his right hand. And then at that hand itself.

At bright steel and dulling brass.

And an odd leather gauntlet.

No, that was his hand.

His...*hand*...

And then he knew.

He was a geen.

A geen with a sword.

No, a geen with *that* sword.

Which was impossible.

"No," he whispered into a moonlit darkness that was wavering into light.

Reality shattered. Moonlight swept away, replaced with rippled rock lit by the last orange flicker of the watchfire. Flat sand swirled and spun and became hard stone. He fell, except that there was no falling, only a realization of lying where he had always been: cloak-wrapped on a rug, with Rann's back warm beside him. No footsteps followed him: raspy hiss across dry earth; but snores replaced them: a hand's worth of uneven, uncertain cadences. His hand clinched on nothing.

No sword.

No sword...

He opened his eyes in truth and saw the cave.

He was also sweating, and the dream still hovered there at the edges of his mind. Too real, it had been. Far too real. It had to mean something, yet the only thing that made sense at the moment was its literal meaning, and that he dared not ponder.

He sat up slowly, not wishing to wake Rann. The cave mouth was a blot of star-spangled blackness framed with stone limned dull red by the fire. Bingg's back was a cutout far to the right, facing outward, blocking the only exit from their sleeping place. The boy's head had dropped forward, however. Probably he was asleep. Probably Avall should rise and chastise him. Maybe even take the rest of his watch, though he had done one of his own already.

But Bingg was only a boy.

Or at least not yet a man, though his body had started the

change, and he had undergone the prescribed one night of release with an unclanned courtesan.

Something told Avall that his cousin would never have a typical boyhood. It also told Avall that Bingg would probably not protest that loss overmuch.

But what about that dream?

It had to be prophetic, but if it meant what he thought it did, it threatened dire news indeed.

If only he had some way to contact Merryn! But the only possible means to that end had been shattered past repair. And that assumed it was sane.

"No," came a whisper close beside him. Startling him from a reverie that had already begun to draw him down to sleep again.

He glanced around, determined that it was not Rann who had spoken, which left—to his surprise—Kylin.

Kylin, who had said nothing since his initial outburst of doom-laced, singsong, quasi-poetic ranting. And now a word. A word one often said while dreaming, granted, but the way affairs had fallen out of late, Avall had no surety that anything in his mind—or anyone else's—was sacrosanct. The Eight knew that his stronger thoughts and emotions slopped over into Rann's often enough. And vice versa. Had the same thing just occurred between him and Kylin?

And what were they going to do with the poor little harper, anyway? He was already blind. He had no harp, so he was now cut off from the only thing he was truly fit to do in any active sense. He couldn't keep watch, couldn't hunt, couldn't fight to defend himself, *could* eat if one put food in his mouth, but that was all.

His would not have been a good situation in Tir-Eron with a phalanx of healers to attend him. Here in the wildest part of the Wild, it was unthinkable.

There were only two alternatives. Kylin would die—or he would revive.

The former was far too easily accomplished.

The latter...

Natural healing—which might never happen, and even if it did occur, might take longer than they dared tarry on the island.

Or unnatural.

And the only kind of unnatural healing Avall knew of was the gem.

The shattered gem.

The broken gem.

But still the gem.

And there might never be a better time to try it than now, when no one was awake to interrupt him. When the world was calm and quiet. When Kylin was himself in repose, but not so far gone that he had forgotten language. When Kylin's brain, while perhaps injured, had not had time to close off those parts of itself that still functioned behind a wall of ever-thickening scars.

Scarcely daring to breathe, Avall slid out of the cloak, waiting long enough to make sure that Rann's breathing did not alter. A quick slide of hands across the rug found the pouch that contained the gem shards. He dragged it to him. Between the firelight and that of the lone moon still in the sky, he could identify the shard he wanted: the smallest of the greater ones. The *safest* one. But maybe, also, the one he needed.

One final moment of risk, and it would be over—or else it would be begun, depending on how one tallied such things.

By common consensus, they all slept with knives close to hand, so it was no problem to locate his particular weapon; yet even as he snared it, he wondered if blooding was really necessary. His palm was still lightly scabbed from his earlier effort, and Kylin's bore the crusty sign of his gripping of the sword. Gnawing his lip, Avall scraped away at the scab in his palm with the knife, and was rewarded with the merest trickle of red. In the end, he had to cut Kylin's hand anyway, but only barely: a slight enlargement of the wound already present.

A final shift—while he prayed that Rann would not

awaken and that Bingg wouldn't notice his movements—and he managed to maneuver himself so that Kylin's head was in his lap, supported by Avall's crossed legs.

This was it, then. Closing his eyes, Avall found the chosen shard by feel and held it lightly between his fingers while he fumbled for Kylin's blooded hand with the other. The rest was a deliberate rush of movement, done as much from reflex as anything, as he strove for all he was worth to lock his mind away from the worst effects of the gem.

Yet his hand still closed around it, even as his fingers laced with Kylin's, trapping the gem between.

Reality slowed—but not as it usually did. *This* was more gradual, and seemed to take the form of a slow synchronization of breathing and heartbeats. He tried to focus on the latter: on the purely instinctive. Not on his own fear or desires, or the madness he could sense yammering around the edge of his consciousness.

And succeeded! Found, for once, a place that was *of* the gem, but not tainted by its more horrific aspects.

And with that discovery, he sensed a recognition, as though countless severed parts of Kylin were flowing out of the gem and returning to the mind of which they had been a part. Avall flowed with them, but as passenger, not commander; his strength was only needed when the flow threatened to cease, or seemed...*blocked* was the only term Avall could find to even remotely define the sensation.

But it was working! He touched the heart of Kylin's thought, even shrouded as it was by a massive clot of pain and fear—for Kylin would have seen Barrax's death and Rrath's destruction as forcefully as Avall had, but in nowise been prepared to meet them.

And then, quite suddenly, something ruptured—or broke—or collapsed—and a vast flood of healing poured through. Avall went with it—and met, to his relief, a true spark of recognition from a Kylin that was *all* Kylin and still in command of his faculties. It was like awakening a friend from a deep sleep: a slight, uncertain grogginess that quickly solidified into a warm, comfortable joy.

Avall was sorely tempted to remain there, for Kylin's mind was unexpectedly strong and cleanly made; the paths to his desires well-defined; his convictions set solidly in place. He was strong, too: strong enough to join his will with Avall's and force away the last of the gibbering dark from the edge of their common awareness.

And then Avall lost himself utterly in a joining that was closer than friendship or sex, for all that it was not as close as the bondings he and Rann had shared. But it *could* have been, he realized. It was he that drew back from it, not Kylin. Though whether that desperate desire for prolongation was because Kylin had simply been lonely for so long, or was born of a genuine liking for Avall in particular, he dared not try to discover.

Instead, very gently, and not without regret, Avall eased himself out of Kylin's mind. If not healed, at least it was better than it had been. And if he were lucky, Kylin would not even know how his healing had been accomplished. No one need ever know, in fact, for Avall knew with absolute conviction that Rann would rake him over the coals for being so rash and reckless.

But Rann didn't know everything, though he often acted as if he wanted people to think that he did. Avall wondered if he should tell him about dreaming that he was a geen who carried the Lightning Sword and what he feared that portended. Probably not. Not now, when survival was uppermost and any distraction a danger.

As carefully as he could, he eased his legs from beneath Kylin's head. It took but a moment to restore the shard to the pouch, and the pouch to where it had lain.

So what did he do now?

Well, he could return to his place beside Rann and hope sleep found him again—without odd dreams this time. But he was awake now, and that seemed a pointless endeavor, so close to dawn. Without truly deciding as much, he rose and steered a course among his sleeping comrades to where Bingg still sat guard by the nominal entrance. The boy had also awakened, to judge by the way he was sitting up, gazing out into nothing. Avall made no move to approach silently. No need to alarm the lad.

"Couldn't sleep," he volunteered, squatting down beside his kinsman.

"Not for a while," Bingg replied softly. Then: "I won't say a thing."

Avall regarded him keenly, but Bingg only smiled a sly, secret, little-boy smile.

"Get some sleep," Avall told him. "I'll finish your watch. I seem to be wide-awake."

Bingg rose gratefully and slipped back into the shadows in the back of the cave.

Dawn found Avall still in the same place, but with the false Lightning Sword lying across his knees. He'd retrieved it half a hand earlier, for comfort—or security; both of which he'd discovered that he needed.

He wondered where the real one was.

But that concern vanished when Kylin's eyes opened, along with everyone else's, at the sounds of Myx making breakfast.

"I had the strangest dream," Kylin announced. And then would say no more.

Nor did anyone ask him to explain, caught up as they were by a flurry of questions and counter-questions: their own about what had happened back at Gem-Hold, and Kylin's queries about where they were, how they had got there, and why.

"Thank you," Avall remembered to say eventually.

"And thank you," Kylin replied cryptically. Avall hoped no one besides him saw young Bingg's grin.

CHAPTER XI:

A New Dawn

(SOUTHWEST OF ERON–HIGH SUMMER: DAY LXXVI–MORNING)

~~~~~~~

Merryn awoke to the scent of cauf boiling and camp-bread being baked.

And thought she must be dreaming.

Then, almost as quickly, she recalled that there should be only one other person anywhere about who could possibly be cooking if she was in fact awake—and was on her feet in an instant, her pleasant drowse falling away like ice from flexing timber.

"Krynneth!" she bellowed, even as she checked herself lest she have somehow been hobbled in the night—even as she strode toward the open door between the windowless inner chamber the two of them had shared and what had been the hold-house's weather-gate—which was the source of what light existed as well as that heavenly odor and not a little noise, some of which seemed to be Krynneth humming.

At which point she recalled that she had left him restrained when they had gone to bed the previous night. Not heavily bound—not enough to hurt him—but sufficient, so she had supposed, to preclude any nocturnal activities of which she was not aware. Like trussing her up again. Like wandering off somewhere. Like—Eight forbid—making away with the remainder of the regalia, or—worse—trying to make it work.

But there he stood: three spans beyond the farther door, with his wrists still manacled and connected by half a span of soft chains. Which apparently hadn't stopped him from rising silently and pilfering what remained of the hold's larder for items that had survived nineteen years of storage, including cauf (very *good* cauf, it smelled like; then again the stuff got better as it aged), and grain meal and flour.

He had also made a fire in what remained of the forge, which was close enough to the house for the cooking smells to find her. At her soft cough, he turned to look at her, fixing her with a disarming and rather silly grin that made her glad she had gone to bed fully clothed except for boots.

"*Eat,*" he announced brightly.

"Eat," she acknowledged gamely, relaxing against the doorjamb. "And drink."

He pointed to a small, oak-bound cask by the step. "*Ale.*"

She nodded and reached for it; breached it, and poured herself a portion into one of three intact mugs they'd found in the kitchen the previous evening. A swallow, and she finally allowed herself to speculate about this place in which she had found herself.

As best they'd been able to determine, Inon's crew had happened on the hold fairly recently, though the place had been abandoned shortly after the plague, nineteen years before. Whether it had been founded before the plague—during the last period anyone had time, energy, the urge, or the impetus to explore beyond the Spine—or during it, by folk fleeing that contagion, she had no idea. The compound looked well built and decently stocked, but also somewhat threadbare—as though whoever had established it had run low on resources halfway through construction. The stonework was good, however, as were the tiles that comprised the roof, though the ones she had examined had been heavily suffused with the local sand—which made sense. The woodwork was competent, but that was all; and the iron bars on the windows showed no more skill at forging than was typical of someone who had navigated the study cycle of all the clans and crafts.

All of which suggested that the builders had been from Stone or one of its allies, with a smattering of other craftsmen brought along for the initial construction or else through marriage or other legal bond. Alternatively, just possibly, the place had been built by clanless folk who had spent some elective time at Stone, since no clan sigils were anywhere to be found.

But where were they now? She had seen no sign of funeral markers; then again, she hadn't really taken time to look. Confounding speculation was the fact that the former inhabitants had not taken their trek-wagon when they departed (either that, or they had abandoned a surplus one), yet the stables seemed to have been closed up properly. On the other hand, the house had not been stripped, which would surely have been the case if its occupants had vacated permanently— though granted, the kitchen equipment and what little furniture and bedding survived was all of the simplest kind: the sort made by Common Clan or clanless under license by the High-Clan Craft Chiefs, which could easily have rendered it disposable. To further compound the enigma, there were no personal items about at all. No outgrown clothes, no broken toys. Nothing.

If only the bath had been intact...

It wasn't. This was near-desert, and the presence of free-flowing water not a given. Oh, there *was* a well in the yard and assorted hand pumps about, including the one in the stable, all of which spoke of some deep spring; and there was a river half a shot away. But though her people prized luxurious bathing as much as anything in their lives, such facilities were not easily contrived in places like this. Eventually the builders of this hold would have added a complete bathhouse, but it would have taken a while, by the look of things.

As for other functions, a garderobe with one of those hand

pumps sufficed. Merryn had seen worse, but she had certainly seen better.

By the time she returned from dealing with necessities, Krynneth had finished breakfast, having added salt pork from the Ixtian's stash to the camp-bread, cauf, and ale.

They ate in silence on a side arcade out of sight of the carnage in the stable court. Which reminded Merryn that they really did have to attend to the bodies, and that such things were better accomplished before a bath than after. Sighing, she motioned Krynneth to his feet. "Fetch firewood," she told him. "I'll strip them and see if I can locate some fire oil. They practice cremation just like we do, though I have to say that it's more than some of them deserve.

"Not all of them," she amended quickly, gazing at the corpse of the boy, Ivk. "The lad was a good sort, as was Tahlone. Inon had delusions, but they made sense from his point of view. And he treated his men as well as he could, and us better than he had to."

Krynneth merely nodded and ambled toward the dwindling stash of fuel.

Two hands later—with a column of oily smoke rising behind them, and with her own sword back in her hand, courtesy of a tour through Inon's saddlebags—Merryn and Krynneth pushed through the remains of the outer gate and started toward the river. The geen tracks preceded them halfway to the shore, then veered north. No change there, as if she'd expected any.

She felt a twinge of guilt at that. She was wasting time, and that was a fact. She was also behaving irresponsibly, and that was very, very unlike her. Perhaps it was the magnitude of the task before her that gave her pause and made her procrastinate. Perhaps her lifelong hatred of futility and lost causes had reared its ugly head. Or perhaps she was merely trying to second-guess Fate by *not* rushing recklessly onward when more practical affairs—affairs that might slow her now but speed her journey later—needed tending.

To keep from rehearsing those doubts indefinitely, she paused to get her bearings. South, behind her, was mostly desert, easing into the more forbidding expanse of the Flat itself. East was the hold, with, beyond it, the dark masses of Angen's Spine, which seemed to flank more desert to the north, though a glimpse at Inon's map indicated that sand should give way to grassland not too much farther in that direction. The western horizon was obscured by swaths of greenery on either side of the so-far-unseen river. All in all, it seemed safe—for the present. As safe as it was likely to be, anyway.

In any case, much as she needed and desired it, she had no intention of bathing until she made sure that Krynneth had done the same. While he attended to that, she would keep watch, maybe wash some of the clothing she had salvaged from the Ixtians, which it had occurred to her might be useful to Krynneth, if not to herself, and generally try to figure out how best to chase down a very dangerous animal equipped with an even more dangerous weapon.

They had reached the river's edge by then, having threaded their way through the first real undergrowth they had seen since leaving the highlands. Soon enough they found the place where, to judge by the confusion of footprints in two sizes, Inon and Ivk had bathed the day before. There were also geen prints, she noted, but only around the fringe of the scrap of sand that made a tiny beach on the outer curve of one of the river's meanders. Rocks marked either extreme of that strand, behind which more of the knee-high underbrush showed beneath a line of low, flat-topped trees of a variety she didn't recognize. The river itself was maybe three spans wide, tannish gray, and impossibly inviting.

But not yet.

"Kryn, come here," she commanded, after confirming that she was between him and the remaining regalia, which she had no intention of letting out of her presence ever again until she hid it away forever.

"You need a bath," she continued, thrusting a well-used square of Ixtian soldier-soap into one hand and a clean but nubby rag into the other, as she fumbled with his manacles. "You can take off your clothes or I can take them off for you."

He started at that, managed a lopsided grin that both amused and alarmed her, then turned and dutifully began to strip, which quickly resulted in a pile of filthy rags of no color in particular. He paused at his drawers, however, and with them on walked calmly into the water until it was waist deep, removed them, and tossed their sodden mass to shore in what Merryn hoped he knew was a gesture of shortsighted modesty at best.

With Krynneth frolicking happily away, Merryn gathered up his clothes and made her way to the area near the beach's northern border where she made a stab at scrubbing what remained of his hose clean, followed by his shirte. The rest could wait until later, besides which Tahlone (who of all the Ixtians had been closest to Krynneth in size) had possessed not one but two spare tunics, both of which were clean and one even of Eronese cut. They would do for now.

She had just finished the shirte and was reconsidering washing Krynneth's tunic, when he came sloshing out of the water. He looked much cleaner, she noted with approval, while also noting the stark contrast between the tan of those areas exposed to the southern summer sun and the near white of the rest of him. But what struck her more forcefully than either was how very thin he was. Eronese men were slim by nature, especially those born to the High Clans. Most had little bulk to lose, and Krynneth had certainly lost every scrap of surplus he possessed. His ribs showed plain along his sides; his chest and belly were marked by the sketchiest lines of muscles; his joints showed as far too obvious knots. Only his famous pale blue eyes were unaltered.

But it wasn't sickness that had wasted him; Merryn knew that much at once. It was pure neglect: his own—at first—and then more and worse from their captors.

Yet even that small scrap of knowledge was a base from

which to begin rehabilitation. He had to care about himself again, had to have something to look forward to. Food, friendship, and fire: Those were the places to start.

It would not be easy.

In the meantime, Krynneth was simply standing at the waterline looking quizzical—which jolted her from her reverie. A quick sorting through the items she had brought with her produced a towel. She tossed it to him, hoping he would know what to do with it.

Fortunately, he did, and likewise knew what to do with Tahlone's tunic and spare hose, his own not yet being dry. Merryn surveyed the result critically. *Much better,* she thought. *Much, much better, indeed.*

Krynneth's refurbishing accomplished, she wanted one herself, if only a hasty one, yet she did not dare leave her companion unrestrained, unpredictable as he was. Which meant, much as she hated it...

"Come here, Kryn," she sighed, motioning him forward. "I'm sorry to do this to you, but I can't quite trust you yet." And with that, she gently took his wrists and resecured them with soft cuffs, then added a chain that was looped around the trunk of a sturdy tree. "You look much better," she added, smoothing his hair out of his face and seeing those eyes again. "Now stay here and be good. I'll only be a moment. You were up early, so maybe you should take a nap."

"Nap," Krynneth repeated though a yawn. "Good idea."

She regarded him narrowly, wondering how much of his atrophied speech was real, then shrugged and sat down in place to remove her boots. The rest followed, down to her drawers and singlet. Unlike Krynneth, however, she had no intention of indulging in a full immersion; rather, she contented herself with wading out to mid-thigh, then rubbing every visible surface vigorously with the soap and a second cloth. She also rinsed out her hair, gave it a light soaping, and another rinse. And had just rebelted her tunic when she heard voices from the direction of the hold.

She was on guard instantly, praying that Krynneth would do nothing to draw attention their way, even as logic dictated that the presence of water would have that effect regardless. At least she had the regalia, the gems, and her own sword.

Unfortunately, she could not *see* an Eight-cursed thing, where she crouched in the scanty undergrowth. The voices had grown marginally clearer, however: clear enough to suggest they might well belong to women—possibly, by what could be the sound of hooves, women on horseback. They seemed to have halted at the hold, too: reasonable enough, considering that she had left five burning men back there, the smoke of whose immolation was present for anyone in half a day's ride to see. Falling onto hands and knees, she scooted forward in the undergrowth until she could observe the compound more clearly.

She was *not* prepared to see a birkit emerge from the corner of the hold opposite the one on which she had fixed her attention and come bounding over the sand in a rush of tawny gray fur.

Already on guard, her heart rate doubled instantly, even as she shot a frantic glance at Krynneth, who had obviously seen the beast as well and was simultaneously trying to free himself from his restraints and to climb the tree with them on—not that it would matter, since birkits could also climb, depending on the size of tree and beast.

Merryn wished she had brought her bow, but it was back at the hold with the rest of their recovered gear. She did have her sword, however—and the magic shield if it came to that, though she was loath to use the latter without the rest of the regalia to balance it.

And so she paused there—waiting.

The birkit paused as well, frozen in its tracks. It glanced about sharply, wrinkled its muzzle as if sniffing them out—which it probably was—then padded half a dozen paces toward them, before turning abruptly and trotting back toward the hold.

—From behind the southwest corner of which two more figures were now emerging, one on horseback and bareheaded; the other hooded, afoot, and leading two more horses while it stared intently at the ground—and all hard to see against the glare of the early-morning sunlight.

Whether the newcomers saw her, Merryn couldn't tell, but there was no way they could have missed Krynneth, what with the commotion he was making. She tried to shush him frantically, but it was actually he who made the true connection and shouted for all he was worth, *"Strynn!"*

Merryn's heart all but froze in her breast—but by then the figures were close enough—and noisy enough—for her to see that it was true. It really *was* Strynn—on horseback. And that was *her* horse that the other figure—surely it was Div—was leading: faithful Boot, who had survived the geen attack and fled.

Abruptly, she was running: a mad pounding through undergrowth, then across open ground, while Div went on alert exactly as Merryn had done, then relaxed as quickly, and yelled, "Merryn" at precisely the same time Strynn did, while Strynn scrambled to get off her horse, and—almost—fell.

Merryn was there to catch her, and that contact merged into a hug so fierce she thought they might weld themselves together, while Div laughed aloud, Boot snorted and fumbled uncertainly, the other horses looked mutely on, and a full-grown birkit danced around them like a kitten: vicarious mental recipient of the joy they were all bound to be emanating.

"Strynn! What—?" Merryn finally dared breathlessly. Then, as realization dawned: "Why *are* you here? Is something—? That is, something *has* to be wrong, doesn't it?"

And with that she released her hold and eased away.

Strynn's only reply was to bite her lip and nod mutely.

Div, meanwhile, was gazing past the bond-mates to where Krynneth had grown desperate in his efforts to extricate himself and entangled himself instead. Nor did she look happy. "Krynneth," Merryn explained quickly, in part to avoid looking at Strynn, which would provoke more concern. "The war broke his mind. He's well intentioned but harmless. That's enough for now."

Div raised a brow, then scowled in turn. "I'll tend to him—"

Merryn shook her head and motioned toward the river. "That's as good a place as any to straighten all this out, though I'll tell you right up front that, in spite of appearances, I'm in a bit of a hurry."

"The regalia—" Strynn began, looking relieved as her gaze found the helm and shield.

"Part of it," Merryn corrected. "The sword, alas, has been...co-opted."

Strynn's face went dark again. She looked—almost—as if she were about to cry. "Stolen?"

Merryn shook her head. "Not in the usual sense, but it's not something I can explain quickly—nor, it appears, should I try, what with you two standing there looking like death who's been up all night and the horses looking somewhat beyond that! Now come on to the river. The horses certainly need water. And there's Krynneth—"

"We *have* been up all night," Strynn acknowledged wearily, as, by unspoken consent, they pushed through the undergrowth. "Most of the night, anyway. Right after we made camp last evening, good old Boot here came stumbling up all lathered, abraded, and covered with claw marks. Div knew what had caused them, and I recognized the horse—once we got her calmed and cleaned up. After that, we knew you were nearby and we knew that geens were involved. But we dared not hope. That is, we were afraid—"

"We gave Boot as much rest as we could, then rode the rest of the night," Div put in. "And then we saw the smoke and didn't know what to think."

"Nor do we now," Strynn added through a scowl. They had reached the beach by then, and Div went off to extricate Krynneth from the tree.

"Sit," Merryn commanded, reaching for her gear and retrieving the last of the previous night's ale. "Drink?"

Strynn took it gratefully, straight from the jug. "There are at least four stories here," she sighed. "I don't know where to start."

"We know somewhat about Krynneth, though," Div put in, ambling up again with Krynneth in tow, his face by turns showing delight, confusion and—still—a mix of resentment and fear, especially when the birkit chanced anywhere within two spans.

Merryn gnawed her lip. "Much as I hate to say it. I suppose I'd best go first. A lot of things will make more sense if I do."

Strynn's faced hardened, as though she weren't at all pleased with the notion. "Very well, but please believe that we're also on an urgent errand."

"Which *we* can explain in transit, if we have to," Div stressed, shooting Strynn a warning glance. "—If transit means looking for the sword. Now…what in Cold has been going on?"

Merryn took a quaff of ale, followed by a deep breath—and told them.

Only the short version, however, stripped of almost all details in order to focus on the raw facts of how she had veered west after leaving War-Hold, met Krynneth, been taken captive by him, then been captured *with* him, followed by their incarceration, the Ixtians' fatal fight among themselves, and the geens' attack.

Strynn's eyes grew huge, then dark with despair, when Merryn related, in greater detail than heretofore, how the geen had appropriated the sword.

"And you think that means—?" Div wondered.

Merryn shook her head. "I don't know *what* it means. It could mean that the thing was acting on pure instinct the entire time. Or that the sword was exerting some influence on it—which is what the geen itself implied. Or that I was. I have no idea, except that I find every option damned disturbing. It ultimately doesn't matter. There's no way to get an answer here, and there may not be even if we find the thing. But whatever the case, I have to consider my quest and my vow to my King before I can ponder the ramifications of what one geen did and why. I—" She broke off, staring at the birkit.

Strynn followed her gaze. "It's been with us since before we reached War-Hold," she offered. "They seem to have an affinity for Div, and that one did help us find you."

"Along with your finding stone and your horse," Div added with a sudden scowl. "You know, that's almost too coincidental: three separate items that pointed us here."

"Fate," Merryn breathed. "You think it's Fate?"

"I don't believe in Fate," Div snorted. "Or didn't. But there are so many patterns in this, so many things that helped us find you when we shouldn't have been *able* to find you…"

"We were days behind you," Strynn put in quickly. "And then suddenly we weren't. As best we can tell, your party took the long way around the end of the Spine to get here: south, and then north again. We came straight through, via a pass that doesn't seem to be on any map."

Div indicated the birkit with a nod. "The beast apparently knew where you were—something to do with reading your presence in the rain that I don't even pretend to understand. And when your horse arrived…Well, you know how birkits are: Sometimes you can read what they're 'saying' and sometimes you can't, but the sense I got from this fine lady here was that the horse had somehow connected with the birkit—and yes, I know they're instinctive enemies—and the birkit guided the horse, and then the horse guided the birkit. It was… strange."

Merryn frowned in turn. "Too strange to think about right now."

Div nodded mutely.

"You still haven't told me what *you're* doing here," Merryn continued after a pause, staring hard at Strynn.

"Looking for you," Strynn replied flatly. "Looking for the

regalia, more properly. And now that we've found you and
it—"

"Not all of it," Merryn corrected.

"No, and that's the problem."

Merryn glanced at the sky. "I'm a fool to stay here any
longer, but tell me—now. And then—well, you already know
one reason why we need to travel." She eyed the horses speculatively. "Though with them, maybe I can make up some time.
I wonder if birkits can track geens," she added. "Or would be
willing to."

Strynn cleared her throat pointedly. "To cut to the bone,"
she began, "as I said, we're here to retrieve the regalia—and
this is why..."

It was all Merryn could do to keep from screaming from
pure frustration by the time Strynn had finished. Even so, she
was pacing around in a narrow ellipse, unable to sit still any
longer. "Damn it, damn it, *damn it*!" she raged, pausing to face
her friends. "And of course you don't know anything that's
happened since you left Tir-Eron, which means that my fool of
a brother is probably sitting at Gem-Hold's gates right now
waiting for me to show up in a blaze of glory and save him."

"I think he's willing to save himself," Div observed dryly.
"And that sounds like you plan to simply jump back up there,
and that is *not* a given."

"He's got the blessed gem," Merryn growled. "He could
have contacted me!"

Strynn shook her head. "It's mad. You know that. He dares
not use it—though I'll bet anything I own that he's tried."

Div frowned. "You still have the other gems, don't you?"

Merryn rounded on her. "What's left of them! They were
burned, Div. Scorched, anyway. I don't know if they still work,
and even if they do, I don't know whether I can jump with
them."

"We did before," Strynn countered. "You and I, when we
rescued Eddyn."

"We were fools, too!" Merryn snapped. "Besides which, I'm

not so sure that I wouldn't be so afraid of what nearly happened before that my fear alone would sabotage my intentions—even if my surface mind wanted more than anything to return to my brother."

"It's a moot point anyway," Div concluded. "For now There's no reason to attempt it until you've recovered the sword."

Strynn rose decisively. She looked utterly drained. Then again, she had spent all night in the saddle—and here she wa about to assay another day's ride. "You don't have to come with me," Merryn murmured. "With a horse, it shouldn't take long—"

"To what?" Strynn gritted. "To get yourself killed? These are geens you're talking about, Merry! The most dangerous animal—or whatever—there is. We're going with you, and that's not subject to argument. I'll—I'll sleep in the saddle if have to, if that's what you're worried about. But I will be there You'll need all the help you can get!"

"You shouldn't," Div warned, too loud.

Strynn glared at her, then looked away quickly, but not before Merryn had caught the exchange. "Strynn," she said softly "is there something you're not telling me?"

Strynn stared at the ground. "I—"

"She's pregnant," Div said flatly. "We found out on the road."

"Then that settles it!" Merryn spat, fighting back a surge of joy that was almost as strong as the mix of concern, confusion and frustration that was already encumbering her convictions

Strynn's face was hard as iron. "It settles nothing, Merry You have a duty, and I have a duty. I don't want to lose thi child. But I don't want to lose the Kingdom either. I don't have to tell you which one would be harder to replace. Besides, th longer I delay, the greater the risk will be."

"No," Merryn stated flatly.

"My chance. My child. My choice."

"The heir to two great clans," Merryn countered.

"My chance. My child. My choice," Strynn repeated, not moving. "And not, except for the addition of geens, a decision I'm only making now."

"Not a decision anyway," Krynneth echoed softly, from where he was sitting calmly at the foot of his tree.

And for some odd reason that settled it.

A hand later—with everything Merryn had preserved from her own gear along with everything of use that could be salvaged from the Ixtian dead or butchered from the more intact portions of their mounts—they were riding north. It was slow going, granted, for the horses were tired—Boot to the point of exhaustion—and they had to make frequent stops to confirm the trail when the geen prints veered over bare rock or stretches of hard earth.

But increasingly, Merryn was heartened to find, they were moving toward the mountains and slopes of true, living green.

CHAPTER XII:

ON THE SHORE

~~~~~~~~~

Avall thrust an armload of freshly harvested "cauf" ferns into Riff's grateful care, wiped soil-stained hands on his tunic, and ambled over to where Rann was crouched at the juncture of wall and floor, midway along their shelter's length. Rann's arms moved rhythmically, accompanied by the raspy sound of metal on stone, and the soft ping of a hammer that made a counterpoint melody of metal on metal. Avall squatted beside him, watching.

"This stone works fairly well," Rann offered without looking up. "Or would if we had decent tools. A quarter here with a brace of my kinsmen, and we'd have this ground as flat as the floor in the Royal Suite, and a good start on getting the walls trued. There's plenty of height for more than one level, and it wouldn't be hard to close off the front if we had to, though I'd as soon leave it open for the view and the ventilation. Or we could—"

Avall stilled the hammer with a touch. "You sound resigned to staying here."

Rann paused, laid down the tools, then twisted around to look at him. A thin skim of sweat moistened his brow; his hair was bound back with a strip of tunic trim. "There are worse places I can think of," he said flatly.

"You're not serious!" Avall blurted out. "About staying, I mean."

A shrug. Rann picked up the broken knife he'd been using as a chisel and fingered its edge absently. "I repeat: There are *worse* places. Mostly what I'm doing is weighing options. One is to stay on this island; one is to establish a base on the shore; one is to hightail it back to the battle and all that entails."

Avall snorted in frustration. "Including my obligation. I haven't forgotten that, you know. It gnaws at me constantly."

"I know. But something tells me that The Eight have taken you out of *that* game for a while. Not that I'd blame you for being concerned—or for trying to return. It's your Kingdom, after all; and your family and friends at risk. And if you do decide to go back, rest assured that I'll go with you. But in the meantime, there are supplies we'll need. And tools. And while this island is a wonderful place, we'll exhaust its resources before we exhaust those on the mainland—if that's what it is—and, geens notwithstanding, we really do need to be over there well before that occurs."

"And of course reaching the mainland is also the first step on returning to Gem-Hold."

Rann nodded solemnly. "It is." He paused, gazing past Avall's head toward a new source of noise in the cave. Avall twisted round to follow his gaze. The remaining foragers were returning—which is to say Lykkon and Myx, since Bingg had assumed cooking duties for the day, and Riff was keeping an eye on Kylin, just in case. The harper seemed fine, if somewhat confused, but kept complaining of a headache and splashes of color before his blind eyes, for which reason he was lying down with a wet cloth across his brow. At least he was ambulatory. And (when not resting) was soaking up anything anyone would tell him about their present situation. "I can make a harp," he had announced already. "A flute would be easier, though."

"Soon," Avall had assured him, not wishing to add that, however highly his countrymen prized music and art, both were luxuries when set against survival.

Myx, it evolved, had speared two more fish, each larger than the one that Bingg had caught the first day out; and Lykkon had shot a bird with bow and arrow—but lost an arrow in the process, which wasn't good, even if Rann said they could strike points out of fire-glass.

Avall cleared his throat meaningfully. "Now that we've secured our day's rations," he began, "I guess it's time to think about the future. Fortunately"—he glanced at Kylin—"we have one less thing to worry about and one more able body."

"Marginally able," Kylin corrected. "I'll do what I can, but I'm not very strong, and most of the things I'm good at—"

"Don't sell yourself short," Avall warned. "You saved me, don't forget. By doing that you saved countless other lives, as well as making the Chief of the Ninth Face look stupid, clumsy, and ineffectual. I've no doubt you'll display similar resourcefulness here.

"In any case," he continued, "it's time we talked about getting off this island. It's a fine place as far as it goes, but we obviously can't stay here indefinitely. We'd already ruled out swimming to the mainland because that wasn't viable with you unconscious, Kylin—and because it would take forever to get any of our gear across. And that was before we saw what lives in the water. That leaves building a raft or a boat."

"A raft would be easier," Riff observed. "If for no other reason than because we could build one large enough to accommodate all of us and the supplies we have here a lot faster than we could build a boat that would accomplish the same things."

Lykkon nodded. "And while there are plenty of trees on this island, they're either way too big to be workable, or too small. Whereas a raft—"

"There's thick-cane down by the shore on the south side," Bingg supplied. "I saw it from up top. There's more up there, for that matter, but the growth onshore is larger, plus we wouldn't have to carry anything we made so far to set it afloat."

"Which means that we spend the afternoon looking for cane to cut and a good place to build the thing once we've secured the raw materials," Rann said with a sigh.

Avall shot him a wicked grin. "Did anyone here besides Riff spend more than a quarter at Seacraft? And if so, did you spend it studying boat-building instead of learning the names of fishes, which is mostly what I did?"

"I studied basic shipwrighting," Myx volunteered. "But it *was* basic. I crewed a couple of fishing boats, read the prescribed texts, and helped hew a half dozen beams and true, peg, and caulk some planks."

"Which might be useful and might not," Avall mused. "In any case, unless someone has a better suggestion, thick-cane would seem to be our best choice. It's light, strong, and it floats unless you pierce the chambers between the knots—and if you do that, you've got more problems than getting from here to shore."

"Which sounds like we've just filled up the afternoon," Lykkon chuckled. "So much for the rural life of leisure."

"The question is," Rann broke in, "do we have anything besides swords that will actually *cut* thick-cane? Knives will take forever, but it wouldn't be good for our primary weapons to abuse them that way."

"I've got a whetstone," Lykkon informed him calmly. "And a saw. I'd suggest we use the latter."

A hand later, fortified with the smaller fish and more augmented cauf, and equipped with their sturdiest clothing and virtually everything they possessed that had an edge (Rann's caution notwithstanding), everyone except Kylin began the trek to the island's southern shore.

For the first third of the journey, they followed the route Avall and Rann had established the previous morning—a route which actually took them out of the way for a while, since it initially tended north. Roughly halfway to the shore, however, the pitch of the path lessened significantly, so that it was possible to turn back south without having to navigate any dangerously steep slopes. The second third of their journey thus ran below their cave, midway between it and the lake, but views of either the nearer or farther coast were intermittent, courtesy of trees, which, though more widely spaced than in other places, admitted sufficient light to support a luxurious understory, which in turn allowed a wealth of head-high ferns and ankle-thick mosses to flourish. The latter made for slow going, but the ground underfoot was soft enough that a functional trail would not be slow in forming.

The last third of the journey was the most difficult, because the terrain turned very steep indeed, so much so that they finally found themselves standing on a ledge looking down at the tops of the very thick-cane they hoped to harvest. The patch itself extended a good way to either side of where they stood, with the left-hand portion blocked by a fissure too wide to jump, beyond which—and higher up, of course—the path continued maybe a dozen spans more to where a handsome waterfall frothed and rumbled beside an all but sheer escarpment that thrust a blade of stone toward the opposing shore. The upper extremes of the patch were swathed in a froth of more ferns and flowers that slopped over the ledge on which they were standing, while the lower reaches were invisible, but clearly fought an ongoing battle with a good-sized crescent of beach. All in all, it was quite beautiful—and extremely exotic, to people born to a cold and rugged land.

"We backtrack," Myx announced, indicating the least steep part of the bank. "Then we can swing around at the bottom. Better not to go down and through," he added. "If this is like what little thick-cane I've seen back at Plantcraft, it's got razor edges on the leaves. And who knows what sorts of poisonous things might live in there."

Bingg rolled his eyes. "That's all I need to hear."

"Lead the way," Avall concluded—as much because Myx had the lone wide-sword, which was good for chopping away undergrowth, as for any other reason.

Because of the detritus on the designated slope, it took far longer than expected to reach the base of the thick-cane patch, and everyone except Bingg slipped at least once, so that they were all blotched with a healthy application of wood mulch by the time they gained their goal. Happily, the beach was even larger than it had looked—easily a quarter shot across, in fact. On the right it was bounded by the rocks atop which the birds Avall and Rann had seen the previous day nested; the back was walled by the canebrake itself; while the left ended at the imposing spear of stone down which the lower reaches of the newly discovered waterfall slid—a fall, they now saw, that emptied into what was more than a stream but definitely not a river.

"Keep a close eye on the lake," Avall advised, though they were south and west of the rocks the water-beast had seemed to frequent. "That creature Rann and I saw might or might not be entirely aquatic, but it was definitely an air-breather. I wouldn't be surprised if it denned on land—and in that case, there's a good chance its den is on this island and close to the coast."

"We should post watch anyway," Rann agreed, glancing at the sky, where a skim of clouds now showed. "Not that we're likely to accomplish much today regardless."

"But this would be a great place to build the raft," Lykkon observed. "Plenty of work space and a gradual slope to the water. Eight, it wouldn't be a bad site for a permanent dock if we wind up staying here—assuming we could improve the trail."

"We should probably explore farther around," Myx observed absently, gazing toward the waterfall. "When we finish,

I mean. We're over a quarter of the way around the island as it is, and it wouldn't be much trouble to add another couple of shots to what we've already surveyed."

Avall nodded, then sauntered over to the nearest stand of thick-cane. To his unpracticed eye, it looked like good, sturdy stuff; though it was hard to tell, since he had never seen any in the wild, the plant being native to Ixti, and only growing in Eron in greenhouses. *This* stand clearly needed no such encouragement, since each stalk was easily three times as tall as he was and most were as thick as his forearm. There would be no trouble finding enough to make any size raft they wanted, either—but there might be trouble cutting enough.

Riff studied the knobby lengths carefully. "We can get two sections out of most of these," he informed them. He paused, did a bit of quick ciphering in his head. "Might be better to use the whole length, in the long run—for stability and to carry more of us at a time." He did more calculations. "So, say we make a raft two spans square, which is about as small as would be useful and as big as we can easily move. And say twenty-four widths per span. That's forty-eight lengths of thick-cane—or more. A railing would also be good, as would cross-bracing. And there's five of us who can do a full man's work, so that works out to about ten stalks each that we'd need to cut. But it's going to take at least a hand per stalk, unless we want to savage our blades...so we're looking at two or three days just to cut enough without killing ourselves. And that, in turn, raises the question of how to join the stalks together. We've got one length of tent rope that came with us, but that won't be enough. We'll have to use vines and probably peg some stuff, and maybe see if we can contrive some glue."

"So we're looking at maybe an eight to get off this place," Avall summarized. "Assuming we spend half of each day scavenging for food."

"It's something to target," Riff agreed. "And will give us an idea how much we have to ration—not that we'll be able to go wild once we reach the mainland, either."

Avall nodded, and reached over to run a hand down a length of smooth, hard cane skin.

"There's better over here," Bingg called, from where the patch angled back toward the escarpment.

They followed dutifully, noting that the waterfall formed a tiny pool in the vee between thick-cane and cliff. The stream ran from that pool to the sea; a dark opening lurked behind it. Avall angled shoreward to investigate the stream more thoroughly—back in Eron such places were a good source of fresh-water mussels and clams. The others moved to the left, closer to the cave.

Avall had actually squatted at the edge of the clear, shallow water when he saw two things at once, both of which set him shouting.

One was the distinct trail of what could only be claw-edged flippers leading toward the cave. The other was a flash of movement inside it, as though something large and leathery lurked there.

"Watch the cave!" he yelled.

Too late.

Something came lurching out of the blackness toward the rest of their party: something as tall as their tallest, owing to a long, supple neck that issued from a squat, turtle-shaped body that was close to a span long itself. The head was the size of a man's head but oval and far less distinct from the neck, of which it looked like a bulbous extension. Teeth showed, too: very *sharp* teeth. And that head moved on a neck like slick, wet lightning.

Jaws flashed out toward Bingg and would have bit him had he not danced back. By which time Avall could see the beast's appendages. And tell, indeed, that they were very like a sea lion's flippers, though the beast itself was clearly reptilian.

The odd thing was the silence. Most predators made noise when they felt threatened. This one didn't.

But at least there was only one, and it a small one—smaller than the one he and Rann had seen, anyway—possibly an adolescent. Which meant that the parents could be lurking nearby. Except that this cave was too small for one of them.

All of which reasoning took Avall perhaps three breaths before he'd unsheathed his sword and rushed into the fray. The beast was not actually *that* large, he realized, it was just that its parts covered a lot of space and moved quickly. In spite of that, Myx was poking at it with his homemade spear, while Riff and Bingg tried to circle it.

"Go for the neck," Rann yelled, a long-knife flashing in his hand, while Lykkon tried to thrust his own sword past snapping jaws to connect with something vital.

Finding a flipper within easy range, Avall slashed down at it, and was rewarded with a gush of dark blood and a shrill, honking screech from the beast. Encouraged, he waded closer to the side, making a pair with Myx, opposite.

But it was Lykkon—Lykkon the scholar—who got in a lucky slash at the neck that severed the windpipe and at least one major artery. Blood fountained everywhere, showering them with gore. Myx and Riff caught the brunt of it.

Rann gave the beast its death blow: a second chop that severed the head.

"Food," Riff grunted. "If no one has a delicate stomach."

"Maybe," Avall agreed, eyeing the shore speculatively, and wondering if it was wise to let the creature's blood reach the stream that fed it. All they needed was for this lad's kin to come honking up, primed for vengeance. "If we're going to work here regularly, we'll need more than one escape route," he told Myx flatly, with another survey of the surrounding terrain.

Myx—who had very sharp eyes—squinted toward the cave. "There's a more gradual slope in the angle," he said. "Hard to see because it's in shadow."

"You and Riff check it out," Avall told him. "Let us know what you find. We ought to get some of these cut today if we can."

"And someone ought to see if there's anything edible on that," Rann added, pointing toward the inert monster. "If it's like most large animals, there's a nice chunk of solid meat along the spine. I'd start with that—unless someone else wants to—"

"I'll do it," Bingg volunteered gamely. "It nearly ate me; it's only fair."

"I'll help," Lykkon chimed in. "I might learn something. We can take turns being lookout."

Avall found himself facing Rann. "Which I guess leaves us to do what we came for."

Rann grimaced resignedly, but doffed his tunic, then his shirte. Avall followed his example. Unfortunately, the thick-cane proved all but impervious to their efforts. A strong hack with their most expendable sword produced sore hands but the barest nick in the hard skin. Knives used in a sawing action worked better, but the process was tedious and progress impossibly slow. Rann's saw worked best of all, but even that was slow, and the blade showed signs of being unequal to cutting as many spars as required.

It was also hot, sweaty work, though Avall found himself enjoying the exertion. It had been a long time since he'd used his muscles so fully, a long time since he'd engaged in simple labor with his friends.

Time lapsed into a long, drifty languor, as everyone found a rhythm to his task and fit himself to it. Voices floated around the clearing, though no one ever relaxed entirely, to judge by the furtive looks constantly aimed at the shore. Still, no other threats made themselves known. And so a hand expired.

"Where're Myx and Riff?" Rann wondered abruptly.

Avall rose from where he'd finally sawn one shaft of cane through, a half span from the bottom. It still remained upright, however; courtesy of leaves tangled with others higher up. "They went to check the area above the cave," he replied, with a scowl. "They should've been back by now."

"They should," Rann agreed. "But they were covered with blood—and there's water..."

"They still should've told us if they were planning to be gone this long." A pause. "Myx!" Avall yelled. "Riff! Please acknowledge."

Silence.

Rann grimaced sourly and shoved the saw back into its leather holder, then scooped up his shirte and used it for a towel. "Think we ought to check?"

"Guess we should," Avall grumbled. He trotted over to where Bingg and Lykkon were freeing the second loin. It would be a lot of white, tender meat—if it proved edible. "We're going to look for Myx and Riff," Avall told them. "If we're not back in a hand, come looking for us."

Lykkon nodded, and wiped greasy hands on his tunic. It was, Avall realized, the first time he'd ever seen Lykkon dirty, sweaty, *and* disheveled.

Rann was waiting for him at the bank. Footprints showed in the soft earth there, one set bare, the better to assay what was a steep but not impossible climb. A ladder placed just so would work wonders. When they had time to build one.

Rann scrambled up a span, waiting for Avall to follow. A convenient vine made a nice handhold, and a moment later, they were above the level of the cave. Another span put them over an edge and onto the continuation of the path they had seen earlier, beyond the troublesome fissure, this side almost completely flat, half a span wide, and covered with soft grass. It ran to their right, where it ended at the stream that, lower down, became the waterfall. The escarpment rose beyond, but it had a back side, they saw, which made it a spear of rock rising upward. The mountain proper loomed to the left as they faced the spear, and the stream flowed from that direction. Their companions' footprints followed it. Another slope soon blocked their way, but Myx and Riff had clearly climbed it, for it was barely twice as high as Avall's head, and since it was covered with vines, it was easy going. That put them on another ledge—and a good six spans above the beach, which was masked by a froth of ferns. The ledge swung left again, with the stream beside.

"Beautiful place," Rann murmured. "No wonder they tarried."

"And another waterfall nearby," Avall noted, cocking his head. "The roar sneaks up on you. You can imagine why they kept wanting to go just a little farther—and that they might not have heard us call above the sound of the water."

"Let's hope," Rann agreed, leading the way around a knife-edged slab of stone, beyond which the trail kinked out of sight. Avall heard Rann gasp, then guffaw, by which time he'd joined his friend, who had halted where he stood. Rann grinned broadly and pointed farther around the rock, even as he motioned silence with his other hand, but Avall had seen enough already.

There was indeed a waterfall where they had expected one. And there was a pool below it, into which it part-slid, part-fell, so that one might either stand clear of the falling water or stand in it.

Myx and Riff were doing the former. Naked, they stood thigh deep in the pool, locked in embrace, their hands sliding across each other's shoulders and backs and now and then lower. They didn't kiss—bond-brothers rarely did. Rather, they were simply sharing closeness. Myx was slimmer and taller, his hair dark, like most of his countrymen's, and his skin was darker as well. Riff was shorter, stockier (though only by Eronese standards), and unmistakable by his fair hair and fairer skin.

Rann grinned again. "Should we let them know…?"

Avall shook his head. "Would you want to be interrupted? They've had no time for this since we got here, and little since we mustered out."

Rann's grin widened. "Maybe so, but I'm hot and sweaty, too—and *not* keen on climbing down again quite yet."

Avall matched his grin. "Me neither."

Eyes said the rest, as Avall took Rann by the arm and drew him back around the corner, assuring their friends' privacy. Wordless, they sank down against the blade of stone. "Could be worse," Rann murmured eventually.

"Could be," Avall agreed. And then more comfortable silence.

Not a long one, however, for Myx and Riff were too conscientious to shirk duty indefinitely (and they *had* been covered with water-beast blood, Rann stressed). It was therefore no more than a finger later that they came ambling around the outcrop. Nor did either seem particularly surprised to find visitors, though Riff's skin reddened visibly. "We found the way up—Majesty," Myx all but stammered, genuinely chagrined. "We thought we'd better clean up, and we got...distracted. It's quite beautiful around there."

"So I expect," Avall agreed with a twinkle in his eye. "Tell Bingg and Lyk that we'll try to be back in a hand. That should be long enough."

Myx nodded and continued down the trail, with Riff close behind.

"Long enough for what?" Rann chuckled as he and Avall dashed around the corner.

"For almost anything—at least once," Avall laughed back, skinning his shirte over his head. Nor, he found a short while later, with a very wet and naked Rann pressed against him, and cool water throwing spray across his body; was that remotely an exaggeration.

"Cutting cane won't be as bad as I thought," Rann murmured eventually.

"No," Avall agreed into the juncture of his neck and shoulder, "it won't be—if any of us actually manage to get any cut."

"We'll have to," Rann said solemnly. "We can't get so mired

in idleness and pleasure we forget caution, responsibility, and danger."

"I haven't forgotten," Avall assured him. "But we can't forget that we're alive, either."

And for the next little while, they didn't.

CHAPTER XIII:

EXPERIMENT

~~~~~~~

"And this is *all*?" Zeff spat. "These are no better than the first ones!"

He snatched the carved wooden box his chief engineer had just delivered to his quarters and stared the man straight in the eye as he inverted his other hand and let the contents fall one by one back into the container. Multiple thumps sounded softly: stone against a padded velvet lining, punctuated by an occasional click. He closed the lid with a snap.

"We were lucky to find those, Chief," the engineer retorted, his voice as hard as his face, which was all angles, as though it were rock that had fractured. "The crawl was mostly blocked, and what we could get through was narrow—and wet. Some refused to work there at all. The rest—"

"Give me their names—those who wouldn't work."

The engineer's jaws tensed as though he had more to say, and none of it complimentary. "There were also bodies. A lot of them. And having been dead this long, the smell—"

"They'll smell their own guts in the field if they're not careful," Zeff snapped. "And don't think I can't tell that one of these had been shattered."

"They're fragile, Chief," the engineer protested. His tone had softened but his gaze had not. "The spade hit that one before we knew it."

"Then use brushes!" Zeff growled, even as he cursed himself for losing his calm. It was the Nine-damned gems, is what it was! That one rash contact with Avall's mind had planted something in him that day by day was eating away at the wall of control and discipline that had given him his position to start with.

He shook the box in the engineer's face. "This could be victory—right here. This could be our way out of here and home. Instead—we may have to face Avall and the Lightning Sword."

"He won't dare," Ahfinn offered from the corner. "Not with his people at risk. Besides, weren't you—" He broke off, his face white, knowing he had said too much.

"You may leave," Zeff told the engineer, with an absent wave of his hand. "I have business with my adjutant."

As soon as the door slammed, Zeff turned his wrath full on the younger man. "Never do that again," he gritted. "Never mention any of my plans beyond those who already know them."

"I thought he *did* know," Ahfinn countered, with a rebellious edge in his voice that had been appearing there with increasing frequency of late. "Else why have him in the mines?"

"To find those cursed gems!" Zeff growled. "Gems indeed! Grains of red sand, they look like—except the shattered one, and curse him for that, too."

He sat down abruptly, face buried in his hands. "I don't need this, Ahfinn," he continued, as though he had not, bare instants before, been furious at the man. "One moment I'm euphoric because I'm told they've broken into the mines and already found gems. The next—they've found gems indeed, but gems the size of peas. And now these: even worse."

Ahfinn looked up hopefully. "Have you tried them yet?

They might not be—that is, size might not be important. You haven't had time to try the *first* ones yet, have you?"

Zeff shook his head, lacking the energy to answer. It had been like that all day: emotions stimulated every which way, and far too many decisions to make because, with most of its population serving as visible hostages, the daily workings of the hold were running on inertia.

For only one reason, too—and maybe a futile one.

To—hopefully—hold off Avall until Zeff could match the King of Eron on the field.

"Are you still planning to wreck the hold?" Ahfinn dared from where he still sat, stone-faced, in his accustomed chair.

"If I have to," came the slow reply. "But that idea makes much less sense than it did. The plan was always that if Avall didn't come here, we would destroy the hold, and High-Clan would then turn on him, him being untried, and so on. Alternately, we would destroy it anyway, and he would be blamed for pressing the issue. But that was when we stupidly assumed we could find more gems. And before I truly knew how loyal—against all reason—his friends are to the man. Now—too many would know the truth, I fear, because they will have seen it with their own eyes. And from what I hear, our brothers in Tir-Eron are not playing their role well, either. They're being far too ruthless, for one thing—for all that they've had to be. This was all planned to be subtle and it hasn't worked out that way."

"We moved too soon—I think," Ahfinn offered.

The rage returned, like a forge flame newly plied with bellows. "You *think*," Zeff snapped. "What do you know?"

Ahfinn regarded him coldly. "I know the people in the southern two gorges made far more demands than expected. I know they don't care who *rules* them as long as someone *feeds* them. If we'd waited, they would have petitioned Avall for food and he'd have had no more than we've had, and they'd have saved us a river's worth of work."

"You're a brave little sod!"

"Someone has to be. Forgive me, Chief—but you have not been yourself these days."

"Have I not?"

"Not since you tried to master Avall's gem."

"I did master it."

"Barely—but it escaped you."

"Escaped—? You think the gem—?"

"It might have. It fits some things."

"And these?" Zeff indicated the box in his hand.

"I think you should try to bond with one of them."

"Largest or smallest?"

"That's hard. The smallest should in theory be less risky, but the largest might give you a clearer idea of what you have to work with."

"Then large it is. You may leave now."

"Are you sure?"

"You may leave now."

Ahfinn rose and departed, good Priest that he was—and probably good man. Better than he was, these days, Zeff concluded—or at least more alert and...focused. But maybe he could fix that. Winter would arrive eventually, and the army would have to withdraw. Of course he would prefer not to spend a winter here, either, but it would give him more time to prepare. More time to seek better gems in the mines, and more time to—

To let the prisoners starve, for one thing, since new supplies would certainly not reach the hold this season if affairs didn't soon shift in his favor. And if they didn't change—Well, one thing was for certain: They would be eating nothing but vegetables—from the hold's greenhouses. And maybe bread, if the granaries were still fairly full by then. But meat—That would be cats, dogs, and rats, in all likelihood, since they would need to reserve the horses.

Not that it mattered. For now he had a goal. Something real and imminent that did not depend on "ifs" and "somedays."

He had a gem—a virgin gem—with which he could try to bond.

And the choices were either to sit there and dread that bonding, or slake his curiosity.

It took blood. That much he knew, and little more—save how it had felt that one time when he'd swung the sword and lightning had replied—and scared him half to death, though he'd told no one. Not how little control he'd had then, and not how much he'd wanted to swing it again and again.

Now—

Best to do it. And with that, he snared a paring knife from the cheese tray and settled back into his seat. There should probably be more ritual, he supposed. Then again, he doubted that Avall had taken special precautions when he had first bonded with the master gem, nor that he took any when he worked with the sword. Rrath clearly hadn't.

Which awakened another sore point.

He would have to attend to Rrath soon; that much was clear. Should have before now, in fact, for Rrath—in his right mind—knew as much about the gems as anyone Zeff had to hand. And if Rrath couldn't reveal that knowledge consciously—Well, perhaps Zeff could enter his mind by means of a gem and ferret out the facts that way.

But all such speculation was stalling, he realized with a scowl. And that was unconscionable in one who still had a hold to run, a siege to endure, and a battle—eventually—to be waged and hopefully won.

And so he wasted no more time making a tiny slice in his palm.

Now to choose a gem. Ahfinn had suggested he use the largest one, and Ahfinn was usually right when it came to practical matters, if perhaps too much the pragmatist. A deep breath, and Zeff opened the box one-handed and selected the largest stone—at that, no larger than a pea. Another breath, and he set it against the tiny wound welling in his flesh.

And closed his eyes.

He felt nothing at first, and almost hurled the gem away in disgust. But then he noticed that the candle flames were flickering more slowly, and that the dust motes that pervaded the air seemed to be twinkling ever so slightly as they described their endless, draft-blown, dance.

So it was working after all. His hand felt warmer, too, and something was trickling into his hand and up his arm. Something that held the same relationship to the mad rush of power he had felt when he had used the master gem as the brush of a feather had to a sword blow—yet clearly the same in kind.

And there was also a vague sort of greeting, though not to him in particular. This felt more like a simple recognition of one presence to another, like a pair of lodestones pulling at each other, maybe; or metal gaining sympathetic heat from a fire. Or even a mirror showing a phantom face when confronted with a real one.

So *something* was certainly occurring.

And maybe, if he added a second gem, more might follow.

CHAPTER XIV:

Something Dead

～～～～

"Something's dead," Merryn announced, giving Boot's reins a gentle tug to shift him to the slowest gait he could manage without stopping entirely. She pointed northwest, where the grassy slope they had been traversing for the last two hands ended in a fringe of trees a shot away. And thank The Eight for that open land, too; it made ambush by geens less likely on the one hand, and made them easier to track on the other. Heavy animals on soft earth typically left clear prints.

Not like a day ago, when they'd had to rely on the birkit's ability to track across hard earth far too frequently, as sand gave away to more fertile, if still sun-baked, soil. At least there was no more desert; they had left *that* a hand past sunrise and were now enfolded by an eruption of ever-higher hills that seemed to sport equal amounts of open meadow and hardwood forests.

The air was clear today—as clear as Merryn had ever seen. Which was probably why she had seen the vultures riding the thermals across the ridge they were approaching—riding them, but using them to spiral down, not up.

"Something big, I'd say," Div offered, joining Merryn at the head of the file. Behind them, they heard Strynn and Krynneth slow as well—on one horse, since the women all took turns doubling with Krynneth. Skinny as he was, he weighed no more than they did. "Places like this," Div went on, "small animals are going to be snapped right up by hawks and eagles and such. Anything that would attract circling vultures would have to be big enough not to be carried away by something else." A pause, then: "A deer, maybe; we've seen plenty of sign."

Merryn glanced around in search of the birkit—it was keeping up with them for the nonce, where hanging back or ranging from side to side as if searching was more typical behavior. Its nose was wrinkled, however, which meant it was sifting odors. "It's alarmed—or anxious," Div supplied in a tone that brooked no argument. "And I'm not sure, but I think I caught of flash of the way it thinks really loud and hard when it thinks about geens."

Merryn tensed. "You think geens—?"

Div shrugged. "Maybe. But they hunt in packs, generally of four. I'd assume that if they killed a deer, there wouldn't be enough left for anything else to eat."

Merryn returned her attention to the terrain. "I wish I knew more about them," she sighed. "It just never seemed important to learn. As you said, I know they're pack hunters, that they prefer to hunt at dusk and dawn, but don't limit themselves to those times, and that they prefer live meat to carrion. That said—"

"They haunt places like this," Strynn broke in, riding up to join them. "Places where grazing animals wander about in the open, while they lurk in the woods until—"

Merryn suppressed a shiver and scanned the forests warily. "No need to worry," Div assured her. "The horses would have spooked long before now."

"Cold comfort," Merryn muttered. "Shall we see...?"

Div was studying the ground. "The tracks we've been following lead toward the birds regardless, but caution might be in order."

"So I was thinking," Merryn agreed, loosening her sword in its scabbard and hearing the rattle of Div retrieving her bow and the hiss of Strynn likewise freeing her blade. Krynneth had asked for one, too, but they dared not trust him with one—yet—though his vocabulary was up to fifty words now, and his eyes looked clear more often than otherwise.

"Nothing learned by staying," Div chuckled, and gave her horse the heel. Merryn followed at a cautious trot, and a moment later, they crested the ridge.

An oval vale two shots long and half that wide opened before them, covered with the same grass they had been traversing, and framed with oaks and maples. What they hadn't expected was the fact that the ridge had hidden a higher sweep of genuine mountains that rose to the northwest—probably too far west to be part of Angen's Spine. An air of peace rode about that place—broken only by the slow downward spiral of the vultures and, very faintly, the stench of flesh decaying in the pervasive southern heat.

"Keep watch," Div told Strynn offhand, not bothering to see if her command was heeded. Merryn smirked at that: a Common Clan woman ordering the Royal Consort about so casually, and the Consort taking no umbrage from it. On the other hand, those roles were tied to Eron and the people they had been there. This was the West, and no one's country but their own, and in more ways than one they were free.

"Merryn?" Div prompted, shaking Merryn from her reverie even as she led the way down the slope toward the source of the vale's disturbance.

"Holy Eight!" Div spat a moment later, from where she rode a few spans in the van.

"What?" Merryn called, but by then she had seen as well.

They all had.

Not a dead deer, but a geen—lying facedown in the knee-high grass, with all four legs splayed to either side and its tail stretched out behind.

Merryn went instantly to full alert. The geen was dead without a doubt, but it hadn't been dead for long—no more than half a day, in spite of the smell of corruption—which was largely a function of the heat. And the only thing that could kill a geen was a man—or—she shuddered—another geen.

"What—?" Merryn whispered abruptly.

Div was already off her horse, prowling about—but avoiding the body. "More geen tracks around," she announced. "At least two sizes, but that doesn't mean much. Want to help me check the body?"

Merryn grimaced, but nodded and resheathed her sword. Strynn was dismounting as well, but keeping Krynneth back—which was probably wise. She wasn't certain how he would react to the sight of geens—or death. "Keep your bow to ready, just in case," Div called. "Folks who hunt geens usually proceed that way."

Holding her breath—for this was as close as Merryn had ever been to a geen, live or dead—she eased around one side of the beast while Div took the other. A trace of smoke scent clung to the air, she noted for the first time, along with, very slightly, the odor of cooked meat. All at once she recognized it, though she kept her silence for the nonce.

"No sign of blood," Div pointed out. "Which is odd."

"It didn't die of blood loss," Merryn replied with absolute conviction. "Help me turn it over."

Div eyed her curiously, but acquiesced. They each grabbed a forelimb and twisted the torso enough to flip it.

"Eight!" Strynn breathed, behind them. "It's—"

"Fire," Merryn finished for her. "Or—more properly—lightning."

For the dead geen showed, unmistakably, the same sort of damage all down its scaly torso that the Ixtians had displayed back at the hold. The Ixtians who had been blasted by the Lightning Sword.

Only this was worse, if only because the smell was worse, and that courtesy of the fact that the blast had ripped the geen's abdomen open, leaving the organs therein free to rupture in the heat. Merryn had to slap her hand over her mouth to keep from gagging.

"At least we're on the right track," Div gritted, likewise swallowing hard.

"Yes," Strynn agreed from farther back, "but do we want to be?"

"No choice," Div concluded, sparing a glance at Merryn.

Merryn started to remount, then paused, gazing back at the dead creature. "If anyone has a stronger stomach than I do, those claws are prized in Ixti. We could do worse."

Div grinned wickedly. "Never bypass a resource in the Wild." Without another word, she wrapped a link of wine-doused sylk across her lower face and spent the next half hand cutting.

Two days later, and closer to the true mountains than ever, they found a second geen, dead exactly like the first one. And three days after that...

"Another one!" Merryn cried, pointing to a now-familiar mound of dark reptilian flesh that disrupted the flow of meadow grass around it.

"Like the others?"

Div shook her head, "This one's so fresh the vultures haven't found it. Two hands at best, I'd say." She rose from inspecting the burn marks down the beast's breast and scanned the landscape critically. Merryn followed her example.

It was late in the day—they would have to make camp soon—and the sky looked as threatening as it had since they had set out, with iron-colored masses of heavy clouds shrouding the entire heavens, broken only when random sunlight colored thin places steel or bronze or copper. Lightning was already fumbling around up there, awakening ominous rolls of thunder. It *would* rain before dark; there was no doubt about that: another reason they would need to make camp soon.

Which made the dead geen all the more troubling. Two hands at most, Div had said; which meant the one with the sword could still be very near indeed. She stared at the woods apprehensively.

They had been lucky so far: The geens' trail had held steady, almost due northwest. It had ducked into the woods by night, but most days it had taken the path of least resistance: marching through a steady series of meadows that ornamented the mountains like a string of beads. The only problem was that the beads were getting smaller, and the woods closer, darker, and thicker with every passing hand. Which would mean a number of things, none of them very pleasant.

Like the fact that they would have less warning of any impending geen attack—unless the horses spooked, or the birkit did.

Like the fact that their own hunting would likely fare less well. They still had venison from a deer Div had killed two days back, but it was starting to go bad, in spite of a hasty smoking. Unfortunately, the only deer they'd seen hide or hoof print of since then had been species that favored open country. So—unless they found woods-deer, which were impossibly wary—they might soon have to rely on small game and birds, which would be harder to kill in the heavy foliage and uncertain light.

And the mountains...It looked as though they would never end. Certainly the geens' trail angled toward yet another ridge, this one fairly wide and running level a good way to either side. Beyond it...more mountains and higher, but those were still a fair ways off. There were mountains to the east, too, which she thought might be part of Angen's Spine, given the way Eron's eastern coast swooped around in an arc to the west.

"What do you think?" Div asked, wiping her hands on her thighs and striding back to join Merryn and Strynn while Krynneth relieved himself a few spans down the backtrail.

Merryn scowled. "I think we need to make camp soon, preferably somewhere with good potential to stay dry. I think we need to set a watch against geen attack and sleep armed and with one eye open even then. I think we're closer to our quarry than we've ever been and in a perfect world with perfect weather, might actually catch up with them today—"

"It," Div corrected. "You've said yourself that there's nothing to indicate there's more than one—the one with the sword—and that they usually hunt in groups of four because they're born that way. We've found three dead ones now: all dead the same way, which makes no sense."

"None of this does," Strynn countered. "There's no reason for it to use the sword to kill its fellows unless it felt threatened or angry. If they're as smart as we think they are, the ones without the sword could well be envious that they don't have one. That could incite anger, which would provoke attack."

"What I wonder," Merryn mused, "is why the thing has kept it all this time. It would have to be carrying it, and the fact that it's killed with it several times—with lightning, not just the naked blade—implies that there's been at least sporadic contact between the gem and the geen's bloodstream—and probably a longer contact than any human has ever endured in the bargain. I keep hoping we'll just find the sword thrown away, but that seems less likely every moment. Which means—"

"Which means," Strynn finished for her, "that when we do catch up with the thing, we may well find ourselves facing the Lightning Sword."

"Which we can't survive." From Div.

"Not likely," Merryn agreed. "Which means we'll have to resort to stealth in order to retrieve it."

Div rolled her eyes. "Optimistic, aren't you?"

"Better say fatalistic," Merryn retorted.

Strynn shot her a scathing look. "I don't need that, Merry."

Merryn rounded on her. "What's that supposed to mean? We're talking about me, here, about my agenda, my quest."

"Makes a convenient excuse," Strynn shot back. "But I'm on a quest, too—which supersedes yours."

"No," Merryn gritted, "it does not. Your quest was to retrieve the regalia, which only incidentally requires that you retrieve me. If I were dead, you'd still be obliged. The Kingdom comes first, Strynn."

"In that case," Strynn raged, "what about the child I'm carrying? It's heir to someone who may even now be dead, but also to the two—when we left—most powerful clans. And Clans outlast Kings, or have you forgotten that, too? And don't forget—"

She broke off, mouth agape. "Merry, I'm sorry. I don't know what came over me, or why." All at once she was crying, and Strynn—like Merryn—almost never cried.

"It's the pregnancy talking," Div advised, glaring at both of them. "And in any case, is a discussion for *after* we find the geens—or geen, as I'm all but convinced there's only the one."

"The most dangerous one that ever lived," Merryn growled, her eyes bright with tears of her own. "I'm sorry, too, Strynn. And whatever else happens, remember—"

"Don't say it," Strynn murmured. "You don't have to. I feel the same way. In any case, we have the same goal at the moment. That should be sufficient."

Merryn nodded silent assent.

"Rain!" Krynneth announced abruptly. And at that very moment, Merryn felt the first drop strike her hand.

"Waited too long," she sighed.

"Shelter looks best over there," Div observed, ever the pragmatist. She used her bow to point to where a copse of evergreens made a darker mass against the pervasive hardwoods. "And I *think* I see a mass of boulders big enough to provide decent back-shelter *and* something solid underfoot as well, though we may have to pitch the tent beside it, if we can't get the pegs in."

"Good enough," Merryn acknowledged and said no more until they were under the arms of the forest.

She did not remain there long, however—only long enough to confirm Div's opinions about the mass of boulders, and to see that the tents were well pitched (to one side of an almost flat slab at least two spans square) and a cook fire under way. The rain had proved a false start. "I'm going out again," Merryn informed them with calculated nonchalance. "Not far, and I promise I won't do anything careless—but we're in need of firewood—*dry* firewood, and there's not much of that around here. I'm going to see what I can find before it all gets soaked. If I'm not back in a hand, come looking." And with that, she strode into the woods.

But firewood was a minor priority, though Merryn hated to lie about it. They were close to the geen, very close indeed—so close she could all but smell it—and now it looked like they were going to lose ground again. If nothing else, the hard rain that was now inevitable would wash away most of the remaining spoor. She was therefore going to track the thing as far as she could in the remaining daylight—or until the rain got so bad that she couldn't. And if she found it... well, there'd be time then to decide on a course of action.

And if it found *her,* there would likely be no decision at all.

It was rash, it was stupid, it was selfish and careless, but Merryn was tired of waiting.

The tracks weren't hard to find, and continued, as they typically did, in a straight line through the center of the meadow. Which took them directly beneath the eaves of the woods on the northwest side—a quarter of the way around the meadow from where they were camped. She hesitated there, for it was getting late and the sky was even more ominous. Yet the tracks led beneath the branches, clear and tantalizing. She glanced at the sky again; saw lightning flash between two clouds. Thunder rolled ominously. *Was that an omen?* She really was being foolish. But she was close, so close...

Should she?

She glanced back the way she had come, saw a flicker of firelight and a trickle of smoke that suddenly spoke all too eloquently of friends, comfort, and home.

Too much to risk.

Still...

It wasn't raining yet; so she would compromise: She would continue onward for another finger—another fifth of a hand—or until it started to rain in earnest, whichever occurred first. That was probably as much as she could expect, and at that, she would have to endure Strynn's fury—and probably Div's—all over again.

Half a finger farther on she found something that confirmed her course of action at last.

The land had been rising steadily since she had entered the woods, with more and more stone showing among the pines: stone of a kind she identified with fire mountains. Indeed, a whole ridge of it had appeared, crossing her trail at right angles, which also put it at right angles to the slope, as though a section of land two spans high had simply been yanked upward there. The resulting low cliff face was cracked and fissured—and one fissure was more properly a true cave.

The geen's tracks ran directly into it.

And even Merryn was not fool enough to track geens in the dark.

On the other hand, the cave would limit the creature's options as well. They had it now—she thought. If they were patient.

But *not* in the dark.

Before she knew it, she had turned and was striding back

toward the meadow. The rain caught her there in earnest, but Fate smiled on her enough to present her with the biggest dry log she could still carry, and with that as peace offering, she returned to camp, where she endured reproachful glances but did not reveal what she had seen. Not yet. Not while she was still pondering what to do about a certain geen in a certain cave.

CHAPTER XV:

ASSASSINATIONS AND ASSIGNATIONS

(ERON-TIR-ERON-HIGH SUMMER: DAY LXXXIII-EVENING)

~~~~~~~~~~

Tyrill knelt in a tiny, open-sided shrine a dozen shots down
North Bank from Tir-Eron's official southern limit and pre-
tended, with perhaps too much fervor, to be praying. It was a
shrine to Life, as it happened: Life, who had risen in favor of
late, both because of the sudden pervasiveness of Death in a variety of troublesome guises, and because it was getting on
toward First-Harvest, and food—which was rarely a problem
when the Kingdom was not engaged in civil war—was suddenly in short supply.

It therefore made sense for poor clanless women—whose
kind would bear the brunt of any shortages that might transpire—to haunt the fanes of that aspect of The Eight whose
province was fertility. And of course it was *their* sons—and
daughters, as well—who had borne the brunt of the recent
war. And though fatalities had been few and injuries light,
still, they were not to be discounted.

Which was why Tyrill was "praying," but not what she was
doing *while* she "prayed."

No indeed! What she was doing, overtly, was studying the
aftereffects of her latest...indiscretion.

The fane was small and out of the way; set, as it was, halfway up a high, steep hill, to which an equally steep set of steps spiraled up from the road—all of which tended to discourage passersby from casual visitations. Which also made it a perfect vantage point from which to observe—if she positioned herself so as to peer through the surrounding pierced-stone half screen—a set of granaries that stood at the foot of the path, across the road from a large wheatfield. Two days ago, there had been four of them. Now there were three—and the occasionally still-smoking stub of the other one.

That one—a largely empty one, by deliberate design—had been torched the previous evening by person or persons unknown, shortly after the last harvesters had departed. And only the intercession of Fate—or Life, since one of Life's fanes was conveniently nearby—had prevented all four from being consumed.

The result, of course, was that the remaining granaries were now under guard by members of Priest-Clan or their lackeys. More to Tyrill's point, however, that guard should be changing any moment. She watched closely, there in the light of the setting sun: watched the last laborers—all of them Common Clan or clanless, where before there would have been a handful of High Clan involved—empty their baskets into the middle granary and amble away. The guards—two of them—watched them go, then spared a moment for a drink and to greet their replacements when they came riding up. At Tyrill's range—a quarter shot up the hill—she couldn't hear more than an occasional laugh or comradely shout. But Tyrill was not about hearing. She was about waiting...just a little longer.

The day guard was leaving now: had mounted their horses and were pounding away, leaving fresh replacements to sit watch through the night.

Tyrill waited until the old guards showed only as spots of

dirty white rising above clouds of dust only slightly darker, and then she moved.

Carefully.

Just enough to be seen by one of the guards below.

A shout ensued, but she chose to ignore it, intent on her false piety.

Another, then a pause that probably masked a muttered comment or an exasperated sigh, followed by the pounding of footsteps on the spiral path. Two pairs, she was pleased to note.

Getting closer.

Closer.

"Who's there?" a young female voice called sharply, the tones tense with alarm.

"What?" Tyrill coughed, as though startled. She twisted around in place, timing her movement to coincide precisely with the arrival at the entrance arch of a breathless, flush-faced young woman. "I'm sorry," she continued, blinking in exaggerated confusion. "I fell asleep at prayer, and it made me groggy, and I...I can't quite seem to stand."

"It's late," the guard said stiffly, though she was obviously trying to be polite. Beyond her, Tyrill could see the guard's male companion pacing about, looking impatient.

"I'm sorry," Tyrill repeated, reaching for her cane, then raising her hand to cough once more.

But she didn't cough. Remaining on her knees gave Tyrill an excellent angle on the guard's unprotected throat. And that close—no more than a span away—even in the rapidly gathering twilight, there was no way she could miss. Not as practiced as she had now become.

The girl looked startled, then grabbed her throat—and started to fall. Tyrill caught her as she rose—and almost fell herself, before she got the two of them stabilized.

"Help!" she called, in what was not entirely feigned panic.

"What?" the second guard cried, arriving at the door. And halting—

Just long enough for another dart to find the back of his neck, from where Tyrill's more mobile and sharper-sighted accomplice had waited behind a piled stone wall farther up the hill.

The man collapsed as neatly as Tyrill had ever seen a man fall: simply folded himself down at each of his joints, like a puppet whose strings had been severed. Still struggling with her own burden, she had to watch him fall and pray no one else saw what had transpired.

By the time she had freed herself of the unfortunate guardswoman, a new figure stood in the entrance arch: a man as disheveled and shabbily dressed as she, though younger. He stepped carefully around the fallen guard and helped Tyrill find her feet, moving with a grace she would have envied half a lifetime ago.

"Good work—for a pair of flute players," Ilfon laughed, brandishing the blowgun he had made when Tyrill had shown him hers—which he had painted (as he had painted hers) to resemble the flutes street musicians used, down to false finger holes. It wouldn't stand close scrutiny, but no one who'd got close enough to discover their deception was alive. With a flourish, Ilfon removed the glass darts from both necks and ground them against the dusty marble beneath his feet, into which they disappeared as though they had never existed. And swatted at something that buzzed his face.

"Good luck, this," he chuckled. "Mosquitoes, I mean. Mosquito bites look a lot like the marks of blowgun darts. And this time of year, this close to the river…"

Tyrill nodded sourly. "Whoever finds them will see what they expect to see."

Ilfon's brow quirked up. "Two guards dead in one of Life's shrines? That may be pushing it, even so. But we won't need to come this way again. Not until they've relaxed their vigilance."

Another nod, as Tyrill slumped down on the rail of the

shrine itself. "It was a good plan, though: lure them south, then ambush them. But we have to be careful not to fall into a pattern. And not to deflect blame where blame doesn't belong. We don't need innocents accused of crimes they didn't commit."

Ilfon scowled a warning. "It *is* going to happen—eventually. You know that."

"But hopefully not yet," a husky female voice inserted, in what was obviously an Ixtian accent.

Tyrill whirled around in place, even as Ilfon went instantly on guard.

"No need for that," that same lower voice advised. "I'm coming to the entrance now—that's how much I trust you."

And with that, a dark, cloaked shape did indeed melt into view just beyond the archway. Tyrill couldn't see the face for the angle of the waning sun and the overhang of the woman's hood.

"Lady Tyrill, Lord Ilfon," that unknown woman continued, dipping her head in formal acknowledgment, "I see that you have become well acquainted with the...flute. Therefore, allow me to introduce myself: the...flute-maker." And with that she swept back her hood.

"Elvix," Tyrill gasped. "I should've known."

"Elvix mahn Aroni mahr Sheer at your service—Chiefs," Elvix grinned through another bow. "Ambassador at large from Ixti, and now at the service of you, who represent, if I may say, Eron's only legal government."

Ilfon looked anxiously toward the door, as if expecting other intrusions. "I'm alone," Elvix assured him. "No one knows I'm in this part of the country except Tozri—and maybe King Kraxxi, if word has reached Ixti by now. In any case, I'd suggest we retire to a less...controversial location. I feel confident that we have all got a great deal to tell each other."

Ilfon nodded sagely and extended his arm to Tyrill. "We've a caravan—if you can call it that—over the next rise."

"That will do nicely," Elvix assured them, with another grin. "I have wine."

And until the last moon set at midnight, the three of them drank and plotted and planned.

CHAPTER XVI:

RAFTING

~~~~~~~~~

They hadn't reckoned on rain...

Three days of the wretched stuff—without letup, and sometimes so heavy they could see nothing but an endless curtain of liquid silver shimmering down from the cave opening's upper rim to where it disappeared a quarter span beyond the ledge that terminated what passed for a floor.

At least there was no dearth of drinking water—but that was the *only* surplus of water that was good, since the rain meant that progress on the raft, which had been running well ahead of schedule, was now running badly behind.

Never mind the effect the incessant downpour was having on their hunting, which was to render it impossible; fishing, which was only barely viable; or gathering firewood, which was the real problem in the long run. Hindsight told them they should have laid in a supply of dry wood against such an eventuality as they now confronted. Instead, they had blithely harvested the closest kindling first, with the result that not only was all the remaining nearby wood too green to burn easily, but they had to go ever-farther afield to find the shrinking portion of the remainder that wasn't. And return soaked themselves, to sit around what little flame they could coax into being, nibble fish and mushrooms, and drink increasingly watered-down cauf—*after* "drying off" on blankets that got damper and damper while they waited for sodden clothes to dry.

At least it was summer, so cold was not a problem. But even so, an unpleasant clamminess pervaded their sanctuary, in very unwelcome contrast to the crisp warmth that had greeted their arrival. The scent of mildew was beginning to tickle the air, too, and with the soap supply all but exhausted, blankets and rug alike were starting to stink of sheep. They staved off some of the problem by going barefoot and shirtless most of the time, and leaving as many garments as they could as close to the fire as they dared. But while common bathing was something they had all indulged in without thought, the cave was *not* a bath-chamber in a hold, and long-ingrained rules of decorum haunted extended casual "indoor" undress, adding to the pervasive edginess.

To fill the time, they made rope from the inner bark of a tree that grew in groves a quarter shot down the path; made arrows from reeds and shoots of thick-cane; and flaked points from fire-glass, which was abundant thereabouts—or helped Kylin with the flute he was making. Sometimes they sang, too; but no one but Kylin had more than a passable voice.

They also played games: notably question games or dare games, and engaged in every sort of athletic contest a hard floor and cramped quarters allowed—which was mostly variations on wrestling. And they groomed each other: trimming long-neglected hair and shaving off sparse beards. Finally, they mended everything they could find that needed mending until they looked set to run out of thread and Lykkon made them stop.

Mostly, however, they simply talked—about the war, at first, but increasingly about what would be required to turn this remarkable location into a viable hold—either here on the island, or in the cliffs that ringed it.

And by all those means, the bonds between them grew stronger. Already comprised of two sets of bond-mates and another set of natural half brothers, with Kylin the only odd lot, they all discovered things about each other none of the rest had known. There was even a little love play—discreet and under covers, with Lykkon and Kylin being the most frequent participants, simply because, without bond-mates themselves, they had endured longest without physical affection. Bingg was an awkwardness in that regard, because he was Avall's cousin, Lykkon's actual half brother—and too young for even courtesy attention from the rest. He needed a bond-mate his own age—which was one thing he would not find here in the Wild. *If they remained in the Wild.*

Which brought them back to that.

Avall was absolutely convinced that he had been shown this place for a reason, and brought there for one as well—though what those reasons might be, he had no idea.

He turned back from the cave's front rim, where he had been standing for at least a half hand, staring out at the sheeting rain. The cliffs that were their goal were out there somewhere, but he couldn't see them. Scowling, he padded back to the fire and asked the question he had posed at least once a day since work on the raft began. "Assuming the thing actually floats, how long do you think it will take to reach the mainland?"

"How fast can you paddle?" Rann retorted, voicing his standard reply.

"As fast as you can," Avall replied sourly. "It's just that we really don't have that much left to do on the thing, and if the rain were to break, we could make the first trip this afternoon."

"Enough 'ifs' to choke a geen," Myx grumbled. "We'd still have to carry the first load down there—and we don't know what shape the trail is in."

"We don't *know* the raft's still there," Riff put in grimly. "If the level of the lake has risen much, it might not be."

"We had it lashed down," Lykkon opined from the corner. "There hasn't been *that* much wind."

"Only rain," Avall spat. "And rain. And rain."

"Don't forget rain," Bingg chuckled from nearest the fire, where he was pounding tubers in hopes of making something resembling bread meal.

Avall glared at him, then eased closer to Myx and Riff, pitching his voice for them alone. "There never seems to have been a good time to ask this," he began, "and it's not really a good time now, but...forgive me if this seems rude, but...are you lads happy here? You seem to be, but you're both betrothed, correct? To women now at War-Hold? If we were to stay—not now, maybe, but someday—"

Myx exchanged glances with Riff. "You're asking would we rather be here or with them."

"We'd rather be here *with* them," Riff inserted. "But that said, you're right: We like it here. We *think* they'd like it here—or my lady would, anyway; since she's from Wood, and The Eight know there's plenty of wood around here."

"Do these mysterious women have names?" Bingg inquired, likewise easing closer. "I don't think I've actually heard you say them."

"Navayn—she's mine—and Tavera," Myx murmured. "Navayn's got a brother about your age. I suspect he'd be up for a trip west as well."

"All of which is ultimately supposition," Avall sighed, leaning back on his elbows. "But I had to know—well, wanted to know, anyway—in case we did decide to come back here on a more...permanent basis."

"After the war, you mean?" From Myx.

"After some kind of resolution," Avall corrected. "The Eight know precious little can be resolved from here. That's why getting to the mainland is so important. Once we get there—"

"You can be King again," Myx finished for him.

"Avall doesn't like being King," Bingg countered, too loud.

"I just wanted to know where you stood on the matter of going versus staying." Avall replied. "I didn't want you to do anything you didn't want to do. Getting to know you two has been one of the joys of the last half year, but I never wanted to take over your lives."

"You haven't," Riff assured him.

"Where you go, we go," Myx added "—allowing for the Fateing, if it ever starts up again."

"And as for Navayn and Tavera, they're more likely to force us to go with you than to try to hold us back."

"Well, that's as much as I could hope for, I guess," Avall concluded. And with that, he rose and ambled back to the front of the cave.

Something had changed out there, he realized. Perhaps the rain wasn't falling so hard, or the drops weren't quite so large. Certainly he could see farther into what was still mostly a sheet of mist. But for the first time that day, he could also distinguish two shades of gray where the opposing cliffs were supposed to be, so that reality had regained a horizon. And even as he watched, the whole world brightened abruptly and one pure beam of sunlight lanced down.

Rain swallowed it at once, evoking a disappointment in Avall so bitter he almost wept. But another beam appeared a finger later, and that one not only remained but expanded, so that by the time another hand had elapsed—it was still barely past noon—the sky was all but clear. A hand after that, they had spread three days' worth of damp clothing on rocks to dry and were all, save Kylin, on their way to the cove to see how much damage the raft had sustained.

Not much, as it evolved. At some point the lake had risen high enough to lap under it and shift it—but in such a way that it had pivoted around one corner, so that the bulk of it was now two spans closer to shore than heretofore. As for actual damage, one section of railing had torn loose, but would be no problem to resecure.

For the rest—it was mostly a matter of checking bindings, adding some new ones from the rope of which they suddenly had a near surplus, and rigging a mounting for the sail they had decided would make a useful supplement to oar power.

"If we stay here," Lykkon mused, gazing at the now-visible shore that was so near and yet so inaccessible, "we should rig a ferry system. It would take a lot of rope, but it could be done, and the first crossing would be the hard one. Once we had one rope stretched across the lake, we could walk either end to the best locations. That would make going back and forth a whole order easier."

"Assuming we stay here," Myx stressed with exaggerated emphasis.

"Right," Lykkon agreed, with a grin. "Assuming."

"Tomorrow?" Avall inquired, dipping his head toward the raft. Sweat glistened on his bare torso, but he looked absurdly happy.

Riff nodded solemnly. "Tomorrow. But it won't be fun, whatever you think. And it could still be deadly, for all we've seen no more water-beasts."

"I've been thinking about them," Lykkon murmured through a thoughtful scowl, as he surveyed the lake. "I think they may only be here part of the time. They could be like salmon: They live in the sea but come inland to breed, and maybe the young ones stay here until they're big enough to dare open water."

"The one we killed was big enough, thank you," Bingg growled.

"Agreed."

"That also assumes we're near the sea," Avall observed. "We've no proof of that, except that we've seen seabirds—but we've seen them as far inland as Gem-Hold, so that's no indicator."

"But there is a trace of salt in the water sometimes," Lykkon countered. "That implies some level of physical connection."

"There's salt in the Flat, too," Avall retorted. "It could as easily be fed by water that flows through that."

"We'll find out tomorrow—maybe," Riff broke, in fixing both Avall and Lykkon with a warning glare. "We may reach the top of those cliffs and find a fine bright city of plague refugees on the other side. *Something* has to have happened to all those folks who went west."

"Most of them died," Lykkon informed him smartly. "There are good records of who left, and most of them were accounted for eventually. Relatively few actually got over the mountains."

"Tomorrow," Riff repeated absently. "Tomorrow."

"Tomorrow," wound up being a seamless extension of "tonight," for the simple reason that none of them slept more than sporadically. Long before sunrise, Myx had stoked up the fire and had cauf going—full strength this time, he said, for celebration as much as fortification. There was fish (there always was), fruit, and a few thin-shelled nuts of a type none of them had seen before their arrival on the island. Finally, there was a sort of semi-bread made from Bingg's pounded tubers mixed with water, salt, and a little of their real bread crumbled, all baked by the fire.

They dressed carefully, in as many clothes as they could wear and still move effectively, but eschewed items like tabards and cloaks that would encumber a swimmer gone overboard. In the interest of maximum safety, in case of attack either by water-beasts or geens, each of them wore every weapon he possessed, and they were careful to have at least one dagger close to hand.

Some items were too large and bulky to consider transporting this trip, of course, notably the table and rug; but most of the smaller items fit neatly into the boxes that had been made for them (they had, after all, come from a camp tent), so that packing was fairly simple. Every one of them carried a box or bag slung on his back, and that would be enough for the first trip. Bingg had the distance lens—triple-tied, to make absolutely sure he wouldn't lose it.

So it was that the sun was a blue-pink promise in the sky when they set out. "We'll be back, though," Avall whispered to Rann. "Even if we return to the war, we'll be back. I know it."

Rann could only smile and slap him on the back—then stagger as the move unbalanced the box on his back, evoking nervous giggles from both of them.

The raft was still where they had left it, and still intact. Nor—thanks to Lykkon's careful planning—did it take long to load the boxes around the mast and lash them down with make-do vine webbing. Kylin would sit with them, back to the mast, because that was the safest place for him. For the rest, Bingg was to the fore as lookout; Riff was in the back as steersman; while Avall and Rann manned the oars on one side, and Lykkon and Myx the others.

That was the plan once they got it into the water, anyway. Unfortunately, that aspect took far longer than expected, because the craft was already heavy, and they hadn't reckoned on the extra weight of the load. In the end, they had to sling vines around it and drag it in small bursts of effort to the shore—which necessitated them wading out almost waist deep—which was also as far as they *could* go, before the bottom fell away.

Happily, the raft floated splendidly, and, once they had all clambered aboard, didn't appear prone to tipping—if they moved with care. There was no wind to speak of, so there was no point in using the sail, but they were young, strong, healthy, well fed, and optimistic, and that was enough to see them out of the shallows with aplomb. A moment later, they were plying the oars (lengths of thick-cane with the bottom half span split open and folded outward to make blades) as if they were life-long boatmen.

They were almost exactly halfway between their departure point and their destination, when something thumped hard against the bottom.

CHAPTER XVII:

IN THE DARK

Avall had not been the only one cursed with impatience that morning.

Merryn, too, had found that she could wait no longer.

Three days of nonstop rain that had them sitting beneath an increasingly leaky stretch of oiled-canvas roof while the world outside seemed set to wash away had seen to that.

Three days watching their campsite become an island amid a swirl of muddy needles, twigs, and leaves.

Three days of listening to Strynn alternately sniff, cough, and sneeze, as she succumbed to what she claimed was the worst cold she'd had in five years. Div was threatening to get it as well, and Merryn herself was coughing more than she ought, though she thought that might be a function of inaction.

Only Krynneth seemed to be prospering. He had doubled his vocabulary again, but still wasn't offering up sentences—unless two-word opinions counted. He seemed impervious to the illness, however, and was proving to be an expert healer as well as a decent forager for firewood, though Merryn took pains to assure that his forays took him south and east: away from the cave and toward what she'd been happy to discover was quite a serviceable river.

The cave...

She had tried to watch it without appearing to, which was hard without leaving the camp. Mostly she contented herself with sitting as close to the edge of the shelter's front overhang as she dared, staring out at the woods and the meadow, and hoping a dark shape wouldn't come skulking out from among the maples.

At least Div had chosen the campsite well: a slab of stone two spans square, with another behind it; both thrown together as though the earth had shaken them free at some unimaginably ancient age and tried to construct a giant's throne there; two sturdy trees as anchors, to give their canvas span enough to embrace the horses if the beasts didn't mind close quarters; and a crevice for the fire they kept going so as to cook, make cauf, and keep their clothes dry. Room for their tents to one side.

But however secure it was, remaining there was wearing on Merryn, who knew that the resolution of their quest lay—perhaps—no more than a few shots and a few hands away.

Of course she couldn't reveal that fact, because she had determined long since that this was her battle—which had manifested in a suspicious calm that both Strynn and Div had noted. Her explanation had been that the geen wouldn't like the rain any more than humans did, and that the creature was probably holed up somewhere. But that sort of careless rationalization had to sound dubious to anyone who knew her as well as Strynn did.

If Strynn hadn't been sick, anyway.

Then had come yesterday's sunshine—but that had arrived so late in the day none of them had seen any point in moving on. Strynn had sounded awful, too, so they'd decided to see what improvement a dry night would impart.

Merryn had already decided how she would spend that night—at least the latter part.

She had planned it carefully, and had positioned herself and her gear just so—and at that, her plan turned, as she was perfectly aware, on an incredible amount of luck. Still, it *was* a plan, and that was more than had existed previously.

It was simple, really, the only complications coming at either end—one of which she was about to undertake.

She had made a point of sleeping on the slab rather than in the tent she usually shared with Krynneth—she needed fresh air, she said; Krynneth was getting a little ripe. And she had considerately chosen a sleeping place near the stone's edge, overtly to give the others room, but in actuality so that she could slip away silently. She'd also been careful to feed the horses more than common so that they would be a trifle groggy, and to sleep in the thickest clothes she possessed that could pass for nightwear yet still be worn under armor. All of which she kept in mind as she carefully raised her blanket and eased out and away from Strynn, who slept nearest. It was still a hand before sunrise, but the largest moon was shining, so that she could see well enough without a torch.

Well enough, anyway—if she moved slowly—to make her way entirely from beneath the tarp and down to the ground beside the rock. The earth was mushy there, and she *had* to move slowly to avoid making sounds that might betray her. But she was Night Guard, she reminded herself. Night Guardsmen knew their bodies; they knew how to move silently, efficiently, and with absolute stealth.

She employed all of it, as she eased around to where she could reach up and secure the remaining items she required—all of which she had positioned carefully for just this eventuality. First came her sword: practicality there. That was followed by the helm—back in its nondescript burlap cover. She set it on the ground while she secured the last and clumsiest item: the shield, which she had left propped up at the back of the sleeping area where the floor and wall slabs came together. She had to stretch a bit, and use one hand where two would have been much better, and at that, the hand guard scraped. She froze where she was, heard Div's breath change cadence, then moderate again. But she had it now, and an instant later, had removed it.

Now came haste. Silent haste. Moving as carefully as she ever had in her life, she made her way through the forests that lay behind their camp until she reached a small copse of oak trees maybe a quarter shot away and within sight of the glistening river—a place she had marked previously as appropriate for what she was about. And also a place where she had left certain other items on previous foraging ventures. It was amazing how sneaky one could be when no one was expecting it.

It was all there, too—of course—her mail and the rest of her armor. And there in the moonlight she vested herself quickly—everything but the helm and shield. Those would have to wait until the last possible moment, and even then she wasn't certain she would actually don them. They were two-thirds of a set and, without the third component, were out of balance. They would try to seek that balance anyway, and in all likelihood unbalance her mind in the process. She might be strong enough—had *proven* strong enough once—barely. She hoped she was more experienced now, and that experience would be sufficient.

And that was a powerfully big hope, she acknowledged. The last person to wear the regalia had been Avall, but he had helped make it, and was close kin to the King for whom it had been fashioned. Still, he was no closer kin than Merryn was, so the gems should recognize her.

Then again, there was poor Rrath, who had also worn the armor and gone messily mad for his pains.

Unfortunately, it was the only thing that made sense. If the geen had the magic sword, the only way to stand against it was with the shield that matched it while wearing the helm that completed the set. If she were lucky—that word again—she would never find out. But *that* depended on the other end of her plan going as desired, and that truly was a dubious proposition.

Ultimately, it all reduced to logic. The geen—*Please Eight, let there be only one*—had to sleep sometime. Hopefully at that time it would relinquish its hold on the sword long enough for her to retrieve it. That accomplished, she would have the upper hand. Even if the sword were unactivated, she would be in good stead to face a sleepy monster. And she could activate all three gems in a breath if necessary. She hoped it wouldn't come to that.

Then again, she hoped many things, as she made her way into the night, alert for the sound of pursuit, but hearing nothing save the drip of leaves shedding water and the absent snuffle of a horse.

And then another thing: one she should have anticipated. A soft, relentless *pad, pad, pad.*

The birkit.

She should have known.

Hunt. The word appeared in her mind. Not a question as much as an affirmation. And not a challenge.

Nor did it surprise her; the gems gave one powers, even unactivated, sometimes—and the ones in the helm and shield were perilously close to *being* activated.

Her first impulse was to spin about and drive the beast home, but she reconsidered. It could raise a cry and ruin her plan. And it was a hunter. One the geen might not expect. A distraction, if nothing else, when a distraction might be needful.

Hunt, the birkit "said" again, and that clinched it.

Half a hand later they had found the cave. Merryn paused by the entrance slit to light the smallest torch she had been able to construct on the sly: a torch she stuffed in a crack in the rock while she donned the shield and helm, taking exaggerated care not to activate them. That accomplished, she returned the torch to her right hand, along with the sword—awkward but necessary—uttered a brief and surprisingly fervent prayer to The Eight, and entered the darkness for an appointment with several of them, notably, she suspected, Death and Fate.

It was slow going, but it was progress—very slow progress through the dark. The cave narrowed quickly, but was still wide enough for passage; it almost had to be, since geens were roughly the same width as humans and somewhat taller. The walls were scoured smooth in places, she noted, especially at hip and shoulder level. And the thin skim of mud on the floor allowed the expected three-toed footprints to show clearly. They went both ways, too—which prompted a chill, indicative as it was that the beast had been out and about during the rain. Still, the most recent set looked to point inward, which was some relief.

It was cooler, she likewise observed, which might make the geen lethargic—or might not; there was debate on whether their blood ran hot or cold. In any case, she hoped she would soon meet that blood firsthand. Maybe then she would know once and for all.

Maybe.

The shield scraped the wall.

The noise made her flinch—which brought her head unexpectedly in contact with a dip in the ceiling. Echoes fled up and down the tunnel. She froze in place, abruptly awash with sweat. The birkit growled low in its throat, but stayed where it was: a span behind. At least its location negated ambush from that quarter—though what the source of such an ambush might be, Merryn didn't want to ponder.

On and on she went, setting each foot precisely, moving just so, praying for no recurrence of the noise she had generated. She sniffed the air, noting mostly a general, moldlike mustiness, but also a stronger musk, along with a low-level stench like rotting meat, feces, and urine. At least there was no sign of the last two. Like all Eronese, she was fastidious about such things.

There were sounds as well—beyond her own breath and footsteps and those of the birkit. Most notably, she caught the drip of water from ceiling to floor, and, more distantly, a low, solemn thrum like something distant beating on the earth. War-Hold had sounded like that sometimes—when the tides ran high. Perhaps this place wasn't as far from the sea as she had assumed; the trees in the most likely direction were too tall to allow more than a cursory reconnoitering.

On and on, as the tunnel twisted and turned, rose and fell. The torch was starting to burn down now—which alarmed her. If it reached the halfway point, she would have to retreat regardless. Or—

The birkit growled abruptly: a half pitch higher than heretofore. *Prey!* The word erupted in her mind, though less a word than an image and a feeling of excitement tinged with fear and caution.

Merryn went instantly on guard. A breath for calm, as she had been taught, then another, and she checked all her grips, readjusted her helm, and started forward once more.

The tunnel kinked right, then left, then right again. Unexpectedly, she saw light that did not come from the torch: a thin shaft of moonlight lancing down from some cleft in a ceiling that was suddenly more distant, and which revealed an abrupt expansion of the tunnel into a roughly oval chamber six spans across. The dark slits of more tunnels marked the lesser darkness of the walls, but Merryn barely noticed them.

She had found it.

The geen.

And the Lightning Sword.

The beast lay curled on its right side along the right-hand wall, with its legs drawn up toward its belly and its right arm folded against its breast. Its neck was thrown back recklessly, so that she could see part of its teeth but not its eyes. But that wasn't what she was looking for.

That gleamed red in the fitful firelight: half a span long, ly-

ing on the floor. At first Merryn thought the sword was un-
guarded—but when she dared a second step into the chamber,
she saw that the geen's right hand was still draped casually
across the hilt.

So, what did she do now?

Speed or stealth: Those seemed to be the choices. The former demanded that she relinquish her sword—either that, or
act in a dangerous gloom. The latter—if she moved very
slowly—might not. The latter was also less nerve-wracking,
and Merryn discovered that she was very, very nervous indeed.
What had she been thinking anyway? To dare such a thing
alone? She had learned what she had come for. She could retreat, inform her friends of what had transpired, and the lot of
them could set an ambush outside the cave and wait for the
geen to appear. They might have to sacrifice a horse to lure it
forth, but that was a small price to pay to regain the sword that
could save a King if not a Kingdom.

The geen shifted.

The birkit growled again—louder.

Merryn discovered that she had advanced a span into the
room—far enough to swing a sword with reasonable authority
if it came to that. The geen and the sword were scarcely four
spans away.

It twitched.

Holding her breath, Merryn crouched down and eased another step across the floor, praying she wouldn't slip, that nothing would scrape, squeak, or rattle.

Another step. Halfway. If she did this exactly right, she
would only be weaponless for an instant. One breath to drop
her sword, another to grab the Lightning Sword by the blade,
a third to yank it free, a fourth to shift it around so she could
grasp the hilt. So little effort, yet such a risk.

The geen moved again. Not a twitch this time, but a
jerk.

Merryn froze, heart thumping as loud as it ever had. The
sour taste of fear poured into her mouth. The birkit bristled;

she could hear its low-pitched growl—protracted now—as it eased back and crouched down. *Please don't let it attack,* she thought. That would spoil everything.

The geen's hand jerked again, tightening on the hilt, and this time it moved indeed: the head slid around; the legs stretched.

Merryn backed up from reflex, even as she realized that what she should have done was move forward and slash the beast's exposed throat while it was still groggy.

It wasn't groggy now.

Faster than she could have imagined, it unfolded itself into a wary crouch. Merryn backed up again, and was shocked when her shoulders slammed against the wall to the left of the entrance tunnel. The helm rang loud. Reflex swung the shield in front of her, even as she tried to manage both sword and torch. The latter would probably stay lit even if she dropped it—it was that well made—but she didn't need that concern, besides which the fire might keep the geen at bay.

Something was, for it was full on its feet now, facing her, with the sword upraised in its fist and blood trickling down its wrist. It looked eerily human, too: The stance was not far off that of a swordsman at guard. Its eyes were the worst; normally yellow, they gleamed red in the torchlight, like some demon from the Not World come to haunt the solid lands. The thinnest of lips peeled back from jaws as long as her shins, in a frightening parody of a taunting grin. Perhaps it was. Forearm muscles twitched in a way she didn't like.

The birkit growled, then scooted right, distracting the reptile.

The arm swung around. Merryn was certain the room was about to explode with lightning.

But would such a move be wise? It would surely kill everything in range, including the geen itself. Unless the sword *knew* as much and forestalled it.

Or maybe not, for the muscles were tightening again, the arm going up, the sword rising...

"*No!*" Merryn yelled all at once. "Put that down!"

To her utter surprise, the beast froze, then wavered where it stood. The tense arm muscles relaxed minutely; its head swiveled around to face her.

"*No!*" she repeated, taking a step forward, shield to left, sword—and clumsy torch—to right. "That's mine!"

Confusion raged into her head—and *not* the birkit's. Anger rode with it, then more confusion, coupled with the oddest confluence of thoughts Merryn had ever experienced, which carried with them much the feeling of being part of a pack, and then ruling that pack, and then losing it.

"Give, give, give," Merryn shouted aloud, while her mind demanded the same—and more. Her hand twitched onto the trigger that awoke the shield, even as the same reflex jerked the back of that same hand up to slam the helm into her forehead, which awakened that gem in turn.

Power flowed into her—eager, but so unbalanced that she staggered.

She didn't care. She felt stronger, and the gem in the helm told her she *was* stronger, and with a confidence her normal self would have considered reckless, she shouted again. "Put that down *now*!"

Whether it was the power of her voice alone, or the power of her thought, desire, and will amplified through the helm, the geen took a step forward, then another, so that they were barely two spans apart. It raised the sword again, and Merryn found herself wondering what would happen if magic sword met magic shield in confrontation.

"*No! Drop! Now!*" She had no idea if she shouted or merely thought so loud she might as well have shouted.

Whatever it was, the tendons in the geen's wrists twitched a third time, and the hand sprang open. The sword fell to the floor.

It was like a light gone out and a light awakened, and Merryn was never certain what happened next. All she remembered was the geen's eyes going dark and feral as whatever intellect had fired them winked out; and then she remembered it leaping toward her—one leap, she thought, or maybe even a rushing stride. That, and raising the shield before her.

A scream—and that scream ended as quickly as it had begun, as the geen thrust itself backward, flailing awkwardly, but with so much speed that it smashed against the far wall. The torch guttered where Merryn had dropped it, threatening to go out, and she could see little more than a flurry of furred motion as the birkit rushed the fallen geen, while a terrible, alien anger thundered through her head.

She felt pain and anguish as well—though neither her own nor the birkit's. And then the torch recovered sufficiently that she could see the geen lying where it had fallen, with its entire torso a mass of blood where the shield had wrenched its flesh away. Ribs showed, and enough muscles had been sent to that "other" place that it could move its arms but feebly. Teeth showed above bare jawbone, too, and the fronts of both thighs ran red with blood above bone. Dark liquid pooled on the floor.

With a gurgling hiss like water thrown onto a fire, the geen expired. She saw its ribs rise one last time, then every muscle went slack.

She released the breath she had been holding, treated herself to another, then forced herself back to wary discipline—and eased over to retrieve the Lightning Sword, careful not to wake it.

But the shield and the helm *wanted* it awake, it seemed, and it took all the will she possessed to shrug off the shield one-handed, then use that same hand to unbuckle the helm and remove it as well. Cool air rushed in to soothe her face and head. Sweat ran into her eyes in spite of the arming cap she wore,

nd she knew that her hair was soaked. Tired in mind as much
s body, Merryn slumped against the wall and slid down to sit
n the floor.

She had won! She had defeated the geen and retrieved the
word! It only remained to collect her gear, secure the birkit,
nd return to her friends in time for breakfast.

The birkit...

The beast was somewhat calmer, now that it knew that the
een was dead. But it still evinced a certain restlessness. A rest-
ssness that played around the edges of her mind in a way that
vorried her, when she wanted nothing for the next little while
ut to sit there and catch her breath. She could find her way
ut in the dark, if she had to—if the torch went out, which
ow seemed likely. *If* she could find the right cave by which to
xit.

The birkit, too, seemed to be concerned, and was now
rowling from dark slit to darker opening with an almost des-
erate intensity. Abruptly, it paused at one and sat down. Her
rain still sharp from gem use, she caught its thought as clearly
s she ever had: *Through here! Now!*

What it wanted, she had no idea, but it wouldn't hurt to in-
ulge the beast, at least briefly, though she dared not tarry.

Sighing, she levered herself up, redonned sword, shield,
nd helmet but did not activate them, and limped over to join
he birkit. Rather than precede her, however, it eased aside, as
hough it would have her enter what it had found.

Very well, but only for a moment.

A moment was all it required.

The cave jogged right, then right again, and the second jog
evealed true light—morning light, in fact, for the sun was
ven now in the act of rising. She blinked against the unex-
ected glare—a glare that seemed to come from two directions
t once—from above the ridgeline she could dimly see beyond
er, and from something that glittered below it.

Water.

A lake.

And on that lake, approaching the nearer shore, a raft bearing figures.

More than one of whom, even at that distance, she recognized.

"Avall!" she shouted into what was suddenly quite a lovely morning.

CHAPTER XVIII:

LANDFALL

~~~~~~~~~

"Avall!"

Avall twisted around, confused. His name had sounded twice—like an echo. Except that one voice had been an octave higher than the other, and there had been an overlap between the two, not a pause.

But hard on those voices—and of far more immediate concern—came a second thump against the bottom of the raft. Myx yipped; Kylin cried out. Lykkon grabbed for the railing, as a third impact lifted the opposite edge of the raft half a span above the surface of the lake. More water sloshed in on the near side. The raft groaned. A binding snapped amidships.

"Avall? What—?" from a wild-eyed Riff in the back, where he served as steersman.

Avall glanced around frantically, even as one hand left his oar to seek his belt knife. He saw nothing at first: merely the glitter of sunrise upon a froth of low waves. But then he made out more: a darkness beneath that surface, angling toward them.

"A water-beast," he yelled—as his name rang out again. But only one voice this time: Bingg, at lookout. Myx and

Lykkon, too, were all vigilance as their gazes swept back and forth across the nearby water. Kylin looked quietly panicked, knuckles white as they gripped the rope bindings of the box on which he sat, staring blindly into nothing but murky light.

Bingg, for whatever reason, was still pointing toward the cliffs that loomed before them, less than a shot away. Even in the ruddy light of sunrise, the boy's face was bright with joy—which made no sense, given that they were under attack. Yet he was leaning precariously far over the rail, oblivious to the danger such recklessness posed to himself and the raft alike.

And Avall's name once more: the high voice, its tones thin and strained in the morning air.

Avall spared an instant to scan the shore, noting absently that his companions were now doing the same in varying degrees of concern or excitement—all save Kylin and Riff—who was trying to watch the water and keep the raft in order all at once.

Another impact—from directly underneath. The raft rose straight up for nearly a quarter span, then jolted back down in a froth of spray that drenched what little of their clothing was still dry.

"Gawk, row, or fight," Riff bellowed. "But not all three. Now what—!"

"*Avall!*"

Again the high voice. And this time Avall saw the source.

The line of cliffs before them was split and fissured all along its face by ridges, shafts, and chimneys running from the water's edge to the summit. But it was stepped back, too, in terraces and ledges, most of which sported some degree of foliage. Even so, some sections were too steep to support more than ferns and mosses, and at the juncture of one of the vertical flutes and horizontal ledges, someone was standing.

Balancing perilously, more precisely, by the way the figure was clutching a swag of clinging vines that depended from the ridge a quarter shot above. Unfortunately, the rocks there were vitreous, and the sun was hitting full upon them, so that they glittered too brightly for Avall to determine more than the fact that the figure glittered, too, as though it were wearing mail.

And might—by the voice—be a woman.

But there was only mail-wearing woman he could imagine meeting in this part of the world—only one who would know his name, at any rate.

"Merryn!"

He hailed her aloud without realizing it, but by then Rann had likewise recognized her—or drawn the same conclusion.

A scrape against the bottom of the raft reminded him that they still faced a threat that would grant no quarter even to happy reunions. "Bingg," Avall snapped, sliding his oar on deck. "Give me the distance lens." Bingg looked confused for the barest moment, then loosened the ties that secured the instrument against loss. An instant later, he stretched across the thick-cane deck to extend it to Avall, who had to strain to reach it.

Praying that no fresh impact would wrench it from their grasp, Avall snared the object quickly and raised it at once, swearing as the focus blurred. But then he found it. It was indeed Merryn, standing on a ledge no wider than her feet, gripping the vine with one hand, and waving frantically with the other. She wore mail, as he'd suspected, though no surcoat, and her hair was plastered to her skull with sweat. She looked tired—and seriously alarmed. With reason, if she had seen the raft heave upward. "Everyone," he shouted, "it's Merryn. Up here on the cliff!"

"Merryn?" Riff was the last to respond. His gaze never left the water.

"You're joking!" From Rann.

"The *Eight* I am!" Avall pointed to the shore, and by then everyone had seen. Without prompting from their nominal captain, they all picked up their oars and shifted their course as directly toward Merryn as they could manage.

But the water-beast had other plans and was evidently tired of playing. A shadow Avall could barely distinguish from the raft's wake suddenly shifted directions, becoming darker and denser as it approached. Then, before anyone could react more than minimally, the beast smashed into the back of the raft right beside Riff's steering oar. More alert to the raft than the rest of them, Riff jerked the oar toward the exposed hump of back, even as he stretched down to stab at it with the dagger that had appeared in his free hand. A thin line of blood showed across what looked like wet black leather, and the beast dived instantly.

Avall alone of the crew saw that happen, and however enthralled he was by Merryn's arrival, he knew that it would be the ultimate caprice of Fate if no one survived to give her welcome.

"Stand to attack," he yelled. "Forget Merry—for now. Watch every side, and prepare for anything. If it moves, hit it. Stab it. I don't care, but *kill* it."

"It" was not cooperating, however. Yet for a long moment the lake stilled. The ripples in their wake subsided as they drifted. He could hear Merryn yelling, but her voice was faint.

And then, like the world's largest sword rising from the depths, an enormously attenuated head and neck shot skyward right beside Lykkon. Reflex made him release his hold on the rail and flinch back—which upset the balance of the raft. It tipped dangerously. Bingg lost his grip and slid into Avall, which further skewed the weight distribution. A box broke its bindings and tumbled past Avall's feet to lodge against the lowest strip of railing.

They poised there for a moment, tilted at a perilous angle, with one side almost a span in the air and the other immersed half that deep in water. The crew grabbed at whatever they could find to keep from falling, and only Riff retained his footing—by twining his toes into a particularly large knot of lashings.

As for the beast...it had vanished—or was invisible beyond

he floor of the listing raft. Which was even worse, since that
out it in a prime position to knock the unbalanced structure
he rest of the way over, which would free it to choose its vic-
ims at leisure.

A cacophony of shouts rattled the air, mostly "Avall" and
"beast" rendered in varying degrees of panic at varying pitches.

And then came the lightning.

A pure white bolt of it rode down from that cloudless early-
norning sky to strike the waters beyond the bottom of the
aft—which was now rather more like a wall.

The air shattered with thunder. Steam hissed. Vapor fled
not past Avall's face. The stench of lightning bittered the
oreeze, mingled with the crisp scent of burning meat. Then si-
ence, followed hard by a long, thin blubbering scream that no
human throat could have uttered.

Riff was the first to regain composure, the first to scramble
oward the part of the raft that rose highest above the water.
The first to bring his weight to bear (and he was heaviest of the
crew by a bit), and the first to extend an arm to Lykkon, who
was nearest (though lodged atop a jumble of boxes beside the
nast). Somehow their hands met, and Riff jerked Lykkon up
oward him. The raft promptly shifted far enough toward
evel for Myx and Rann to make up the difference.

"Is it—?" Bingg dared, as he untangled himself from Avall,
atop whom he had fallen.

Riff scanned the waters on his side, then turned and nodded. "It is. It's floating out there—in two pieces. But what—?"

"Merry—and the Lightning Sword," Avall replied, heaving
himself to his feet, hands questing for his dagger, the distance
lens, and his oar all at once.

Bingg had reclaimed the lens, however, and was scanning
the shore intently.

"What's she doing?" Avall called, as he settled on the oar
and set it in the water once more. They had drifted, he
noted—but fortunately the line of that drift was shoreward.

"She's trying to get down," Bingg yelled back. "But she

can't. The vine's too short and the ledge is too steep, or she
can't find handholds, or something. I think she's—yes—she's
going back inside the cliff. She waved, and made a 'wait' sign,
but she's gone."

Gone.

Avall felt the word like a weight of despair.

"She'll be back," Bingg vowed with conviction. "She has to.
We just have to be patient."

"We have to make landfall," Avall countered. "We have to
get up there."

"We can't—not there," Rann told him flatly. "There's simply no anchorage."

"Then we'll have to find one!" Avall snapped.

"We can wait," Riff put in firmly. "If we have to, we can
make a circle of this place and find a way up top. If Merryn's
inside the cliffs, she has to have entered somewhere."

"She looked as surprised as we did," Bingg added. "And as
glad to see us."

"She wouldn't have left without good reason," Avall conceded, somewhat more calmly. "Probably to find some way to
get down."

"Or us up."

"She's surely got rope somewhere," Rann agreed.

"So what do we do?" Kylin asked the group in general: the
first time he had spoken.

"Try to hold position," Avall sighed. "And wait."

Holding position proved more difficult than expected, but in
the end, they managed, though more than one set of eyes swept
anxiously across the lake in search of anomalous shadows.

Happily none were forthcoming, but most of a hand still
elapsed in an agony of waiting before Merryn returned—with
three companions in tow. Strynn was with her—as was Div,
and a worn-looking man they didn't recognize. "Strynn look

bad," Rann muttered, as he lowered the lens they all were sharing now.

"Just be glad she *looks,*" Avall shot back, then glanced up at the cliffs again. Merryn was maybe a quarter shot above them, which was a lot of rope. Most likely, she would have to find a second landing and throw from there. Or a third.

The latter proved to be the case. Merryn managed to find sufficient handholds in the vines to work her way to where a wider ledge jutted out a good eight spans lower than her initial perch: a ledge from which more vines depended. Div followed, while Strynn and the stranger remained behind: more proof that at least one of them was ailing.

Once on the ledge, Merryn reached up to receive a heavy coil of rope that Strynn and the man were lowering from the cleft, using what looked like torn-up strips of a Warcraft cloak to constitute the line. Once she'd freed it, Merryn secured the rope to a stump and tossed the remainder down to the raft. Avall watched it uncoil, fascinated, praying it was long enough to reach them. Unfortunately, it came up a span and a half short.

There followed the most frustrating morning Avall had ever spent, with both his wife and beloved sister so near and yet so far, and their presence all but proof that at least one of their quests had succeeded, and every breath bringing them closer. But there was no time for casual greetings as they called directions and encouragements to each other and tried to finesse the raft into a position from which someone could make up the difference between cliff wall and lake, while Merryn made her way down to a precarious perch a scant two spans above the water's edge.

And then the raft was bobbing within reach of the cliff, and Bingg was stretching as far up and overboard as he dared, fingers questing for Merryn's, which she in turn stretched down toward him one-handed, while the other hand held the rope and both feet anchored her at an angle from the cliff.

But Bingg was not quite tall enough to make contact, and the raft was proving unwieldy in the sudden wind that had kicked up and was raising waves that now threatened to suck them away from their goal, now to dash them into it.

And then one of those waves spun the raft a quarter turn around, which put Avall on the shoreward side. And while Rann jabbed frantically with his oar to keep the rock away, Avall reached out and—with his extra height an advantage—managed to clasp Merryn's fingers.

Power surged through him—or joy so strong it was effectively the same. And then Merryn was pulling, drawing him to shore, while Rann shifted over to seize Avall, and Bingg worked his way between them to tie one of their makeshift ropes to the end of Merryn's while Myx and Lykkon secured the other end around the decking near the mast.

All of which brought the raft even closer to the cliffs, where Bingg was finally able to loop the rope around a finger of stone that looked like it would hold the raft securely and keep it relatively stable.

"Should I come down?" Merryn called.

Avall thought for a moment, then shook his head. "We were already trying to get to shore. We'll come up. But what—?"

"Later," Merryn and Rann chorused as one, though both Rann and Div (who had claimed the next ledge up the rock face) were having a hard time keeping their eyes off each other.

"Right," Avall agreed regretfully, gazing around to where his crewmates were already untying loads in anticipation of landfall.

Riff however, looked troubled. "If we're not careful, we may lose the raft," he warned. "A little care now could save a lot of grief in the long run. I'd suggest we off-load the most irreplaceable items regardless, then try to stabilize the raft as best we can."

"Actually," Rann mused, stroking his chin, "if we tied it off a little better, the lot of us might be able to hoist it as far as that ledge Merry's on."

"Sounds as good as anything we're likely to come up with in a hurry," Avall agreed. And with that, he slung a pack onto his back, grabbed the nearest length of rope, and with Merryn's assistance, struggled ashore. Thanks to the near-vertical slope, he had to climb hand over hand, and it was touch-and-go at times, yet before he knew it, he had reached the second ledge, where Div awaited. There was no time for reunion in either place, however, merely a pause to tie his burden to the fabric rope Strynn and the stranger commanded, and watch them heave it up to where that third group of allies waited.

By which time Bingg was clambering up the rope and Lykkon was getting ready. Only then did they realize that Kylin might be a problem. For, blind as he was, and no stronger than Bingg for all he was larger, he might have trouble climbing—yet the trek was too perilous for him to assay unassisted. Kylin, however, disagreed vehemently—and amazed them all by shinnying up the lower rope with uncanny ease, only slipping once, right at the end.

Riff—as nominal captain—was the last to come ashore, and that only after he had checked the knots that bound rope to raft four times. That accomplished, they set their backs and arms to it and heaved from Merryn's perch. The raft rose, if slowly and awkwardly, for it was heavy, and they were all tired from their morning's exertions. In the end, they only managed to raise it half its own width above the water, where, fortunately, a pair of rocky knobs provided rests atop which it could lodge—which, with the slight slope, provided minimal security at least. Not that Riff didn't risk a potentially deadly fall securing the corners to a few stray roots, scraggly trees, and sturdy vines.

Bingg, who was the lightest, made one final trip down to

confirm that the remaining supplies were securely lashed to the deck, and then he, too, joined his fellows on land.

And then the rope was coiled again, and Strynn was pulling it upward, and the rest of them were climbing the vines—which proved far easier than the rope had been.

By unspoken agreement Avall went first, and so was first to scramble over the upper edge and find himself suddenly in Strynn's arms—and utterly at a loss for words because of it.

It was as though she read his mind—which perhaps she did. "We've basically succeeded," she told him tersely, obviously holding back what, if his own heart was any guide, was a flood of emotions, all of which distilled down to the look in her eyes: joyful, yet grave and troubled. "I've got a cold, but I'll survive, and Krynneth's . . . not himself, but improving."

It took Avall a moment to absorb even that much information, and another to peer through the rough-cut hair and sunken features in search of the Krynneth he had known. The man looked awful—clearly something terrible had befallen him, and perhaps the rest of them as well. But he was also grinning and thrusting out his arms for an embrace Avall was not slow in granting, awkward as it was in the narrow tunnel in which they had found themselves. "*Avall!*" Krynneth crowed, in an oddly childlike tone. "Avall. Avall. Avall."

"That's me," Avall murmured, gently prying Krynneth's arms away, while his gaze sought Strynn's anxiously. "Come, Kryn," he continued, we have to get out of the way. There're other people—"

The next few moments were another study in chaos, as the tunnel proved barely more than one-person wide, even without packs to consider, which resulted in Avall and Strynn being at the head of a line that was pushed farther and farther into the unknown of the cliff face.

And then they were twisting around a corner and then another, and morning light became no light became firelight again, as they found themselves entering a large chamber lit by three small torches.

But the chamber was not empty.

The messily dead corpse of a very large male geen lay against one wall, with a handsome female birkit worrying at one well-muscled haunch. And against the other wall—

Avall had no choice but to leave Strynn and rush toward it, kneeling in the mud as he regarded what might yet save his Kingdom—if he could get it there...

The royal regalia he had sent away what seemed so long ago—though why it was here, he had no idea. Surely this was not the hiding place Merryn had chosen.

Not with a freshly dead geen to guard it.

But he would get no answers now, not with the rest of the crew crowding in to join them. Merryn made her way toward him through the chaos. "Not how I'd thought to meet you, brother," she chuckled, finally enfolding him in the hearty embrace necessity had delayed for so long, "but I'm beyond glad to see you—thought not here. We've got a camp a shot away on the other side. That would be the best place to figure out what in the name of The Entire Eight is going on."

"Sounds wonderful to me," Avall agreed, adjusting his pack. "I've had enough water for a while—though we'll need to go back to the island at some point to retrieve some things."

"All in good time," Merryn sighed. "For now, we really do need to get back to camp. We left the horses unattended, and as you may have noted, there are geens about—and you know what they like to eat."

"We've known," Avall replied offhand. "About the geens, I mean. We've seen them on the cliffs."

Merryn nodded absently, then started abruptly, and whirled back around to face him, face hard and intense. "*Them?* There wasn't just the one?"

Avall shook his head. "I don't know how many. Several.

Though we haven't seen them lately. It's been"—he glanced at Lykkon—"how long?"

Lykkon scowled. "Let's see, we've been here eleven days. We saw them the first morning, and every day after that until the rain—"

"So there could still be some around," Merryn spat, suddenly all business. "Come on, we have to get back to camp!"

CHAPTER XIX:

JEWELS IN THE WILD

(SOUTHWEST OF ERON–HIGH SUMMER: DAY LXXXV)–MIDMORNING)

To Avall's surprise, it was barely four hands past sunrise when they made their way out of a second cleft in the rocks and once more beneath open sky. More surprising, it took a moment to adjust to terrain that, instead of sloping sharply downhill, ran off gradually through woods that would have seemed perfectly ordinary had at least a third of the trees not been of a kind he had never seen before. Lykkon hadn't either—nor Riff, who was connected, via Shipcraft, to Wood and ought to know. And that difference as much as anything confirmed the fact that they were very far from home indeed.

The ground was soggy underfoot—from days of rain that had penetrated even to the undercover—and Avall found himself scanning the leaf mold for the distinctive tracks of geens. He found none—no one did. But that didn't stop Rann from foisting his pack on a startled Krynneth and jogging off with Div in advance of the rest of the party—overtly to check on the horses, but equally likely to secure a few moments' privacy with his lady.

Not that Avall wasn't glad to see Strynn as well. Yet somehow the present reality of their reunion failed to match the image of that event he had carefully tended in his mind, with the result that everything seemed slightly unreal. Given the way they always had to relearn each other after every separation, he supposed it would take a while before things between them regained a comfortable level. Now that they had the regalia again, he hoped he would *have* that time.

He was carrying the Lightning Sword because someone had to; while Merryn took charge of the helm; and strong, stocky Riff shouldered the shield along with the largest pack. It was a practical arrangement in the extreme, but such casually cavalier treatment of valuable artifacts once again put Avall off—probably because it was yet another example of the reality of an event having no relationship whatever to how he had expected it would be. Beyond that, he had also realized that far more information needed to be imparted than a simple explanation of why half of Eron's High Council was here in the middle of the Wild. Like Zeff's latest ultimatum, for instance, and Rann's rebellion, and the circumstances that had precipitated them here—all of which now seemed more like an extended, and not entirely pleasant, dream, than any real series of events.

Nor were Merryn—or Strynn or Div—likely to be pleased with what they heard. And who could tell about poor Krynneth? Whatever happy reunion anyone was anticipating would dissolve into argument and anger sooner than anyone thought, once certain hard facts were made known.

All thanks—yet again—to the Eight-cursed gems!

Which was another oddity, Avall reflected, as he strode through the dappled forest shade, angling toward the brighter light of the meadow now visible beyond the farther trees. *When had he grown so accustomed to the notion of staying here, anyway?* Either on the island itself or on the cliffs around it, both of which showed promise of possessing more than enough raw materials to construct a nice serviceable small hold? And now all that was about to change just as he'd begun to accept it. Eight! Before long—maybe even within a hand—

he would be marching off to war again! He wondered if he was remotely ready.

But they had reached the eaves of the woods by then, with the meadow beyond, and the sheer beauty of the place jolted him back to the present, so that, for the too-short while it took to reach the camp, Avall forgot how ephemeral happiness could be.

Fortunately, the horses were alive, healthy, and no more nervous than typical, though Div was handing out sugar treats in a manner so profligate it prompted a scowl from Merryn.

"We've got food," Bingg volunteered, shedding his pack and gazing about anxiously. "If no one minds eating water-beast."

"I'm sure it's better than horse," Merryn sniffed—and that settled it. "We've got cauf," she added, with a twinkle in her eye. "I don't suppose you lads do?"

"Some," Avall retorted loftily, "though ours is, uh, some-what...adulterated."

"You were on that island *how* long?" Merryn muttered. "Didn't someone say eleven days?"

"It's a long story," Avall sighed. "Perhaps we should all sit down." And that comment seemed to be the cue for everyone to unload their packs, divest themselves of unnecessary cloth-ing and war gear, and find places on and around the rock that anchored the camp. "The first thing you should know," Avall continued when the din had more or less subsided, "is that we didn't *choose* to be here."

And for most of the next hand he explained why. At that, he only touched the high points, but neither Merryn, Strynn, nor Div had heard anything of what had transpired after Strynn had departed Tir-Eron in search of Merryn: not about the progress of the war itself, nor the coup in Tir-Eron.

"That will have spread by now," Merryn opined when he had finished. "There's no way this Ninth Face won't have co-ordinated attacks in all five gorges."

"They wouldn't have to in Half or South," Avall grumbled.

"Those two were already well on their way to chaos when the Face made their move." He broke off, raising a brow at Strynn. "Though if anything *had* happened there, surely someone would have sent word to War-Hold. I don't suppose you heard anything, did you? Assuming you went by there?"

Strynn shook her head. "Nothing."

Avall flopped back against the rock and folded his arms across his chest, frowning intently. "One troubling factor is that the nature of the attack makes me think that not only is the Ninth Face involved, but that they have access to some form of distance communication."

"Gems?" From Merryn.

A shrug. "Maybe. But I'm thinking it might be Wells. I'm finding that the more I deal with them, the more there seems to be some commonality between the effects of the gems and those of the Wells. At minimum, both affect a person's mental powers. Beyond that, one seems to allow *communication* across distance, the other *seeing* across distance—and maybe time as well."

"But how do you *know* that?" Merryn shot back, brow furrowed by a frown of her own.

"Because the last Well I drank from was the Well beneath the Ninth Face's citadel, which should, in theory, owe no loyalty to me—or to the King, rather—yet it showed me a vision of the lake we just came from."

"But I saw it, too!" Div countered. "In a dream. And I've never drunk from a Well in my life, nor had contact with a gem in eights."

"You've had contact with the birkit, though," Strynn observed. "And they *also* seem to be some kind of catalyst."

"Or repositories," Avall gave back, returning his gaze to Merryn. "And I suppose I should add that I dreamed about the geen with the sword, which might tie them into the mess as well. We need to talk about both those things, too—but not until after we've walked the straight trail. For instance, did

Strynn and Div catch up with you before or after you'd hidden the regalia? Obviously you have it now—but that doesn't mean you hadn't hidden it earlier. Though why you'd be here—"

Merryn cleared her throat, took a long swallow of cauf (augmented with some of the remaining brandy) then sighed—loudly. "If you're through arguing with yourself, brother, there are a couple of things you ought to know, one of which will likely please you, the other of which almost certainly will not."

Without waiting for reply, she launched into the whole long tale of her capture—first by Krynneth, then by the Ixtians—which was followed by an equally lengthy account of the geen's theft of the sword.

Avall was frowning like thunder when she finished—but as much at Div and Strynn as at his sister. "You should have kept a closer eye on her," he growled at them. "You know how she is."

"If they had, you'd be floating around the lake in pieces," Merryn replied airily, but her face was traced with guilt—like a little girl caught at something dangerous by her elders. "It was act or argue," she continued, frankly. "I knew that time in which to confront the geen was limited, and that it was ultimately my fight. But I also knew that Strynn and Div would insist on coming along if they knew I was going—which would have reduced us to arguing about who would stay with Krynneth, who was too much risk to take along. Div would ultimately have won, because Strynn was simply too sick to make an effective second—if nothing else, because she was likely to sneeze or cough, and thereby alert the geen or geens. But if Div and I had been killed, that would have left Krynneth in the care of someone who might—forgive me, Strynn—die herself, so I had to be sure there was someone strong in camp, and that left Div. It was pure logic, brother, nothing more."

"We'll talk about it later," Strynn sniffed. "Besides, there's an even more important reason I couldn't go—one that Avall certainly needs to know."

Avall lifted an inquiring brow. "And that is?"

"I'm pregnant—about an eighth now."

It took a moment for the words to sink in—though if anyone voiced a reply, Avall didn't hear it. Only when Rann and Lykkon slapped him on the back at precisely the same time did he truly realize what his wife had said.

"Pregnant," he blurted out.

Strynn nodded through a very self-satisfied grin. "Twins—I think. I should have told you earlier, but things had just got so grim and serious when we should all be happy—"

"However briefly," Avall broke in ominously, as emotions warred across his face. "You know that we'll have to act quickly now that I've got the regalia back. Or *I* will, at any rate." He closed his eyes and clamped his hands to either side of his head. "But—Oh, Eight damn it! This is just too *much*! There are too many things to confront all at once, too many choices, too many Eight-cursed if-thens!"

With that, he rose and stalked away, but Merryn was on her feet in an instant, restraining him with a hand on his arm. "Is there a *reason* you have to confront it now? The ultimatum's been expired for over an eight, in case you've forgotten. Whatever's happened in regard to that *has* happened."

Avall turned on her fiercely. "*Has it?* Maybe it has and maybe it hasn't, but the fact is I'm still King and I've gone off and left people I care about in perilous straits, and people I'm responsible for imprisoned under threat of their lives, never mind what's happening in Tir-Eron. And that's not even considering that Zeff could well have found more gems by now—he's had more than long enough to dig his way down to the mines, especially if he uses everyone in the hold as slave labor."

"And you can fix this? You yourself?"

"Give me the regalia and you'll see! And the other gems—our personal gems you demanded of us."

"What for?"

"So I can jump back to Gem-Hold. Even if Zeff has found more gems, I'm bound to be his equal simply because I've been dealing with gems longer and have three very strong ones properly installed in housings designed for them."

Merryn shook her head. "You can't."

"Can't what."

"Jump back."

"Give me those gems and I'll show you!"

Merryn grabbed Avall by both shoulders and shook him firmly but gently. "You *can't*, Avall. They were damaged. They were burned in the fire."

He glared at her. "You've tried them?"

A deep breath. "I haven't dared. I remember what happened with the master gem recording Barrax's death. These may have done that as well, and if they have—are you man enough to face another man's death by burning?"

"The gems can be cured, Merry."

"Can they?"

"The master gem—it was getting better before I broke it."

"And the fragments?"

"We're still testing. That's why I wanted to use the other gems."

She shook him again. "And what about us, Avall? Your friends? Your family? Your wife? Your bond-brother? Everyone you love is here right now. What about us? Would you abandon us all to who-knows-what just so you can return to Gem-Hold and—quite possibly—die?"

"I won't die," Avall retorted. "The cursed gems won't let me."

Merryn's eyes flashed fire. "The same gems that are shattered or burned past risk of usage? Do you think they owe you any favors now? You said they protected you, but look how we've treated them! Would you risk it, Avall?"

"You're saying I shouldn't go back?"

She shook her head. "Not at all. In fact, I'll kick your

backside for you if you don't try. But you go with the rest of us. And maybe you go via the gems. *Maybe*. We've got three good ones in the regalia; maybe you can jump with them. But you won't do it alone." She paused, grinning fiendishly. "You know, what would be true justice would be for you to jump into Gem-Hold in secret and plant the burned gems where Zeff can find them—and let him go pleasantly mad."

Avall couldn't suppress a chuckle. "This is the same sister who didn't want me jumping?"

She released him with a chuckle of her own—and a warning pat. By unspoken consent, they began to walk together, away from the camp. "Madness and genius are opposite sides of one coin," she said eventually.

"And we'd be fools to decide anything until everyone knows as much as possible."

She regarded him seriously. "You know what we have to do, don't you?"

"You'll tell me anyway, won't you?"

"Only that in order to determine what we can and cannot do, we'll have to test every one of the gems, both alone and in every possible combination, not only to assess their present condition but also in case some combination of them might still allow jumping—which I will concede is the fastest way back there, if also the most—I'm very tempted to say 'foolhardy.'"

Avall felt his blood run cold. "You're right—much as I hate to admit it, you're right."

Her expression didn't change. "*And* as soon as they're determined to be even minimally safe, the rest of us need to try to bond with the various gems as well—including the burned ones *if* someone can determine that they're safe. And maybe even if they're not."

"That's insane!"

"Maybe so, but hasn't it occurred to you that maybe the gems have different effects on different people, or that people have different effects on them? Strynn has said, for instance, that the birkit told her that she's a strong thinker."

"So is Kylin," Avall acknowledged. "He was able to link with me through a gem neither of us was touching."

She grinned. "Then there you are. And there's also the small fact that we all need to be as familiar and facile with their various…powers as we can be, simply because there's no telling when one of us might be incapacitated or have to work with an unfamiliar gem. But beyond all that, there's one final thing I think needs to be done—and this one you *really* won't like."

"I've a feeling I know what it is, too," Avall sighed. "You're talking about the regalia."

She nodded. "You have to try it again to see if it's sustained any damage. But we also have to be prepared for the possibility that you may not be able to use it when it's needed—because you're dead, injured, didn't make a jump you expected to, or for a double-eight dozen more unpleasant and unlikely reasons that nevertheless could occur. The point is: A weapon that can only be used properly by one person isn't much of a weapon. Which means that, much as I dislike the notion, I should try it, in case I have to substitute for you—and then probably Lykkon and Bingg, since it seems to have an affinity for Clan Argen minds. After that, I'd say Rann should try it—with supervision. He's not our blood, but he's the closest friend we've got who isn't, and I think we need to know how the regalia would respond to that. And before you say that Strynn's closer, I'd remind you that she's also pregnant and carrying the heirs to two important houses—and that those children may be even more important now that the High Clans have been decimated again. That said, she should try it—after she's delivered."

"And Myx, Riff, Div, and Kylin?"

"Them, too, though I notice you didn't include Krynneth. Still, if it accepts them, fine. If it doesn't…Well, if nothing else, the attempt could become a kind of loyalty test."

Avall shook his head. "No it will not! When this is over, if I'm alive, or anyone else is alive who owes allegiance to me, I'm going to do what I started out to do: have anything that smacks even slightly of gems hidden away beyond temptation. Maybe in that geen's lair, in fact."

"There's a lot wrong with that idea," Merryn snapped.

Avall turned and started back toward camp. "Maybe so, but tell me later. For now, we need to tie up a few loose ends, then play question-and-answer in case we've left out anything important, and then—I don't know about you, but I barely slept at all last night, besides which, I'd like to spend some time with Strynn." He paused. "She is all right, isn't she?"

Merryn shrugged. "I'm neither a healer nor a midwife, but it looks like a simple cold, complicated by the fact that she's pregnant."

Avall took her hand. "So, then, as soon as we feel up to it, we start investigating the gems—obviously we can't do all this testing you propose in one day—probably not even in an eight. But regardless of all that, we need to head north as soon as possible, optimally tomorrow. With this many people and only three horses, it'll be slow going, but at least it will be some kind of progress. And we can work with the gems on the way. And if we should find out that jumping is an option—"

"Enough for now," Merryn said. "I'm as tired of the if-then game, as you are."

More discussion awaited them at the camp: discussion that eventually shifted to the hard points of actual logistics—notably where, exactly, they were, and how long it would take to return to Gem-Hold—if such a thing were possible—before the winter snows.

"It shouldn't be hard," Lykkon put in, after a good hand's intent listening. "I can tell a fair bit by where the stars are and the way the sun and moons rise and set. Tied in with what Merryn's told us about the overland route she took, I've got a pretty good idea of where we are. Of course it would help if I had my maps, but, idiot that I am, I pulled ours out to check something before we left, got distracted—and inadvertently left them on the island." He blushed furiously.

"We can return," Riff assured him. "It'll take time and effort, but it should be possible."

"Tomorrow," Merryn concluded with conviction. "Tonight's going to be long enough already."

CHAPTER XX:

PLAYING WITH FIRE

(SOUTHWEST OF ERON—HIGH SUMMER: DAY LXXXV—LATE AFTERNOON)

～～～

Avall and his companions spent the latter part of the morning and most of the afternoon putting the camp in order and retrieving their gear from the raft. Though they had not been able to bring everything from the island—the worktable, rug, and Lykkon's mislaid maps, to name three—they had brought nearly everything else that was small, portable, and applicable to either defense or most crafts, along with the bulk of their food, save one case of wine. Of course they hadn't been planning to feed four extra mouths, either—but neither had Merryn's crew expected to have to provide for seven, so it evened out in the end. Merryn and Strynn still had a decent supply of trail rations, along with a few more items they had secured from the Ixtians. Avall's group had a fair store of fruit and nuts from the island, plus a nice supply of luxury items Lykkon had been hoarding, which included some very good wine he *had* brought along, the consumption of which was justified now that there was cause for celebration. For the rest, they had canvas for tents and awnings, and blankets for bedrolls, so that the result of half a day's intensive labor was that they all but tripled the size of the original compound. Myx and Riff took charge of the horses and strung up a make-do rope corral around them, as well as volunteering to stand guard against marauding geens. By unspoken agreement, the raised rock slab itself was dubbed the Royal Pavilion, mostly because Avall had moved his gear there so as to be with Strynn. The rest of the sleeping arrangements were yet to be decided.

What with Merryn's excursion in the wee hours, a morning's worth of exertions for most of them, and an afternoon's excitement, punctuated by more physical endeavors, they were all hungry well before the usual mealtime. Bingg and Rann volunteered to cook, claiming they had fewest other conflicts, since Lykkon was frantically recording everything he could remember about the day in his journal.

The meal itself was quite a feast, given its impromptu nature and the circumstances under which it was contrived. The main entree was a stew of horse, water-beast, and a third of the remaining Ixtian bacon, mixed with local wild mushrooms and tubers. There was also fruit, wild salad, and pan-bread with cheese; while they quenched their thirst with water, saving the wine for dessert, as they were saving their precious supply of cauf for breakfast.

And while the amounts consumed would have raised no eyebrows in Tir-Eron, life in the Wild had accustomed everyone to lighter fare, and so no one went away hungry.

With three hands still remaining before sunset, peace settled across the camp—but also a certain degree of anticipation. People kept glancing at Avall, then glancing away, as though they hoped he hadn't seen them. They were waiting for him to act, he knew. Waiting for him to remember that he was King.

Which was odd, he considered, as he leaned back against the upright stone at the rear of the camp and took his first long sip of Lykkon's wine. Yesterday he had been one of a group of equals; better at some tasks than some of his fellows, worse than others. And less useful overall than Riff or Myx, if for no other reason than because he was younger. Today, he was King again. He wondered what made the difference. He had the regalia, of course, but that was a symbol of power, not power itself, at least as far as this group perceived it, for they knew he would never use it against them.

But Merryn was back, as was Strynn, so perhaps *they* made the crucial distinction. Merryn was certainly more decisive than he, yet she deferred to him. Strynn was all but his legal equal and also strong in her own right. But again, she deferred to him.

So, he wondered, where did the division lie between that which was symbol and that which was truly Avall?

He caught himself drowsing and shook himself. This was no time to waste on dreaming when there was work to be done if they were going to accomplish anything at all beyond vanishing from Eronese history—or being recorded there as slothful dilettantes.

"I need to do something," he announced, and rose.

Merryn and Rann, who stood nearest, caught his eye. "There's no reason to wait," he continued, for their benefit alone. "I can dread what I know I'm going to have to do, or I can get it over with. I don't know how much progress we can make before sunset, but I guess it's time we determined the current status of at least a couple of the gems.

"Lykkon," he called, louder. "You need to be here to watch and record. And to abort things if it looks like anything untoward is about to happen."

"What *is* about to happen?" Lykkon inquired, ambling over to join them.

"I'm about to test the gems and regalia," Avall told him. "As days progress, we'll all need to work with them, but we're starting with me because the majority of them are most attuned to me."

Lykkon, who had effectively taken charge of the fragments of the master gem, nodded. "Where do you want to begin?"

Avall sat down on the edge of the slab of rock around which their camp was built. "I've got some idea about how the broken ones function, and Merry just used the regalia, so I suppose the logical place is to begin with the burned ones, since they're the primary unknown quantity. I'll try to bond with them, starting with the one that used to be mine, and go from there."

Merryn stared at him. "Not to be contentious, but...why you? Two of those gems were tuned to Rann and Strynn; they could just as well be the ones to test them. And since Strynn—"

"I'll go first," Rann broke in abruptly.

"You will not!" Avall challenged. "I've shirked responsibility long enough, and this, as nothing else, is my responsibility."

"But you haven't worked with these particular gems," Merryn gave back. "No one has, since they were burned. They're a whole new...category."

"Besides," Rann chimed in, "I've contributed almost nothing in gem lore, so it's time I did. Just one of you be ready to pull me out if things go badly."

Avall glared at him. "I haven't said you can do this yet—and I *am* still your King."

The glare Rann returned him was as fierce. "And my duty is to *protect* that King, and since we both know there's a risk involved—"

He paused, tense as a harp string, all but gasping for breath, then: "But forgetting that for the nonce, I will say this once and never, I pray, again: but as you are my friend and my bond-brother, Avall, do not ever, ever, *ever* pull rank on me in a matter like this again. We both know what's at risk, and I'm not talking about the gems—not anymore."

Merryn's hand was actually on her dagger, the situation had grown so tense. But she laid a hand on Avall's shoulder. "We'll gain more new information at less risk if Rann tries first," she murmured. "If he succeeds, I'd say the next step would be bonding with you, and then...we shall see."

"Will we?" Avall growled. But already his will was weakening in the face of cold, hard facts. A risk *was* involved. Rann was more expendable, as far as the Kingdom was concerned, and Rann served the Kingdom as well as the King—and the Kingdom always came first. Besides which, he was willing.

"Do it," Avall said finally. "I'll concede this argument. But be warned, I will not concede the next one, not if it's a matter of who uses what gems how."

"That's—" Rann began.

"Not fair," Merryn finished for him. "But probably reasonable, given what's at stake."

And then, abruptly, silence.

"Are you going to try for any particular effect?" Lykkon dared at last, to break the uneasy tension. "Merryn's right: We *should* all try the same things, optimally with all the different gems in all their states. For now—Well, as I understand it, the main effects aside from bonding are protracted time sense, heightened senses in general, and the ability to distance-speak—but that last probably won't work at present, since all the likely targets are surely wide-awake right now, and 'speaking' works best if one is dozing but not yet full asleep. Oh, and there's jumping, of course."

"Jumping," Avall echoed sourly. "But probably not with these." He eyed Rann warily. "If you *do* try something that stupid, be sure your target is within recovery range—by which I mean somewhere from which you can walk back here in no more than a hand—like the geen's cave, only I forbid you to target that."

Rann rolled his eyes. "Give me a gem and let's get started—before you talk me out of it entirely and we have the whole damned argument to do over."

Merryn fished in a pouch and brought out what had been their personal gems before she had claimed them to be spirited away with the regalia—which was before one of the Ixtians had walked into a fire with them in a pouch at his side.

Rann studied the three gemstones carefully, trying to identify the one that had been his own personal gem—the one that had, to all intents, chosen him. It had been the smallest one, though not the weakest. But it was hard to tell now, for the fire seemed to have changed them, dulling their sheen a little and shifting their hues to more subtle shades. "This one," he announced at last, choosing one. Wordlessly, Avall passed him his knife. "Please," Avall added tonelessly.

Rann locked glances with him for the briefest moment: a moment full of equal parts challenge, fear, and farewell. Then he looked down again, took a deep breath, and drew the knife across his palm. That accomplished, and before he had time to fully consider what he was about, he grasped the fire-damaged gem with his bloodied hand.

Perhaps it was his own mind that warned him; perhaps it was Avall's whisper ringing impossibly loud in both physical and mental ears; in any case he heard it: *Beware, Rann, there is a death in there.*

And death there was, but it was a weak voice crying in a crimson-stained darkness, not the horrendous, loud, impossibly immanent effects Avall had experienced. Rann's rational part attributed the difference to the fact that Barrax had been in actual blood contact with Avall's gem when he had died, whereas Inon had only held them in a pouch; thus, the gems had not tasted death so close at hand—and in that he was fortunate.

Yet they *had* tasted death—but of a different kind entirely. It was as if he could hear a kind of keening, as though the gem itself mourned the death of part of its own strength. Or, more accurately, like a person might mourn the loss of vigor in his limbs, or diminution of sight and hearing with old age. It sounded—there was no other word for it—tired.

But it welcomed him, too: like an old friend returned, and it sent that expected surge of power into him, but not with so much force or energy as heretofore. He sensed relief and liking along with it. But he also sensed a new eagerness to be at one with him that he found disconcerting. Without quite knowing how he accomplished it, he erected a balance point whereby the gem's power could enter his bloodstream at a certain rate and he could enter the strange place of gem power at the same time—but slowly, carefully, disturbing nothing. And once he had passed into gem's domain, he began to explore his limits.

The first thing he did was to try to contact Avall. That was reasonable enough, since Avall was close at hand and they had shared so much gem-bonding previously that their thoughts often resonated with each other even without external intercession. He therefore tried to picture Avall's face in his mind, and then to *think* at that face the one thing he most wanted Avall to know, which was that he was safe, and the gem also seemed to be reasonably intact and sane, except that it was weaker.

And he thought—*thought*—that he sensed Avall acknowledging that contact. Yet without actually bringing Avall into the bond, or Avall bonding with his own gem, there was no sure way of knowing.

But should he try to jump now, in spite of Avall's prohibition? He had never done that before, never mind done it with this gem, so he wasn't certain it would even allow such a thing.

Should he even try?

Actually, he wasn't sure how to do it, save that it involved absolute desire—and he found that he could not muster sufficient force of will. He wasn't angry enough, he supposed—or hurt enough, or desirous enough. Not that he didn't try something simple anyway: nothing more complex than the basic urge to be closer to Div, who was no more than a span away.

But maybe that was *too* easy; his mind too aware of how frivolous such a jump would be. And so it resisted.

Which made him angry. But with that anger came something unexpected.

Pain. Like fire. And worse, the torment of a man's last thoughts as he found himself irrevocably consigned to flames. Flames in contrast to which death was blessed relief.

The pain had been there all the time, he realized; he had merely been shielded from it. Now he had unwittingly shat-

...ered that shield, and the full force of the pain had found him: ...he pain of a man's body dying and his senses fleeing and his ...oul giving itself up to despair. And also the pain of the gem it- ...elf in danger of being destroyed.

He could not endure it—and so he fled. And as he did, a ...art of him that had grown more dangerously distant than he ...ad realized took control of his body and opened his hand, ...ropping the gem into his lap.

Enhanced senses watched that slow, tumbling journey, and ...eard stone strike tunic wool loud as thunder, then slide down ...he threads with the roar of an avalanche that quickly subsided ...nto a rush of air he thought was a summer storm, but which ...roved to be merely himself inhaling.

And then he opened his eyes and saw Avall's face, tight ...ith concern—but only for a moment before sweat ran into ...is eyes, blinding him. He was soaked with it, he realized, as ...hough he had stood too near a fire.

"It works," he told Avall. "But it's weak. And it does indeed ...ontain a death, but only a little one, and that death is cloaked ...n fire."

And with that, he picked up the gem carefully, wrapped it ...n a scrap of sylk, and stored it in his pouch. Nor did anyone ...rotest, though Merryn frowned as though it had been her ...wn. For Rann's part, he shifted his gaze to Strynn. "Do you ...vant to try yours now?"

Strynn shook her head. "Not until I'm better—not that I ...eel bad right now, but I suspect that's less cure than eupho- ...ia— There'll be plenty of time later."

"Speaking of which"—Avall sighed, glancing at the sky— ...that took longer than I anticipated—though it probably ...idn't feel long at all to you."

Rann studied the sky as well, surprised to see longer shad- ...ws than had been present when he had begun the bonding. ...What now?"

Avall gnawed his lip, looking by turns tired, eager, and anx- ...ous. "As best I can tell, there's only time for one more round this evening, tired as we all are. And since the most important thing to learn is also the least risky—in that it's the only one that involves gems that haven't obviously been altered— think that I should try on the regalia. After that—if there's still time— No, we'd be better off not worrying about that. For now...let's assemble the regalia."

Had it only been an eighth? Avall wondered. An eighth since he had stood atop a tower in the Citadel in Tir-Eron and let Rann and Lykkon fasten the regalia onto him, so that he could embark—then as now—on a test that would properly assess the regalia's properties?

That had been the last time he had used any of the gems with confidence, he realized—save when he had tried to reach poor Rrath through the second, and lesser, of his personal gems. After that—after Merryn had taken gems and regalia away—he'd only had the mad one. And though he had worked with that one endlessly and had, in fact, noted some improvement in its...demeanor, he had never looked forward to those workings. Which, he supposed, had tainted his attitude toward the gems in general.

Now, however— He supposed he would know soon enough, because Merryn was holding the shield, and Lykkon had the sword, while Rann was raising the helm over his head then lowering it and buckling the chin strap. "Better you than me," Lykkon murmured. "And certainly better you than Zeff."

"Or Orkeen—or a geen." From a vigilant Merryn.

Avall didn't move. The world had narrowed abruptly to a slit of woodland glade through which a setting sun sketched long dark shadow among tall trees. The helm blocked the rest—nasal, earpieces, browridge: an archaic design and impractical, but traditional. *As though his countrymen would tolerate anything else!*

But this was not Tir-Eron, and the rocks around him no battlements, the trees no invading army. Merry and Rann and Lykkon—Well, he had seen them all in soldier's gear, but they wore simple tunics now, and well-worn ones at that.

"I'm King of the woods," he announced, voicing words that had come to him from out of nowhere. "I'm King of the Wild."

"A greater kingdom than Eron, and older," Rann muttered back. "Now, stop stalling and do what you have to do."

"Not here," Avall retorted. And with that he strode out into the nearby meadow, not halting until he had reached the approximate center. Once there, he faced as close to northeast as he could figure, and only then did he squeeze the hilt and grip, and slap the back of his sword hand into the helm. Pain pricked him, and blood ran more freely than was its wont at any other time, but power also flowed into him like wine into the mouth of a parched traveler. Nor did he sense more than a shadow of the odd pauses, wonderings, and queries that had greeted him the last time he had donned the regalia: the ones that reminded him that the equipage had not been made for him, but for another King entirely: one who was now—in all but the most literal sense—dead.

It was like being himself and himself all over again. Not only that, he could sense other resonances as well: a ghost of misplaced loyalty and resentment that was Rrath; an exhaltation at the use of raw power unleashed that came from the sword in particular, and which he identified as Merryn; and a strange, primal, primitive power that spoke, unmistakably, of geen.

But those *were* powers, he realized, things to be incorporated and used, not impediments.

But what should he do with them? He had been raised to think that one should never use power frivolously, and this was more power than existed anywhere else in the world.

Perhaps that was enough for now. Without further pause,

he raised the sword on high, moved body, thought, and will in a certain way that pierced the Overworld, then swung the sword down again—and tore the sky asunder.

"Zeff of the Ninth Face," Avall roared, through the wind and lightning he had summoned and was about to release, "your fate is mine, and it starts for you tomorrow!"

And with that he aimed the sword at the top of a distant mountain. And once more he clove the heavens. Fire blazed up on the horizon, as a tree he could not see, yet knew existed, exploded into flame.

He was on the verge of calling the lightning yet again—until a firm pressure curled around his sword arm, and fingers pried at his palm. "No, brother," Merryn whispered. "It's a joy and a temptation. But never forget that first and foremost it's a weapon."

Rann reached up to unbuckle the chin strap. "It's rained for three days," he chuckled. "I hope that'll be sufficient to forestall any fires your...impulse may have ignited."

"Not for Zeff," Avall retorted. "Not ever."

CHAPTER XXI:

MOVEMENT IN THE DARK

(NORTHWESTERN ERON, NEAR MEGON VALE—HIGH SUMMER: DAY LXXXV—EVENING)

~~~~~~~~~

"Do you *really* think he's coming?"

Tryffon leaned back from the Council table and laced his fingers across his belly. "It's been eleven days, lad; optimism is a fine thing, but like any good thing, it can be indulged to excess." He took a sip of wine for emphasis, and regarded Vorinn keenly.

Vorinn tried not to flinch beneath that stare, which had not been aimed at him with such intensity since he was a little boy. "Do you think I like this?" he retorted as calmly as he could manage under the circumstances—which wasn't as calmly as he liked.

"The troops are getting…anxious," Tryffon continued. "Are you aware of that? Every day they sit out there, a dozen spans from the enemy, wondering when they're going to have to fight. Every time someone moves on the other side of that palisade, their hearts leap, their guts run cold, and their balls retract if they've got any, because they think that this is it: This is when they find out if their training was worthwhile or in vain; whether Fate favors them or someone else. What it's like to slice into a real live person, and what it's like to have a person try to slice into you."

"I know all that," Vorinn growled, rising and starting to pace. The movement set the stubby candles that illuminated the tent flaring in their stands. "I've felt exactly the same thing. But you know as well as I do that I'd have been through that palisade long ago if Zeff hadn't come up with that hostage ploy—which effectively makes it impossible for us to use any weapons that aren't absolutely precise. And that's assuming I can get the army to attack, when every soldier here has close kin on the other side of that picket."

"You could have fired the fence. That wouldn't have been hard."

"Yes I could," Vorinn snapped, whirling around in place to glare at his older kinsman. The wavering light gave his features a demonic cast. "I could've fired it—and when the Face went out to fight it, we could've taken them, rushed in, and freed the hostages. But that's assuming they *would* rush out—which is not a given. They could just as easily have retreated into the hold, killing hostages as they went. And let me remind you: Members of Priest-Clan claim no other clan-kin after they vow to that clan."

"No, but they take a vow not to kill the innocent."

"As do we."

Tryffon rolled his eyes—and filled his mug again.

"'Half of war is patience,'" Vorinn grumbled. "Isn't that the first thing we're taught in strategy? Not to swing at a foe until we're ready to swing? Not to shoot at a target until it's clear? That's what I'm doing here. The problem is, there's more than one kind of patience. I *can* wait for Avall to return—which I still think he will do, because his alternative is complete loss of honor forever, and honor's too important to him to forsake if he can avoid it. But even if he doesn't come back, Merryn will, because she's got as much honor as he has, on top of which, she likes to fight. That he hasn't returned means that he's either dead—which is possible, but which wouldn't stop one of the others from finishing what he's started—or that he hasn't found a way back here yet. And since we assume he has the physical ability to jump back here anytime he wants—given that he jumped away with six people and half the contents of a tent—we have to assume that the reason he hasn't returned is that something has forestalled his efforts—or else he has no reason to. Now let me add that I am *not* happy about having so many 'ifs' controlling my actions. And maybe I'm expecting more of human loyalty than I've a right to, but I have to think, based on everything I know, that Avall will get back here as soon as he can, but that he won't bother coming back at all until he knows he can win, and there's only one way he can do that."

"He could've won with the sword he had."

"Maybe. Or maybe it would have driven him mad. Would you want to risk that? And if it had driven Avall mad, rest assured it would've made short work of me. Stronger, I may be, as a soldier, but he's got more raw willpower than I have."

"Geenshit."

Vorinn shook his head. "It's true. Back when we were children—or Avall was; I was well into my teens; seventeen I think—I happened on him in the forges. Eddyn was taunting him and picked up a bar of iron, stuck it in a brazier, and dared him to hold on to it as long as he could. Well, he took that dare and grabbed hold—and kept it, even when the other end of the bar had started to glow. He was sweating all over by then, but he still held on. He'd probably have suffered damage if Tyrill hadn't caught them at it and made them stop, and even then, Avall got mad at her, not at Eddyn."

Tryffon shrugged. "Pain isn't hard to endure if you ease into it gradually."

Vorinn frowned at him. "Maybe so. But you want to know something else? I went down there later that day when no one was around but someone I knew from War that I knew wouldn't tell on me. He'd seen what Avall had done, and I got him to stoke up the same fire exactly as hot as the earlier fire had been, and then I took the same rod of iron and tried to repeat what Avall had done. And I couldn't. And that's why I know Avall has more will than I've got."

Tryffon mirrored Vorinn's frown. "I've never heard that story."

"Ask Tyrill."

"She only saw half of it. And she may be dead by now."

"And the fellow who saw me fail died in the war, so I guess I've no way to prove it. But surely we've got better things to do than sit around doubting each other's veracity."

Tryffon didn't reply.

"So, back to waiting," Vorinn sighed. "I'll concede that I'm playing with the nerves of my army in the sense that they don't know when they'll be called to fight, any more than they know whether—should that occur—they'll find themselves fighting among the staked-out bodies of their kin, or be watching that kin being butchered.

"But on the other hand, Zeff's playing with nerves, too—because there's no way he could know we have neither the false sword nor the real regalia. He probably suspects as much by now, but he doesn't *know*. And that has to be driving him crazy. Look at his method of defense. It's designed precisely to prevent attack from anything that's not very, very selective. Which means he assumes we *do* have it. On the other hand, he's completely disrupted the functions of the hold, except that he can't afford to do that for very long. Our soldiers only have to be soldiers. His have to be ready for as much violence as ours are ready for—and do everything else a hold requires along with it. And he's bound to be digging like mad."

Tryffon drained his mug. "He *will* reach the mines, you know."

"More waiting," Vorinn conceded, "and that's a fact. The longer we wait, the more likely he is to reach them—and that does concern me."

"What happens then?"

Vorinn took a deep breath. "I don't know. I'll know when I get there. By that time, it will be a choice of evils."

"Or you could simply pack up, return to Tir-Eron, and try to set things right there."

"And face possibly the same tactics there as here? Never mind that I'd be leaving an enemy at my back with nothing to restrain it but fear of attack from Avall."

"Which would mean even odds of Zeff seeing our desertion as cowardice or arrogance."

"Which would still keep him guessing."

Tryffon rose. "I'm going to bed, lad, but think about all this. And think about all the people out there and what this is doing to them."

"What about the people in the hold?"

"Most of whom are outside it right now? There are more folk in your army than there are in the hold. At some point you have to consider greatest good for the greatest number. I—"

Tryffon broke off, cocking his head. "Something's happening." He reached for his sword and strode toward the entrance flap.

Vorinn moved as quickly; his hand, too, was on his sword, and he was in the lead as they burst into the Council Tent's vestibule—exactly in time to see Veen come running up with Ravian in tow. "Activity beyond the wall," she panted. "We can't tell what for sure, but it looks like they may be removing the prisoners."

Tryffon gaped incredulously. "*Now*? In the dark? He must know we'll attack as soon as—"

"That has to be what he wants to happen," Vorinn broke in. Then, to Veen: "Sound the alert, and start lighting torches along our palisade." He paused to snatch up his helm and shield, having never removed the rest of his armor. A moment later, he was striding through the camp toward the palisade. The air was thick with smoke, and heavy with moisture from a brief afternoon shower that had quelled the dust but not yet laid a layer of mud on everything. But other things thickened the air as well: the low buzz of excited voices, the thumps of rapid footsteps, and now and then a shout. There was also an unseen energy born of expectation, fear, and relief. And—soon enough—runners: toward the front and away from it.

Abruptly, a young woman in Watchers' tabard skidded to a halt before the Regent's party. Her face was damp with what Vorinn realized was a return of the earlier rain. It wasn't heavy—yet—but it could become a problem. "They're moving the hostages, sir—the ones closest to the hold: They're unstaking them and leading them away."

"And those closer to us?"

"Not yet. Not when I left, at any rate."

"Follow me and continue your report," Vorinn ordered, striding off again, noting as he did how more and more torches were starting to flare atop his own palisade. "Were they freeing them quickly or slowly?"

"...Methodically, I would say."

"Were they being harmed?"

"Not that I could see. Though of course they were weak and staggering, not having moved in days. Their circulation—"

"I know," Vorinn snapped. "Trust me."

They had reached their palisade by then, the central part of which had acquired a second, higher level in recent days, along with a walk half a span wide behind it. Every fifteen spans, a flight of stairs rose to that second level. Vorinn scaled the nearest two at a time, and was pleased to note that his arrival at the top was greeted at once by one of the other Watchers handing him a pair of distance lenses.

The overcast made it difficult to see, and it was starting to rain harder. But if Zeff hadn't moved hostages to keep them dry earlier in the day, he was unlikely to be doing so now. Had he therefore chosen this *particular* time to act, with the weather simply a fortuitous coincidence? Zeff had weather-witches, which the Royal Army didn't, a fact Vorinn tended to forget. Perhaps it was time to reconsider that, too. Weather-witches were part of Priest-Clan; their loyalty was therefore suspect.

But surely, with all Eron to choose from, one or two could be found who supported the Kingdom over the rebellious few.

But that was for later. For now...

He raised the lenses, found them fogged with moisture, wiped them on his surcoat, and raised them again. Behind him, he heard his squire of the night trot up with his cloak and the rest of his war gear. He let the lad settle the cloak across his shoulders and flipped the hood up absently.

By then he had seen—

Something. He was not at first certain what, in fact, he beheld.

It began as a creeping darkness around the foot of the hold: a darkness that was easy to distinguish against the structure's white stone, but hard to tell from the ground in the absence of light from the moons.

But then the flash of torchlight caught a rippling, reflective surface.

"Water," he said aloud, without knowing it.

"What?" from Tryffon, who was fumbling with a second pair of lenses.

"Water—water's leaking out from somewhere."

"From under the hold, you mean?"

"Can you think of anywhere else? The question is: Is it by accident or design? And in either case, where is it coming from? Could it be from a ruptured cistern?"

Tryffon shook his head. "Not likely. They're mostly on the back side of the hold, for one thing, and the way they're situated, they'd either dump into the Ri or fill up the basements long before there'd be enough to run out here."

Vorinn felt a bolt of dread stab his heart. He turned to face Tryffon, his eyes cold and grim, his mouth a hard, thin line. "That means the river, then. The Ri-Megon flows through mostly natural channels below the hold, correct? Channels which are also below the entrance to the mines? But there's still no reason they couldn't dam it up from inside—in fact, it would be fairly easy, especially if they've got a surplus of rubble from the mine explosion, never mind the water gates they use to regulate runoff."

"But why?" Tryffon protested. Then: "Oh, Eight, boy! I'll bet you're right. They know that the prisoners are the only reason we've not brought the attack to them, but they also know they can't leave them outside indefinitely, so they've had to come up with an alternative. And since the hold is built in a low place in the vale, instead of surrounding it with prisoners, they're going to surround it with water!"

Vorinn slapped the fence—hard. "So much for waiting."

Tryffon laid a hand on his shoulder. "There's nothing we can do—now. If we press the attack, they'll leave the people there to drown, knowing that there are others still to hand that they can put up on the galleries to ward off trebuchet attack."

"Meanwhile, they move the hostages a few at a time as the water rises, and then they evacuate themselves via the raised platforms behind the palisade."

"And let the water do the rest. Wily bastards."

Vorinn lowered the lenses again. "How high do you think—?"

Tryffon shrugged. "Based on the lay of the vale, I'd say that the water could easily rise to more than a span deep along most of the length of the place. Deeper to the north, maybe; not so much at the south, but there are actual walls down there— walled and terraced gardens, more properly: built for decoration, but they can still flood behind them, making them easy to defend. Never mind that we couldn't get the towers in there to them."

Vorinn braced himself against the rail. "Oh, Eight, Uncle— the towers."

"What about them?"

"What's to say the water won't rise up to them? Up to where our forces are? 'Water knows neither friend nor foe, merely its own level'—isn't that the proverb?" A pause, then: "Dammit, much as I hate to say it, I guess I'd best give the order. Tell the soldiers to stand to alert, but start packing their gear from the first ranks back. Tell them to wait until the water is three spans away—which will probably be a while, if it even rises that high—but if it does, tell them to back up a span at a time as the water advances and to stop as soon as it stops. Get folks moving the towers as well—I know it'll be uphill in the rain, but use the horses, and start at the north end because the ones there will be at risk soonest. And finally...tell the archers that as soon as the last hostages are moving inside, to fire that wall. It'll help morale to see it burning, and if we have to fight through there, I want no hidden obstructions."

Tryffon dipped his head toward the two heralds who stood nearest. "You heard the orders. Have them sent." The heralds left at a run, one north, one south. Barely ten breaths later the first fruit of that command began to manifest, as Vorinn saw the vanguard of the nearest band of troops rise as one to join their fellows, who were already standing. Torches flamed off shields, swords, and helmets, as ground rugs were gathered, rolled neatly, and stored in anticipation of evacuation.

And still the water continued to rise. It was hard to tell how deep it was at the base of the hold—maybe half a span—but it already stretched a third of the way across what had been the open land between the hold and the palisade. And that in only a quarter hand.

"It has to be the river," Vorinn spat. "It has to be."

Tryffon nodded gravely. "Which means they've already flooded the lower levels of the hold. Including, I'm sorry to say, the forges."

Vorinn caught his breath. "The forges—"

"Aye," Tryffon replied, even more grimly. "And if they're willing to abandon the forges—Well, I don't have to tell you what else is on that level."

Vorinn felt his blood run cold for the second time in a dozen breaths. "Oh, Eight, Uncle, you're right. That's also the primary access level to the mines. If water starts flooding in there, it'll fill the mines in no time."

Tryffon nodded again. "We should know soon enough. When it reaches that level, the water out here should slow its advance—for a while."

"But that means—He can't! He's not that stupid."

"No, but he might be that mad. Regardless, there's only one rational reason why Zeff would seal off the very reason he wanted this place to start with, and that's—"

"That he'd found more gems!" Vorinn finished for him. "Damn, oh damn, oh damn."

"It could mean that," Tryffon conceded. "Or it could mean that he's given up on finding any and returned to his former plan. For that matter, he could have found gems anytime after Avall left, and only now figured out how to use them."

Vorinn raised a brow. "In any case, I suppose the balance of power has shifted again—and not in our favor, now that we get to wonder what, exactly, Zeff is up to."

"Maybe so," Tryffon agreed. "But remember, lad, from their point of view this still gives them no more than parity— assuming they haven't found enough gems to give every mother's son of them one of his very own."

Vorinn scowled thoughtfully. "You really think that? Even I'm not crazy enough to believe that someone as power-mad as Zeff would ever share that much power. It would only take one person to disagree with him, and we'd see that hold come down."

"Which is also—probably—a good reason to suppose that they don't have gem-powered weapons yet. And even if they did, we'd surely have seen the effects of them being tested."

Vorinn scratched his chin. "I don't suppose we could dam the river upstream."

Tryffon shook his head. "Far upstream, maybe; closer in, the channel is so steep it would be all but impossible to reach it. And by the time we could manage anything useful, Zeff would already have his moat. Oh, it might drain off slowly, but would it be slowly enough? Still, I suppose it's something we should consider."

Vorinn chuckled grimly and slapped Tryffon on the back.

"What's funny?" the old Chief inquired.

Vorinn gestured to the rising water. "That. If nothing else, it gives us a time frame for action."

"How so?"

"If we wait long enough, we can ice-skate over!"

"We'd better not be waiting that long," Tryffon rumbled. "There's always a chance Priest will gain enough control of Tir-Eron they can afford to put an army at our back."

"They can't," Vorinn countered with conviction. "They won't. I won't let them. Before that happens, I'll go find Avall myself."

"And how will you do that, boy?"

"I may not be able to track him," Vorinn replied with a grin. "But I'll bet I know some birkits that can."

"I'll believe anything now," Tryffon sighed—and fell silent. And for the next two hands they watched the water rising... rising... rising...

CHAPTER XXII:

HEALING

(SOUTHWEST OF ERON—HIGH SUMMER: DAY LXXXV—EVENING)

Avall lay propped up on his elbow, staring down at Strynn, who had drifted into a heavy slumber after the evening meal. *Should he wake her?* he wondered. She obviously needed rest, else she wouldn't be sleeping now—not with so much going on. But he, in turn, needed her—needed to see how she really was, if nothing else.

Besides pregnant.

—With *his* children, now, not those sired by another man. Which made him wonder about Averryn. He barely knew Eddyn's son—and would not have known him well in any case, since children were traditionally raised by their one-parents. But Averryn had been in Tir-Eron during the massacre on Mask Night, and he had heard nothing about the boy since. Not about Averryn—and not about his own mother.

That last shocked him. *Had he grown as cold-hearted as all that?* To forget people so closely tied to his blood, simply because they were not part of his day-to-day routine? As he sometimes tended to forget Strynn when in the presence of those he had known longer and more comfortably, if not more intimately? *Would it be this way every time they were apart?* A period of fumbling uncertainty as they became reacquainted with each other? He didn't require that with Merryn, nor with Rann—or even Lykkon. Why should it be so with his wife?

Should he therefore wake her and ask her—gently—to spend some time with him. Or would that, too, be viewed as selfishness?

"You shouldn't worry," came Merryn's voice behind him: soft and low, but strong for all that. "She's had very little rest for two eights—never mind being sick and pregnant. This is the rest of relief you're seeing: She's accomplished what she needs to accomplish, and for the next little while, she doesn't care. It's nothing to do with you."

Avall reached around to find his sister's hand and draw her up beside him, even as she pulled him away; the better—he knew—not to awaken Strynn. "Eddyn told me a long time ago that I didn't deserve her: that I would never be able to give her what she really needs. And I'm afraid—I'm so afraid, Merry, that he was right. And I'd hate for him to be right, I'd *hate* it."

"What did you tell him, then?" Merryn murmured back, as they eased away from the twilight camp.

"I told him...I told him that nobody ever deserves anybody."

"Do you still believe that?"

"I don't know. It's so easy to reduce everything to favors and revenge, and all that. Take Myx, for instance: he tended me when I suddenly jumped into his room in the tower, and his life promptly fell apart, but he gained power and prestige for it, and lost nothing except an ordinary life, in place of which he's got an extraordinary one. But is he keeping score with me for that? Will he walk up to me one day and say, 'we're even,' and disappear forever?"

Merryn regarded him keenly. "Is that what you're afraid of? That we're all going to disappear on you?"

He eyed her askance. "Most of you have, at one time or another."

"Most of us have *had* to. But we've all come back, haven't

we? Whether you believe it or not, even I was planning to come back after I'd hidden the regalia. I know Strynn would've come back. Rann would live in your skin if he could. Kylin risked his life to try to get you out of Gem-Hold; and, accomplished as he is, even Lykkon would like nothing more than to grow up to be you, as would Bingg."

Avall shook his head. "And what's so special about me? I'm only good at one thing, and that's making fancy things out of gold. Beyond that—I'd say I was good at choosing my friends, but that assumes I actually do that. Most of them just seem to wander into my life unsought. Beyond that—I don't—"

A finger at his lips hushed him. "Don't say 'deserve' again, or you *will* deserve what I give you, and you won't like it, either. Besides, you're forgetting one thing you're good at, Avall, and that's the one thing Eddyn never had—nor a lot of people we know. You're good at caring."

"Aren't people supposed to be?"

A shrug. "So our ethics teachers would say—not that I've witnessed it much in practice. Then again, my feeling is that we care *more* than our elders do because we're the first generation to reach adulthood after the plague, and the adults we saw around us were still so sore with grief they didn't dare to care, because everyone they had cared about had died. They closed themselves off, and it's up to us to reopen them."

Avall found a tree and leaned against it. "Where is everyone?" he demanded, choosing not to respond to his sister's flirtation with philosophy.

Merryn squinted into the surrounding gloom. "Bingg's sitting watch with Rann and Kylin. Everyone else has gone in search of geens. Not to hunt them," she added quickly. "Just to see if any are about. This is the time of day they like to forage, don't forget: because this is when big prey animals venture into open spaces."

"And if they find any?"

"Rann's a span away from the Lightning Sword; that should be sufficient." She paused, looking at the ground, suddenly shy as a girl. "Speaking of caring," she murmured. "I actually came seeking you with a question that involves that very thing."

A brow quirked up. "And what would that be?"

Merryn gnawed her lip. "Krynneth. I've been thinking about him ever since I heard how you healed Kylin on the island."

"You aren't supposed to know about that!"

Merryn lifted a brow in turn. "According to your story, he was mad when you jumped the lot of you here, but he's clearly recovered now. I wondered how that happened, but wasn't sure how Kylin would respond to direct queries, so I asked around. Took two tries, and then... well, I assume you know who knows and who doesn't."

"I didn't heal him," Avall growled. "I just... helped him."

"Which is all I want you to do for Krynneth. It shouldn't be that hard. As far as I can tell, they both simply shut down from shock. The only difference is that it happened to Kylin suddenly; with Krynneth, it happened over time."

Avall grimaced sourly. "I guess there's no good reason not to at least make the attempt, given that Krynneth is not only my friend, but has done untold service to Eron. And that's not counting what he is to you." He paused, looked Merryn in the eye. "What *is* he to you, anyway?"

Merryn shrugged again, though she—almost—smiled. "Mostly a possibility, I'd say. I don't know if I'd ever love a man enough to wed him. But I might love one enough to try a year-bonding. And Krynneth is one of those men."

"I see."

"He also likes you—a lot. More than you know, in fact. I was thinking that maybe, between the two of us, we could bring him to himself again. I really think that all he wants is to feel safe and wanted."

Avall snorted. "He didn't feel that way at court after the war?"

"He did, but he had a burden of guilt on him then—a

burden I understood and may, frankly, still be carrying around. And something I suspect you understand a little better now. But that's beside the point. It'll be night soon, and I know you want to start back north tomorrow. Forgetting ethics, Krynneth's the most unpredictable person in your entourage right now. Wouldn't you rather be able to trust him?"

Avall patted Merryn's hand. "You don't have to convince me of the need, sister, only that it's necessary now."

"This may be the best time," Merryn replied soberly.

"Well," Avall sighed, "lead the way. Where is Kryn, anyway?"

Merryn grinned wickedly. "We were all so preoccupied after dinner that I was afraid he'd wander off, or do something rash or stupid and get himself hurt. So I made sure he drank a lot, on top of which I put some sleeping herb in his wine, then helped him to our tent and left him there."

"'Our' tent?"

"We share one. Div and Strynn did, too—before you arrived; it was safer than putting Div in with him."

Avall could think of no reasonable reply.

They could see the cluster of boulders that marked their surrogate home by then, and hastened their steps that way. A small tent rose on the far side of it, midway between the stones themselves and the rope perimeter: close enough for inclusion, far enough away for privacy.

"Will this be noisy?" Merryn inquired, as they paused beside the entrance. "I don't want to wake Strynn."

Avall couldn't suppress a smirk. "Shouldn't be. We'll see."

Merryn undid the ties, then motioned Avall in ahead, before joining him. There was room for three lying side by side on the ground, with maybe half a span extra in either direction. Krynneth lay in the middle, flat on his back, legs crossed at the ankles, arms folded on his chest, breathing peacefully, all in the efficiently precise manner Eronese children were taught to adopt as soon as they were old enough for quarters of their own.

Avall blinked at the soft, subtle light where he had been

expecting near darkness, since the outside world was quickly slipping from twilight into true night. But then he saw the source: a glow-globe in the smallest size anyone could make, nested on a tripod of small stones in the farthest corner.

"Lykkon," Merryn offered. "He had a few among his stores. He said he didn't think they were needed on the island, so he was saving them."

"Typical," Avall growled good-naturedly. "That's why we love the boy."

"More a man now, in case you haven't noticed," Merryn corrected. "His birthday is coming up soon. He'll be twenty, and eligible for Fateing."

Avall shook his head. "I'd almost forgotten about that! I wonder if Priest-Clan is even bothering to implement it. Or if that institution, too, has fallen by the way."

"That's one I personally could do without."

Avall's only reply was to claim a place on the ground close by Krynneth's torso. "It's one of the few things that *does* work: the way we educate people."

"Doesn't matter now, anyway," Merryn murmured. "Do what you came to do."

Avall bristled a little at being dismissed so casually, but began to compose himself as best he could. Which was difficult in light of the day's events.

But maybe this was good for him, he reflected. And maybe Merryn knew that and was finding a way for him to calm himself. In any case, there was little to lose by trying.

"Should we wake him?" Merryn asked seriously, as she scooted around to Krynneth's other side.

Avall shook his head again. "Kylin was sleeping when I did what I did with him, so that's probably what we should do here. But I'll tell you what: You can do the cutting."

"Cutting?"

"How soon you forget, sister. I'll need access to his blood. Mine, too, but that should be no problem, given that I just used the regalia."

He left her to it, seeing her only from the corner of his eyes as she reached for Krynneth's hand, while he fumbled in the pouch for the least innocuous gem, which was also the one that had healed Kylin. He found it by feel as much as anything: a sliver of glittering red folded in a square of sylk. It was fragile: so fragile that he feared he would break it.

He withdrew it carefully and unwrapped it, then stretched himself along Krynneth's right side, while Merryn did the same on the other. It took a moment to find a comfortable position, but then he had one: lying on his left side, with his left hand curled above his head and his right ready to clutch Krynneth's now-bleeding hand, which Merryn had just laid on his chest.

"Anything I can do?" she asked softly.

"Watch and wait—and break the contact if anything untoward occurs."

"Will it?"

"It hasn't—not with this gem. But that doesn't mean it won't."

Merryn nodded silently, then, to Avall's surprise, reached up to stroke the curve of Krynneth's jaw. "He doesn't deserve so much pain," she whispered. "And I know exactly what I mean when I say 'deserve.'"

"Yes," Avall agreed with conviction, "you do."

With that, he closed his eyes, trying to relax, for this was something better done by feel than by sight. Already—after only that oh-so-brief contact with the gem—he could feel his senses shift to a finer pitch. The gloom in the tent took on brighter, if still subtle, colors. Breath sounded louder, but with a comforting susurration, like distant waves. He smelled the earth and the tent, leather and whatever soap Merryn had used last, mingled with a fair bit of mildew and sweat. He smelled Krynneth, too—the man definitely needed a bath, but Avall understood the complications of him actually getting one. In any case, it was nothing he hadn't endured before with Rann on their first impossible overland trek. Indeed, he found him-

self recalling the interludes of quiet fellowship that had punctuated that reckless mission, which in turn helped him relax.
This wasn't that different, actually: approaching darkness, and
a tent, though the other time it had been Rann close beside
him, and both of them tired from a day's exertions, but grateful
simply for each other's presence, each other's warmth...

Without quite knowing when he did it, Avall slid the gem
into his palm, and as soon as he felt the power start to draw,
joined that hand with Krynneth's.

Power joined them, too, but not the expected strong surge
of it; instead, there came a steady, almost gentle, rush. Avall
welcomed it cautiously, and tried to direct its flow away from
himself and into his friend. He was aware of Krynneth's hand
now—more keenly than would normally have been the case;
could feel the bones and know where muscle belonged that
sporadic diet had worn away; could touch the calluses on his
fingers and know which came from sword work, which from
working wood—for wood was Krynneth's birth-craft as well
as Riff's.

All at once, he was simply riding along, journeying with
Krynneth's blood in search of Krynneth's brain.

Which was odd. Most of the other times he had bonded
with someone through a gem, he had met the intellect as soon
as he met the body, or even sooner. Even with poor Rrath.

But maybe that was because he had *wanted* to meet those
minds. He might—troubling notion—actually be *afraid* of
Krynneth's. Especially if, as Merryn had suggested, Krynneth
had tucked his higher self away to hide from guilt. And guilt
was something Avall knew all too well. But maybe Merryn
had known that, too, and had arranged this healing as much
for him as for her friend.

But that would be subtle even for her; and depended on
information she did not possess. Or *shouldn't* possess, he
amended—though, given that she was his twin, she still
might—especially with all that gemwork in which they had
both indulged so recently.

Where was Krynneth, anyway? This wasn't like Rrath's situation, where the victim had walled himself away beyond reach. No, Krynneth had simply hidden—apparently by diverting anything that resembled thought or personality away from a large portion of his recent memories. Which didn't mean they weren't still present—as Avall discovered when he blundered into a batch of them: mostly memories of fighting along endless corridors. He knew those corridors, too, had walked them himself, in fact: long ago when he'd done his own quarter at War-Hold. But Krynneth wasn't there now.

Or was he?

He felt Krynneth flinch when Avall paused at those particular recollections, as though someone had touched a wound that was far too tender.

He tried to call to him: to summon him from his pain and fright like a timid deer at the edge of the wood. But Krynneth wouldn't come.

Yet somehow Avall knew that he *would* come—that part of him wanted to come—if only he could avoid those parts of his memory that tortured him. Once he did that—maybe—Avall or Merryn or one of his other friends (he wondered, suddenly, if Krynneth had a bond-brother and if not, why someone so brave, handsome, and accomplished didn't) could go with him and confront them an item at a time.

But was he the person for that? He tried to determine who might be best—who, of everyone Krynneth knew, he trusted most. Yet Avall's efforts at that were clumsy, and once again Krynneth flinched away.

He doesn't trust me, he realized. *He identifies me with the problem, even though I wasn't there. But I was part of the war. He remembers me as a soldier, not as a smith and not as a friend.*

But what about Merryn? She and Krynneth had been close indeed, almost lovers—as Merryn had admitted.

"Merry?" Avall murmured, so softly he wasn't certain he spoke with his mouth or his mind alone. "Join me. Cut yourself and join me. He needs you more than he needs me. There's a barrier between him and me I don't think he'll breach, but he might breach it with you."

"If you're sure. I'm not good at this."

"You will be. I'll be with you—at first. And then I'll slip away. He'll never miss me. And while you and I are together, I'll show you what I know, and what I think needs to be done."

Avall felt her hesitation, but he likewise felt her resolve. And he also felt—in some odd way, though they were not physically connected—Merryn cut her hand and slide it onto Krynneth's chest beside his. Finally, he felt the moment when their blood touched and mingled and the moment the gem acknowledged Merryn's presence and drew her into their bond. Avall moved deftly, then—both in body and in mind. He slid his hand free of the gem, but in such a way that it was now lodged between Merryn's hand and Krynneth's. And then he slid his mind free as well, letting Merryn fill the space where he had been.

But he never withdrew completely, for there was a terrible comfort there, like someone come home at last, or seeing a treasured friend once more.

"I'm here, Kryn," Merryn assured him. Whether aloud or through the gem was irrelevant.

"Merry . . . ?" And that *was* spoken.

"Kryn."

"I hurt. In my soul, I hurt."

"I know, Kryn. But we can fix that. Given time, we can fix that. And so much of you *doesn't* hurt."

"I—"

Words failed the rest, as Krynneth succumbed to a flood of emotion that was well-nigh overpowering. And atop that flood came a heartbreaking longing to be cared for simply as himself, not as a sick man, or a handsome man, or the best warrior Wood had produced in a generation.

But along with that longing came need: unfocused desire to be touched in body as well as mind. Avall slid his hand away from Merryn's, then upward and across Krynneth's chest, stroking him lightly, which was all he could think to do, for he could feel the bond decreasing. But he could feel Krynneth's appreciation, too, and his desire that those caresses continue.

He could also feel Merryn's alarm. Only it was not so much alarm as startlement. Avall knew what had to happen now. Gently, gently, he returned his hand to where Merryn's hand still twined with Krynneth's, and ever so slowly began to slide them both downward along the length of Krynneth's body until they found the ties to Krynneth's hose. "You know what to do," Avall whispered, as he let his fingers linger there, working at the simple knot. "You've wanted it for a very long time; he has, too—and now he also needs it. I don't think you'll even need the gem, though I'll leave that sliver with you. And if you do—it should be easy to renew the bond, with both of you still bleeding."

With that, Avall moved his hand away, leaving Merryn to remove what clothing she would from both of them. A moment later, he left the tent entirely.

It was more than a hand after his departure that Merryn likewise emerged, looking serious, smug, and sated.

Avall started to speak to her, but she hushed him—as was getting to be a habit—with a finger, then pointed back toward the tent. A dark head emerged from the opening there. But instead of a blank stare, Krynneth's face split in the silliest grin Avall had ever seen. It was just as well the sun had set, Avall concluded, else he was certain he would have seen his sister blushing.

Abruptly Krynneth's grin vanished, so suddenly Avall feared he had hidden himself away again. But then he spoke once more, only this time his expression was perplexed and solemn. "I'm better," he said carefully, as though surprised to discover that he could speak. "Not well, mind you, but on the road to mending. Thank you."

"And I," Merryn added loftily, "will be there to explore every twist and turn with you." She looked at Avall and winked. "Did you know he has a mole—?"

"No," Avall told her firmly. "And I don't want to know, unless *he* chooses to tell me."

Merryn shrugged wickedly. "You know," she drawled, "I got up way before dawn this morning; I think it's time I went back to bed." Without another word, she pushed Krynneth back into the tent, leaving Avall to stare at the encroaching night.

The hunters were back by then—empty-handed, which was just as well, but eager to swap tales with Bingg, Rann, and Kylin around the fire they had stoked up again.

For himself—Avall was like Merryn: He'd had a very hard day. Strynn was still asleep, but there was room and more than room beside her, and Krynneth wasn't the only soul desperate for comfort. It had been a long time, he reckoned, since he had awakened beside his wife. But she was there when he drifted off to slumber. And she was still there, awake and smiling at him through the clear light of dawn, when he reawakened.

Interlude: A Visitation

~~~~~~~

Evvion san Criff y Argen-a had come to despise the night, when once she had loved it far, far better than the day. Loved it for the peace it conferred, she thought—and for the softness it spread across the world: wrapping all harshness with shadows, easing contrasts between dark and light, hiding the harder things in life, or rendering them remote and unreal and thereby less threatening.

That was before night had become irrevocably linked in her mind with fire —Fire from Mask Night, the unrestrained chaos of which she had always loathed, so that she had, as had become her habit, fled Tir-Eron in anticipation of it. That departure had probably saved her life, too—and that of Strynn and Eddyn's child, young Averryn, who even now wriggled and twisted in her arms as she paced about the common hall of the suite she had been given in this, Stonecraft's most formidable citadel.

A citadel that was ringed by more cursed fires now, courtesy of a besieging force—not quite an army, but formidable for all that—that could not, so far, come closer than the narrow shard of beach that showed below Canarra Isle's sheer cliffs when the tides in the Ri-Eron ran low. Most times they waited:

a small armada of Ninth Face boats surrounding the island, their deck-torches proclaiming as eloquently as words that while Evvion and the other refugees who had found themselves stranded here after the coup on Mask Night were safe from Ninth Face swords for the nonce, they were not safe from the grimmer demon of starvation.

Or from winter, when the Ri-Eron might well freeze solid this close to the shore—solid enough, at any rate, to support the weight of trebuchets.

And so Evvion waited—and paced, and drank very indifferent wine, and tried only to think of now, and of protecting what was not, and never would be, Avall's son.

Which did not imply that Averryn was not important or that she did not love the little boy, now almost half a year old and growing quickly; only that she had a practical streak, and had reserved a portion—the best portion, she hoped—of her love for what would be the true fruit of her son's loins.

She wondered how that son fared, there in the west. The last report she had received before the coup stated only that Avall's army was rather more than halfway to its destination. Since then—nothing.

Nothing.

Nothing but waiting. And waiting. And waiting.

A cough at the chamber door startled her, making her start and spin around in a manner she normally found unseemly, and which Averryn patently did not like. A hall page stood there, clad in Stonecraft gray and black, which most of the staff now wore in preference to Eemon's midnight blue or Criff's yellow and cream. For while Eemon blue was not the same shade of blue the Ninth Face wore, it was close enough to bring that hue to mind—and the Ninth Face came to mind often enough already.

The page was a boy, she saw—her favorite, in fact: young Talisso—and he looked by turns excited and concerned as he cleared his throat again, then stated plainly: "Lady, you have visitors—from *outside*."

"Show them in," Evvion replied with more calm than she felt, even as she moved toward Averryn's cradle. *Visitors from outside indeed! Surely the boy knew the stronghold was besieged, with no one going in or out.* Still, it was not in her heart to chastise the lad.

"They" arrived sooner than expected—exactly as Evvion was snugging the blanket beneath her adopted-one-son's chin.

At first she did not recognize any of the three people Talisso escorted into the room, clad as they were in nondescript browns and grays of no particular cut, besides being cloaked and hooded. Indeed, it was not until the tallest—and the only male—spoke that she recognized even one of them. "That is the most important child in Eron right now," that man said softly, in tones Evvion knew.

"Lord Ilfon," she cried, astonished. And then the shorter woman with Lore's deposed Chief swept back the hood that had overshadowed her features, and more important, her cloud of snow-white hair, and she recognized Lady Tyrill as well. And felt a flood of relief more potent than winter wine surge through her soul.

As for the third—that woman had darker skin than the other two and foreign features—Ixtian features, in fact—and it took Evvion a moment to put a name to her, for all she knew that name very well indeed, though mostly by reputation.

"Lady Tyrill," she said automatically. "And…Elvix, is it? Sister to the Ixtian Ambassador?"

"More his mistress of assassins," Tyrill shot back in something between a bark and a laugh. "I imagine you're more than a little surprised to find us here," she continued, with her characteristic brusqueness.

"Surprise is…an understatement," Evvion stammered, as the page busied himself dragging four chairs into the defiant circle of candlelight before the chamber's solitary window, positioning them so that none faced the outer world—and the besieging army with its brighter and more threatening fires.

"You wonder how we got here," Ilfon inserted smoothly, helping Tyrill to a seat before claiming one himself. Elvix sank down in another, leaving Evvion the last. She was gaping like a fool, she realized—and shut her mouth abruptly.

Tyrill—almost—grinned. "Suffice to say that not without reason is the Chief of Lore considered the third most powerful man in the Kingdom after the Sovereign himself and the Chief of War."

"'Authority, might, and knowledge,'" Evvion quoted the old proverb. "'On these rocks is a Kingdom built.'"

"Knowledge," Ilfon echoed. "And the most potent knowledge, wouldn't you say, is secret knowledge? And among the most potent secrets a man might carry in his mind alone and never commit to writing is where the secret entrances to most of the older holds lie—this one included. Unfortunately, this hold is a fair way downriver from Tir-Eron, and we three have had pressing and ongoing business in the city, so that only tonight were we able to make our way here and move a certain tile in a certain riverside shrine two shots upstream, and thereby access the tunnel by which we passed under the river and so came where the Ninth Face, so far, cannot."

"And by which you can escape, should you so choose," Elvix added, speaking for the first time. "Ixti stands ready to give you and the High King's heir sanctuary, should you feel inclined to dare the journey."

"I— This is much to digest in a short time," Evvion choked, refilling her wineglass and motioning for the page to bring more. The chamber was now guarded, she saw when he opened the door: Zolan and Ilb stood in the corridor flanking the entrance, solid as the stone of the mountains. Then, finally: "Why did I not know of this secret?"

"Because only Clan-Chiefs and the Chief of Lore know of such things," Ilfon replied. "And your Clan-Chief is dead."

"Which is only one of many secrets we must discuss tonight," Tyrill added impatiently. "And only one of many grave tidings we must convey. And the gravest of those, I fear, is that the former High King, Gynn syn Argen-el, is dead as well."

Evvion felt her heart skip at that: the death of a King reported so matter-of-factly, though why the death itself should surprise her, she had no idea. Gynn had been effectively dead since that unfortunate moment last spring when a rock hurled by an explosion during the Battle of Storms had shattered his helm and, along with it, most of the back of his skull. He could breathe, moan, and eat with difficulty, but that was all.

"We know little," Tyrill continued, studying Evvion's face intently. "Those who had been nursing him were all loyal to the King—and we know what has befallen those with that loyalty." She paused, cocked her head. "Or do you? How much of what transpires beyond these walls *do* you know, anyway?"

"A few messengers arrived before Priest-Clan's soldiers did," Evvion replied. "And a few message birds have come since then. From them we have gained some sense of what transpires in Tir-Eron, but mostly we are left to imagine."

"Which can often be worse than reality," Ilfon put in. "Though I doubt that is true in this case."

"Gynn," Evvion prompted.

Ilfon shrugged. "It is as Tyrill said: Those who had him in their care...passed from that position, though whether through death or imprisonment, we do not know. With them absent—or simply less vigilant—it is easy to see how a man who teeters on the brink of death could tumble from that precipice."

"This was...announced?" Evvion asked.

"It was. Which in itself is unusual for the Gorge's new masters. But I suppose they thought it better to be aboveboard about such things, so as to preserve the illusion that they rule honestly and openly, if not by right."

Evvion gnawed her lip. "So it would seem. But tell me, then: Why are you here? You spoke of other business—"

Elvix grinned like a fox, but it was Tyrill who answered. "It appears, Lady," she began with a wry chuckle, "that I have become a warrior in my old age." She motioned toward Elvix. "And to give credit where credit is due, I have had aid and inspiration from an unlikely source—a source with whom, two quarters ago, we were at war."

Elvix nodded acknowledgment of the compliment but did not speak, though her sharp bright eyes obviously missed nothing.

"The fact is," Tyrill went on, "our primary allies seem to be outlanders. We have made some contact with the northern gorges, and may have aid there—possibly even the aid of Strynn and Vorinn's brother, who, for all his youth, is both a leader of men and a man of action. Report is that he is gathering an army to march south before winter. But we cannot rely on that, and it is out of our hands in any case. No, what we— Ilfon, myself, Elvix, and a few others—have done is to mount our own small secret war against the Ninth Face. Elvix gave us the means—outland blowguns—which, I must say, work passing well if one would commit murder quickly, clandestinely, and with minimal fuss. So far we have confined our efforts to guards, since they are the most visible and the most vulnerable—"

"And the most susceptible to having their fears played upon."

"Which we have done," Elvix chuckled. "We have played them like a harp. Sounds that have no source. Two of three guards dead and the other left to wonder. Or simply men vanishing—especially those posted farthest from the Citadel. But we have killed soldiers closer to it, too—though not many, for the risk of discovery is high, what with none of us being what one would call inconspicuous."

"And what of Ixti?" Evvion demanded. "I know King Kraxxi swore eternal friendship with Avall. But can we count on him?"

"Kraxxi will come if he is asked," Elvix replied carefully, "but Avall, or someone whom Kraxxi knows represents Avall without shadow of doubt, must do the asking. His own position is not strong enough for him to set what remains of what I have to admit is a worn and dispirited army marching across the Flat again on personal caprice alone. No, much as he hates it, Kraxxi knows he would be better served to remain where he is until his throne is more secure. All that said, he might still come north himself—with his personal guard, who are all utterly loyal to him."

"And who would rule the Kingdom, since Kraxxi has no son?"

"My brother, Tozri, most likely," Elvix replied.

"But," Ilfon stressed, "if an army left Ixti tomorrow, it could not reach here for almost a quarter—almost until Sundeath. And Sundeath, we fear, is the time the Ninth Face have targeted to set one of their own on the throne. And that assumes that army is unopposed."

"But what about Avall? Avall is King. Surely he—"

Ilfon and Tyrill exchanged troubled glances. "Lady, you do not know—?"

"Know what?"

"Your son was taken prisoner by the Ninth Face before he could reach Gem-Hold. His army continued on with Rann, Vorinn, and Tryffon effectively in charge. And then something very strange occurred: Avall escaped—by what the one report that has reached us indicates must have been gem-born magic. Yet he did not return to camp—or if he did, it was only for an instant."

"And now?"

"And now,"—Ilfon sighed heavily—"no one knows where he is or what he is about." Evvion did not reply. Rather, she calmly refilled her glass yet again, drank half of its contents, then stared at the blood-dark vintage for a long moment. "If my son were dead," she said at last, "I would know."

And then, in a stronger voice: "And until I know for certain, I will remain where I am, in case he needs me."

Ilfon nodded. "I thought you would. But now, Lady, let us

address another matter, and perhaps the most important of the several that brought us here."

"Let us," Tyrill put in, "address the matter of sanctuary."

"Sanctuary?"

"You are not the Hold Warden," Tyrill continued, "but your voice carries more sway than your rank. And I am here to say that we have means to bring others here for safety—and supplies along with them, if the hold is willing to accept those who bear them. And then, perhaps, someday, we can retake Tir-Eron—or if not, at least preserve the best of what was— and will be again."

"Sanctuary," Evvion repeated slowly. "I must say that word has a marvelous sweet sound. Very well," she continued. "Let me hear what you propose."

And, until shortly before dawn, she heard them.

The fires were still there the next night, though Evvion's visitors were not.

But Clan Eemon's strongest citadel also had more men to defend it than heretofore, and more supplies with which to defy what was no longer quite so perilous a siege.

But Evvion still loathed the night, if only because that was the time she had most cause to wonder what strange stars watched over her son and daughter.

CHAPTER XXIII:

TO THE NORTH

(SOUTHWEST OF ERON—HIGH SUMMER: DAY LXXXVI—MORNING)

Avall woke—for the second time that morning—to the sounds of camp being struck and the smell of cauf a-brewing. And to Strynn sitting beside him, tickling his nose with a feather.

He grinned up at her, even as he batted the instrument of torture away. "I take it you're better?" he yawned.

She grinned back. "Much. I—" She paused, looking contrite but too happy to feel much of it. "I did something I probably shouldn't have, Vall. Once I knew Rann had survived contact with his gem—well, I changed my mind about trying mine and asked Merry for it. And while you four were out starting forest fires, I contrived to cut myself, and...bonded with the gem."

"Strynn! Do you have any idea of the risk—?"

"As much as you," she replied gravely, setting the feather aside. "But I also remembered that the gems have healing powers, or that mine eased my first pregnancy, at any rate. And I was so sick of—of being sick that I thought it was worth it. And guess what? I learned two things. I learned that my gem doesn't contain either as much fire or as much death as Rann's evidently does, and I learned that you're right: Not only can they heal us, we can also heal them—at least I think we can. You know how we can tell who they like and who they don't? Well, this time I also felt something like...gratitude. It was very weak, kind of like an old person when they're sick. But I'm sure I felt it. And I think you're right about something else, too, Vall; I think they really are alive." She paused again. "In fact, let me put forth a radical notion that only this moment occurred to me. Suppose it's not so much that they're alive, as that they're actually life itself. Life frozen into a crystal, or something."

Her eyes went huge, even as Avall's did. "That's way too much to think about this early in the morning," he groaned. "But I suppose it *is* worth considering."

"That's all I ask," she murmured lightly—and with that, she yanked the cover off him and pushed him out of bed.

Except that "bed" had been a sleeping pad at the edge of a sloping shelf of rock, so that "out of bed" was also off the rock. Avall "oofed" as his bottom struck the ground. Fortunately, the earth on that side of the stone sported a healthy growth of moss, so that nothing was injured save his pride.

Of course Rann and Lykkon picked that precise moment to glance up from where they had been coiling the rope that had defined the camp's perimeter. Both burst out laughing, forcing Avall—clad only in his shirte and drawers— to retaliate by rushing toward them. Lykkon sidestepped neatly, but Rann was a breath too late in assessing the situation, with the result that Avall was able to snare him around the waist and wrestle him to the ground. A moment later, they were rolling through the leaves like the boys they still almost were, with Avall laughing so hard he could barely breathe. And then Lykkon chanced to offer one comment too many about style, which prompted both combatants to turn on him. One moment Lykkon was on his feet, the next Avall and Rann were sitting atop him, one pinning his arms, the other his legs.

"Tickle his belly," Bingg advised, sauntering up to regard

the proceedings with interest—from just beyond easy access range.

"They do and you die!" Lykkon choked, through an ill-suppressed giggle.

The commotion had attracted Myx and Riff by then, as well as Krynneth, the former two of whom moved casually to flank Bingg. "You know," Myx drawled, taking the boy by the arm, "if I'm not mistaken, being ticklish is inherited—and since young Bingg here is Lykkon's brother—"

"*Half* brother!" Bingg corrected, as he tried to bolt.

Too late.

Riff's hand shot out like a whip—and suddenly the boy was prisoned upright between them. And though strong for thirteen, Bingg had not yet had his adolescent growth spurt, while Myx and Riff were full-grown, well-trained soldiers ten years his senior. It was therefore no real contest.

"Pull his shirte up." Myx laughed, yanking at the garment's thigh-length tail with his free hand. Riff added his own efforts, deftly avoiding any number of failed shin-kicks and foot-stomps, so that barely a breath later they had Bingg's torso exposed from waistband to armpits. "I think a...comparison of sensitivity is in order," Myx continued. "Who wants to do the honors? Strynn, do you still have that feather?"

Strynn flourished the object in question fiendishly. "On whom should I begin—and where?"

Div came charging up, flush-faced, with a sweaty Merryn in tow. "What The Eight? We thought someone was being murdered!"

"Someone will be," Lykkon growled. "Probably several someones."

Strynn advanced with the feather. "Ah, but you're a gentleman, Lyk; and I know you'd never hurt an expectant mother."

"Not while she's expecting," Lykkon gritted back, risking an experimental twist, which failed utterly. "But pregnancy is a temporary condition—and I have an excellent memory."

"I do, too," Bingg added indignantly, daring a twist of his own.

Div regarded Merryn smugly. "I wonder," she asked Merryn casually, "if they've noticed that the groundcover on their wrestling yard is mostly itching ivy."

Five sets of gazes immediately sought the earth—six, if one counted Lykkon, who was still pinned by the shoulders with a face full of hair.

"Oh Eight!" Myx spat, disgusted. And thrust Bingg playfully away.

Avall likewise noted that the hands pinning Lykkon's shoulders were knuckle deep in a patch of the irritating herb, and released his grip at once, scrambling awkwardly aside to avoid the rest of the patch, while Rann gave Lykkon an arm up.

Lykkon—who did tend to take himself too seriously—scowled at them in triumph. "I *do* keep score," he huffed. "And I know where everyone sleeps."

"So do I," Avall chuckled. "No hard feelings?"

Lykkon shot him a dirty look, but shrugged and stalked away, yanking his shirttail down from where it had become wadded in his armpits.

Avall couldn't resist one final prank. Shooting Rann a conspiratory wink, he ran up behind Lykkon, yanked the waistband of his cousin's hose out far enough to show cleavage, and emptied the handful of itching ivy leaves he was for some inane reason still clutching down the garment, then let the waistband go and ducked for cover.

Lykkon continued on, airily unconcerned, though he was certainly walking funny. Bingg, behind them, burst out laughing like a crazy man.

"Evil!" Rann chided, as he jogged up to join Avall.

Avall reached over to wipe his hand along the angle of Rann's jaw. "Could be worse," He smirked. "I could have dropped 'em down the front."

The three women—who had all been observing the proceedings with tolerant restraint—rolled their eyes at one another. "And now they'll have to bathe," Merryn snorted. "And wash clothes, probably, which means—"

"There's no way we're going to get away before noon," Div finished for her.

Strynn sniffed in cheerful disgust and regarded the chaotic camp. "And you know what? If I didn't know better, I'd swear they contrived that just to get out of working."

Div grinned back. "Fine with me, besides which, *I* control the medicine kit, and it's going to take a lot more than river water to wash all that itch-juice away."

Kylin chose that moment to poke his head out of his tent: victim, it seemed, of very sound slumber indeed—or possibly of too much drink the previous night, given his tendency to overindulge in spirits. He cocked his head, listening. Counting breaths, Merryn decided. "Where is everybody?" the harper asked eventually, followed by a truly impressive yawn.

"The sane ones are here," Merryn snorted. "The rest—Listen hard and you'll hear them being silly down by the river. I'd suggest you join them. I don't want to see another man until noon."

Kylin took a deep breath and ducked his head underwater, then rose again in place: there where he was *just* managing to keep his feet in the deepest part of the river in which standing remained an option. Behind him, the stream widened into a pool twenty spans across and deep enough for honest swimming, its farther shore consisting of a long, steep bank of ivy-covered stone thrice as high as a man and running, nearly level—so his companions told him—as far as they could see to north and south. A narrow beach twenty spans to the north on the nearer side offered the only real access through a fine growth of laurel that otherwise grew down to the water's edge. Their clothes blotched the strand now: blots of faded color against a duller brown. Newly scoured with soldier-soap mixed with river sand, the rest of the wrestling party was paddling about behind him, indulging in what Rann said might well be their last good chance for a casual bath in what could easily be eights.

Kylin didn't like to swim, but he did like being clean—and good, simple camaraderie—for which reason he was lingering there, as he often did, on the edge between two worlds.

Which was why he heard it.

Something ...

A heavy, cautious tread and a hiss of breath, where there ought to have been nothing but the whispery silence of forest. And along with those sounds came a sudden rustle of small animals disturbed and fleeing through the leaf mold, followed by a succession of tiny splashes as what he presumed was a phalanx of frogs leapt into the water.

"Something's wrong," he announced. And by that time his gaze had turned toward the forest trail by which they had reached this place. A blur of light was all he could make out, of course: sky above the darker mass of land. Yet even that much was comforting—usually, but certainly not now.

Riff, who happened to be closest, heard him when the others—apparently—did not and promptly swam nearer, breasting the water with long, clean strokes. "What?" he gasped, when he reached speaking range.

"Too much noise and then too quiet—all at once," Kylin muttered, suddenly feeling as vulnerable as he ever had in his life.

"I'll trust you on that," Riff replied as he found footing and waded a span beyond Kylin. "No, you're right. Can you tell—?"

"Quiet," Kylin hissed, turning his head in a steady arc from right to left, then pausing just when he could twist no more without moving his whole body. "Footsteps," he whispered, as a chill raced down his bare skin. "Heavy tread. Geens—I think. At least one; possibly more."

"Oh Eight," Riff groaned. "And us bare naked without a weapon in sight."

"Can geens swim?"

"When they have to. They don't like the cold, though—and this water is pretty damned chilly. But more to the point," Riff continued, "their advantage lies in speed as much as size—and water ought to slow them down. They can't use their talons to slash if they're using them to swim, and—"

"Hold," Kylin cautioned. "They're coming closer."

"We have to back up," Riff rasped in his ear. "We have to warn the others. They probably couldn't hear you because of the sound of the rapids farther down."

"And then?"

"We look for another way out and try to get back to camp."

"If the geens haven't been there already."

"They haven't. Any attack would have brought out the Lightning Sword, and we'd have known if that was being used."

"*Is* there another way out?" Kylin dared, even as he began easing backward, careful of his footing.

"Maybe. There's a fairly heavy growth of vines on the bank behind us. Maybe we can climb out there. I—"

He said no more for the footsteps had intensified, and this time Kylin knew, by the way Riff's breath caught, that he had heard them, too.

"I don't suppose there's any way we could reach our weapons?"

Riff shook his head. "The geens would be on us before we were out of the water. And we're fools to have left them there."

More sounds, then: a soft *thud, thud, thud* that suddenly intensified into the dreadful steady patter of running geens.

"Now," Riff snapped. "No, relax, I'll help you—" as Kylin felt a strong arm slide around his chest and sweep him backward into deeper water. In spite of that, his head went under briefly, and when he broke surface again it was to hear Riff shouting at the top of his lungs, "Geens! Geens! Geens! Get to the other side and grab those vines."

It was the worst experience of Kylin's life: being utterly helpless in the face of one of nature's most painfully lethal threats. For he could truly think of no worse fate than being eviscerated alive, while simultaneously having the flesh ripped from his bones and, quite possibly, drowning. They were in open water now, the bottom having long since dropped away, and Riff was swimming strongly toward what Kylin knew, by their cries, was the rest of the party. As for the geens—Well, it was all poor Riff could do to keep them both afloat without him trying to provide complex descriptions.

The others clearly knew about the threat, however, to judge by the shouts now mingling with a sharp intensification of splashes, as their comrades headed for the possible safety of the bank and the vines there. He doubted that this was a good time to inquire whether geens could climb.

And then he sensed solidity near him, and Riff was steering his hand to a hold on something hard and dry that he recognized as a good-sized vine. "Hold that and don't let go," Riff said tersely, his voice the only clarity amid a cacophony of splashes and shouts. Kylin found no call to argue.

For once, Riff envied Kylin his blindness.

Dying was one thing, but to see that death approaching and be unable to do anything about it— Well, that was another thing entirely.

At least he would not die alone.

Or without a fight, he told himself, as that timeless moment of personal fear dissolved into the chaos around him. He had done his duty: taken care of the weakest of their number for the nonce. Now it was time to address his own survival.

Which—to his amazement—they were all doing quietly. Or perhaps they, too, had seen their own deaths approaching and were pondering them in silence.

The geens were in plain sight now. A fourfold pack of them had just stepped out of the cover of the woods, apparently from the north. (Some comfort there: The camp was to the west, and the way the wind was blowing, they might have missed the scents of men and horses.) They were moving warily, too, their heads held low to the ground, but there was an air of unconcern about them as well.

"Probably come for a drink," Myx advised to Riff's other side. "Maybe they won't notice us."

"What about our clothes?" Lykkon challenged from farther up. "They have to smell like—"

"They'll smell horse first if the wind shifts," Myx gave back. "And that'll lead them straight back to camp."

"And give us a chance to retrieve our weapons, right?" Bingg added nervously.

"Have they seen us, do you reckon?" That from Rann.

"Hard to say," Myx retorted. "As much noise as we were making, they'd be hard-pressed not to know *something* was over here."

"Thank The Eight for these vines," Riff panted, shifting his grip on the one he held, even as he noticed that the river had undercut the bank there and was trying, none too gently, to drag his feet beneath some hidden overhang. "We can climb out—eventually."

"I'm not worried about eventually," Avall grumbled. "I'm worried about now."

Unfortunately, at that very moment the vine to which Bingg was clinging, and had indeed started to climb, broke, precipitating vine and boy alike into the water with a loud splash.

Four geen heads shot up immediately. One scaled head stared straight toward them.

An instant later, eight taloned legs attached to four lithe bodies stepped, as though possessed of one mind, into the river. And a moment after that, the first of them was swimming—straight toward the bathers, its tail describing zigzag arcs in the water.

The bathers, however, wasted no time. Unable to swim north because of the current, or south because of the rapids, they had no choice but to climb—which they did—awkwardly, but with reasonable dexterity (though Lykkon had to help his brother find a stronger purchase, and Riff found himself seeking handholds for Kylin as well as himself). Which might give them respite, but only for a moment.

The first and largest geen had reached midstream now, and was swimming strongly. Focused as he was on his next—and hopefully higher purchase—Riff nevertheless could not resist twisting around now and then to check—and every time he did, he got a closer look at those fierce eyes and deadly teeth, and those terrible claws that now cut water as effectively as they could cut his flesh. And suddenly he had no doubts whatever that these geens, should they so choose, could climb. Weight might be against them; then again, weight was doing him no favors either, as the stone in which the vines were anchored was proving so porous and powdery half of his would-be holds ripped free as soon as he put more than minimal weight upon them.

One just had—

He grabbed for another as he felt his remaining hold start to rip free as well.

A hand slipped, then a foot. Stone raked blood from his thigh and shin, and a toenail caught and tore. He scrabbled for a hold furiously, but Fate had claimed him by then, and he fell.

Fortunately, he had sense enough to kick free of the vine, but all he could think of as he entered open air was what waited below.

And then he was actually on top of it—and then *below* it as he dived for the bottom, thinking that perhaps geens could not hold their breaths.

Too soon he found the bottom, but along with it, the

current found him. It dragged at him relentlessly, but he fought it, intensely aware that he had left friends in peril, but also realizing that he—perhaps—might be in a unique position to help them. Maybe. If he could find something hard or sharp—a broken limb, perhaps—with which to make a spear.

He felt about desperately, finding nothing but smooth, moss-covered stones and, now and then, a vine.

Meanwhile, above him, he could feel as much as see the chief geen treading water as it—apparently—sought to climb up the wall where his friends—he hoped—were still scrambling for safety.

No luck, and his lungs felt fit to burst. And then he had an idea. It was a long shot, but anything was a long shot now. Still...Maybe...

A quick scrabble along the bottom located another length of vine, one that seemed rooted there. An experimental tug did not free it and that one test was all he dared. A fumble in the gloom showed him that the vine was in fact quite long. Maybe even long enough to—

He acted as he thought. A quick surge upward brought him directly beneath the geen. Risking accidental evisceration, he snared one scaly leg, quickly looped the vine around it—and pulled with all his might.

The geen had apparently already found some purchase on the bank, and he met resistance at first, but then the tension released and he reeled the vine in at once, even as he backed away to where his earlier flailings had told him was a section of fallen tree trunk.

Maybe if he could loop the vine around that, he could secure the geen. Maybe, if he was lucky, it might even drown.

Assuming he didn't drown first, for he was in dire need of air himself.

Something swished close to his face—a claw he assumed—and he flinched away.

But something else swished by his shoulder, this time close

enough to draw blood but also close enough for him to see that it was no claw but something white and narrow.

And then he could see nothing but a cloud of blood in the water above him.

He let go. He had to. At the same time, he thrust himself away from the geen and downstream.

When he surfaced again, it was to see the geen struggling to keep its head above the water while yet another carefully aimed arrow thumped home in its throat. More blood followed, and that blood seemed to have awakened the innate bloodlust that characterized all geens, so that an instant later, the victim's fellows were tearing at their erstwhile leader, even as more arrows picked them off one by one.

Arrows that could only come from one source.

Fighting the current, Riff struck out for the farther, and now friendlier, shore, and when he thought it was safe, turned to watch as the geens, one by one, succumbed to the careful bowmanship of Div, Strynn, and Merryn. As for his other companions, it was hard to tell for sure because of the greater distance to them and the water in his eyes, but he thought they all were safe.

And then his feet touched sandy mud, and all at once he was splashing noisily up the shore toward the beach. Div drew a bead on him as he emerged from behind an outthrust clump of laurel, but her bow swung back around as quickly when she saw that he wore skin instead of scales, and sported neither talons, deadly teeth, nor tail.

"Are they—?" he gasped.

"I think so," Div gritted. "If your friends will show sense and dive in below them, and then do like you did—underwater."

Riff needed no further prompting. And with so much noise from confused and dying geens, functional noise was suddenly no danger. "Dive if you can," he shouted. "Do like I did. We'll cover you."

At first they seemed not to hear, but then he saw Lykkon start, point, and then, when Riff had nodded again, leap into the water.

The others followed, with Myx—bless him—taking charge of Kylin.

A moment later, they were all standing dazed and shivering on the beach, scrambling into the clean (and hopefully irritant-free) clothing they had left there, while Merryn rained imprecations on them about carelessness.

"If you and I hadn't bonded last night," she raged to Avall in particular. "If you hadn't mingled enough of your blood with mine that I felt your fear come upon me and knew that something was amiss—"

"I know," Avall replied glumly as he reached for his drawers. "It was rash, and stupid, and I'm sorry."

"You can't be that rash again," Merryn retorted. "Now, get dressed, we need to start traveling as soon as you can."

"That's no way to address your King," Rann snapped.

Merryn turned in her tracks and regarded him coolly. "King?" she drawled. "All I see is a half dozen foolish, very lucky, and nearly naked men."

By the time everyone was dry, dressed, and fed, and all their possessions packed and put away, it was early afternoon. At least the men didn't insist on pissing on the embers of the fire, as Merryn had feared they might, giddy on juvenile masculinity as they all seemed to be. Still, she supposed they owed themselves some frivolity after their near brush with disaster—and found herself mildly jealous of the way Avall was so casually physical with his friends. She had once enjoyed the same kind of reckless sparring with him herself, and not that long ago. *Had she changed, or had he?*—for she could not imagine carrying on like that with either Div or Strynn.

Well, maybe with Strynn. If they were drunk. And no one was around to provide commentary.

Still, it felt strange to leave the pile of boulders, for all she had only rested there for five nights and Avall's cadre barely one. The Wild could reclaim it now. Rain would wash away the ashes and fill in the postholes; savaged foliage would grow back, and the odd scraps of food left about would be gone before nightfall, courtesy of insects and small animals.

But it was part of history, she reckoned; one of those points at which history might well hinge, in fact; for she had no doubt whatever that they were walking into history at that very moment.

It had been decided from respect for ritual as much as royal right, that Avall, Strynn, and Merryn should ride the horses as they set out, with the rest of the party walking—at least as far as the top of the ridge that housed the geens' cave. They planned a short stop there, in order to overlook the lake and get their bearings—which basically meant identifying a target on the horizon as close as they could manage to due north. It would be rough reckoning at best, but that was all they had to go on for now, since it would have taken most of a day to retrieve Lykkon's maps—which, in spite of their earlier frivolity (or perhaps because of it) was a day they no longer felt was theirs to squander. With time being of the essence, the straight route was the only reasonable alternative, though backtracking the way Merryn had come would have been more certain. Still, Lykkon seemed confident that he could manage even without his maps, by a combination of star observation and mathematics. She would have to trust him to it, she supposed. The Eight knew any math beyond that required for smithing (which was mostly geometry) was as mysterious to her as the sea.

In any case, it was a fine afternoon, with the sky as blue as flawless glass and the landscape as beautiful as a dream, for all she knew that dreams often concealed dangers unsuspected. So it was that she found herself surveying the eaves of the forest anxiously, searching for other geens that might still be lurking around. But the woods were empty of any obvious threat, more proof of which came from the horses' utter lack of concern for anything but ambling, and the birkit's sudden urge—perhaps prompted by her human companions' antics of the morning—to act very much like a cub.

So it was that they traversed the meadow and entered the woods half a shot west of the trail that led to the cave where the geen den lay. Nor were they long in finding a place where the slope was gradual enough for easy going. And then, quite suddenly, they reached the summit. The ground fell away precipitously a dozen spans ahead, but a new trail—probably a game trail—kinked left there, paralleling the ridge crest for another quarter shot or so, aiming slightly uphill toward what looked to be an open space among the trees.

Caught up by the spell of the place, they all turned toward the clearing in silence, with Avall and Strynn still in the lead. A moment later, the trail ended abruptly atop a slab of stone big enough for their entire party—and twice as many more—to stand upon. And then Merryn gasped indeed.

There was the lake, and there was the island within it: a near perfect circle of dark, vitreous stone, festooned by swags of greenery. But that wasn't what amazed her, though it was as beautiful as any mortal place she had ever seen. No, what took her breath was what she saw when she looked left.

The land sloped steeply to that side, curving around a sort of bay or cup in the side of the ridge that encircled the lake, as though some impossibly huge creature had taken a neat bite from the rim. That, with the slope, permitted the first truly comprehensive view they had yet achieved of the land to the southwest. And there, halfway toward the horizon, lay a sheet of what could only be water: water that Merryn knew with absolute conviction was the signal mystery that had haunted her imagination since she was a child: the much-rumored, seldom-seen enigma that could be nothing else but the western sea.

The presence of gulls wheeling in the sky thereabouts all but confirmed it, as did the fact that Avall had said that the lake water held a faint salty tang, as though the two bodies were in somewise connected.

"Well," Merryn announced happily, "I've seen what I came west to see; now I can leave this place content."

Lykkon, however, looked more sober. "So near and so far. It's a pity we don't have time to investigate more. It would be wonderful to say one had swum in both seas."

Avall nodded in turn. "It would indeed. But in any case, the trail looks to run that way for a while, so we'll at least get to come a little closer. And there's another thing," he added. "It's one more reason to return."

Merryn grinned at him. He grinned back. But Myx was the first to turn his face away and gaze, yet again, at the opposite horizon. "That way lies Gem-Hold—and Eron," he said solemnly. "And that way, for now, lies the future."

PART II

PART II

CHAPTER XXIV:

CHALLENGE

(NORTHWESTERN ERON: MEGON VALE—NEAR-AUTUMN: DAY 1—MORNING)

~~~~~~

"There's a herald on Gem-Hold's ramparts," Veen announced breathlessly, from the entrance to Vorinn's tent. His guards rushed up on either side of her, barring nearer approach with crossed spears, their faces flushed with chagrin beneath their duty helms.

Vorinn tried to suppress a grin. Veen would have brushed right past them in her haste: she who was most conscientious of the entire Regency Council about ceremony and propriety. But then the import of her words struck him in fact.

"*A herald?*" He was on his feet in an instant, reaching for his formal cloak, sword, and helmet. "Is that all? Was Zeff with him? Has someone informed Tryffon and Preedor?"

"He's got a parley flag," Veen replied quickly, dodging deftly aside as Vorinn brushed by her in his haste. "He's alone—and I've already sent my second to inform the Chiefs."

"Took long enough," Vorinn muttered in passing. And with that, he thrust through the outer entrance and into the brighter light of the morning camp.

It was the first day of autumn, he realized—or of the quarter that contained it, more precisely; the Eronese calendar was quirky that way. Summer and winter were honored with entire quarters—one for joy, one from fear—and lasted forty-five days either side of their respective solstices. Spring and autumn had to make do with eighths centered on the equinoxes and crowded, in autumn's case, by Near-Autumn and Near-Winter before and after. Which didn't change the fact that summer was to all intents over and winter not impossibly far away.

In any case, this was an auspicious day—because he had already decided, long before the herald had appeared, to call Zeff down to parley at a hand past noon. That Zeff had preempted him was not important, though he could think of any number of possible reasons why that might have occurred, the most plausible being the same one that had prompted Vorinn himself to act: that only another eighth remained in which an army might return to Tir-Eron in time for Sundeath and the Proving of the King. Who that King would be, if not Avall, Vorinn had no idea. He himself nursed aspirations in that direction, but perhaps Zeff did as well; it would be just like him. And a sovereign from Priest-Clan would certainly be one solution to the current disaffection—though not one Vorinn could endure.

He supposed he would know how things lay soon enough. The way he saw it, Zeff would either call for Vorinn's surrender or offer up his own. Vorinn had long since prepared replies to either eventuality.

He had reached the palisade now, and saw its primary gate opened before him by a tide of eager-faced soldiers who seemed to have caught the same impatient excitement that had infected Veen. His horse was waiting, too, but he eschewed it. Now that Zeff's moat effectively filled Megon Vale, it was only a dozen strides to the siege engine that had become the royal viewing tower. He mounted it in haste, waiting for those to catch up who would.

And then slowed abruptly. Heralds were *not* Chiefs or Kings, and were entitled to less ceremony and deference. Vorinn therefore mounted the last few steps—the ones that would take him into full view from Gem-Hold—at a deliberately leisurely pace. It wouldn't do to appear *too* eager.

So it was that he had stilled his face to calm serenity when he stepped out onto the platform, adjusted his cloak about his shoulders, and set his helm upon his head, making certain that the Regent's circlet was fully displayed. He doubted that Zeff would have seen it earlier, which would add to the herald's confusion, since he would likely be expecting either Avall or Rann.

The herald registered no surprise, however; then again, he wasn't supposed to—and knew, moreover, what *he* was about to say. Which gave him a slight advantage—but only a slight one.

He was a proper herald, too: clad in precisely the prescribed regalia, save that every item was pristine Ninth Face midnight blue and white. He even held a staff, while a lesser herald stood beside him with a speaking trumpet.

For his part, Vorinn advanced to just behind the railing, folded his arms for a moment, then motioned for his own horn to be brought forward. Only when that had been accomplished to his satisfaction did he speak.

"Herald, I see you," he intoned the ritual acknowledgment, his amplified voice echoing up and down the vale. "Do you have words for me?"

"I have words for the King of Eron," the herald replied. "Is this Avall syn Argen-a I see before me?"

"It is his Regent, acting in his name. And in that name, I have authority to treat with all and sundry."

The herald paused briefly, as though taken slightly off guard, then composed himself with exemplary haste. "You wear the Regent's circlet of Eron, so it appears to me, which is sufficient proof that you are empowered to hear the message with which I have been entrusted."

"And what message is that?"

The herald stood straighter and began to speak, not reading: "Be it known this day, the first of Near-Autumn of this year and reign, that Zeff of the Ninth Face does hereby challenge Avall syn Argen-a or his appointed champion to single combat with swords at a place and time to be hereinafter named, so long as it please his opponent and betrays not the security of either combatant."

"I hear this challenge," Vorinn called back clearly. "I would also like to hear where this place might be in which our champions could meet so securely, for it seems to me that they would either have to swim or deliver themselves up to an enemy."

"Such a place can, however, be provided," the herald answered. "Though it will require some preparation. If, however, you would do this thing, we will send word how and when, for your approval."

"I would hear this 'how and when,'" Vorinn responded. "And I will wait."

"I will convey this word to our Chief, Lord Vorinn. But would you do us all the courtesy of announcing who your champion might be?"

"Ah, sir herald," Vorinn retorted, with a grin. "For that I fear it is Zeff who must wait."

"You have not formally accepted," the herald reminded him. "I hear it implied in your words, but you have not expressly stated—"

"I accept, in the name of Avall and the Kingdom of Eron," Vorinn shouted. "And may Fate smile upon the most deserving."

"May Fate smile indeed," the herald called. "By your leave, Lord Regent, I will convey your words. I will return to announce time and place."

"My leave you have," Vorinn replied. And stepped back from the railing.

"I hope you know what you're doing," Tryffon growled through his beard. "The Face was the challenger; it was for you to name weapon, time, and place—yet Zeff clearly had all three predetermined."

Vorinn shrugged, though part of him agreed with Tryffon's assessment. He had, indeed, been rash. But no rasher than he had already planned to be. "It makes no difference in the long run," Vorinn told his kinsman. "I had already planned to challenge Zeff today, which would have given him choice of time and place anyway—I would have had to be that magnanimous. But that would also have betrayed the fact that I am to be our champion. This way, they won't know who it will be until it is almost time. That plays into our hands. Anticipation alone could skew the battle."

Tryffon regarded him keenly. "You don't look like you believe that, not entirely."

Vorinn slumped against one of the corner posts, gazing around reflexively to see who else might be listening. A glance and a nod sent Veen and the rest of his entourage toward the stairs. Tryffon raised a brow.

Another shrug. "Easier than going all the way back to the tent to talk, especially when we're waiting."

"I'm listening. Though I think I already know what you're going to say."

Vorinn scowled. "Ah, then you've already considered the implications."

Tryffon scowled in turn. "I've considered some of them. The Eight know if they're the ones *you're* considering."

Vorinn sighed heavily. "So... we can spar or we can talk. Very well, what I think is this. While we've all but told Zeff that Avall is no longer in control here, he does not know that as an absolute fact. The most he *can* know is that Avall isn't actively in control, and that he's sufficiently incapacitated to require a regency—and the most *that* implies is that the regency can better be served by me than Rann."

"We've covered this much over and over, boy."

"Fine. But hear me. With all that's gone on lately, we tend to forget that Zeff's original ultimatum was for us to surrender the regalia. He must therefore assume that we have it with us. Whether or not he *believes* it, he can't omit that from his plans entirely. And while he must have guessed by now that the replica regalia was indeed intended as a ruse, he still cannot discount the possible presence of the genuine article. The Eight know we've tried to second-guess him on that, on why he'd think we haven't deigned to use it. Certainly he's predicated his defense upon that assumption."

"Get to the point, boy."

"The point is that Zeff is willing to face us now, while suspecting that we have the Lightning Sword and the regalia that goes with it, and *knowing*—from his point of view—that we have the replica sword, which is nearly as powerful. It therefore stands to reason that he thinks he can stand against them and probably win. And since we know that he has flooded the mines, and a fair bit of time has elapsed since then, the only reasonable conclusion is that Zeff has managed to contrive a weapon of his own that he thinks can stand against anything we can bring to bear."

Tryffon blinked like one dazed, then folded his arms and frowned even more deeply than heretofore. "All that makes sense, boy—fearfully, logical sense. Which then raises the question of how you think you can possibly beat him, given that we have neither sword, shield, nor helmet."

"Hope, determination—and the fact that I'm the better swordsman."

"You're mad! Or a fool!"

"Both, probably. But it's the only solution I can see, unless we want to sit here until Deep Winter, making up excuses for Avall and waiting for Priest-Clan to consolidate its power past breaking. And believe me, Uncle, we either break its power in the next quarter, or we lose any reasonable chance of breaking it at all."

"I—"

"Hsst, Uncle," Vorinn broke in. "Here comes the herald."

"In Gem-Hold's—what did they call it? Viewing plaza?" Preedor gasped, half a hand later. "Are they mad?"

"That remains to be seen," Vorinn replied, with slightly more control than he had evinced with Tryffon earlier. Excitement did make him rash; that was a fact. But at least the warring factions had broken their long impasse.

"And how do they propose to manage this?"

Vorinn took a deep breath. "First, remember that I can't go into the actual hold, with or without escort; even I'm not that big a fool. And keep in mind that Zeff won't come out here for the same reason, and that the only way we can possibly arrange anything resembling neutral ground is either by choosing a site that gives everyone equal access, or no one. We could manage the first after a fashion, if Zeff drained the moat, but he won't do that. He can, however, drain it partway, and redirect some of the rest—enough, apparently, to give us access to a raised pavement in the viewing plaza above the water courts on the south end." He paused, reached for paper, and drew.

"There were already walls around that end of the hold, Two-father," he went on, sketching rapidly. "Notably, there are walls around the forecourt twice as tall as a man. They were built for decoration more than defense, but they're more than adequate to hold in water, which Zeff has made them do."

"I know all that, boy," Preedor growled. "I spent three quarters here twenty years before you were born."

"Fair enough," Vorinn replied. "But things can change in twenty years, and one of the things that has changed fairly recently is that, to the south of the forecourt and raised one level above it, there's now a flat walled area about fifteen spans square that was carved out of a spur of the mountain and which serves, in part, as a place from which to look down on the water courts, which are lower. From the outside it still looks like mountain, which is why we've tended to forget about it during our planning—not that we could climb that side anyway, or get a siege tower to it—and the only access to it from the outside is by way of a narrow flight of steps that have, until this morning, been under half a span of water at their base and double guarded from above. Anyway, once you actually get there, this plaza is ringed by sets of steps and so on, but in the middle of it is a raised platform that, conveniently enough, is big enough for two men to fight on. There's a walkway from our side of the walls leading to this platform, which is apparently about five spans from either side and five spans across."

"What about access to the hold?" Preedor inquired.

"Actually," Vorinn replied, "the only access from the hold is via an arcade from the second level that runs from above the west side of the forecourt to the top of the steps that ring the plaza. Those steps would normally be underwater, but Zeff's men apparently think they can build a pontoon bridge out to the central platform. Access would be limited for both of us—since neither access route would be more than a span wide, which isn't wide enough for any worthwhile battle, plus they know we can't fight in water, which would still fill the plaza about waist deep."

"And they're going to drain the moat for this?"

"Enough to uncover the bottom part of the outer access stair—*and* this central platform and the access walk from our side, to the depth of a hand below it. That will still leave water half a span deep around the platform. And while it will also require draining the rest of the moat somewhat, the main edge of it should only draw back maybe a span at best. In other words, it would present much the same deterrent it does now."

Preedor snorted loudly. "It sounds preposterous and ridiculously complicated, but it's probably the closest thing to neutral ground that can be found. So I suppose it will have to do."

Vorinn regarded him gravely. "I know you don't approve, Two-father, but I'd be glad to hear any halfway reasonable alternative."

"That's just the trouble," Preedor huffed. "I can't think of any. In any case, to my mind the crucial question is this: Assuming we do manage to defeat Zeff, does he have the au-

doors were closed now and—as early reconnaissance had shown—filled in with stone from within. And none too well either, for water oozed from around them, but never enough to indicate danger of collapse—or, more to the point—vulnerability to battering rams. More walls continued to the left in an artful marriage of new masonry and the raw stone of the mountain. A narrow paved path paralleled them, running below the level of the South Road until, halfway along its length, a simple stone stair barely wide enough for a single man to traverse angled up their flank. Veen had once proposed attacking from that quarter, but Vorinn had pointed out that to reach that stair required any attackers to move single file directly beneath five spans of well-defended wall. That was before the wall had been crowned with bound Gem-Holders, of course, and before the lower span of the stairs had been flooded. They were visible now, though still damp, and Vorinn supposed that the hold's new wardens had contrived some way to direct the flow of the Ri-Eron's waters in various directions as suited their intent.

Whatever the mechanism, the stairs were accessible for the nonce, and dry enough to climb if one observed caution. This Vorinn did, feeling impossibly vulnerable as he made his way up the side of the wall until he reached the top, where a waist-high bronze gate had been opened by Ninth Face warriors half a hand before. He turned through it, and found himself standing upon the topmost of five wide stone platforms that kinked around the plaza to form terraces that could double as seats. For the first time since their arrival, no armed warriors stood atop that wall.

Veen had accompanied him eight paces back—right behind his seconds—but not Preedor or Tryffon, for someone would have to retain command authority if the worst scenario occurred, and those two were best equipped for that station. Indeed, Tryffon was already—against his wishes—designated Acting Regent, though the bulk of the army did not know that. As for the others—they were soldiers chosen by the ranking on-site Chiefs to represent certain clans, namely Argen, for the absent King; Eemon, for Rann; and, to everyone's surprise, Common Clan. Crimson, maroon, black and gray, and beige. The third was not technically proper for Eemon, but that clan's midnight blue had been deemed too close to the Ninth Face's livery, so Eemon's representative wore Stonecraft's heraldry instead.

And then, with the sky blazing blue overhead and Gem-Hold white before him; with the mountains of Angen's Spine looming beyond, and the forested heights that surrounded the vale at his back, Vorinn syn Ferr-een marched out to meet his fate.

As he stepped down onto the raised causeway that arrowed into the plaza where the white stone slab that would be the field of combat gleamed in the crisp autumn light, a door opened in the arcade opposite, and a length of wood two spans long and as wide as that doorway thrust out into the water that lapped about the plaza's half-drowned walls. Floats barely visible beneath it buoyed it up, and as soon as it was in place, another followed. It took three of the objects to reach the dueling platform from that side, and a moment more for soldiers in Ninth Face surcoats to fix it firm, which they accomplished with practiced dispatch, whereupon they re-formed ranks and marched back into the arcade.

Precisely as the gong sounded again, to mark noon, Zeff himself appeared.

He was dressed as he had been dressed every other time Vorinn had seen him in official capacity, which is to say in full Ninth Face heraldry of dark blue surcoat and white-velvet cloak, all over what looked like a mail hauberk above dark blue leather armor on arms and legs, save where cups of finely worked metal protected elbows and knees. He wore no helm at the moment, but one of his attendants carried one, as another carried his shield and a third his sword. All of which was prescribed; Vorinn's seconds carried exactly the same, though he had twisted protocol slightly by shrouding all three items, the better to keep Zeff guessing.

Vorinn scanned Zeff's regalia carefully. It was well polished; that was obvious. Indeed, the sun shone so brightly on both helm and shield that they hurt to look upon. It therefore took him a moment to realize that he, in fact, faced two parts of the false regalia. There was a red glitter within that metallic glare, too; one he didn't like, though it was also one he had expected. By squinting, he could even make out the source: Between the helm's eye ridges showed a fist-sized ring of all-too-familiar ruddy gems. They were small individually, but appeared to be of sufficient number to equal the mass of the single gem in the "magical" royal helm. The shield showed no such augmentations; then again, the gem in the "magic" shield had been on the inside, protected by steel and rare alloys from the bite of any normal blade. And Vorinn knew without bothering to look that the sword would likewise sport, either in the grip or the guard, a similar set of jewels. And though Vorinn was chilled to the bone by their very presence, he also knew that there was no particular reason why Zeff could not be playing Avall's own game and trying to trick him with false panoply.

It was too late to worry about that, anyway.

By the rules that governed this kind of challenge, there would be no heralds and no marshals. And the combat would be, unless one of the combatants conceded verbally, to the death.

Vorinn waited until Zeff was on the last section of bridge before he himself progressed farther, so that they entered the platform at precisely the same moment. His cloak belled behind him in a gust of sudden wind, which he chose to call an omen of victory. Long since trained in the form of such things, the seconds took up positions of their own, two to a corner, facing their equivalents, even as the combatants faced off.

In spite of Vorinn's higher rank, Zeff was challenger. It therefore fell to him to speak first. "I am Zeff of the Ninth

Face," he announced. "I welcome you to what I hope we both agree will be, for this time and place, neutral ground on which no blood may be shed but our own. And I would now ask, as is my right, who it is I have the honor of facing on the field of honor?"

Though he stood barely four spans from Vorinn, Zeff held his head so that he appeared to speak to the Vale at large, and made a point of staring about as though seeking someone who was not present.

Vorinn cleared his throat. "I am Vorinn syn Ferr-een, Regent for this time for Avall syn Argen-a, now and until his death, for everyone here assembled, and for you and me especially, our anointed and rightful King. And likewise," he added, once again breaking form, "brother to Strynn san Ferr-een, Consort to that King."

Zeff nodded stiffly, but his face twisted ever so slightly with a mocking grin. "This King of which you spoke—"

"Is indisposed. Any victory I achieve will be in his name and no other."

"This indisposition—"

"Is not our concern today."

Zeff shrugged. "No, I suppose it is not. In any case, it is time we were about our business. With time, place, and weapon already decided, do you see any cause for additional delay?"

Vorinn puffed his cheeks thoughtfully, playing for effect, then spoke. "Lord Chief," he began, "I have agreed to meet you here as champion of the rightful King of Eron and as commander of his lawful armies. I have granted you all you asked, though it was my right to name these things: time, place, and weapon. I therefore crave a boon."

Zeff raised a brow ever so slightly, though he had surely been expecting something of the like. It was part of the ritual, after all: threat, taunt, threat, and counter-threat.

But to deny any boon now would be unthinkable. Zeff's power had to rest in large part on his own personal honor, and to refuse a boon would degrade that.

"If it is within my power and a just thing, I will grant this boon," Zeff called confidently.

Vorinn spared him a tiny conciliatory bow. "Very well, my boon is this. You have determined what our weapons are to be. You have said nothing of our form of defense; therefore, it is mine to name. And I name it now. We will have *no* defense. We will fight with neither helms nor shields. By sword alone shall we meet our dooms."

Zeff stiffened for the merest instant, and Vorinn felt a tiny thrill of anticipation. He had been right: Zeff had been expecting to meet the full achievement of magical regalia. Now he would not have to face the shield, which should increase his chances, not diminish them. But since he knew that, he would also suspect Vorinn of some trick.

"I will meet you thus," Zeff answered, a breath before Vorinn expected. "Now, if we may match our swords, we can begin."

"As you will." And with that Vorinn claimed his sword from his primary second and stepped forward, even as Zeff did the same.

Matching swords simply meant that both men set the bare points of their blades on the ground before them in the center of the dueling platform and measured their length one against the other, so that each man would know the limit of the other's reach. Happily for Vorinn, it would also give him a chance to examine Zeff's weapon more closely. Which he did, noting that a spiral of tiny red gems did indeed weave their way among the gilded spirals on the hilt, each connected, as best he could tell, by a thin filament of bloodwire.

Which confirmed what Vorinn had already suspected: that Zeff had deduced the theory that underlay the making of gem-powered weapons. Still, that did not concern Vorinn over-much, for Zeff could not know even half of what Avall had known and had put into the royal regalia, for the simple reason that Avall did not know it all himself. Much of what had determined the regalia's final fashioning had been seen in

Strike!

Left/right/left/right.

Up/down; aim for the head, then for the body, then the head again, then the legs.

Zeff met them all, though he was clearly on the defensive.

But every moment that Vorinn waited was a moment longer in which Zeff could prime himself to act.

Even as Vorinn plotted his next move, blood oozed from between Zeff's fingers.

It was now or never.

But that did not mean that Vorinn was not careful or controlled or precise. Indeed, Tryffon said later that he had never seen the ensuing move executed with more finesse.

For as Zeff raised his sword again, Vorinn swung with all his strength—but not to bring blade against blade or body. Rather, he sought to bring his hand against Zeff's own, and follow with his whole weight.

Even so, their blades took the brunt of it and smashed together hilt to hilt, quillions locked, blades raised between them like the horns of the fabled Ixtian oryx. Vorinn could hear the hiss of Zeff's breath as he strove to disengage without making himself vulnerable to the follow-through. He could see the sweat that already sheened his foe's brow, and could smell the tang of polished steel, clean velvet, and well-oiled leather sharp in the brilliant air.

He thrust backward, and Zeff staggered but did not loose his grip. Zeff's lips curled back from perfect teeth as he concentrated. Vorinn saw his eyes go blank for the briefest instant.

Vorinn released his sword at once. Zeff's blade sliced past his face as Vorinn's hilt stabbed the ground between them. But by then he had reached out and seized Zeff's sword just above the quillions. Pain flashed through him, so sharp it was exquisite, as good steel parted excellent glove leather. Oblivious to the agony, he continued to bear down, forcing the blade away by strength alone, and forcing his exposed flesh around it. Steel touched bone and his nerves sang. Blood was everywhere.

More to the point, blood was coursing down the blade past the quillons to join with the blood already welling from Zeff's hand—which controlled the gems.

And then Vorinn forgot to breathe—because, for a timeless moment, he simply *wasn't*. And then he was two people again, and then—abruptly—one person with two conflicting wills.

You dare not! one of those wills protested.

I have dared, the other asserted.

And then nothing but fear, anger, and determination so closely mingled that he could not tell which thoughts were his and which his foe's.

Their hands had not moved, but reality had slowed, and Vorinn could suddenly feel the slow pulse of power seeking him through his blood—power that knew him, yet did not know him; that recognized in him something familiar and good, but which yet worked for a countermanding end.

Was this what Avall had felt? This recognition from the gems? Vorinn knew well enough that they more or less "liked" Avall, and that all subsequent gems based their reactions, in part, on how their wielders reacted to Avall in turn. But Zeff's gems should never have known Avall. And Vorinn had never bonded with anyone.

Which meant that—maybe—it had come down to wills, and he prayed that his will was stronger. *What would Avall do in this situation?* he wondered, in that moment of frozen time that looked, indeed, to those gathered round, to truly *be* frozen. He wished Avall were here to tell him. He wished he had Avall's strength and skill and courage. Dammit, he wished he knew everything Avall knew about these wretched gems! And even as he wished, he sensed Zeff wishing as well.

Or hating, which was itself wishing of a kind. And Zeff was wishing about Avall, too: wishing he was forever removed from this or any equation, which in effect meant that he was wishing that Avall was dead.

Yet while they stood thus locked together, Vorinn's body

went right on pressing the physical advantage granted him by greater weight and height—and eventually inertia interceded.

Zeff staggered backward. Vorinn went with him, not daring to release his hold, yet still his body pressed forward. Zeff could not resist, and fell. His hip struck the pavement, and Vorinn actually flew over him, yet never released his grip on Zeff's terrible blade. Indeed, such was his momentum that the force of his flip brought Zeff into the water with him.

And then water closed over their heads, and Vorinn felt nothing at all save the pain in his hand and that other, strange, not-quite pain that was water assailing the gates of his breath. Red dyed that water: a murky cloud emerging from where their hands still joined steel and flesh and jewels.

And where, in an odd way, their wishes also mingled.

But...the water was welcoming them! And then Vorinn felt something incredibly, impossibly strange: He felt himself dissolving. And then there was no Vorinn left but raw desire.

And then—finally—a sense of upward motion.

CHAPTER XXV:

TRIAL BY WATER

~~~~~~

Avall had barely crouched down to wash his hands in the clear, fast-running shallows of the nice-sized river beside which his party had chosen to take its midday meal, when the deeper channel in the center erupted into spray.

With it came a concussion like thunder without the noise, and the unmistakable sharp metallic stench of unseen lightning. Taken off guard, he recoiled—and sprawled on his backside in cold water, aware, even as he fell, that the river was somehow singing to him. Or singing to that which was *within* him, anyway. It was like when he drank from the Wells, sometimes: doors opening in his mind and doors closing. His poor, burned, personal gem pulsed like a wind-fanned coal on his chest, while around him, attenuating in a way that was all too familiar, time began to slow.

So it was that he had ample opportunity to note the wide river valley around him, with the river straight ahead ten spans wide, bordered on either side by a graceful sweep of shore paved with countless rounded stones which in turn stood as a bulwark against a fringe of low-grown scrub that fronted impressive stands of taller hardwoods.

Across the stream—beyond that place where the fountaining water had suddenly frozen to a near stop—more trees grew closer in: aspen, beech, and yew. Mountains rose behind: a hard surge of purple stone with the sparkling white of eternal snow draped around their peaks like lacy shawls.

Farther down to the right, he could hear the long slow gulps Boot made as she drank down the river, while behind him, he caught the slow shouts of his companions acknowledging that they, too, had seen what he had seen and were amazed. He could even feel their thoughts, a little; frozen, as was everything else: mostly thoughts of relief that the morning's trek had ended, that they would rest here for lunch and assuage a reasonable hunger. Thoughts that the mountains ahead were the most tangible proof yet that, after six days on the nonexistent road, they were finally approaching the first of what would surely prove to be many goals. And then thoughts that all that had been shattered by a sudden insertion of the strange.

But only for a moment, as reality cried out to him, then slowed once more, so as to command his full attention.

And then normal time resumed again, and he knew without doubt that this was no vision but a real event that was happening before his astonished eyes.

The fountain that had begun it all subsided, but rising from its heart came two figures.

Two *men,* Avall realized: dripping wet and locked in mortal combat, with their hands clamped around something that glittered in the noonday light so brightly it was like frozen fire— or light itself solidified—until the water sluiced away from it to reveal a sword. A *single* sword.

A sword one of those men had suddenly wrenched free and pointed toward the heavens.

Avall covered his ears, but that barely shut out the shout of thunder, the crackling snap of what was closest to lightning, yet not remotely the same as that even more perilous power.

Yet whatever it was struck the water from a cloudless sky, wrenching out a heavy veil of steam that obscured the combatants for a moment—though Avall saw them fly away from each other as the force that one of them had summoned wrenched them both apart.

Even as he scrambled to his feet, he was cataloging colors. The one on the right had worn red of a particularly rich and vivid shade that could only be Warcraft crimson. The other: midnight blue edged with white. Not Eemon, but...

Priest-Clan. The Ninth Face, rather. But what were they doing here?

And who were these two men?

And then came the truly impossible: The water brought him the answer. More properly, it brought a set of images in what was clearly some kind of vision or far-seeing: Gem-Hold encircled with water...a formal combat about to ensue—to the death, using what appeared to be at least one gem-powered weapon...and then those combatants falling into water—and vanishing.

But whose thoughts were these seeking footholds among his own? Thoughts of glory and anger and fear and triumph and amazement and despair. Thoughts of him: reluctant admiration. And thoughts of him: raw, unadulterated hate.

Faces appeared abruptly, matching themselves to those thoughts.

"Zeff and Vorinn!" he yelled, as reality surged back even more violently.

He was back on his feet now and wading clumsily into deeper water, while the whole shore behind him seemed to have gone mad. Horses neighed, whinnied, and threatened to bolt, while voices he had no time to sort out tried to keep them calm. Others were shouting names—questions—or simply curses or yelps of alarm. The birkit—which Avall could see from the corner of his eye—seemed to have forgotten it was a this was no time for theory, what with the siege still hanging at a crucial juncture.

Yet the images remained: the images his mind had sieved from the water. Like pools among stones, they were: each reflecting the sky—except that these pools reflected events. Nor could he resist gazing among them. One of them had caught his attention even now: the hold flooded, and the water rising from where the river flowed beneath it, then finding the hidden entrances to the mines that no men knew, and rushing into them, where they found, at last, the deep-hidden seams and veins where the few remaining power gems remained. And when the water touched those gems, it somehow touched *all* gems that touched the same water. And touched blood in that water as well, and anything in that blood that had met with the gems before.

For the briefest instant, Avall saw all the water in Eron, like a golden network spread across the land. And saw also certain places where parts of that network were brightest.

Places that already had names.

"Wells."

Avall whispered the word aloud.

"What did you say?" Merryn demanded.

He looked up at her. "Wells. You know that I've always said that some of the gem effects feel like what happens when I drink from Wells? I think I know why now—except that I'm not certain I can explain it, except to say that as best I can tell, whatever's in the gems... may be everywhere. But it's only in the gems that it's concentrated enough to have much effect. And only through our blood—and maybe our thought and will—that any of that effect can be manifested."

He broke off, shaking his head. "I'm sorry, folks; I can't manage this right now. The war's come back to haunt me, and we haven't even finished testing the powers and limits of the gems we've got already—and now we find that Zeff has more of the wretched things, and that there are even more beneath Gem-Hold, and that the gems themselves may be influencing events more than we thought. All of which means—I don't know what it means. One thing it means is that I don't even know how much of me *is* me, anymore."

"The part we love," Rann said simply. "And what you've just said—though I don't understand half of it with my surface mind—well, it still resonates in my gut. And it confirms what Merry and I came here to urge you to do."

"And what's that?"

"You have to go back. More to the point, you have to go back now—as fast as you can. You have to take the sword, the shield, and the helmet and return to the war. It's hanging on Fate's thread, Avall. There's bound to be confusion there—you could probably *tell* what's going on there if you dared touch your blood to the water—that's my guess. But the fact remains. You have to go. At once."

"The others—"

"If you tell them, we'll have to discuss everything and argue everything and explain everything," Merryn said. "Obviously gem power can bring a person—or more—here. Therefore, it can take as many people back."

"Let me stress that," Rann added. "You're going nowhere without me, no arguing, and you need Merryn."

"Strynn—"

"Is as strong as steel, and she'll still have all she needs in the way of allies. We'll come back for them if we can. And if we can't, they'll understand. But this can't wait, Avall. The Ninth Face has literally lost its head, and while I'm certain that there's a chain of command, that chain is probably kinked up in confusion right now, what with Zeff having vanished. Besides, do you think Tryffon would sit still through all this? This is his chance to push that siege he's been wanting for eights. Fifteen spans of water half a span deep to an undefendable door. He won't be able to resist."

"No," Avall sighed. "He won't."

He rose at that and gazed back toward the impromptu camp a quarter shot up the shore. An eruption of bushes screened part of the group, and none of the rest were watching, intent as they were on Vorinn's narrative. "I'll go get Boot," Merryn volunteered. "I'll pretend I'm bringing her down to drink. That's when you can get the regalia."

Avall rolled his eyes. "You're asking a lot."

"No more than I think you can accomplish."

"Not of me," Avall flared. "Of the regalia. Of the gems in it. We've never used them all at once to jump; we don't know if they even can, since they all seem to behave differently, and who knows what the combination might do—or not. And even if they can get someone back to Gem, we don't know if they can take all three of us."

"And a horse," Merryn added—"if possible. You'll need it to make a proper entrance—and maybe to make a proper escape, if it comes to that."

Avall rolled his eyes again. But by that time, Merryn was already jogging toward the pickets.

Avall gave up thinking. Better not to, for the nonce. There were too many ways to think at once. Better he let instinct take control. Rann seemed to sense his trepidation and laid an arm across his shoulders. "A hand from now, it will all be better."

"A hand from now everyone I know could be dead," Avall shot back. "I'm willing to do this because I truly have no choice, given the time frame—but have any of you thought about this in the larger sense? The gems are giving us something for free. Over and over they do that. That can't be right. There'll have to be an accounting. One day...who knows? Maybe someone will jump and not come out of the Overworld. Maybe we'll bond and never be able to separate. Maybe the gems will overwhelm us utterly."

"Later," Rann said sadly. "Here comes Merry."

Merryn was indeed returning, with faithful Boot in tow. And now that she was screened from the rest of the camp, she was wasting no time divesting the mare of the regalia. Rann collected it as she passed it to him. Shield first, then sword, then helmet. "Up you go," she told Avall, nodding toward the horse.

Avall said nothing at all, simply stuck his foot in the stirrup and vaulted atop Boot's broad back. Sturdy though she might be, Boot was not a warhorse. He hoped the poor beast was up to this—whatever "this" turned out to be.

Still not speaking, Rann passed Avall the helm, then held the reins while he donned it. Merryn gave him the sword, then Rann the shield. He fumbled for a moment, not having bestrode a horse in full caparison in a while. Nor did the fact that he was trying not to awaken any of the gems make his efforts easier.

But then—far too soon—he was ready.

"One more thing," Merryn said at last. And with that she passed up Zeff's severed head. "He'll have to ride in your lap," she continued. "Probably not pleasant for you, but you'll need proof."

Avall nodded—and tried not to flinch as he nestled Zeff's head between his crotch and the pommel. It was only so much meat, he told himself. The soul was fled. And thanks to the gems, he knew that the soul—at least in part—outlived the body.

"You two?" he demanded, to distract himself.

"Behind you, if you don't mind. We're only going a dozen spans. Boot can manage that."

Avall was too agitated to argue. If this was going to happen, he wanted it done and over. Yet when he felt Rann slip up behind him, and Merryn slide on farther back—in what had to be a very perilous seat indeed—it seemed too soon.

"Now or never," Rann whispered in his ear. And before Avall could stop himself, he set heels to Boot's sides and rode into the river. The middle channel was deepest, but still not deep enough to reach higher than Boot's breast, which was a problem they had not considered.

"Fate help us now," Avall muttered. "I can't."

And with that he slammed his sword hand into his fore-head, tripping the blood trigger there, then clamped down with both hands as hard as he could on sword and shield alike, let go the reins, and—relying on balance alone—thrust both hands into the water, one to either side.

Willpower did the rest.

Wanting this done and over was enough, and "done and over" meant returning to Gem-Hold-Winter.

Avall tried to drag his hands back above the water, but the water knew him, and sang to him, and then it seized him and pulled him apart like waves eating up a sand sculpture at the seashore.

The last thing he saw was mountains above woodland above river. The last thing he heard was Vorinn splashing through the water behind them yelling, "Not without me! Not yet. No!"

CHAPTER XXVI:

LULL BEFORE THE STORM

~~~~~~~

"What just happened?" Ahfinn demanded of the tall soldier standing at his right, who was gazing, as was he, at the chaos that had just engulfed the dueling ground. *Empty* chaos, perhaps—for the focus of that duel had vanished. Yet even now the square was filling with eight men from two factions, all rushing forward in utter confusion to stare over the platform's side into less than a span of water, where, it appeared, two other men had, not ten breaths earlier, vanished without a trace.

"It's the same thing that happened the other time," the soldier told Ahfinn sourly, reaching for his sword. "And curse them for it, too. Damned tricksters."

"I'm not so certain," Ahfinn retorted through a scowl. "Did you see Vorinn's face when—?"

"All I saw was his blood on his hand," the guard gritted. "All I *want* to see is his head."

"Orders," someone panted at Ahfinn's other side. "Do you have orders?"

Ahfinn blinked at the man. And only then did he realize that he was now facing the impossible responsibility that Zeff had laid on him that morning in Gem-Hold's assembly hall, before most of the Ninth Face force in residence.

"*I go to fight*," Zeff had announced. "*I go to meet our foe in order to end this impasse. We could all fight here, and many could die, and still nothing would be accomplished. Or I can fight their champion. I have that in my possession which all but assures my victory. Our foes have nothing but pride. They sought to trick us with false goods, but we have seen through their deception, and any weapon they may have with them, be assured that we have better. I will be our champion because this has been my venture from the first, and because the law of our order demands that no man ask of another what he would not himself willingly undertake. I have always been a fighter. I will fight.*"

Silence had followed—for a moment. Then, from a young woman: "*And if you lose?*"

"*There are better warriors in this hold, and better scholars, and better theologians. But there is not a better man to oversee all these things than Ahfinn. He will take my place. His orders will be my orders.*" A pause, then: "*Torai, you will retain command of all strategy and tactics, save that Ahfinn himself will ordain fight or flight. Ganaron, you oversee our hostages. Pyvv: supplies. And now,*" he had concluded. "*I go to prepare for this battle. I will see you all at dinner—where we will all laugh at how moot these orders have been.*"

Moot indeed! Ahfinn snorted as he pondered the unhappy present. The whole mess had begun to unwind when Vorinn had tricked Zeff out of the rest of the regalia. Not that Zeff had really had any choice once affairs had been set in motion. But he could have anticipated, could have established a contingency.

And now...

"Orders," someone prompted.

"Secure the hold," Ahfinn yelled back from pure reflex. Then, to a young man who had come rushing down the stairs, and who he knew to be one of the lookouts: "What's Eron doing? Not those we can see, those we can't!"

"Milling about like ants whose hill has been upset. But they're armed. I saw swords everywhere—drawn, and those who wield them pressing forward."

"Into the gap? Or have they come through it already?"

"They're as...hesitant as we, it seems. I think what just happened surprised them as much as it did us. I—"

"They *are* gone, sir," a young man panted, having just run up the pontoon bridge from the dueling square. Ahfinn recognized him as one of the seconds—the one with Zeff's helm, in fact, which he still bore. Ahfinn snatched it impulsively but did not put it on. A ring of gems sparkled on the forehead. Zeff had set them there, trusting no one else, relying on smithcraft learned in his youth. The rest was Avall's work—in replica. And still the most beautiful helm Ahfinn had ever seen.

"Someone give me a sword," Ahfinn snapped. "And bring Zeff's shield—the one he should have worn in that accursed duel. I'm no soldier, but it's still my duty to lead. And if I die, that is my duty as well."

Both shield and sword appeared, as if by magic. Ahfinn paused to sheathe the sword in his belt, then, with the shield in one hand and the helm in the other, strode onto the pontoon bridge. "Dammit! Secure the bloody *hold*!" he shouted, as he reached the center, turning around to face the arcade's door. "And get this water rising; Tryffon's bound to be scenting blood. Now find me a herald and prepare for attack. I'm going to try to parley, but I want a secure hold at my back. Move every archer we've got to this end. And get the hostages back on the galleries. No, never mind. We don't have time for that."

And with those orders still ringing in the air, he continued on, trying to match his steps to the bounce-and-jounce of the bridge, and not entirely succeeding. He met Zeff's remaining seconds there, looking as confused and apprehensive as he felt. The Royalists clumped at the other end of the platform, near the causeway, looking no more certain of what had transpired than Ahfinn's men.

"What happened?" Ahfinn demanded. "Are they—?"

"Truly gone, as far as I can tell," a Ninth Face warrior replied. "They hit the water, and then it was like seeing the shadows of two fish in there, and then blood was flowing, and we couldn't see a thing, and then it was like the two of them... rippled, and they were gone as if they had never existed."

"Sorcery!" one of the King's men spat.

"If sorcery, it is yours!" Ahfinn shot back, turning to glare at Vorinn's four allies. Sturdy men, they were. Grim men. Men in their prime. Men who, by the rules of the contest, had no swords. Unfortunately, by those same rules, neither did Ahfinn's.

Steps slapped loud on the bridge behind him. A young man dashed up, flush-faced, but in a herald's tabard. "You asked for—"

"Go find Tryffon syn Ferr—or whoever is Vorinn's deputy. Demand to see Avall. If they deny you, tell them—tell them that a hostage dies every day until he shows himself."

"Sir," the herald challenged bravely, "once we have done that, there will be no reason for them not to level this hold."

"While the water stands, their arrows can't reach it, and there's the same problem with the trebuchets they've always had. Now don't argue. No, wait— Tell them that... what just happened was neither our wish nor our command. Tell them I will stand here undefended save by my own hand until I have reply; that I do this as a sign of good faith."

"As you will, Lord," the herald replied with a curt bow. He turned neatly and strode with cold dignity past Vorinn's seconds, who, respecting the sanctity of the youth's office, parted to give him passage.

Without a word, the Royalists turned and fell in behind the herald, not hurrying, though their backs faced enemy arrows unprotected.

Ahfinn found himself alone in the center of the platform, with all of a besieged hold behind him and an angry Kingdom on the verge of facing him down. This was a balance point, he realized: a crux of time, space, and history.

Time passed.

An eternity for Ahfinn, but no more than a hundred breaths in fact.

He heard the thunder of hooves before he saw them, and knew at once that it was not his herald returning.

It was Tryffon, Veen, and old Preedor, all sitting fully armed on horseback, with what looked like the entire Royal Army, some afoot, some mounted, pouring through the gap behind them onto the newly uncovered ground. And every third one of them, to guess, carried a scaling ladder—which could reach the battlements of the viewing plaza, now that the moat had been pulled back and no soldiers—or hostages—commanded the heights above them. The horses couldn't get up to the plaza, granted, but in this kind of fighting, horses didn't matter.

The hold was vulnerable, too, if only at the door behind him. The attackers would have to fight in rising water, but so would his own soldiers. And the controls that worked the locks that dammed the river were only two rooms behind the entrance to the arcade. And if the Royal Army got that far...

The Ninth Face might well be doomed.

More boots rang on the bridge behind him: many pairs, and heavy. Mail jingled; leather creaked; metal clanged against more metal. Ahfinn turned casually, trying to appear calm, and saw Ninth Face soldiers marching out of the single door and across the narrow bridge. Not an endless stream, but a steady one.

"We came to fight," the first one announced. His fellows crowded up behind. "We've had enough sitting, the lads and I. We'll die here, or not, but we're not going back inside. The rest—it's their say, but your orders. But we won't leave you to die out here alone, and we can't let you be captured." Without another word, those knights fanned out to either side—maybe thirty of them, effectively filling the platform. Ahfinn, paused for a breath, then passed his shield to a soldier for as long as it took to don Zeff's helm. That accomplished, he retrieved the shield again, but remained where he was, waiting for the first man to come over the wall. A glance behind showed the door closing at last; a glance to where the water that surrounded the platform lapped against the wall showed that it might have risen a finger's width. Or perhaps that darkness merely marked where it had splashed. Unfortunately, the locks could only be closed so fast, and the Ri-Megon would not be hurried.

Breath hissed loud in his helm, and sweat streamed into his eyes, but still Ahfinn remained where he was—waiting.

It occurred to him, then, that he wore Zeff's shield and helmet and that both were very likely...magic. They would have blood, Zeff had said; blood would power them. The helm would enhance his will. The shield would absorb any force brought to bear against it. At least that was what Avall's regalia had done. He had no idea whether Zeff's versions would evince those same powers, for Zeff had never confided anything about his work with the new gems.

But Zeff was not Avall.

And he certainly was not the *smith* Avall had been.

Yet if Ahfinn had a fault, it was curiosity, and if he had two, the second was impatience. It was therefore no surprise that he found that he could wait no longer. A deep breath, and he slapped the helm hard enough to bring forth blood from the barb within it, which was also hard enough to send that blood to the gems in the war helm's brow. At the same time, he squeezed the grip within the shield.

Power answered—but not enough; he knew that in an instant. It was weak and tentative, and eased into his body like warm syrup, not hot wine. Yet for all that, his shield arm suddenly felt stronger, and his vision had grown more acute, so that he found himself staring at the forces still crowding their way through the gap half a shot away, and could now hear their voices, as though a wall had lifted from between them.

Yet so intent was he on those odd new sensations that when the first scaling ladder slammed into the wall six spans from his feet, he started—for to him that impact had sounded like thunder. Without thought, he dashed toward it, even as the more seasoned knights around him surged past him on either side, swords hissing from their scabbards, shields rising to cover knee to chin. He was awash in a sea of blue and white, and then, somehow, he had moved past it—exactly as the first head showed above the rampart. He hewed at it from reflex, but a sword stabbed upward beside it, narrowly missing his throat. He hewed again, and again the sword swung—but this time he met it with his shield.

And felt nothing. The sword might as well have been paper. And he who had wielded it drew back—not a completely destroyed blade, as contact with Avall's magic shield would have produced, but one whose edge, nevertheless, was dull and smoking.

And since Ahfinn had not had to absorb the force of that blow with his body, he had strength to push forward instead—and slammed the shield into the face of the man who had now scaled another two rungs to meet it. The man screamed and toppled, hanging by one hand for a moment before falling to the ground four spans below. Someone beside Ahfinn grabbed the top of the ladder and pushed. The ladder swung backward into the air, but not far enough. It smacked into the parapet again.

And then another touched down right beside it, and all Ahfinn knew was fighting.

It was thirty to three hundred, however—or three thousand—and Tryffon, like Ahfinn himself and most of his Ninth Face brethren, was tired of waiting. Ahfinn therefore found himself and his companions quickly forced back by Royalist elite. The water was higher now: lapping across the edges of the platform. In another hand it would be too deep for anyone on foot to essay. As for himself, he had maybe another dozen breaths in which to decide a course of action from among the three choices he confronted: to die there, to let himself be captured, or to retreat.

The latter was most likely, for already he was in the center of the platform, with the Royalists making slow progress along the narrow walk that led to it. Some slipped and fell, and some of those fell victim to his comrades. Some of his comrades, too, had jumped into the water and were hewing at the feet and legs of the Royal Army. Yet fighting was all but impossible when water was rising around one's ribs and the range of possible blows thereby limited.

"Do we retreat?" a man gasped beside him: the first time anyone had posed that question so nakedly. The man's face was calm but grim. He had brown eyes, Ahfinn saw, which was rare.

"We—"

Ahfinn never got to finish his sentence, for, with a roar like a waterfall exploding into being, the water to his right burst upward in a bubble of white, gray, and blue that became a lacy geyser that seemed to freeze in place for the briefest instant before subsiding. And rising from it came—impossibly—a slim young man on horseback, gold-helmed, with a shield of the same, and waving a sword that could only have one name.

Two others rode with him, one behind the other: a man, and, pressed hard against his back, a woman. Both—incredibly—held on as the beast surged out of the water, and—in one impossible leap—landed on the platform between Ahfinn and the vanguard of Eron's army.

A twitch of the rider's arm sent lightning arcing across the hold beneath the lowest gallery. The woman was off the horse and on her feet by then, and reached up to snatch something from the sheltered place between soldier and saddle. She flourished it aloft for all to see, not bothering to unsheathe the sword she also wore.

Ahfinn recognized her in a flash, though he had never met her.

Merryn.

Merryn san Argen-a: Avall the High King's sister.

And in her hand...

Black hair, blank eyes, slack mouth, stump of neck still dripping red...

Zeff.

With a flourish of her wrist that precisely matched the disdainful sneer that curled her lips, Merryn dropped the head to the pavement. It splashed in the finger-deep water there, and rolled onto one ear, gazing up at Ahfinn.

Ahfinn felt his blood turn to ice.

And then Avall syn Argen-a raised the Lightning Sword, and Ahfinn knew fear indeed.

CHAPTER XXVII:

THE HARROWING OF GEM-HOLD

(NORTHWESTERN ERON: GEM-HOLD-WINTER—NEAR-AUTUMN: DAY II—SHORTLY PAST NOON)

It was one of the hardest things Avall had ever done: holding that sword motionless in his hand. For—in spite of the helm, the shield, and the balance they in theory provided—the Lightning Sword was clamoring for release. *Full* release—in thunder, lightning, and storms. He could feel the whole weight of the Overworld poised there, invisible at its tip, demanding to be called into Avall's realm as raw, naked power.

Whether this was the darkest side of his own will manifesting or the power of the gems themselves trying to act in his behalf in the most profligate manner possible, he had no idea. All he knew was that, after the first bolt—which had still been weak, as he himself was still weak from this latest jump—it was all he could do to control the thing.

His only option was to let go—slowly—cutting off all but residual blood from the gem.

While trying not to show it.

"Lower the floodgates now!" he shouted. "Or I will bring this hold down around you. One blast of this sword and everyone before me burns—or boils—alive. One on that door and

we enter however and in what number we will. You have
lost—whoever you are. I will now receive your surrender."

It was a good speech, anyway, Avall supposed. And maybe it
would save some lives. But this was not the time to contemplate
such things, as he sat there waiting for reply—it seemed forever,
though he knew that perception was in part a function of the way
the gems shifted his sense of time. His heart beat loud. He could
feel the sun on his back, already sucking the moisture from his
clothes. River water ran into his eyes, but he managed not to blink.

And before him, moving as if in a dream, a young fellow—
not much older than he was, he suspected—wore the helm he
had made as a replica of his own master one, and carried the
shield that twinned the one upon his arm. That other's sword,
however, was plain.

"Your name," he barked, to break the restless silence that
was suddenly a weight around him.

"Ahfinn," the young Ninth Face warrior replied, with no
trace of hesitation whatsoever—which could reflect either
bravery or fanaticism. Avall prayed it was not the latter.

"Do you command this hold?"

"In the name of—of Zeff—I was *given* command of it."

"To hold against your King, or to surrender?"

"To do either as my will and conscience demand. But I am
only one man, Majesty. Each and every warrior of the Ninth
Face must act as his heart requires."

Avall shook his head. The sword twitched. Like many
other people—like Vorinn and Zeff, and Merryn and Rann,
and probably this Ahfinn as well—he was tired of playing
games of feint and parry. And deathly tired of waiting.

His hand squeezed—once—and as quickly released. But
that one gesture was sufficient. All that pent-up power arced
from the sword and slammed into the wooden door seven
spans behind where Ahfinn was standing. It also struck two of
his loyal guard who had retreated there. One toppled where he
stood; one fell into the water. They had played the soldier's
gamble; one had lost, the other had even odds.

The door itself was blown to splinters.

"Remain where you are," Avall warned Ahfinn frankly, "and I will either ride through you or over you, but neither way will you survive. Pass to the side now, and you will live. You will undergo trial as a traitor, but you will live—until Law—which belongs to your clan, not mine—rules otherwise."

Ahfinn did not move for a moment, and then, with quiet calm, he removed his helm and passed it—to Avall's surprise—to Merryn. His shield he bestowed upon Rann, and then, without looking either to right or left, he laid his sword on the pavement before him—and joined the throng of loyal Eronese behind Avall.

"Stay close," Avall called to him over his shoulder. "I will need a guide." A pause, then: "Tryffon, if you will assist me?"

Tryffon made his way forward. Somehow he had managed to get himself drenched with blood in spite of the very brief battle, but he looked happy, if wary and surprised, as Avall—who did not wish to relinquish the regalia yet, however much it cost him—climbed down from faithful Boot. "Where's Vorinn?" Tryffon rasped into Avall's ear as their heads came close together.

"Well, but far away. I had to leave him, else I would not be here now. That's all I know, and all I have time for at present. Look for him in a breath—or in a season. The same applies to all of them. For now, we have a hold to reclaim, a situation to reassess—and still a narrow way to travel if we are to reach that goal. Likely a fair bit of resistance, too—which I am sure will delight you no end. But I see we now have a spare magic shield and helmet."

"My own will be more than sufficient," Tryffon rumbled.

"Go by my will and with Fate's blessings," Avall told those soldiers—mostly members of Common Clan, he noted—who had gathered around him. One maneuvered Boot aside so that Tryffon and the bulk of what remained of the Night Guard could make their way across the pontoon bridge. Avall expected them to meet at least token resistance there and in the arcade beyond, but no such opposition was forthcoming.

A hand later, the southern fifth of the hold was secure, and the water around it was receding at roughly a quarter span every hand—they dared not drain it faster for fear of damaging the locks, as well as the quays and fishing holds downstream. Which was not to say that the harrowing of the hold was not slow going, for they had to progress a stair, a hallway, and a room at a time, checking all doors and hiding places as they went. And there were indeed pockets of resistance, though those were few—Zeff had evidently maintained loyalty mostly from force of personality, or, more recently, fear of what was reported by many of his men as something close kin to madness. Most of the holders they found neatly bound—some in their clan quarters, some in the weather-locks adjacent to the arcades, a few as though they had simply been trussed up in haste and left in place once that initial binding was complete. He prayed they would find them all; slow starvation in a closet would be a grim death indeed.

As for those few Ninth Face knights who chose to stand and fight, most quelled after he brought Ahfinn up to march alongside him—especially after Ahfinn was given Zeff's head to carry. To Ahfinn's credit, he did so with dignity, though he was clearly scared to death. They were not so unlike, Ahfinn and himself, Avall supposed. Both were competent at many things, talented, and smart. And both had been thrust into positions of power for which they were not suited by temperament, but for which circumstances had nevertheless equipped them, uniquely, to bear: Avall, because he understood the most powerful force in Eron as much as anyone did, and in some small wise controlled it—or was controlled by it, he feared; Ahfinn, because in a hold full of scholar-specialists, he was the only one Zeff, for whatever reason, had dared entrust with knowledge of his weaknesses. What would happen to Ahfinn now, he had no idea. That was for Law to determine.

For the present, Ahfinn had information Avall needed, and that was enough to ensure his survival. "Crim," Avall demanded of the Ninth Face's erstwhile commander. "And Rrath: as soon as may be, take me to them."

"Crim is in her quarters, tied to her bed—or should be."

"With how many fingers?" Tryffon snapped.

"All she was born with but one," Ahfinn answered calmly.

"Pray you speak the truth," Avall muttered. "And these quarters, I believe, are—"

"Farther on—Majesty," Ahfinn finished for him.

It was another hand before they found the former Hold-Warden, courtesy of a particularly persistent pocket of militant Ninth Facers that had to be cleared out. There couldn't be many left, Avall reckoned, for word of its liberation had spread through the hold like fire, and as the Royal Army advanced through it, not only were more of his soldiers available to take captives, but the former hostages often as not rose up in advance of their liberators and delivered their captors to them. More than one party of Eronese warriors came upon groups of Ninth Face knights neatly tied up for their disposal.

They found Crim's suite easily enough—locked—and had to break through the door. And once inside, they found the deposed Hold-Warden as well—bound to her bed, as Ahfinn had predicted—but also with a gaping wound across her throat, and her sheets dyed crimson with gore. "Dead," Avall said dully, for he had liked Crim as well as he had known her, and respected her administrative skills as much as anyone's he knew.

Rann took it even harder. He rounded on Ahfinn, murder thick in his eyes. "Do you have any idea who—?"

But before Ahfinn could reply, a pair of Night Guardsmen came tromping up—with a white-faced man squirming in near panic between them. "Ishvarr syn Myrk'," the taller guard volunteered, indicating himself. "And loyal cousin to Hold-Warden Crim, I might add. We found this scum in Gem-Hold colors, trying to escape. I didn't recognize him—but I *did* recognize some unique pieces of jewelry he had with him that once belonged to my kinswoman."

"He has blood on his hands, too," the other Guardsman supplied. "And was trying to rid himself of a bloody dagger."

Avall's face went hard and grim. His blood seemed to run colder in his veins. "You have this dagger?"

"Aye."

"Give it to this man." He indicated the wide-eyed Ahfinn. Ishvarr hesitated but an instant, then did as commanded. Ahfinn blinked in confusion. Avall fixed him with an icy stare, then nodded toward the ash-faced prisoner. "Your man: your clan: your justice," Avall informed Ahfinn coldly. "You know the sentence for murderers. If he leaves this hold alive, this man's fate will be the same—but he will suffer longer."

Ahfinn's face turned whiter than the accused's, but bit his lip and, before anyone expected it, stabbed the murderer-thief beneath the ribs, then drove the blade upward with a sharp, deft twist. The man whimpered once, then went limp. Ahfinn left the weapon where it stood as the Guardsmen released the lifeless body and let it topple.

Ishvarr relieved the thief of the stolen treasure and returned it to Crim's suite, then gently closed the door and rejoined Avall's party in the hall. Leaving the corpse in a spreading pool of his own blood, they continued down the corridor.

"Rrath," Avall reminded Ahfinn curtly. "Now."

"He should be in Zeff's private quarters. At least that's where I saw him last," Ahfinn replied carefully.

"He had best be alive, is all I can say," Avall growled.

The suite Zeff had claimed as his base was more austere than Avall would have expected of even a minor Chief, then again, Zeff was Priest-Clan, and they prided themselves on asceticism. A door to the left led from the common hall to what was clearly Zeff's sleeping chamber. A small wooden box stood on a bare stone table there—nothing remarkable, yet it drew

Avall's gaze like a lodestone. Ahfinn saw him looking. "Majesty," he said impulsively, "if I may..."

"Careful," Tryffon warned. "It could be a trap."

"No trap," Ahfinn countered. "On my life."

"Which belongs to us, in any case."

"Let him," Avall broke in. "We're waiting."

Ahfinn deposited Zeff's head in what had most likely been the Chief's favorite chair, to judge by the patterns of wear, then retrieved the box. It rattled when he picked it up. Avall was taken aback when Ahfinn approached again, knelt suddenly before him, flipped the box's lid open, and raised it so that he could see inside.

Red glittered there.

Gems.

Magic gems. Not many, and most were small—some smaller than the fragments he had salvaged from his own smashed master gem—yet it was without doubt a treasure trove, and a power trove along with it. "All we could find before we flooded the mines," Ahfinn explained, rising. "The rest are in the sword, shield, and helmet Zeff took to the duel. If there are more—"

"I doubt there are," Avall murmured. "At least not here."

Tryffon regarded him sharply.

"Rrath," Avall prompted, looking around. "And could someone find Esshill? He will want to be here."

"He's here now!" someone called from the outer chamber. "If you mean that little former Priest who's been following us around." A moment later, and not without a bit of pushing and jostling, the crowd of Night Guard in the doorway parted to admit a slight figure still clad in the Argen-a livery he seemed to have adopted as his own. Then again, Esshill probably did not feel comfortable claiming his own clan just then. He bowed deeply when he saw Avall, then stood up straighter. "Majesty?"

"I thought you would want to be here," Avall told him simply. "I heard how you conspired with Kylin to effect my rescue. Sleeping draught, wasn't it? To give Kylin time to sneak out of camp so he could be taken prisoner here? And while I don't approve of your methods, I do approve of loyalty to Sovereigns—and to bond-mates. I also understand it very, very well." He turned back toward Ahfinn. "Well, where is he?"

Ahfinn dipped his head to the right. "Last door to the right. There's a corridor—"

Tryffon bent close enough to mutter into Avall's ear. "Might as well try them all, lad—just in case. And if they're locked, do what you must to open them."

"I've got the keys," Ahfinn murmured under his breath.

"Then use them!" Avall snapped, tired of having his patience tested.

Ahfinn nodded smoothly and reached for his belt pouch. "As you will."

The first room contained only a chair, a tapestry, and a rug, and was clearly a private meditatorium. The second was a strongroom of some kind, and contained, among other things, an impressive stone table-safe. The last gave onto a short corridor off which more rooms opened—possibly guest rooms for whoever claimed the main suite, but easily enough converted into cells. Kylin had stayed in one, Avall recalled—from which he had been brought out to play on command, like a pet or a toy.

The third one contained Rrath syn Garnill.

At first Avall thought he was as dead as Crim had been, for he was lying in almost the same position Crim's corpse had displayed: on his back, with his hands folded on his breast, and everything below his armpits hidden beneath a blanket of dull tan wool. In spite of the covering, it was obvious that he had lost weight—which he could ill afford, given that he had been shockingly thin already. But then Avall saw the slow rise and fall of his chest and breathed a small sigh of relief himself.

Veen—who had done a double tour at Healing, and had attached herself to the army's healers in her free time—checked his pulse and pronounced it slow, but strong and even. "He'll live," she informed Avall, who had not entered the room. Esshill was hanging back too, probably grown afraid of what he might find. But now that he had heard—

Avall eased aside for the priest to enter, watching as the man immediately sank to the floor beside Rrath's bed and reached up to grasp his bond-brother's hand, oblivious to everyone present. "I'm here," Esshill whispered. "I won't ever leave you again, and I'll do whatever I can to help you recover."

Avall watched for a moment longer, then leaned over to Veen. "There's nothing to be gained by staying, and nothing to be harmed by leaving him here for now," he whispered. "Just don't forget them when we leave. And—" He paused. Something had just occurred to him. He still had the box of gems Ahfinn had given him—and he now had proof positive that such gems could sometimes, in time, heal damaged minds. Impulsively, he eased over to where Esshill sat, hunkered down beside him, and opened the box. "Esshill," he murmured, extending the container, "maybe one of these will help. You'll have to choose, and I can promise nothing, but Veen can show you when things are a bit more settled. For now—look at these, and see if one doesn't...connect to you. Touch them if you have to, or—"

He got no further because Esshill had reached out and taken the third-from-smallest stone—less than half the size of a pea—between two fingers of his right hand. "This one," he announced with conviction.

"Take it—for now," Avall told him. "Work with it. See what you can do. I'll need to have it back, of course—and you'll have to remain under watch while you're working with it. But it's the least I can do for the two of you. Believe me, I truly do understand."

That small kindness accomplished, he rose and returned to the corridor, moving thence through Zeff's bedchamber to his common hall.

He had just strode into the larger corridor outside when he felt the floor buck upward beneath him, then subside. A general quivering followed, as though the hold were some vast beast trying to shake itself free of water.

"Earthquake!" someone shouted, as stone dust trickled down from a ceiling that—fortunately—held.

"Maybe," Rann agreed. "Or maybe not."

Avall met his gaze, eyes grim with concern. "What do you mean?"

"It could just as easily be the hold settling," Rann replied. "With all the lower levels flooded, never mind the mines, there's no telling how much damage has been done to the structure of this place. In fact," he added, to Merryn, Tryffon, and Avall alone, "I fear it may have to be abandoned—or leveled to its foundations and rebuilt from scratch."

"What about the gems?" Merryn hissed.

Avall patted the box he still held. "I think we've found all there are to find—here. And I think that if there *are* any more, we have the means to locate them."

Merryn scowled and looked as though she were about to speak, before she finally settled on nodding.

Avall caught Tryffon's gaze in turn. "In any case, Chief, I'd suggest we conclude this sweep expeditiously. I'd also recommend—no, make that command—that, as much as I know people will hate it, everyone sleeps outside tonight. That includes former hostages, present hostages—everyone. If Rann doesn't trust this place, I certainly don't. People can gather what they will until sunset, and we'll let smaller groups in to salvage for as long as they need to do so afterward; but until we can get some folks up here from Stone—people I don't need with *me*, Rann—we had best consider this place restricted. Which also means we'll have to post a guard."

"Which wouldn't be a problem," Merryn retorted, "if it didn't look like we'd need everyone we have and then some if we're ever going to retake Tir-Eron."

"Sister," Avall sighed, squeezing her hand, "once again you have read my mind."

CHAPTER XXVIII:

PLOTTING IN A MAZE

~~~~~~~~

"It's too big a risk," Ilfon hissed. "And it's certainly too big a risk to take right now. I don't have to remind you that neither of us is what one would call unobtrusive."

Tyrill glared at him from a shaded niche in the much-neglected hedge maze behind Smith-Hold-Main. Pale new growth along the edges shielded much of the interior, including the stone bench on which they sat, facing each other, feet drawn up before them. Long cloaks the color of fading foliage draped their shoulders, while hoods far overhung their faces, so that only their bright eyes showed.

"We couldn't be more unobtrusive than we are now," Tyrill muttered back. "I can barely see you, and this is broad daylight, and you half a span away."

"You know what I'm talking about, Tyrill."

She reached over and tweaked his nose playfully, as she had not done to anyone since she was a girl running wild behind this very hold. As she was now doing *many* things she had not done since then, she reflected. Like playing hide-and-find within this same maze—often as not with Eellon in those days. That seemed a thousand years ago, too, not eighty. That was before the plague had taken more than half of her adult kin, before rivalry had sundered her from Eellon, who should by rights have been her closest friend. Before anyone had dreamed of a handsome young Argen-a King named Gynn. Before the names that now rattled in her head in a litany of the living mingled with the lately dead had, any of them, been born. Eddyn—he always came first. And Avall and Merryn and Strynn. And then Rann and Lykkon. Nor could she omit Preedor or Tryffon, who had sworn in open council never to share space with her again, unless the King command it. There had been plague and war; but they had consumed barely two years between them. The rest—there had been wonderful things: friends and travel and the crafting of marvelous things out of metal—including, she was secretly proud to say, the sword, shield, and helmet that comprised the new royal regalia, which were by all reasonable standards the marvels of that, or any, age.

Ilfon grunted and rubbed his nose, jolting Tyrill back to the present. "What was that about?"

"We could always break it again," Tyrill chuckled. "If you think the new shape isn't disguise enough."

Ilfon spared her a warning grin. "Let me remind you, Lady, that there are still parts of you that could be broken without imparing your . . . functionality. You've far too many teeth for a clanless goodwife, for instance. And, to be serious for a moment, we really should think about obliterating our clan tattoos. Yes, I know you don't want to do that because it's something the Ninth Face does, but it truly would afford some protection."

"It would," Tyrill conceded, "but most of life reduces at some point to what one wants to worry about. I choose to worry, first of all, about my country, my clan, and my craft, and that's why I'm here with a blowgun up my sleeve. If I just wanted to be warm and fed, there are any number of places I could be. If making was still my concern, I could head north, hire on at a Common Clan hold, and probably live there in peace making horseshoes and dinnerware until Priest-Clan stumbled on me. And at that, I'd lay odds of my dying a natural death in bed before that occurred. If you've noticed, for all their pride before the coup, they're not very good at actually making things happen."

"That's because most of their really good people are doing what they've always done, and ignoring the new power structure entirely."

"And since most of the other really good people are dead or in hiding—by which I mean our fellow Chiefs, among others—that leaves their least-well-equipped people to handle the most difficult tasks. Eight, Ilfon, even I didn't know how much depended on the system of clans and crafts until it shattered. It makes me feel proud, in an odd sort of way."

"Not that you need an excuse to feel proud," Ilfon snorted.

Another glare. "You don't have to stay here, *youngster*. I can do what I came to do on my own."

Ilfon scowled at her. "May I remind you that I can't leave until dark—now that you've actually got me in here."

"You should have considered that when I suggested we sneak in here before dawn this morning."

"What I was considering was an old woman—and an old friend—putting herself at considerable risk for something stupid. As you said, Lady, it was what I chose to worry about."

"Well, you shouldn't!"

"I—" Ilfon broke off abruptly. Something had rattled twigs nearby. Tyrill held her breath, even as he did. The rattle became a full-scale symphony of small outdoor noises: twigs, leaves, and branches being bent, pushed, and strewn about. And then came a flash of gray right past their hiding place, and a graceful arch of curving tail—with, right behind it, a larger splash of pursuing yellow: squirrel and cat, in their age-old game, with two birds behind, cheering on the action.

"Someone else who isn't worried about the Ninth Face," Tyrill laughed.

Ilfon's face went serious. Holding his breath, he thrust his head outside and gazed quickly at the sky. "It's getting close to time, if you're still determined to do this crazy thing."

Tyrill patted her voluminous sleeve. "We're running out of darts, in case you haven't noticed. I've got exactly five glass ones, and that's all—and Elvix says she can't get more until Tozri returns at Sundeath—"

"—Which he may not do, if he hears what's going on here."

Another snort. "Either that, or he'll return with Kraxxi leading the Ixtian army—overtly to restore his friend and ally—who has not, let me remind you, officially been deposed—but one would have to wonder."

"Ambition dies slowly," Ilfon agreed. "I have only to look across from me to see clear proof of that."

Another glare. "The fact is, Ilfon, that we need more darts if we're going to continue our little subversive action. We can't get more glass ones, but if I can get some bloodwire, I could make some that would do almost as well. The problem is, there are exactly two sources of bloodwire right now: One is in the forges beneath the Citadel; the other is in Smith-Hold. The first is out of the question, which leaves the second. Unfortunately, the only viable time to get into Smith-Hold is when the place is least well guarded, which is the middle of the afternoon. The guards are lazy then—because they've become used to most of the trouble happening at night—and there are so few of them that most of those that *are* present are half-asleep, because they've already worked a shift. Besides, if we—I—*do* encounter anyone, there's a good chance it will be an ally, or at least someone who won't betray me. *Besides,* old beggar women are everywhere, or haven't you noticed?"

"Not at a major hold's usually well-secured back door."

A shrug. "Some old women are also confused and stupid. And...Fate will attend the rest."

And with that, Tyrill thrust her head from beneath the arbor. A quick check of the sun's position in the blessedly cloudless sky, and she unfolded herself from the bench, leaving Ilfon to decide for himself whether the time had come for action.

Yet for all their free speech earlier—which really had been safe, since no one could possibly come upon them unawares in the maze—Tyrill was suddenly as silent as Eddyn's statue in the water garden two courtyards to the east. It was a skill she had been forced to cultivate, and not easy at all for someone who could barely walk unassisted. Except that, however ruthless a taskmaster she had always been to Smith-Hold's apprentices, she was ten times as ruthless on herself. Pain was only *a* thing, she told herself over and over. It was not *the* thing. It might pain oneself to walk, but pain was clothes on one's legs, or paint on a coach. The object—and the action—could exist without it, though she had never quite convinced Ilfon of the fact. And if she still needed a cane . . . Well, that was as much for balance as anything, because balance was harder to control in a hurry.

So it was that she had already retuned her movements, emotions, and senses alike to stealth as she made her way out of the maze, the twists and turns of which she had memorized eighty years gone by. Ilfon had no such memories to guide him, and therefore had to rely on her—which she found amusing, since it meant he had to creep along in her wake, and him barely half her age.

They were now one turn from the maze's entrance, and nearing one of the few places where the hedge wall thinned enough to permit a view of the lawn beyond, which could not, however, be entered thusly without cheating the maze. It also made a convenient place from which to observe the back of Smith-Hold-Main.

The part best seen from their new vantage point was the oldest part of the entire hold, built in haste for maximum size, space, and serviceability, before the clan had grown rich enough and accomplished enough—and had married into Stone enough—to produce the more elegant, better-proportioned, and better-detailed structures to either side. Ivy covered most of it now, and close-grown trees gave shade in the few places where light wasn't needed, while also masking a host of architectural sins.

What Tyrill needed was simply to see one door—and see if that door was guarded, for, if nothing else, Priest-Clan tried very hard to be thorough. Certainly, every clan- and craft-hold was guarded, optimally by two soldiers per entrance. But with the Ninth Face's resources stretching ever thinner, and some holds amazingly vast and sprawling, there was no way every entrance could be adequately policed at all times. Happily, this particular door to Smith-Hold was one of the latter. True, it was guarded faithfully every night, and until noon every morning, but after that, Smith's secondary entrances were left unwatched by a complicated but real rotation—one it had taken Ilfon's peculiar brand of logic to puzzle out. Then again, he was Lore, and therefore accustomed to observing such things.

And if things went as they ought, the guard would be leaving his post just about now. If it was the same fellow who usually manned that position, he would yawn a couple of times, scratch his backside, and amble off toward the postern gate to rejoin his Ninth Face fellows.

And there he was, as regular as Argen-el's best clockwork! A nice-looking young man, he was, too, save for a wine-colored birthmark across otherwise fine high cheekbones, which disfigurement he tried to hide with sideburns that were far too wide. Tyrill felt sorry for him. As obsessed with beauty as most of her kind were, he would have stood out at any hold—which perhaps explained why he was a Priest now. No one was ever *born* to Priest-Clan; and they tended to take in all comers.

In any case, his Ninth Face tabard swung jauntily as he started down precisely the path Tyrill had predicted. Which brought him within easy range of her blowgun, had she been fool enough to use it.

She was not. For all her stealthy intentions, the guard was far too visible—and a dead body would be visible far longer than it would take an old woman in a dark green cloak to navigate three spans' worth of paces. Besides, this was daylight, and, while Tyrill was willing to kill foes whose faces she could not distinguish, she had qualms about killing those whose faces she could.

So she waited, resisting a rising urge to let the blowgun slip into her hand.

...rustle, rustle, rustle...

Tyrill nearly jumped out of her skin, and Ilfon was so alarmed for her that he covered her mouth with a hand.

What The Eight had that been?

Ilfon shaped the answer with silent lips: "Cat."

Which would have been perfectly fine, had the noise not made the guardsman turn. For a moment Tyrill thought he was going to ignore the matter and continue on. Indeed, she could all but feel him weighing the decision: *Should he investigate, here at the end of his shift, knowing it was probably nothing, but also knowing that it would be his head on the Citadel's gate with several others if he let anything untoward transpire on what was still, officially, his watch?*

To his credit—and Tyrill's chagrin—the lad proved conscientious. He sighed again, and strode straight toward the hedge—straight toward the thin space behind which Tyrill was hiding, in fact. A hard tap on Ilfon's thigh made him back away, which happened to be toward the entrance. Which was fine. The hedge was thick and dark there, and the entrance wall kinked around both its corners for half a span to form walls, in the angle of which one could hide reasonably effectively.

More rustling, then a loud meow. "Cat! Damned cat," she heard the now-unseen guardsman growl in a scratchy tenor that hinted of an autumn cold. As if to confirm that assessment, he sneezed.

And seemed to be going away—until he suddenly turned again and marched back to the maze's entrance, not a quarter span behind Tyrill's back. Her heart double-beat, then seemed to stop entirely as she waited, trying to free her blowgun silently only to discover that it was stuck. At least if they killed him—if they *could* kill him—he had reached a place where it would be easy to hide the body.

What was he doing, anyway? And then she knew. Fabric scraped, mail jingled, leather hissed, and then more fabric; followed by the sound of liquid striking the foliage behind her with considerable force, accompanied by a low, relieved sigh. Her eyes went wide and Ilfon's wider as fear warred with amusement on both their faces.

And then over.

...rustle, rustle, rustle...

That damned cat again, and closer. If only the lad would ignore it and go on his way. Smith-Hold's cats were no concern of his.

Once again Tyrill's luck held.

And then came the unthinkable.

She sneezed.

She tried desperately to make it a little cat sneeze. But it came on her so suddenly that it rushed out with full human noise and splendor.

"Who's there?" The guard again, with his trews done up and no nonsense at all in his voice.

And then, impossibly, another sneeze.

Tyrill fumbled for her blowgun, but it had lodged between her cuff and the lining of her sleeve. For his part, Ilfon was so alarmed that he was simply staring—only for a breath, granted, but a breath was all it took for a young man to dash into the maze, look first right, then left, and see, however dimly, that he faced, to all appearances, a Common Clan crone and—possibly—her one-son.

At least that would have been the likeliest assessment had Ilfon not that moment managed to free his blowgun—exactly as Tyrill likewise untangled hers from her sleeve—neither with time to load them.

When Fate played games, it appeared, Fate played extravagantly.

"I don't know who you are," the guardsman snapped, leveling his sword at the two of them, while maneuvering himself in such a way that he neatly boxed them into the corner. "What I do know is that there's no way on Angen that you two are flute players, or that those are flutes. In fact, you're"—he stepped closer—recklessly, but it caught them both off guard—and flipped back the edge of Tyrill's hood—"Lady Tyrill. And you—"

Ilfon acted. He heaved himself forward toward the guard, but Fate still had one cruel trick to play and had let a twig in the hedge snare Ilfon's tunic, so that as he leapt forward, it yanked him back again. Which was all it took for the guard to whirl around and slam the flat of his sword into Ilfon's ribs.

"Lady, you will come with me," the guardsman growled. "As for you—" He scowled at Ilfon anxiously, then, with casual, calculated precision, swung his sword's point delicately across the juncture of Ilfon's calf and ankle. Tyrill heard the tendon snap and Ilfon's hiss of pain and anger as blood spurted out upon the green.

"You won't die," the guardsman told him with calm dispassion. "But I don't think you'll be going anywhere, either—not before I can get this one in chains and return with reinforcements."

Tyrill said nothing at all. There was nothing left *to* say. Which left it to Ilfon to lie on the ground and bleed, sweat, and try very hard neither to cry nor swear.

CHAPTER XXIX:

CHOICES

~~~~~~~

"Dammit, I need to *be* there!" Vorinn growled. He was pacing up and down the riverbank, precisely at the juncture where rounded stones gave way to sandbar—stones that he kicked often as not, oblivious to what such useless violence did to his boots. Sand, he simply ignored. It was a beautiful place—or would have been had he not needed to be somewhere else. Lykkon walked beside him, along with Myx and Riff— and for some odd reason, that wretched birkit. *What did they mean, anyway, letting something that wild travel with them like a pet?*

As if hearing his thought, the beast bared its teeth at him, growled, and danced away.

"We don't even know if Avall made it there," he told Lykkon. "All we know is that he isn't here. That none of them are."

"He has to be there," Lykkon retorted quickly. "There's no reason to assume otherwise, given the way you got here."

Vorinn rounded on him, fighting down a rage he certainly had a right to feel, though not to direct at Lykkon—or any man he liked or had soldiered with. "Yes, but assuming he *is* there, he's fighting my fight and probably getting himself killed for his trouble."

"It was *his* fight before it was *your* fight," Lykkon replied calmly. "And he's got better weapons than you had and a lesser foe. The Lightning Sword is the thing the Ninth Face fears most, which is why they were out to get it. Well, they've got it now, and from what you've said, they've got it in a way they can't oppose. They gambled, and they lost."

"That's not why you care, though, is it?" *That* had come, uncharacteristically, from quiet Riff.

Vorinn stopped in place and glared at the younger man. "What are you saying?"

Riff stepped up to him bravely. "What everyone in camp has been thinking since you returned to Tir-Eron: that you want to be King, and would probably make a damned fine one; but that you're too good a man to take the crown from your sister's husband unless you win it fairly."

Vorinn's breath caught. "Do you believe that? Not about me being a good man; I'm not so vain as to need to probe that notion. But about people thinking I would make a good King?"

"I *do* believe it, if that helps. Avall believes it, for that matter, as, I'm sure, does Rann. And I will tell you this absolutely: While Avall was here, he was far, far happier than I ever saw him in Tir-Eron. Maybe not as happy as when he's smithing, but I didn't know him before he got all tangled up with the gems and the war. He doesn't want to be King, but he thinks he's required to be King, anyway, so he's making the best go of it he can."

"Which is why he sent the regalia away to start with," Lykkon put in. "Oh, true, he knew it was a temptation to anyone interested in power—an example of which we've just witnessed. But he wanted it gone a lot more because it was one of the things that had made him King to start with. Anyone who has that much power—explicit or implicit—people expect you to use it, and as many will try to foist it on you as will try to take it away. Gynn might have been the King of Balance, but Avall values balance even more than Gynn did. You, however—this is going to sound strange coming from me, since I tend to analyze everything—but you'd be a good King simply because you'd be a good King. You want the job, and you've got the right allies and the kind of skills we need right now. Avall's both too soft and too hard."

"And," Riff finished for him, "that could kill him—and the artist in all of us knows that would be a crime."

Vorinn cocked a brow. "So you're saying…"

"That Avall should do what he's good at, and so should you."

Vorinn paused, staring at the river. "It's probably over by now, anyway."

Myx shrugged and lifted a brow. "Might not be."

"And how to you propose that I return to Gem-Hold, when I don't even know how I got here?"

Lykkon chuckled softly and laid an arm across Vorinn's wide shoulders, drawing him back toward what was rapidly becoming a proper, if impromptu, camp. "That should be obvious."

"Not to me!" Vorinn grumbled. "I know it has to do with the gems, but that's all. When I came here, I was just trying to get the sword away from Zeff."

"That sword's still here, and all the power it contains."

"You're saying that I could—"

"I'm saying that you might be able to. It makes sense to me, and I know a fair bit about those things. To jump apparently requires three things. It takes a gem, preferably a big one that likes you, but apparently a bunch of small ones will do just as well; it takes blood to wake it and usually warm bodies around to power it; and it takes will. We've got all of those things. As far as I can tell, all you have to do is blood yourself on the hilt and wish. And something tells me you'll have no trouble with the wishing."

"What about the rest of you?"

Lykkon folded his arms and frowned, kicking at a stone. "I don't know. We could add our wills, but that might also cause problems, since one of us might want something else more than you wanted to get back to Gem-Hold. Or one of us might think we wanted one thing and find we were really wanting another—like what probably brought you here."

Vorinn regarded him incredulously. "I already knew you were brilliant, Lykkon. But I never knew how much so. Whatever happens—if I survive, and whether or not I become King—there'll always be a place for you where I am."

Lykkon grinned, and Vorinn remembered all over that the lad was still only nineteen. For another few eights, at least.

By which time they had reached the camp. Strynn looked up at him from where she was calmly drinking dilute cauf with Div while studying what had been Zeff's sword. "Not bad work here," she announced, "though the edge could be a lot better. The gems...they're small, but I can feel the power in them. They're probably tuned to Zeff, but I've no doubt you could master them, since they seem to like me, and I'm blood kin to you. If you're lucky, they won't even contain a death, which seems to be the worst thing that can happen to gems—and even that can be cured."

Vorinn stared at her. "You're all like this, aren't you? Eaten up with the wonder of those damned things."

"It's a matter of survival," Strynn replied with a wary smile. And with that she laid the blade across her forearm and extended the blade, hilt first, to her brother. "You want to go; you need to go; I think you probably have to go—and now you've got a way to go. There's nothing else I can tell you."

Vorinn chose to ignore the weapon for the nonce. "What about the rest of you? I can't in good conscience leave you, but if you go—" He glanced at those gathered around: Strynn, Div, Riff, Myx, Lykkon, Bingg—and poor tortured Krynneth and blind Kylin. "Some of you aren't soldiers," he finished roughly.

"Soldier enough to save Avall," Myx retorted, looking at

Kylin, who was saying nothing at all. Krynneth's eyes were as hard as Vorinn's last words had been. "Soldiering doesn't always mean swinging a sword."

"In any case," Strynn continued, "it's everyone's free choice. We're not in Eron, by any reasonable definition, so Eronese law doesn't hold, save as we acknowledge it. And even if it did, I'm Queen by implication and Consort in all but fact, and that gives me power to decide such things in the absence of the King. Nor are you King yet, oh my brother."

"But you. I can't leave you here—but you—you can't stay here unprotected! You're—"

"Actually very wise to stay here," Strynn replied tartly. "There hasn't been time to tell you, thanks to your unorthodox entry and apparently hasty exit, but I now bear Avall's heir—heirs, actually, since I think they're going to be twins."

Vorinn's tense expression broke into a grin. "Twins! Does...does Avall know?"

"Of course."

Vorinn shook his head. "Yes, naturally he does. It's just that there are so many things these days that people *don't* know—"

Strynn regarded him levelly. "Yes, I know." A deep breath, then: "Brother, there's something else you don't know and probably need to know. It's something so new in my thinking—in our thinking, actually—that sometimes I hardly know it myself."

"Go on."

Another breath. Strynn's gaze swept around those assembled there as if seeking permission to speak further, then met his gaze again. "You brought it up all unknowing, so I might as well finish it," she began, then paused again and went on, with obvious difficulty. "I really am thinking of staying here more or less permanently. We all are, actually—once all this is settled."

"You're mad!"

Strynn raised a hand to silence him, in a gesture Vorinn knew better than to challenge. "No, hear me! The men started it first, mostly as a function of practical speculation when they thought they were stranded here—an eight south of here, to be precise. I'm not talking about anything as major as a craft-hold or anything," she went on quickly. "In fact, I wouldn't want that. But that's getting off what needs to be our focus here. To return to where we were, we've found—and this surprises me as much as anyone, let me tell you—we've found that we—none of us—are happy with all the rules and rites and responsibilities that come with living in Eron. We think—*think*, mind you—that we could get by here without a lot of them, still have a decent life, and all be a whole lot happier."

Vorinn could restrain himself no longer. "Who," he snapped, "is we?"

Strynn's voice remained calm, though she frowned ever so slightly. "Basically everyone who was here when you arrived, with some qualifications. No one would have to stay," she stressed. "But everyone who was here is warm to the idea in theory—and yes, that includes Avall. Myx and Riff, in particular, like the idea, and think their consorts would like it as well. We'd have to work hard, of course—much harder than we might be used to—but we've all got a solid grounding in basic survival skills, and we could recruit people—carefully—from Eron, though no more than twenty or so, I think."

"Why carefully?"

"Because we wouldn't want anyone to know we were here, not least because people might—rightly or wrongly—try to link us to the Lightning Sword and come seeking it, which could ruin everything."

Vorinn's frown deepened. "So Avall hasn't changed his thinking about that?"

Strynn shook her head. "Only in the short term. But I can't imagine him changing it in the long term, either, since any plan to retain it in Tir-Eron would simply put him back where he was—a miserably unhappy man cut off by circumstance from pursuing what he does best and loves most."

"Sister, do you know what you're saying?"

"I think I do," Strynn replied carefully. "Let me stress that this is new thinking—dreaming around the campfire kind of stuff. But it would solve so many of our current problems. In fact, the only problem it would really create beyond the obvious is how we would resolve our ingrained sense of responsibility with this. But Merryn has the most trouble with that idea—and she's warming to it herself, if for no other reason because she thinks she has to protect me and her brother."

"But—"

"This wouldn't be exile, Vorinn. We would still visit Eron when and if we wanted to and needed to. We've our own fortunes to finance a lot of this, and no lack of contacts—if they live—who would help us, surreptitiously, with supplies and such. We—"

"What about Averryn?"

"What about him? He's in very good hands, from everything I've heard. And there's no reason those hands—or others like them—can't bring Averryn here."

Vorinn regarded her incredulously. "You really do mean it! You're going to stay here."

"Maybe. If enough other folks agree to stay—or join us—to assure a reasonable life. Rest assured, brother, I'm far too spoiled and selfish—and far, far too much a hedonist—to want to spend the rest of my life foraging for food. But it would only take a few people with the right skills to set up a decently functional hold. And very little time—for the simple reason that the winters won't be as bad over here."

"You know this?"

"Lykkon all but knows it, and I'm willing to trust him."

Vorinn exhaled heavily and stared at the sky as if daring the day to progress. "Fair enough, then, I'll say it simply: I have no choice but to return to the war as soon as I can, assuming I can get there, and that's exactly what I intend to do. Anyone who wants to accompany me is free to do so, but should be aware that we may not get there at all, or that the mere fact of that person's presence may render return impossible—" He looked at Lykkon when he said that. "Am I right? I think you're all fools to consider staying over here, though I can see why some of you might think you can. But frankly, there's no time to talk about any of that now. As for going back with me: I'll need to hear how you stand—now, if you don't mind."

Strynn regarded him calmly. "I'll stay here. I really have no choice, since I have no idea what jumping might do to my un- born children, and I will *not* put the heirs to two great clans into the kind of combat situation in which you may very well find yourself. I will remain in this place for two days, awaiting some kind of word, then return to the lake. Anyone who wants me can find me there."

"I'm with her," Div chimed in. "We've become good friends, and I know the Wild. I can teach everyone what they need to know, and I think I can do it without setting everyone at each other's throats. The birkit also seems to like me, and birkits make far better allies than foes."

"Myx?"

Myx exchanged glances with Riff. "I'd like to stay here at least until Strynn and Div get settled and there are more men about. Not that I doubt the women's strength or skill, but there are things at which men are simply better. I've also got some healing skill, and Riff's good with wood. Though I've no right to speak for him," he finished awkwardly.

"Riff?"

"What Myx said, to which I'll add that this was never my war, and I thought it was stupid from first to last—which doesn't mean I don't think highly of those who had to fight it, or understand their motivations. But sometimes— I guess I'm saying that sometimes you need to forget about ideals and focus on facts. Survival's a fact. Making things is a fact. Who runs a kingdom for what reason—that doesn't mat- ter."

Vorinn started to reply that by staying where he was, Riff was all but assuring himself of a role in running a kingdom, however small. Back in Eron he could, in theory, return to being either a woodsmith or a soldier. Instead, he raised another objection. "You both have consorts."

Myx shrugged. "They'll come. This is exactly the sort of thing they'd relish. It only remains to get word to them, and arrange...transportation."

Vorinn rolled his eyes. "Krynneth?"

Krynneth looked startled, as he often did these days, as if the question had dragged him back from some other place—or, perhaps, time.

"I'll stay here, if no one objects," he said slowly, pronouncing each word with deliberate care. "I think I'll fight again someday—but not today. Today, I fear I would do more harm than good."

"And I," Kylin broke in before Vorinn could address him, "I've done what I can—for now. Any good I happen to accomplish henceforth will be done here, and I'm not sure how much that will be. As for the rest...I'm blind, and no one here is a fool."

"I didn't expect you to go," Vorinn told him frankly. "But it is your right. Even now I won't try to stop you."

"You won't have to," Kylin assured him. "There are as many songs here as there, so here is where I'll stay." He punctuated his remark with a shimmer of notes on his harp.

"Lykkon?"

Lykkon took a deep breath. "I'm in a quandary," he began slowly. "I'm not needed here as much as some of us are, and I'm not overly fond of living in the Wild. On the other hand, there's a lot to be learned here, so whatever else I do today, I certainly plan to return here eventually. That said, I'm also the Royal Chronicler, and seem to have become Avall's closest friend after Rann, Merry, and Strynn, and he'll need me in that capacity, if nothing else. Which I guess means that if I'm going to finish the Chronicle properly, I need to see as much as I can firsthand; therefore, if possible, I'd like to go with you. I don't think I'm duplicitous enough that my deep brain would contradict me. As for Bingg—"

"Bingg's his own man, here," Vorinn cautioned.

"Bingg goes where Lykkon goes—for now," Bingg laughed. "I'm like him in that I like to know things, but the things I most want to learn are in Eron, not here. I'm at the beginning of something Lyk's at the end of, and I'd like to see it through—assuming there's a Kingdom left for me to do that in. But if there is, I want to be there, and if our efforts somehow fail, I don't want to spend the rest of my life wondering whether my presence could have made a crucial difference."

"In other words," Strynn summarized, "you don't want to spend your life decrying the lack of something you didn't help to save."

Bingg regarded her shyly. "Thank you. Eloquence is one of those things I need to study."

"Which means you're going?" Vorinn concluded.

"Which means I intend to make the attempt," Bingg corrected. "There's also the fact that I'm the smallest person here, and Lykkon's no bigger than Myx, so if size *is* a factor in returning, that should play in our favor."

"Spoken like my brother," Lykkon grinned, sparing him a rough hug.

Vorinn looked at the river. "Do we need...?"

Lykkon shrugged. "I don't know. Maybe. That's what Avall did, and I'd trust him."

"Well, then," Vorinn sighed, "you lads armor up, assemble what gear you have, and let's get moving. There could still be fighting at the hold."

"As you will, Lord Regent," Lykkon agreed—and trotted off to begin sorting through their packs. Vorinn watched absently as he began redonning his own clothing. It was still damp, naturally, but would be wet again so soon that it scarcely mattered.

Fortunately, he had arrived in full war gear, excepting his shield and helmet, and equally fortunate, Lykkon's armor had come with him during their jump. Bingg had no armor on this side of the Spine, but Myx—who tended to remain in his guard persona when the group was traveling—was shrugging out of his mail, with able assistance from Bingg. "It's the smallest we have to hand," Strynn offered from beside him. "Myx won't need it as much as Bingg will. He's practical that way."

"I hope Bingg won't need it either. I hadn't intended for him to fight."

"No, but that won't stop someone else claiming him as a target. He's smart enough otherwise to keep himself safe. And if there really is a battle, he should find a sword soon enough. As for a helm—look: he's trying on Myx's, but it doesn't fit, which means Riff's won't."

Vorinn watched the nascent warriors for a moment longer, then shrugged, shook his limbs to loosen them, and smiled down at Strynn. "I'll have that sword now, if you don't mind. And whatever happens, though it's been my honor to serve my Kingdom and my King, it has been a far greater honor to serve my sister."

"And I to be served by you."

With that, she offered him the sword again, and this time he took it—then shifted his gaze to the ground, blushing furiously, suddenly afraid to meet his sister's eyes. "Strynn," he stammered, "I...have no wife—nor even a year-bond, now; nor a bond-brother. But I..." He paused again, as words deserted him. "I would have a kiss from you, for luck."

"And I will be glad to give it," Strynn replied formally, raising her hand for Vorinn to assist her up. The kiss—on either cheek, then the lips—was as chaste as it ought to be between siblings, but somehow it touched something new in his heart. And maybe, for the first time in his life, Vorinn truly felt that he was loved.

He started to speak, but Bingg and Lykkon came jostling up just then, eager-faced, and, now that they were once again clad more or less the same, looking more than ever like brothers. Lykkon had retrieved his personal sword, and Bingg—who, again, had none on this side of the mountains—sported Riff's second-best hunting knife.

"I'll have one of those kisses, too," Lykkon smirked, looking at Strynn with a twinkle in his eyes. "If you've got any to spare, I mean. And one for my brother, please."

Strynn tapped her lips experimentally, then smirked in turn. "Yes, indeed, there do seem to be a few left. So I suppose—" She didn't finish, simply leaned forward and planted her lips firmly against Lykkon's cheeks and mouth, then did the same for a blushing Bingg.

Vorinn was staring at the river, obviously agitated. "I think I see why Avall left so precipitously," he muttered. "It spares all this."

"It spares a lot," Strynn agreed, "but I'm sick of Avall always leaving. Or me leaving," she appended pointedly.

None of which prevented the rest of their group coming forward for hugs, wishes of luck, and victory kisses of their own.

Myx shook Bingg roughly by the shoulders, like a brother. "You know why I'm lending you that mail, don't you? It's so that you'll either have to bring it back or be in my debt forever."

"I'll remember," Bingg affirmed. "And I promise that as soon as I can, I'll make you a new set."

Riff raised a brow and elbowed Myx in the ribs. "He's Argen-a, brother, the best smiths in the world; you'd better be sure he makes good."

"Never fear," Myx and Bingg chorused together.

"Let's go!" Vorinn shouted. And all at once the lot of them were trooping into the river. Strynn and Kylin halted when the water got calf deep, but Myx, Riff, Div—and Krynneth—pressed onward until it lapped against their thighs. Vorinn tried not to look back, but could not resist doing so once, and saw them all standing there, waiting. He wondered whether they were watching the end of something or the beginning of something better.

And then he turned, braced himself, and continued on. "What do we do now, Lyk?" he murmured, when the water reached his ribs.

Lykkon gnawed his lip, then nodded decisively. "We should try to duplicate exactly what you did to come here as much as possible. Bingg and I will grab the blade—just enough to blood ourselves—you should then do that as well—and then we'll grab your hand, dive under ... and wish."

"Under?"

"Most of this is wishing," Lykkon reminded him. "If you're underwater, you generally wind up wishing more fervently—not to drown, if nothing else. More to the point, your body's wishing along with your brain. That should help considerably."

"I guess I'll just have to trust you," Vorinn grumbled, and extended the blade. Lykkon slid his palm down the metal with easy confidence, revealing red at once. Bingg had to try twice, but likewise managed to ensanguine two fingers. Vorinn hesitated for a pair of breaths, then shifted the hilt to his other hand and ran his right palm down the blade, wondering why the previous wound there seemed almost to have healed already. Another shift put the sword back in his dominant fist.

As soon as those two other reddening hands joined his on the hilt, he triggered the barb that waited there, and, the instant the power answered, sank down where he was in the middle of an unknown river in an unknown land and wished to be back in another place entirely: a place that was no less beautiful or bloody, but rather more familiar.

Somehow, impossibly, he heard two other minds wishing that as well. And then water closed over his head, and he felt himself torn asunder.

He tried not to think about it this time—as he had *had* no time to think about it earlier, intent, as he had been, on survival. But this ... It was odd, it was strange, it was distinctly unpleasant, and he wanted it over.

For a moment he simply *wasn't*. And then, for a much longer interval, he felt himself stretched impossibly thin, as though his whole body were become a wire thousands of shots long.

And then that wire was coiling again, and he was—

—Somewhere else.

He knew that instantly: by the cloudy blood in the water around him, by the feel of smooth stone beneath his feet as it forced him toward the surface, by the muffled sounds of shouts and running feet seemingly everywhere...

And then, like a spring rewinding, he compacted back to himself, which, along with his will and what felt like a thrust from some place deeper than the pavement, propelled his body upward.

The first thing he saw was Avall.

CHAPTER XXX:

REUNION

(WESTERN ERON: MEGON VALE—NEAR-AUTUMN: DAY II—MIDAFTERNOON)

It took Avall a moment to acknowledge what he was seeing—and even so, reflex made him flinch backward in alarm—which brought him hard into Tryffon and Merryn, who, like himself had just stepped back onto the pontoon bridge outside what was still the hold's only accessible door. Metal clanged. Mail rustled. Armor creaked and snapped.

Tryffon "oofed" and growled an irritable, "What is it, boy?"

Avall ignored him entirely. He had no choice, really.

Perhaps one day he would get used to things like this: seeing the water to the right of the dueling platform appear to thicken—if that was the right word—then start to foam, then surge upward abruptly, only to collapse upon itself, revealing—

—*Vorinn*—with, beside him, their hands still sliding away from his sword to grasp blades of their own, Lykkon and—he blinked— Could that grim-faced, cold-eyed warrior really be young Bingg?

All three went instantly on guard for all they stood in water to their crotches. But then Vorinn's eyes went wide, and what had begun as a snarl segued into a gape, then widened into a grin.

"Please tell me you've left me someone to kill, cousin," Vorinn blurted, his practiced warrior's gaze still darting about in quest of prospective foes.

"Actually," Avall replied from pure, numb-brained reflex—"we're effectively through with all that." Then, as realization truly dawned and joy replaced fatigue: *Vorinn! You're back! And Lyk and Bingg! You're back*—and you're safe and—you're too late, and I'm sorry, but it didn't take long once it happened. And—oh Eight, all of you, just come here!"

Bingg was already out of the water by the time Vorinn had sheathed his sword and begun to clamber out in earnest. Lykkon was on the platform almost as quickly. Together, they hoisted Eron's war commander out of what was now a rapidly draining pool.

Avall had reached the sodden party by then. He and Vorinn had differed on many issues in the past, but those differences were forgotten as he snared his brother-in-law in a hearty hug which only ended when Tryffon claimed his turn—which gave Avall time to greet his two young kinsmen properly. It had barely been three hands since they had seen each other—if even that—yet to Avall it seemed like forever, as he felt an overwhelming mixture of joy and relief flood through him.

He was wet from the shoulders down where Vorinn had embraced him—and didn't care. All that mattered was that the problem that had plagued him for so long that he barely remembered when it had not been a factor in his life was well on its way to resolution.

With that in mind, he crowded close to his friends again. Close enough to hear Merryn lean to Vorinn's ear, and whisper, "Strynn?"

Avall felt a jolt at the mention of that name. He should have *noticed* that, damn it: how only three of all that number he had abandoned in such haste had returned. Not that Strynn was truly a warrior—but that was in nowise to say she couldn't fight. And then he remembered: She was pregnant, which was cause enough to remain behind. And, he suspected, in light of assorted campfire conversations during the last eight days, there might be other reasons.

"She *had* to stay," Vorinn replied loudly, for Avall's benefit as well as Merryn's. "Things are as well as they can be there, but that dish makes a better meal than a snack. For now"—he made room for himself among the increasing numbers jostling about—"what's happened here?"

Avall likewise glanced around—and was immediately taken aback by the number of people scurrying hither and yon. He only hoped they were allies; all he needed was for the Ninth Face to produce some terrible new strategy now, when victory seemed at last within his grasp. As for Ahfinn—*Where was the man, anyway?* Oh, yes, there he was, securely in custody of Lady Veen, who had bestowed Zeff's head on someone else while she bound Ahfinn's hands before him.

But Avall's folk seemed to be everywhere, most especially on the gallery closest above and behind him, and still crowding through the cleft in the hills that led to the hold's southern approach. And since this was still the only real portal in and out—until the water lowered another span, at any rate—this platform and the narrow walk that served it were becoming impossibly crowded.

"Let's go back to my tent," Avall suggested, avoiding Vorinn's query. "Anything that needs our attention can be pursued as well there as here."

With that, he flung one arm around Vorinn and the other around Rann—both of whom had been, at various times, his Regents—and nodded for his ever-attentive escort of Night Guard to open a path for him away from the hold.

Yet he paused again where the causeway met the outer wall and the route started down the narrow outside stair. It was a good place to see from, and a good place to be seen—and, since a good third of his army was crowding in below, it was also as good a place as any from which to give worth its due.

Taking a speaking horn from a herald who had attached

herself to their party, he leapt into the embrasure between two merlons and, oblivious to the dizzy drop below, raised the horn and shouted to the suddenly attentive throng crowding into Megon Vale.

"People of Eron," he began. "Knights of Eron and people of Eron and everyone who has, even once, borne the most excellent rank of soldier!"

And with that, as though they thought with one brain, everyone in the entire vale and the hold behind him fell silent.

"Hear me, all you good folk," Avall continued. "Today we have the victory—in proof of which we have the head of he who gave us so much grief. And without its head, the body will soon wither and decay. So shall it be here.

"But that is not why I address you," he went on. "I stand here not for my own sake and my own glory, small though that glory may be, but to present to you another: the man who endured longest and risked most to bring us to our present happy pass. All good people of Eron—I present to you the man who truly is your savior: the Lord High Commander of all the Royal Armies: Vorinn syn Ferr-een!"

Perhaps Avall had heard a louder cheer when Vorinn joined him on the ramparts, but he doubted it. It began as applause and shouts of acclamation from those close-packed ranks below: those best stationed to hear his words. But from there it quickly spread up the hollow and into the gap, even as more applause erupted from behind: applause that was soon joined by hoots and cheers and bellows. And then someone began beating a shield, and someone else a drum, and a third someone a helmet; and a flute was found, then a trumpet, then two more, and to Avall's utter amazement, the whole world dissolved into joyous noise.

Even the earth seemed to be celebrating, for it was shaking, too. It took Avall a moment to realize what that portended. "Wonderful as all this is," he whispered in Vorinn's ear, "we probably aren't as safe here as we could be."

Without further debate, Avall and his companions—and Vorinn after a final pause to wave at the ecstatic crowd, which prompted another swell in volume—started down the stair.

They walked back to the camp because it was a fine day; and though they were all tired to the bone, it was a fatigue that was not worsened by action. Not when a cheering mob flanked their every step and followed them all the way. Many of that number were Gem-Holders, Avall noted, wondering how they had managed to get outside so fast.

It was just as well they were here instead of there, he supposed, if what he feared about the hold's stability was true. Still, he banished that and other dark thoughts from his mind as he led what had been most of his Council and a good part of his court back to the Royal Pavilion.

"Wine," he called to the chamber squire—who had arrived but a dozen breaths ahead of them. "The best there is in the camp, and keep it coming. Some of us have had to stint for far too long, and for now—I don't care. Everyone have what they will, and let's relax, and then, much as I hate to say it, we need to consider a number of important matters."

And with that, Avall flopped down in his chair of state—where he remained exactly long enough to note that everything he had on was somewhere between damp and sodden, whereupon he disappeared into what had been his private chamber and found a pair of fresh house-hose and a long robe, both in Argen's colors. Not bothering with shoes, he belted the robe with a plain black belt and returned to the outer chamber, which was rather less populous than when he had departed.

Most of his court had followed his example regarding dress, it seemed, and came trickling back by ones and twos, drier and without armor, with Lykkon and Bingg last of all—by which time the chamber squire had managed to secure the requested wine, along with a spread of cold meat, cheese, bread, nuts, and an assortment of sauces.

Though plain fare for a Royal Court, to Avall, who had not seen its like in several eights, it seemed a feast indeed. Helping himself to a slice of roast venison with hot mustard on dark bread, he tallied those before him: Merryn, Rann, Lykkon, Bingg, Vorinn, Veen, Tryffon, Preedor, and a number of men and women he barely knew, whom he assumed Vorinn had appointed to replenish the Council's ranks when Rann had abdicated. These last traded uneasy glances with each other, as though wondering if they should, in fact, be present. Avall, in turn, wondered what they thought about sharing the room with Rann and Lykkon, whom some of them surely considered traitors.

"Welcome, all!" he cried when the silence grew too strained. "Things have changed somewhat since I was here last, so I apologize for any discomfort, either physical or otherwise, you may experience. I also see a certain amount of concern on some of your faces as to whether you should indeed be here, so let me address that first. All here are welcome here, and welcome to remain here until we return to Tir-Eron. Your presence implies both competence on your own part and the confidence of those in whom I place confidence in turn; therefore, welcome all. But be warned: You will soon learn that I conduct affairs in a certain manner, so do not be surprised at anything you hear—or see. Not that anything is likely to surprise anyone after today."

"No indeed," Tryffon snorted. "Not hardly."

"Now then," Avall continued, after a deep breath, "I know that we all want to catch up on what has transpired of late, since we've all been separated in a number of interesting ways and at a number of interesting places. Unfortunately, much as I hate to say it, the particulars of that should probably come later. Frankly, too, I don't have the energy to rehearse it all again, having just done a short version of that very thing earlier today. For now"—he paused, gazing around the table—and beyond, to those who had found no seats there and settled for benches against the wall or, in Bingg's case, the floor—"we need to address two things before any other. One, of course, is how to conclude our business here; the other is what our business henceforth will be. There is one obvious answer to the latter, but I would like to hear the latest word on that before anything is decided. Which leaves us with our present situation."

"What *is* our present situation?" Vorinn inquired, with scarce-controlled impatience. "I never made it into the hold, as you remember, and you never properly answered my question when I arrived. I assume, however, that the Ninth Face has been defeated."

"It has been defeated *here*, as far as we can tell," Avall acknowledged. "They fell victim to a fatal moment of indecision and disarray, and from investing too much authority in one person. Which may be a kind of national curse of ours," he added. "Comes from all those damned rites and rituals—but that's not what we're here to discuss. So, to continue with your answer, Vorinn: we have taken Zeff's second—his adjutant, officially—a fellow named Ahfinn—prisoner, and he will be tried in Tir-Eron, either by our folk or by Priest-Clan, if we can get them back in their place. For the rest, Zeff's people didn't put up much resistance once we got into their hold, which implies that theirs was, in part, a cult of charisma, not of dogma. In any case, there were more of us than of them, and more of us all over again, as we began freeing the hostages in the hold. There were casualties—a few. Crim was murdered, and justice has already been served for that. Several Ninth Face soldiers killed themselves, and there were a few fights and some wounds taken on both sides, but we suffered no fatalities—which I know is hard to believe."

"But good to hear," Vorinn countered, nodding.

"We also find ourselves in something of an awkward situation, for two reasons," Avall went on. "First of all, we have to decide what to do with the people we've just freed—"

"Leave them here, those who want to stay," Lykkon broke in. "Appoint a new Hold-Warden, and find a Lore Master to see who's where in their rotation and if any vital skills will be needed."

Avall shook his head, frowning ever so slightly. "Won't

work—not like that, anyway. First of all, while the hold—any winter hold—always has more than year's worth of supplies on hand, most don't have their population effectively doubled during the summer, and certainly not at the same time that shipments of supplies are curtailed. They should have been stockpiling for the winter all last quarter, but the only new resources to have made it here are ours, which I'm afraid *we* will need if we're to accomplish what we intend. In fact, I rather suspect we'll be on short rations ourselves before we get back to Tir-Eron, and maybe after."

Rann cleared his throat, glancing at Avall for permission to speak. "There's also the matter of the safety of the hold itself. I know it's hard to think of something so huge and solid being vulnerable. It was built for the ages, and looks it. But Merryn will tell you that War-Hold looked that way, too, and one third of it now lies in ruins. In this case, however, the problem is that while a good portion of Gem-Hold was hollowed out of a subsidiary peak of Tar-Megon, part of it—the front third, in fact—was built over the Ri-Megon, which was harnessed for various purposes inside—and which was turned to the hold's defense when they closed it off and flooded half the vale. Trouble is, they flooded the mines as well, which has rendered them, and with them the entire foundation, unsafe.

"Not that I know firsthand," he added quickly. "I haven't been down there yet, though I plan to go later today. But I *have* found the former Mine Warden—one of the few survivors of the initial explosion—and he confirms it. In other words, until their safety can be assured, the mines are useless, which effectively negates the reason for this hold. Moreover, those parts of the hold that give access to the mines have suffered the most damage, and the raw fact is that the whole place is in danger of collapse. The north end may be fairly safe, but my feeling is that no one should live there until we can give it a thorough inspection. Now, with that in mind, I *would* suggest that you leave a team of stonesmiths here over the winter to undertake such an inspection. There would certainly be resources on site to accommodate fifteen or twenty, which is all that would be required—and all we can spare in the bargain. There's also the small matter of winter. Winter will be especially hard on this place because water will have reached places where water has never been, and will freeze, expand, thaw, then freeze and expand again. All of which will render the hold less stable. Which is another reason it needs to be abandoned for the nonce."

Silence, briefly, while everyone stared at each other.

"There should be no problem with people retrieving personal goods," Rann went on eventually. "As long as they realize they're acting at their own risk. But unless this Council rules otherwise, I'd say the place should be closed until we can determine for certain that it's safe."

"What about the...magic gems?" From Tryffon. "They're the reason this started in the first place."

Avall regarded him squarely. "As far as I know, there *are* no more gems of that kind—not here, and let's say I have a good reason for that assumption. And if there do turn out to be more, I have every confidence that a means exists to retrieve them. And about *that* I will say no more."

"And the Ninth Face prisoners?" Veen inquired. "What do you say about them?"

Avall started to speak, but noted that Vorinn was seeking recognition. "Lord Vorinn? You have a suggestion?"

"We can't leave them," Vorinn stated flatly. "We can't, because we can't trust them. But it occurs to me that they owe a massive debt to Gem-Hold, above all else. What I would therefore suggest is that they bear the brunt of carrying whatever goods need to be salvaged by their former hostages. We would have to chain them, but surely with so many able smiths about, there'd be no problem contriving sufficient fetters."

Everyone laughed at that, including Avall, but something about Vorinn's casual tone made him uneasy. "That's until we get back to Tir-Eron," Vorinn continued quickly. "Once there...we have a number of options as to their specific disposal, depending on what kind of resistance their clan-mates mount. But in any scenario I can think of, the idea of Ninth Face knights stripped naked and tied to tabletops seems to figure prominently."

More laughter followed—but not from Avall this time. "I would prefer a more humane option," he said carefully. "That said, labor is more humane than death, so perhaps we should give your idea consideration. Your *real* idea," he added.

"What about Tir-Eron?" Merryn broke in. "I'm sorry to speak out of turn, especially when the rest of you may know things I don't, but it seems to me that if we're going to return to Tir-Eron, we should have some idea what we'll find when we get there."

Avall chuckled. "You doubt that we've got spies there, or will have? I've more faith in Tryffon than that!" He peered at Tryffon expectantly.

For his part, Tryffon looked as uncomfortable as Avall had ever seen him, to the point of shifting in his seat. "The fact is, lad," Tryffon began, "we don't know as much as we'd like. We've sent people there to find out, of course, but you have to remember that Eron Gorge is a long way from here, even with good horses in high summer, and that's not considering the fact that one isn't wise to make a direct approach to the place if one's intentions are other than they appear to be. The whole west end of the gorge cuts through grassy plains, after all, saving those ridges to the south where we fought that last battle, so one can't come upon it by stealth, not from the nearest end. The only chance for that is to follow the north rim farther east, find one's way to the bottom, then work up-gorge again. Which we've done, I hasten to add."

"And?" Avall prompted through a sudden yawn.

"Actually," Tryffon went on, "what we've found most reliable has been a series of messengers that have been sent by various folk in the gorge. Tyrill sent several, then seems to have run out of trustworthy squires, but from what we've been able to determine from them and by other means, things are bad there and getting worse. Priest-Clan apparently intended to kill as many High Clan Chiefs as they could manage and slot themselves into those positions, post double guards on everyone else, and assume it would be business as usual. They assumed Common Clan would bend to their will, but Common Clan relies on goods from High Clan, and High Clan goods were suddenly not forthcoming."

He paused for a long draught of wine, then went on relentlessly.

"As far as goods and the distribution of same, in which category I include food—well, to put it bluntly, everything south of Eron Gorge is still in chaos. On the one hand, you've got the traditional poor, who've always depended on royal largesse, but who have suddenly found that royal largesse has dried up, so they're petitioning Priest-Clan for help. Only now they're finding out that those truly good Priests who used to help them can't anymore, because most of Priest-Clan's southern resources were decimated along with everyone else's; never mind that the planting's been done late if at all; and their seniors in Tir-Eron have been too busy keeping a peace they destroyed in the first place to oversee planting and harvest up there; and all *that's* ignoring the fact that they've got their hands full of refugees."

"Which means," Preedor took up, "that they went looking to their local Priests for help, and when those—mostly—good men and women tried to help, they found they couldn't. Which has them angry at their seniors."

"Which basically means that Priest has made enemies among the poor when they sought to make allies," Lykkon summarized.

"And as for what stirred them up to start with—the fact that Priest said we had a means to access The Eight directly and weren't sharing—they're suddenly having to explain why The Eight have let things get so bad when it's Their minions who are supposed to be in charge."

"Which isn't even counting the refugees," Tryffon took up

again. "Normally, they would have been absorbed back into their clans, propped up, helped out, and sent away again with whatever they'd need to rebuild, and Common Clan would have made a good profit selling their own licensed wares and whatever surpluses they'd managed to buy up cheap now and then. But suddenly their home clans aren't there anymore, and half the subchiefs from South and Half are prowling through their armories in search of weapons while trying to figure out who they can get to fight for them in order to defend their property against their own, even more unfortunate, countrymen, along with trying to restore order in the name of absent Chiefs and an absent King. Fortunately, honor is pretty deeply embedded in anyone who's wound up with any kind of chieftainship, but what was supposed to have been a neat little change for Priest hasn't worked out that way at all."

Avall puffed his lips thoughtfully. "That's a lot to digest in a small space. I wonder again why you didn't abandon the siege and return."

"Because," Vorinn replied quickly, "we were almost here when we got word of the coup, and then they took you prisoner, and we felt like we couldn't leave you. And then, when you disappeared, we expected every moment that you'd return with the Lightning Sword and everything would be better. But even if we had left as soon as you vanished, we would have been taking a risk, because that raised the possibility that we would find ourselves with foes before us and behind us, both."

"And now we've got an even larger army—in theory," Preedor added. "If we can figure out how to feed them. In fact, I'd suggest we start recruiting from Gem as soon as possible. We should at least be able to acquire a spare hundred or so. We might even—*might,* let me stress—get a few from the Ninth Face, if you make them swear mighty oaths, say on the Sword of Air."

"All of which means," Vorinn finished, "that we may actually have helped matters in the long term by waiting. We're stronger, while Tir-Eron is in worse chaos than before, and therefore better primed for retaking. The problem is going to be toppling those in command without ourselves running afoul of other, lesser opposition, and getting tangled up in that. But I think we can manage that," he concluded. "We make a pretty formidable team, all things considered, especially now that we've got more magic than we've ever had before."

"Which we need to use with extreme caution," Avall warned. "There was a reason we sent the regalia away to start with. I'm willing to use it now—and Zeff's new sword as well—which I guess should become yours for the present; The Eight know you've earned it—but after this. Well, I'll decide after we resolve affairs in Tir-Eron."

"Before or after Sundeath?" Tryffon asked pointedly.

"*After we resolve affairs in Tir-Eron,*" Avall repeated quietly, and said no more, though he knew Tryffon was referencing his oft-stated intention of ruling only until Sundeath, and then trying, very hard, to step down.

"Now," Avall continued through another yawn, "I think we've said as much as most people can digest as full of good food and wine as we are, and so soon after a major battle. So what I'd suggest is that everyone disperse to quarters and take a bath—or a nap. Whatever you can manage. Let your squires, subchiefs, and seconds-in-command run things for a while; it's what they're supposed to do. We'll reconvene at supper and hash out more of this then—and get what reports we can regarding hard points, like number of people who'll be coming with us, number of prisoners and casualties, potential supply problems, and that sort of thing. And tomorrow—not at dawn—let's say at noon; we all need to spoil ourselves a little—we ride out for Tir-Eron."

"For Tir-Eron!" everyone shouted, leaping to their feet. "Tir-Eron!"

Avall watched them file out by ones and twos, until only Merryn, Rann, Lykkon, and Bingg remained, all of whom regarded him expectantly.

He took a long draught from his glass of wine, filled it, and took another, savoring the vintage. "Merry," he said at last, "something tells me that you've got a season's worth of anger built up in you, and that that you didn't get to do nearly as much fighting today as you would have liked. So how about you go find young Ahfinn and squeeze everything out of him you can—and I mean that literally, if you have to. It wasn't Priest-Clan that tortured you during the war, but Ahfinn's friends were in camp when Barrax did, and they could have helped you and they didn't. Remind him that all the Ninth Face are legally traitors because of that. See what he says. It strikes me that Ahfinn likes information and the kind he likes best is the kind that keeps him alive."

Merryn grinned, rose, and managed the sketchiest of salutes before departing. Avall turned his gaze to Lykkon and Bingg. "Lyk," he said, "your tent should still be here, but I doubt there's much left in it that would be of use to you. Feel free to move in with me—you and Bingg both—until you've got your own gear like you want it. You might also want to keep an eye on Myx and Riff's kit, since no one else will be around to do that and I'm sure they've got some keepsakes in their quarters."

"Which is a polite way of dismissing us," Lykkon chuckled, as he, too, rose to his feet, giving Bingg, who had dozed off, a wickedly effective yank in the process. "Come, cub," Lykkon muttered. "Let's find you some proper squire's livery. You're *way* too small to be a soldier."

Suddenly Avall was alone with Rann. Rann moved up two chairs to claim the one beside Avall: his former Regent's Chair. "I know what you're thinking about," he said, "or rather, who."

Avall raised a brow but did not reply. Instead, he slid the bottle toward his friend. Rann took a sip obligingly, then stared at it dubiously and drained the bottle. "Actually, what I'm thinking," Avall murmured, "is that, now that the 'problem of Gem-Hold' does seem to be over, we'll be moving farther away from them than ever. I don't like being that far away. Especially when I don't even know how far away 'far away' is."

"It's hard, isn't it?" Rann agreed. "When they're with you, sometimes you wish you had your own space again—your own distance. But when they're gone..."

Avall patted his hand, then grasped it fiercely. "Only a little longer, Rann. I keep telling myself that. Only a little longer. But I keep waiting."

"For what?"

"Waiting," Avall sighed, "to be happy. No, let me change that—I'm relatively happy now. Let me say... waiting to be content."

Rann regarded him levelly. "Something tells me that's never going to happen to either of us—at least not in Eron."

"At least not in Eron," Avall repeated sleepily, and said no more. And then fatigue ambushed him indeed and gave him contentment of another kind: in soft and dreamless slumber.

CHAPTER XXXI:

BENEATH THE CITADEL

(ERON: TIR-ERON—NEAR-AUTUMN: DAY XI—MORNING)

~~~~~~

Of the myriad possible ways Tyrill had thought to end her days, none had involved incarceration in a prison cell. And *certainly* not in the ones beneath the Citadel, where the only light came from a rationed one candle per day and what could be coaxed down a dozen levels from outside by a system of shafts and mirrors. Unfortunately, today was gloomy, cold, and rainy, and the outside light was dim—which was probably just as well. Her spirits were dim, too: the dimmest they had been since she had begun her back-street rebellion. How *that* was going now, she had no idea. Elvix hadn't told her whether she had distributed more blowguns to would-be partisans, and in that Elvix was probably wise. As for Ilfon: she had heard absolutely nothing—not since her own imprisonment began. Priest-Clan could be gathering evidence against both of them, she supposed, but a more likely supposition was that the Kingdom was in such disarray there wasn't time to see her properly disposed. Which could be good—if they managed to forget about her long enough for someone (she had no idea who) to effect a rescue—or bad, if that chaos resulted in summary execution without trial.

In any case, it was good to be indoors and relatively warm, for the weather had changed abruptly and the wind and rain were cold—the kind of cold that made her bones ache at the best of times, which these were not. She doubted, frankly, that she would have been able to maintain her previous level of activity much longer anyway.

But the waiting was getting to her. Pacing hurt too much, and the light was too uncertain to read by; she was therefore reduced to sleeping and remembering. Inevitably, too, many of those memories centered around her two-son, Eddyn: dead now, and a hero and a traitor all at once—which seemed to be the lot of her sept of the clan. He had even been imprisoned, for destruction of a masterwork—for which offense, oddly enough, he had never stood trial. She wondered suddenly if he might not have been housed in this selfsame cell. It was certainly possible.

In any case, she waited, and then she dozed, and when she awoke again, it was to the sound of booted feet approaching in the corridor beyond the thick oak door. She sat up where she had lain, swung her legs off the bed, and composed herself, wishing she had a comb and a mirror, but grateful that her captors had given her a warmer and more serviceable dress than the one she had been wearing when she and Ilfon had been taken. Sooner than she had really expected, the tread stopped, a loud knock sounded, and a woman called, "Lady Tyrill, your trial will begin in one hand; I have come to see that you arrive in the Hall of Clans in a manner befitting your station."

A key promptly rattled in the lock, and an instant later the door opened to admit a hard-faced, middle-aged woman in Ninth Face livery: a woman bearing a pile of neatly folded clothing. Two men stood guard in the hallway behind her, but withdrew when the woman closed the door, though Tyrill did not hear them depart.

"I appreciate your consideration," Tyrill acknowledged tightly. And calmly began sorting through the garments. They were *her* garments, which surprised her—a full set of ceremonial kit in Argen-yr's colors and heraldry, in fact, but only in the colors of a rank and file member of that clan. There was no Craft-Chief's tabard, for instance, nor any other sign of special status, the omission of which had to be deliberate. Not for the first time did she wonder who, exactly, now exercised sovereignty over her former domain. Someone from the sept of Priest-Clan devoted to Craft, she had heard, which made sense, even if it was not encouraging. But which someone, she had no idea.

Far too soon the last laces were tied, the last buckle set, the last sash cinched and Tyrill found that she was ready. Her attendant—she never knew the woman's name—reached for the cane in the corner, but Tyrill shook her head. "Today," she said stiffly, "I will do without it."

The woman scowled as though she were about to protest but had thought better of it, and nodded instead. Crossing to the door, she rapped twice, then called out, "Servants of the Ninth Face, we are ready."

The lock rattled again and the door opened. Tyrill took a deep breath and, without looking back, stepped into the corridor beyond, where she fell in line between the two guards. Her legs pained her dreadfully, but she persevered. Literal pain of the body was nothing to the pain in her heart. Yet when two more guards joined them at the top of the stairs, she could not resist leaning close to her female attendant's ear. "Four guards for one old woman?" she rasped. "What do they think I am? Or, a better question: What do you think they fear?"

"You are the most feared woman in the Kingdom," the woman replied flatly. "That is a fact, and always has been."

Tyrill could only ponder that comment as she continued on. And wonder how she could turn that knowledge to her advantage.

Unfortunately, she had reached no useful conclusion when she found her party ascending stairs again. Soon enough, they were entering one of the various holding chambers that encircled the Hall of Clans, where the Council of Chiefs, in the presence of the King, conducted the affairs of Eron's legal government.

They tarried there barely long enough for her to note a flurry of conversations taking place beside the outer door—and then her guards closed in upon her and ushered her down yet another corridor and through another door. It opened soundlessly when she arrived, and at a whispered, "Lady, if you will, go forward," from he who seemed to be chief of that small band, she found herself walking through a door she had never expected to pass through—and certainly not from that direction.

Called the Door of Law, that ornate bronze portal was one of eight that opened onto the dais in the Hall of Clans, in this case, between the statues of Law and Fate. The Throne showed ahead and to the left, with the Stone invisible beneath it. No one sat the Throne, Tyrill noted, which was a small blessing in that it implied that Priest-Clan had not yet usurped the Sovereign's role along with everything else, though with Sundeath approaching, it was certainly no given that they would not. It would be interesting to see, she supposed—if she lived long enough to see any such thing at all.

She did not get to tarry on the dais longer than it took to march, under escort, to a chair carved from solid marble that had been set up at the point where the Hall's radiating aisles met before the Stone. The Chair of the Accused, it was: the chair only erected for and occupied by those under trial for treason. Which she should have known, since treason was the only crime that could be tried before the Council per se.

But it would require the Council to ratify a conviction, and she saw no Council here. Not that she had time for a sure accounting—the soldiers blocked too much of the view for that, never mind the fact that she had to look down to be certain where to set what were suddenly very unsteady feet. Even so, it was easy enough to observe that close to three-quarters of the seats on the floor of that vast, domed, and faceted chamber were vacant, and that even the observers' galleries, where in the past a selection of clanless chosen by lot could observe government in progress, were not as crammed with the curious as they, by rights, should have been.

There was a limit, it seemed, to Priest-Clan charisma—or coercion.

Not that she didn't recognize a few faces out there: mostly former sub-subchiefs from minor septs of less powerful—and therefore hungrier—clans and crafts, like Itakk of Wax and Afai of Paper.

Condemned she might soon be, but that condemnation, it appeared, would not be rendered, as Law required, by anyone who was in any true sense her peer.

She would find out soon enough, she supposed, though without the King to sign a death writ, no execution of High Clan man or woman was even remotely legal, and would constitute murder in its own right.

Not that such niceties seemed likely to stop Priest-Clan now.

And it *would* be Priest-Clan conducting this travesty of a trial, she saw, as their traditional door opened and all eight of the Chief Priests filed in. No, all *nine,* she amended with a start; there was a new robe, mask and color at the end of the familiar file, this one dressed in white and midnight blue. She found herself straining forward, gazing at those figures that now ranged themselves across the dais in a semicircle behind the Throne and Stone, seeking to recognize even one from her countless appearances before them in her capacity as Craft-Chief. She could not be certain—masks, robes, and cloaks deliberately obscured most of the bodies that wore them—but she would have bet everything she had ever owned that not one person before her had worn those masks and robes before the coup. Which effectively confirmed the widespread rumor that Priest-Clan's former chiefs had either been killed, exiled, imprisoned, or forced to abdicate. She would find no allies now, she feared. And felt more alone than ever.

Yet custom had not been abandoned entirely. One of those who entered—it should have been whichever Priest had presided over court most recently—carried one of the Royal Crowns, which she (as the Priest's voice later revealed) summarily deposited on the seat of the Royal Throne, signifying the King's implicit sanction, if not presence. That accomplished, the same Priest produced a large, eight-sided die from a pouch at her side, which she proceeded to roll upon the top of a small table that stood at one side of the dais solely for that purpose.

Tyrill could not resist a smirk. No one had found time to contrive a nine-sided die.

"I remove myself from consideration," the Priest intoned, as if to answer Tyrill's concern. "And Fate has ordained that Man will oversee these proceedings." With that she melted back to her place among her fellows.

Another stepped forward immediately, this one wearing a mask of finely carved and painted wood, of which one side was subtly different from the other so as to represent male and female. As also did the cut of the Priest's loose-woven robe of natural wool, for Man—as Man existed within The Eight—was androgynous. The Priest likewise carried a leather-bound staff—the leather being, it was said, human skin taken from some previous Priest of Man upon his or her demise.

The Priest had reached the prescribed position now: to the right of the Throne, facing Tyrill. A pause, and Man rapped the staff smartly on a tile of a particular type of stone known for its resonance. "Chiefs, Clansmen, and clanless, all!" he (by his voice and shoulders) began. "This session of the Council of Chiefs is now open, for ancient rite ordains that it be open this day, with or without the presence of the Sovereign, who has not deigned to grace us with his presence in nearly a quarter of a year."

A pause, then: "We are nevertheless charged to conduct the Kingdom's business, and are come here today to assure that so important and ancient a charge is obeyed. Alas, foremost

among those items we must address today is the matter of the
Kingdom's security as manifested in those entrusted with that
security, in the persons of this Council and—in the absence of
royal security—in the security provided by my comrades here
and elsewhere in Priest-Clan.

"With that in mind, it is therefore my sad duty to pro-
nounce a charge of treason against the person you see before
you, who once was a member in good standing of the fellowship hereabout. And in light of that, and in light of my selection as Priest and Officer of the Day, it falls to me to read those
charges."

Another pause, while a scroll was brought forward by one
of the guards who flanked the assembled Priests at either end.

Man took it without looking, and let it unroll, feeding it
slowly through his hands.

"Be it known to all within hearing that upon this day, the
Eleventh of Near-Autumn in the first year of the reign of
Avall I (incipient), and in his name in absentia, that a charge of
high treason is herewith proclaimed against Tyrill san Argen-
yr, of late Craft-Chief of Smith, acting Clan-Chief of Clan
Argen, and Regent in Tir-Eron in the absence of His
Sovereign Majesty until her abdication of all these duties in de-
fiance of proper rite and procedure."

It was all Tyrill could do to sit still, and the tally of charges
not truly begun. How dare they accuse her of abdication, when
it had been these very Priests who had orchestrated that—well
it certainly had not been an *abdication*! Never mind that she
had indeed presided over the selection of a new Clan-Chief—
who had barely taken office before she was assassinated. As for
the Craft-Chieftainship—that was a matter for election within
the clan, and none of Priest-Clan's concern.

In any case, Man was continuing.

"Be it known that a charge of treason shall be leveled for
any act that by effect or intent seeks to undermine the duly
consecrated power and authority of either the Kingdom of
Eron or its Sovereign, especially in such wise that these actions

cause unwanted death or destruction of the property of the Kingdom and Crown or those charged with the protection of this property or the execution of the Kingdom's Laws."

Which was *not* the text Tyrill recalled. Then again, Law *was* one of The Eight, so perhaps His Priest had been granted a revelation.

But not by drinking from Law's Well. *That* was still sealed, she was pleased to have heard reported.

"In light of these names and conditions," Man continued, "be it therefore known that Tyrill san Argen-yr did at diverse times hereinafter listed contrive the unlawful death by assassination of those charged with enforcing the security of this City, Gorge, and Kingdom while said City, Gorge, and Kingdom were in a state of crisis and under Council Law in the absence of either the Regent or the King, and by so doing did, by all intents, threaten the security of this Council itself, its officers, and through them, the State. Be it known that these assassinations numbered at least thirteen, with others being suspected. And know that not only did Tyrill san Argen-yr contrive these assassinations, but that she coerced others into equivalent acts of civil disobedience, in which we see even more clearly her true intent to undermine the lawful government.

"And know that His Majesty having been given more than ample time in which to address this matter, in which time he has done and said nothing to contravene it, this Council therefore has no recourse but to claim that authority unto itself, for which there is ancient precedent, and set forth this trial in a fit and timely way."

Another pause for breath, and to let the words sink in, then the Priest of Man spoke one last time.

"Evidence to support these charges having been given to this Council in writing in advance of this assembly, does anyone have anything to say in defense of the accused?"

Tyrill's heart leapt, though she knew it was hope in vain. Yet surely, somewhere in this assembly there was someone with a fragment of nerve, guts, or backbone. Someone who would remember Tyrill-who-was. Tyrill who had given all she had to give in support of her Clan and Kingdom.

But there was only silence.

Nervous silence, perhaps, punctuated by coughs, clearings of throats, and the scraping of uneasy feet.

But not one word in her defense.

"Cowards," she said clearly.

The word broke the silence like a scream in the depths of night.

"Cowards," she repeated, as she strove to stand—which took more effort than she ever displayed.

"Cowards," she said a third time, and this time she faced them fully. "And no, I do not speak out of line," she snapped, glaring at the Priest of Man. "I know the Law to a finer degree than you will ever know it, and I know that I am entitled to make a statement now. I have merely spared you the trouble of formalizing that request. I hope you appreciate the concern I feel for the well-being of those who have entrusted themselves with the keeping of this Kingdom.

"And now that I have freedom to speak," she continued, "I will do so, fearing nothing, for pain I can endure, as I endure it now, and I have nothing to fear from death. How is this? you may ask. Listen, and I will tell you how this is so.

"Whether you convict me now—which I have no doubt you will do—or convict me later, makes small difference. I am old. Old people die. If I die now, I die in command of my faculties, but full of pain, and in both regards death would be a blessing. If I am cleared of charges and yet remain incarcerated, my life becomes my own to take when I find the means. If I am returned to the freedom that is indeed mine by right—for I am innocent of these charges, since all these acts of which I am accused were perpetrated out of self-defense—I will return to precisely the same means and methods that sustained me before my arrest.

"But that last will not occur. It will not occur because everyone here is a coward, bribed with power on one hand or protecting their own heads on the other. This I understand but do not forgive.

"And so, I imagine, within a quarter hand, I will be condemned to death. Yet I do not fear death. Death has no hold over me. For I know absolutely that the best part of me—that which makes me unique and powerful—has but a temporary bond to my body. I know this because I have seen sign over and over that this is true. I have seen my kinsmen speak mind-to-mind more than once, and been party to that speaking—peripherally—as well. I have heard my kinsman Gynn syn Argen-el and my kinsman Avall syn Argen-a speak of visiting the Overworld, and whatever else these men are, they are not liars.

"I could say more, example after example, and so give lie to rumor. But I will not. Ignorance punishes the ignorant more than it punishes those with knowledge, regardless of who wields the power of life and death. But I will say this. You claim to speak for The Eight, but The Eight speak not through you. This court—nay, this entire Council—is a sham and a lie, and the more so because your lawful King still lives and pursues the good of this Kingdom in distant parts. Yet he will return, and when he does, The Eight have mercy on you all, for Avall will not. I hope I am here to see that return, but I fear that will not be so, in which case I have every confidence that my soul—my essence—will observe your downfall from afar.

"That is all I have so say, but this: that this is a sad day for this—nay, for *any*—Kingdom; and that I only regret that I must end my days surrounded by sycophants and cowards."

Once again, there was silence. Tyrill tried not to heave the sigh she could feel impending as she reclaimed her seat. She couldn't believe it! She had actually said her piece—as much as she could improvise in a hurry—without interruption. Of course the Priests were all glaring at her as though she were some loathsome insect that had crawled upon their dinner table, and every guard but one had his hand on the hilt of his or her sword.

But she'd had her say, and now she would endure what came after.

Man cleared his throat and stamped his staff again. "Thank you for saving me the trouble of addressing you, Tyrill," he acknowledged with heavy sarcasm. "Now, then, members of the Council of Chiefs, the time has come for judgment. Black means guilty; white means acquittal. I trust you know where your heads and your hearts must stand."

Tyrill did not watch what ensued—not that she *could* have witnessed the actual proceedings, the way her chair was stationed. Yet she knew without looking what transpired in the chamber behind her. Everyone in a legal Council seat—every Chief of Clan or Craft—had a bag of black and white marbles to hand. There was a hole in the arm of each seat, and that hole connected by a system of chutes and levers to a tallying device, which would do the actual counting. That accomplished, a mechanism inside the statue of Fate behind the dais would reveal how the Council had voted by raising that statue's sword or lowering it.

Tyrill did not see the voting, either, though she heard a low rustle of conversation, a fair bit of anxious breathing, and the click of marbles falling.

But she did see the statue of Fate ever so slowly point its weapon toward the floor.

A quarter hand passed, as rite required, and then Man spoke once again.

"Tyrill san Argen-yr, you have been found guilty of High Treason. The sentence for this crime, as prescribed by Ancient Law, is death. The Council of Chiefs acting in concert with the Priest of Law will determine the proper time and place for the enactment of this sentence."

A pause, then: "Guards, you may escort the condemned away."

"There are not enough guards in Tir-Eron to escort even the condemned I see before me," Tyrill muttered, as she rose like a woman half her age and let four Ninth Face knights usher her back to her cell.

CHAPTER XXXII:

A VISITATION

(NORTHWESTERN ERON–NEAR-AUTUMN: DAY XV–LATE MORNING)

~~~~~~~~

"It's a balance," Avall confided to Lykkon, who was riding beside him that morning. "Information against time."

He reined his horse to a halt and stared thoughtfully at the vista before him, remembering the last time he had seen it, which had been at dusk with him bound into the saddle of a very different, though equally smooth-gaited, steed.

To the casual observer, it would have resembled one of those sudden upthrusts of stone that dotted the land between Gem-Hold-Winter and the place where the Ri-Eron made a sharp turn to the south. Though the Trek Road ran almost straight between the two, Avall had elected to waste a day by riding north into what was supposed to be the uninhabited and largely unmapped northwest section of the Wild, so that he could come here to this place where so many things had ended and so many more begun.

For, according to what Merryn had determined from her ongoing interrogation of Ahfinn, that vast upwelling of dark stone housed the Ninth Face's primary citadel. They had others, of course, but his sister had not yet coerced the location of those from Zeff's former adjutant. It would take imphor, she said—a lot of it—and there wasn't that much of the right kind to spare in the camp. There might be more in the abandoned citadel, however, which was another reason to investigate it.

Whatever else it was, the place was certainly impressive—as raw landscape, if nothing else; never mind as the site of a hidden hold. Easily fifty spans high, and close to that to a side, it was more than large enough to house any number of well-trained scholar-soldiers—not that one could tell that it was inhabited simply by looking at it. What few windows it possessed were carefully concealed within the vertical fissures that marked the walls and were either of dark glass, well shuttered, or set so as to follow the shape of those cracks precisely. And since the stone was vitreous already, and the place well, if clandestinely, guarded; by the time one was close enough to discern windows one was too close for that observation to go unmarked or unheeded.

As for the locale—it rose from one of those places where forest made war with stonier ground, and where geysers and fumeroles spat steam and smoke into the air, to produce a place of otherworldly enchantment—and implicit threat. Not all those openings into the ground were what they seemed, either; at least one provided access to the citadel's bowels. Avall knew; he had been there—and escaped via one, only to be recaptured and taken prisoner to Gem-Hold-Winter.

Rrath had been with him then, if unconscious. Nor had that been Rrath's first foray into that citadel. Why, even Eddyn had been there once—and had probably seen more of its interior than anyone.

Of course Eddyn was dead, too, and that death at least in part a function of his sojourn here.

But Avall could think of any number of things that justified this detour, not the least of them being the use of the place as possible housing for those folk evacuated from Gem-Hold who were not hale enough or venturesome enough to return to Tir-Eron. Or who simply wanted to start their lives over again. There were some three hundred of those, according to

Lykkon. More than enough to man this hold exceedingly well—with men loyal to the King.

So here he was, on a bright, clear, Near-Autumn morning, gazing at it expectantly, and waiting for Merryn to return with news that Ahfinn had, by choice or coercion, agreed to show them the way in. Of course Avall could always take the route he had taken during his aborted escape the first time he had been inside, but that had been no more than a tunnel and viable only for people, not for horses. Never mind that it took him through a place he was not yet ready to reveal to the rank and file.

Rann, who had fallen back to talk to Tryffon, urged his horse up beside Avall's, then reined in.

"Looks promising," he began. "It was good thinking to house the refugees here, and a nice piece of balance—again. Since the Ninth Face depleted Gem's resources, it's only fair that the Gem-Holders deplete theirs."

"*If* we can get in," Avall grumbled. "How's Merry managing with Ahfinn? Last night she was trying to find out how much he values his foreskin. Today—I have no idea; but I think it's back to a mix of alcohol, imphor, and intimidation. Where Merryn's concerned, the last alone would be enough for me."

"But he worked with Zeff for years," Lykkon retorted. "I suspect he's acquired quite a thick skin—fore or otherwise—never mind that anyone who's conversant with torture is usually conversant with ways to resist it. But she'll come through, and if not, you've always got the sword. You could simply find a likely place and start blasting."

Avall scowled at him. "I would never do that. I've learned my lesson about using that thing capriciously or for personal gain. Don't ask me how this has happened, but ever since I *jumped* while in the river, I seem to have learned lots of things, many of them things I don't know that I know. Most take the form of hunches, but—well, it's just hard to explain."

"You could always do it through bonding," Rann

murmured. "You and I haven't done that in a while, and I've got my gem back now."

Avall reached over to clasp his hand. "I'd love to, when I've got time to enjoy it. For now, I'm either too busy or too tired, and that isn't going to change even slightly during the next day, at minimum."

"You think it'll take that long to get the displaced folk settled?"

"Probably not, but I want someone—probably it will default to you, me, Merry, Lyk, and Bingg—to prowl through that place looking for records; in particular, looking for records that might reveal other Ninth Face citadels, even minor bolt-holes, and absolutely revealing any safe places or bolt-holes they might have in Tir-Eron. If we could find a back way into Priest-Hold, for instance—that would solve a multitude of problems."

"It would," Rann agreed. "But do you know what I'm looking forward to?"

"What?"

"Sleeping in a proper bed and taking a proper bath. If nothing else, we can surely manage that in there. Ascetics the Ninth Face might be; they're still Eronese. I don't care if the sheets are plain white cotton and there's no mosaic in the bath, all I want is something softer than stone or stretched leather under me, and an endless supply of hot water. I—"

He broke off, for one of the more distant geysers had chosen that moment to shoot a cloud of steam into the crisp air.

Avall grinned at him. "You won't have to argue with me there. Now, shall we see what's holding up Merry? Or I really may think about using the sword."

Rann eyed him askance, suddenly very sober. "There's something you're not telling me, isn't there? I just caught a flash of it across my mind: mostly intense anticipation, I think, but *not* of bed or bath, yet not exactly of information. It had something to do with being King."

Avall's grin became a frown. "If you know that much, why bother asking?"

"Because," Rann replied sadly, "you've a tendency to take risks without telling anyone. Besides which I...I just like it when you tell me things."

Avall forced a second grin. "Fine, then, I'm telling you that I want to be riding into that place by noon. Now, let's go find my sister."

Merryn, as it happened, was already on her way to meet them, a broad grin on her face. "He told me," she crowed, when she came into speaking range. "I gave him last night to ponder a number of suggestions, most of which affected his standing as a man. He just told me where the secret entrance is—or the one that can accommodate horses, anyway. He also swore there were no traps, but I'm making him ride in the vanguard just in case."

Avall raised a brow. "Why this change of heart?"

"You mean besides preserving the integrity of his scrotum? He said that whatever else it was, their citadel was an architectural wonder the equal of any major hold, and that any efforts to force it open could result in irreparable damage."

"Damn!" Rann muttered beside them. "He really is Eronese."

"Get him up here," Avall commanded. "Put all the Ninth Facers under double guard—and blindhood them—then lead the way."

The Ninth Face's secret gate did not prove so impressively secret once they finally found it. Mostly it consisted of a jumble of fallen trees beside a medium-sized stream on the outcrop's northwest side. Flood wrack, many would have called it—unless one moved a broken limb in a certain way, whereupon two more fallen trees lying athwart each other atop a slanting slab of stone that ended in the river rolled half a turn aside. *That* revealed the sides of a vee-shaped opening in the earth, of which the stone was the cap, and the pivot and third side of which were masked by running water when the gate was down. The slope was fairly steep for horses, but not that bad, considering. And the stone kept foot- or hoofprints from showing, as did the water into which it slid.

More surprising was the fact that glow-globes showed down there, and since Ahfinn was already approaching the bottom, with Vorinn and Veen not far behind, accompanied by twenty Night Guard, Avall found a balance point between vanity and caution and fell in with the second rank.

One moment he was watching the sides of the gate rise up around him, the next Boot was making her way down a paved stone slope and he was ducking to avoid the top of the opening. The place was still a shot from the obvious roots of the citadel, however, and despite the strategically placed glow-globes, it was not until Avall found the route sloping upward again, eventually to disport itself into an impressive ring of stables, that he truly felt at ease. Ahfinn, still chained and with his feet bound into his stirrups, was gazing anxiously around as the chamber began to fill up. "This hold will accommodate most of you," he said flatly, "but not all—unless they like sharing beds. In any case, I have given you what you asked, and pray that you will remember it. Now then, unless you wish to sleep with horses, I would advise those who would claim the sort of quarters to which you are doubtless accustomed to take the stair to the right and continue up, up, and up." He looked straight at Avall. "Zeff's quarters are twenty flights up," he continued. "I hope your legs prove equal to the task. If not, I'm sure some of my brothers will be glad to carry you."

"I'll walk," Avall said curtly, and dismounted.

Zeff's quarters were indeed on the top inhabited level of the hold and offered a splendid view, though the mechanism of that view was heavily disguised. There was even a turnpike stair leading up two more levels to the outcrop's summit, where a nice small garden still survived, its edges artfully contrived so that no one gazing upward from ground level could see it. It would be a wonderful place from which to watch stars, Avall concluded, noting even as that thought appeared, how star paths were laid out across the stone. Yes, it was certainly an impressive place, and Avall felt slightly giddy, as though he could take a running start, leap from the edge, and soar off into the afternoon sky. He wondered if the gem—or what it had left in him—would save him then. It had saved him from death by cold and by water. But from falling? It had not saved that unfortunate Ixtian from death by fire. Besides, it would be tempting Fate, and he owed Fate too much already.

"We should come up here again," Rann acknowledged, "*after* dinner. It would be wonderful to watch twilight arrive from this aerie."

"It would," Avall agreed. "And I hope we can do that very thing. But there's something else I want to do first—have to do, really—and a lot will depend on how that resolves."

Rann glared at him. "That thing you wouldn't tell me?"

Avall schooled his face to calm, which he hoped made him unreadable. "I'll tell you everything, if it goes as it ought."

"And if it doesn't?"

Avall laid an arm across Rann's shoulders and drew him toward the stair that led down to what had been Zeff's suite, where the evening meal was already in preparation. "Tell Vorinn that I hope he makes a good King, and see if you can convince Strynn to marry either Lykkon or Kylin."

Rann froze in place. "It can't be that big a risk. If it is, I won't let you—"

"You can't stop me," Avall shot back fiercely. "Besides, the worst that can happen won't. I don't see any way that it can. It's just worth remembering that no matter how minor a task one undertakes, death is always an option."

"Yes," Rann snorted derisively. "Remind me to kill you if you die."

"I've decided that you can come with me," Avall told Rann four hands later, in Zeff's formal banquet hall. They had just finished a magnificent dinner that had been contrived simply by raiding Ninth Hold (as they had taken to calling the outcrop citadel) of its very best. Most of it was stored food, granted, so there was a paucity of fresh meat, but Avall barely noticed its absence.

"Something could happen," he continued, "and I'd prefer there was a witness, but I can't allow you to try to stop me."

Rann regarded Avall dubiously, but eased in beside him as he exited the feast, moving casually, as though he sought a garderobe.

Which, in a sense, he did, for the entrance to what he sought was located by moving a pair of tiles in one. This Avall did, standing aside as a section of mosaicked wall slid back, revealing a spiral staircase leading down. Rann raised a brow. "How did you know about this place?"

Avall couldn't suppress a grin. "I found Zeff's journal back at Gem-Hold; it had references. Once I knew that much, I made a point of prowling through his private records before dinner. I found a complete set of plans for this suite. Those people were nothing if not thorough about their documentation—to their sorrow, now that we control their documents. Now...shall we?"

"Lead the way."

With no more reply than another lifted brow, Avall turned and stepped onto the landing, leaving Rann to watch the door slide closed behind him. The stair was steep—not good for legs used to the sprawl of open land—but fortunately, it was also decently lit by glow-globes in another testament to Ninth Face affluence. Still, he was sweating when they reached the corridor at the bottom, at the end of which a single door was set in a recessed arch. He paused there, breathing hard. Rann was sweating, too, he noticed, but Rann had also possessed the foresight to bring along a flask of wine. He took a long draught and offered the rest to Avall. Avall accepted it gratefully, but only granted himself the smallest sip. "It's going to be hot," he told Rann. "I'm going to strip to my hose, I'd suggest you do the same."

Rann's reply was to follow Avall's suggestion. A moment later, bare to the waist, they confronted the door. Avall produced a key.

Rann raised a brow. "More diary records?"

Avall nodded, then inserted the key in a lock and entered.

Though he knew what to expect from what lay beyond, he was still not prepared for the amount of hot steam that gushed out at him. His body was soaked in an instant, his hair reduced to a cap of limp black tendrils. "Apparently the heat is somewhat variable," he told Rann with a nervous chuckle. "Not that it really matters. What does matter is that we're entering what is effectively a sacred place, so behave with that in mind. As I said, you can watch all you want, but don't try to stop me unless you feel that my life is in danger. You've been around gems enough that you should know the signs."

Rann's eyes went huge. "Gems? *Here?*"

Avall shook his head. "No, but their kin, perhaps. Now, come on. And close the door but don't let it latch."

He didn't wait to see if his orders were executed, merely stepped boldly into the swirling steam. "It's a cavern," he murmured to the dark shape in the mist that was Rann. "Happily, there are glow-globes."

Even so, it was hard to see through the thick white vapor, though he continued to make his way forward, groping a little when the stuff grew too opaque to reveal distinguishable landmarks. Fortunately, the ground was fairly level, though he stepped in pools of water once or twice before he realized that there was an actual path: a strip of white sand half a span wide that rose a finger above the surrounding terrain. Pillars of natural stone showed all about, rising from the ground or dripping down from the roof, often to meet in the center. Glowglobes had indeed been strewn about at intervals, like nests of brighter white upon the natural dark stone.

In spite of their illumination, it took considerable time to locate what he sought. He had been in that place before—once—but not from that direction. Still, when he finally reached his goal, there was no mistaking it. A small pool—no more than a span across—showed among the pillars, surrounded by more of the white sand, and facing it, with its back to the side from which Avall had entered, a low seat had been carved from one of the dripstone columns. Avall sank down there, grateful to be off his feet and enjoying the healing heat of the steam, even as it threatened to boil him alive. A finely wrought gold chalice sat on the ground to the right of the seat, precisely placed to be found by feel alone. Avall's fingers curled around it, and he studied it for a moment, probing the hard knobby gold work with sensitive artist's fingers. "Behold the Well of the Ninth Face," he whispered to Rann, who had squatted to his left. Without further word, Avall leaned forward and scooped the chalice full of water from that Well.

Pausing but briefly, he closed his eyes and drank. His hand was already moving to replace the vessel when the first vision found him.

The last time he had been here—shortly before his capture—he had been visited by a vision of the island in the lake. He'd had no idea what it meant then, only that it was a thing to be desired. He had come here this time purposely seeking some vision of the future, so that he had some surety that his efforts would outlast the moment.

What he saw was Strynn—asleep, with Div beside her, and Kylin close by, curled up like a kitten as he typically slept, though not so close that Avall had cause for jealousy. It was a camp in the woods, but not the camp he remembered, which gave credence to Strynn's comments to Vorinn about returning to the isle in the lake—The Eight knew there had certainly been time to get there. But now that he had seen her, he wanted to talk to her with an intensity he had not experienced since this escapade had begun. And somehow—much as it felt when the gems let him speak across distance—words formed in his mind that he knew were also forming in her head.

Strynn?

Avall?

*I am here. I—*And then some more primal instinct took over, and he was telling her everything that had transpired since he had departed—but not as words; rather, he spoke with feelings, images, and ideas; as if all his memories were flowing from him into her, much as he had felt when he had earlier shared Vorinn's memories of the battle. He had no idea how long it lasted, only that it was amazing. More important, his wife now knew that he was safe and sound, that the battle had been a success, and that all their mutual friends—and her brother in particular—were well and relatively happy.

Yet at the same time, he learned of events on the trek. There was a certain sameness to them that made them hard to dwell on, but he did learn that the party had been attacked by a band of adolescent geens, which had been summarily dispatched, and that the birkit seemed to have taken a mate. They were making slow progress, now that they were down a horse, but no one was in any particular hurry, though they did want to have a permanent shelter in place by winter—in the former geen's den, if nowhere else. Everyone was prospering, and Krynneth had finally gone hunting with Div and Riff, and had come back with two rabbits—and a grin that could have lit a hold. He looked healthier, too, and Div thought he might soon be declared healed.

That was all. Love was exchanged, but it was a natural flow of trust and affection that flowed with the other information, like leaves drifting along in water. And then, quite suddenly, that contact dissolved.

Another image replaced it.

Another sleeping woman.

This woman did not lie on a bed pad beneath the stars, however, but on the plainest of cots within a small stone chamber. Avall would have blinked had he possessed actual eyes in that place, for it looked enough like the cell in which Eddyn had been incarcerated to be the same.

But this was no tall, strapping, dark-haired, High Clan Eronese youth with the broad brawny shoulders of a smith. This was a frail old woman with a cloud of star-white hair fanning around a face that was like fine paper molded across an ivory skull.

Tyrill! It was less a cry than a gasp.

And unlike Strynn, who had never truly awakened, Tyrill did rouse enough to realize that actual conversation was possible.

Avall? So this is what "mind-speech" is like.

Tyrill? I had not planned this. The Well of the Ninth did this. Where are you?

A third of the way back to Tir-Eron. We have won. Tyrill, take heart, for my army approaches. Then, suddenly, as he recalled her situation. *You are in prison!*

A grim, unheard chuckle. *Not only that, Avall, I am condemned. If the usurpers here have their way. I will be executed for treason at dawn tomorrow.*

Tomorrow? Avall was aghast.

Aye. And Ilfon as well—at noon.

But tomorrow? It is not the time and season, and no one can execute High Clan without direct consent of the King.

They reckon such . . . inconveniences no longer to be important. And even delivered thus, Tyrill's sarcasm was like the crack of a whip.

It took Avall a moment to think of a response, so completely confounded was he, but then: *Tell me the rest, Tyrill: everything you can recall. Do not bother with words. Memories and impressions should be sufficient.*

Sufficient for what?

To effect a rescue, of course. I do not know how or why yet, but we cannot let this thing happen.

You are two hundred shots away, Avall.

Distance does not always matter, Avall replied. *Not under some circumstances. I cannot bring an army, but maybe I can bring that which is as strong as one.*

He felt a wash of hope briefly dispel Tyrill's overwhelming despair. There followed a rush of images, most having to do with clandestine assassinations, but also including Tyrill and Ilfon's discovery, arrest, and her trial, along with confirmation of where her cell was located. *I will not hope for rescue,* Tyrill told him when her tale had ended, *but I will not be surprised. And I will try my best to be ready.*

And I cannot promise when or how, but it will be as soon as I can manage. Only remember one thing Tyrill: time does not matter to the gems. But, from what I can tell, you apparently do.

And that was all. Whether he severed the contact in his eagerness to act, or Tyrill did, sensing that any time Avall spent speaking to her wasted time that could be spent effecting her rescue; or whether the power of the Well water had run its course, Avall had no idea. But one thing he did know: There would be at least one more battle. And that battle would come far sooner than he had anticipated.

CHAPTER XXXIII:

MASSING IN THE DARK

(NORTHWESTERN ERON: NINTH HOLD—NEAR-AUTUMN: DAY XVI—JUST PAST MIDNIGHT)

Maybe this will be the last time, Avall mused, as he waited for the remaining members of his Council to arrive from the various duties, diversions, and errands from which he had hastily summoned them close to a hand gone by. Unfortunately, the enormous honeycombed monolith that was Ninth Hold, though laid out with exemplary logic and precision, was more than large enough to confound the careless to the point of getting them lost entirely, or for even the competent to accidentally elude those dispatched to find them. The upshot was that it had taken most of a hand to get word to the relevant personnel that the King had called an emergency council as soon as could be managed, said meeting to occur in Zeff's former quarters, which Avall had made his own.

And that was way too long, Avall reckoned, especially when the fate of two of his staunchest allies in Tir-Eron hung in the balance. Time was flowing away at a fearful rate, the way he saw it, and at a still more fearful rate for Ilfon and Tyrill. And the worst thing was that he wasn't certain that there was anything that could be done to prevent their impending executions. At least waiting for his Council to arrive gave him time to do some planning, as well as allowing him and Rann an opportunity to change into dry clothes: war gear in his case. Rann had raised a brow at that, but Avall reminded him that not only would it save precious time in the long run, but would underscore the urgency of the still-half-formed plan he hoped, very soon, to be enacting.

And then—finally—Tryffon came grumbling in, having been located, after much searching, in the armory taking inventory. Which is exactly where he ought to have been, though perhaps not so close to midnight. A moment later, the last two delinquents arrived, armed with a mixture of gasps and apologies, and Avall could finally get down to business.

He had ordered cordials and cauf, but the only food to hand was leftovers from the feast. Alertness was needed now, and a full stomach was no ally to alertness.

Once again he tallied them: Rann, Merryn, Vorinn, Tryffon, Preedor, Veen, Lykkon, and Bingg (who had attached himself to the Council, though he was years away from being of age); along with a young woman who had wound up being acting Hold-Warden of Gem (which basically put her in charge of the refugees) and the subchiefs from Ferr and Stone, whom Vorinn had appointed to his Regency Council, and who had never had their warrants revoked. It made for tight quarters around the handsome polished table, and the blue-and-white decor put Avall on edge because of the unpleasant associations it recalled—but there was no time for residual squeamishness now.

No time for anything except quick, decisive action, and maybe not even for that, if what he was about to propose worked with less than absolute precision.

"Lords, Ladies, Chiefs, and Councilors," Avall began. "I apologize for summoning you at so late an hour, especially when I had promised you that, for the first time in a quarter, you could actually sleep in beds tonight. Unfortunately, that may now have to be postponed—for one more night, at least. For what reason? you may ask. And in reply I tell you that I have, a hand ere now, received news that is dire indeed, yet also news, which, if we act on it apace, may save us a great deal more trouble later. Necessity requires that I keep explanations short, but in essence, the situation is this…"

And with that he recounted the tale of his trip to the Well of the Ninth and what had transpired there.

"And you believe this…sending to be true?" Veen inquired.

"I believe it with absolute conviction," Avall assured her earnestly. "The last time I was gifted with a vision there, it showed me the island in the lake. This time—I'm not certain why I was given a contact with Tyrill, beyond the obvious, but it was clearly for some larger reason."

"You think it is The Eight intervening in our lives?" Gem's new Hold-Warden—Deenah was her name—ventured.

"I think that's possible. How else would They intervene save through otherwise random events? Or when our own minds have changed in such a way that we may more easily access Them? But this is not the time to argue theology. No, the question is not even whether to act, but what that action will be and when. I had thought to approach Tir-Eron with an army and perhaps win the day through threat or negotiation, but that choice, it now appears, has been taken from us. Priest-Clan has changed the rules—or chosen to ignore them—therefore, of rules we are likewise free."

He paused for a sip of wine, and to try to read the faces of those ranged around the table. Some—the new councilors, mostly—looked confused or uneasy. But there was no time to spare their feelings. "I am not asking for permission or a vote here, comrades," he continued. "I have a proposition to make, and when I am finished, I will ask for volunteers, though I have some in mind already. But I think what needs to happen is this:

"You all know by now that we have means in our possession to jump from here to…many places, apparently, though not without risk, and not with certainty. I say this last because the gems do not always take us where we intend to go, or when we want to go there, and that almost all jumping seems to require what might be termed an excess of desire—that is, that for the instant of the actual attempt, whoever would jump desires nothing else in all the world but the goal to which he would have the gems deliver him. Anger is an excellent catalyst—or fear. Maybe even love, though we haven't tested that much yet. The presence of water also seems to make some aspects simpler, but we'll need to do a lot of testing to find out how that works, and we don't have time for that at present. In any case, what I'm proposing is actually fairly simple. A group of us—no more than three, because that's as many as we have proof can jump the required distance of their own volition—will attempt to jump to Tyrill's cell and then jump back here with her. There should be no problems, and if there are, we will be armed. I say 'we,' because I will be one of those who jump—because I know most about the process and because, though I loathe the notion, I will be wearing the magical regalia, which only I can properly wield. More to the point, I will use it to power the jump. We know it can take three people and a horse, so three people going and four—with Tyrill—coming back should be no problem."

"But what about Ilfon?" From Lykkon, who idolized the man.

"If Tyrill knows where he is, we'll get her to show us, and try, at minimum, to jump him out of harm's way. That said, we may have to make two trips—and frankly I don't know if we can do that. The gems—or our bodies—may not let us. Still, it is incumbent upon us to try."

"Why not simply jump to the Citadel, then?" Preedor inquired through a yawn he tried to stifle. "Or to Priest-Hold, and set them all to rout. The sword would surely be adequate for that."

Avall shook his head—not that he hadn't considered precisely what Ferr's old Chief had suggested. "Because we might wound the body mightily and still not kill the head, and while

I think popular support has swung back in our favor, I would be loath to be seen raining lightning bolts down on Priest-Hold. As for the Citadel, it's unlikely we could catch everyone we would need there if we are truly to defang them."

"But they might be at Tyrill's execution," Tryffon countered. "Why not wait until then to attack? Seize her, call down lightning on them, then jump away."

"Mostly because that requires cutting the timing too tight," Avall replied. "And don't forget, jumping isn't always precise. Sometimes it takes you to the place or person you desire, sometimes it only drops you close by."

Merryn nodded sagely. "I agree with Avall, and not because he's my King and my brother. Spiriting Tyrill and Ilfon away quietly *is* clearly the way to go, if it can be managed. Imagine the confusion—the excuses and accusations—when they arrive at her cell to take her to execution and discover that she's vanished from what is presumed to be an escape-proof prison."

"It would be worth seeing," Tryffon agreed. "Not that we'll get to," he finished sourly, glancing sideways at Vorinn.

Avall ignored the rather too obvious hint. "In any case," he went on, "if we can get Tyrill and Ilfon back here, we'll have access to their information, which will help tremendously in planning the rest of the campaign."

Vorinn stroked his chin, then cleared his throat. Avall acknowledged him. "Vorinn?"

"I was just thinking, Majesty. You say you will lead this excursion, and I will not contest your right to do so. But it is a risk, especially if you plan—as now seems likely—to dare this endeavor twice, which you must do if you would rescue Ilfon. But I would remind you that we have not one set of magical regalia, but two. Granted, the set Zeff contrived is not perfectly made and may well be wildly unpredictable, but at least one part of it *was* of sufficient quality and power to jump two grown men on one occasion and three slightly smaller men on another. Would it not therefore behoove us to send two groups, perhaps a finger apart: one to rescue Tyrill, one to seek Ilfon?"

There was a murmur of approval at that, and, though the idea had not occurred to Avall, now that he considered it, it did have considerable merit. "And who would lead this second expedition?" he asked, though he already knew the answer he would receive.

"I would," Vorinn replied promptly. "I've had some experience with Zeff's regalia—more than anyone else here, at least. And if it comes to actual fighting, I'm as good as anyone hand to hand."

Avall gnawed his lips. "But if you go and I go, and we take those I suspect the two of us might choose, and then something terrible befalls us, it leaves the army under...whose command?"

Rann cleared his throat. "Perhaps we should hear suggestions as to who will comprise these groups, then decide."

Avall—almost—glared at him. "Very well. Since time grows short, I had thought to ask Merryn and Lykkon. I wanted you back here to command the army, Vorinn, but I know Merryn's as good a fighter as we've got, if it comes to that, and that Lyk's as good with the gems, if it comes to *that* plus he simply thinks well on his feet. Though frankly," he added, "I can't imagine suffering much injury if I'm wearing the regalia, especially in a closed space like a cell."

"And now?" Veen prompted.

"I stand by those I have named," Avall said flatly. "Vorinn, who would you propose accompany you?"

"My uncle, Tryffon," he replied at once. "He can fight, and he can play the power game if necessary. If anyone can bully down Priest-Clan, it would be him, but that should only be a factor if we get captured."

"And you would only take one beyond yourself?" Avall challenged, scowling.

"I had thought I might also take Veen," Vorinn conceded,

"for much the same reason Your Majesty wanted to take Merryn."

Veen looked startled but flattered. "Which leaves who in charge here?"

Avall vented a heavy sigh. "My bond-brother, Rann, if he will take it. He's been Regent before, and, from what I hear, was actually quite good at it. He'll have Preedor to advise him, as well as other good folk. Besides, that's only a factor if we fail—and I don't see how that can happen if we act expeditiously."

Rann checked the time candle in the corner. "If you're going to give yourself a comfortable pad before dawn, you'd best be at it," he said. "It's going to take another half hand to get everyone ready. And you still have to figure out whence you want to depart and what your targets will be. Oh, and I have one more suggestion: I think Vorinn's right: his group should leave a finger after Your Majesty's group, in case Your Majesty's group is in need of aid. Of course he might not be able to help, but I truly do think it would be useful."

Seeing nothing more to be gained by further discussion of minutiae, Avall rose abruptly. "Well, good Councilors," he announced, "I thank your for your presence, your advice, and your eagerness to support your King and kinsmen in what may indeed prove to be an ill-conceived endeavor. That said, I think that if we do not act, we will be cursing ourselves for the rest of our lives, and not only that, assuring that our names will be cursed forever. Merry and Lyk, I will meet you on the top of this hold in half a hand if you can be ready by then. Vorinn, Tryffon, Veen, you be there as well if you can manage. Anyone else who wishes to see us off is welcome, but do *not* seek to interfere."

"As if anyone would," Rann murmured into Avall's ear, as Avall went to help Lykkon change.

Avall met his personal target time with almost a finger to spare; then again, the quarters he had chosen were closest of all to the top of the hold and separated from it only by a private stair, which he, Merryn, Lykkon, and Rann used. Vorinn would be coming by another route, from the quarters Clan Ferr and Warcraft had claimed, and by the "public" stair.

In spite of their haste, they had managed to do well in terms of arraying themselves for what they hoped would be stealth but which might as easily prove to be public display. With the former in mind, they wore hooded black cloaks—but they wore them over surcoats of Argen maroon and the best mail and leather their own, or raided, resources could provide. Merryn and Lykkon had swords, small targe shields, and half helms, the better to see in close quarters; Avall had the regalia, newly freed from the table-safe in which it was kept while traveling, but still in the individual cases to which it had been consigned.

While they awaited their companions, they claimed places on four stone benches that faced inward around a tiny, glass-smooth pool. Shrubs surrounded it, along with a few small trees, and there was even a low, rustic-looking pavilion that faced a larger pool that was obviously meant for swimming. None would be visible from the ground, of course, and Avall felt vaguely guilty just sitting there. It was the soft time between midnight and dawn, and, as Rann had predicted, the sky was ablaze with stars, a situation abetted by the fact that one moon had not yet risen, one was a hand before setting, and the third one was already down. There was no wind, and the air was warm, but a fair bit of that warmth was the last of the previous day's heat melting from the rocks, the upshot of which was that Avall was sweating. An eighth from now the weather would be markedly different, he supposed. And one beyond that, this outcrop would be capped with snow.

He hoped he was alive to see it. So much could change between now and then. For one thing, Sundeath would be over, and with it the grace period he had granted himself in which to choose whether he would claim the crown in truth or abdicate it. Still, he had more choices now than he'd had two eights ago, while a fair number of people had fewer. Or none.

But what was keeping the others? Time really was of the essence, and though he had not naysayed them, he had massive misgivings about letting so many of his best strategists and fighters commit themselves to so risky a mission without backup.

Of course Fate would decide, as Fate always did, and Fate did seem to favor him. But what about this supposed Ninth Face? He had drunk from that Face's well twice, and both times it had seemed to act to his benefit. But, again, he wondered.

And then light showed from the door in the cleverly disguised turret opposite him: the one that anyone from the ground would have seen only as a spire of hard, dark stone twice as tall as a man. An instant later, Vorinn led Veen and Tryffon through it. They had dressed much as Avall's group had, down to wearing their own colors—Ferr's colors—beneath black cloaks. And if Warcraft crimson was perhaps too bright to ensure proper stealth, still, it was also a color that most in Eron were conditioned to respect, if not actually fear. Even Priest-Clan, if history prevailed. Even the Ninth Face, if those who opposed that rebellious sect were lucky.

Tryffon raised his sword in salute. Greetings and admonitions of luck followed quickly, and then it was time for business, as Rann began to uncase the royal regalia. Avall waited to be vested. It was better that way, he told himself, and helped him focus his thoughts for what he was about to attempt. Veen and Tryffon, he noted, took their cues from him.

First came the shield, then the sword, and finally the helmet. Rann made a fuss about adjusting straps and setting the helm's chin strap, but Avall understood, even if it made him sad. That was another thing this might eliminate: these endless rounds of partings.

In any case, with the lowering of his helm, the world abruptly narrowed to what he could see straight ahead and a few degrees up and down and to either side. He could feel the gems, too, waiting there a twitch away from his palms, so eager to taste his blood that they were already singing to it. *Had they always done that?* he wondered. *Or was this a new attribute of the regalia that had only manifested since he had used that regalia to jump through the waters?*

"Time passes," Avall said tersely, to distract himself from further speculation. "Assuming we actually manage this thing," he added, facing Vorinn but including them all, "wait half a finger—Rann will tell you when—and follow. If you don't arrive, we'll assume you've failed and act without you. Whatever happens—assuming *we* succeed—we'll try to jump Tyrill back here—or to the safest place we can find—and return for Ilfon just in case. Remember, the only way this is going to work is through absolute desire. And be careful: The gems can detect desires your surface mind doesn't even suspect you possess."

"Heard and acknowledged," Vorinn replied soberly— "Your Majesty and my King."

And with that he returned to his fellows.

Avall likewise turned away, then took a deep breath, and murmured a quiet, "All right, Lyk and Merry, it's time to blood yourselves." He waited for them to draw their weapons, but, to his surprise, they reached forward and slid their hands down the naked steel of the Lightning Sword instead. He heard Lykkon gasp at the pain, but his cousin was up to it, he reckoned, and the gems, when they had time, would heal any physical damage he might have incurred.

This was it, then. A final breath, and he closed his eyes, slammed his fist into his forehead to set himself bleeding there, and squeezed the triggers in the sword and shield. Power flooded into him at once, like a river that had breached a dam and now sent its waters outward, seeking equilibrium among three distinct tributaries. And this time—It was hard to explain, but it seemed as though the regalia felt more comfortable with him, as though it had accommodated itself to him, though it had been made for High King Gynn.

"Merry, Lyk," he called softly, "I can feel it awakening now, so put your hands on my hands on the sword, and as soon as you feel anything untoward start to happen, try as hard as you can to completely merge with me, and if you're thinking anything at all, wish with all your might to be where Tyrill is."

He felt their hands slide over his, so slick with blood he could barely distinguish them—and then it didn't matter, because their power was pouring into him along with the power of the gems, and with it came their consciousnesses and their wills. And where they touched his deepest self, parts of that self awoke that normally stayed quiescent: parts last stirred by Strynn and Rann, not his sister and his cousin. Yet his self welcomed them eagerly, and bound them to him, and directed their power into strange new channels, which made him stronger in turn.

He wasn't certain, but he thought the sword began to glow. *Wish now!* he thought at the others. And then there was nothing but the flow of power and the power of wishing.

He thought he heard the snap of their bodies vanishing from atop Ninth Hold, but could not be certain. The only surety was that he *wasn't* for a moment, and then he *was* once more, and that two other shapes were pressed close against him, then falling away, gasping in surprise and relief, while their blood vanished with his into the sword.

It was Merryn's muttered curse that warned him that things had not gone as expected, though he felt the stirring of wind against his face even as he heard it, and opened his eyes the barest instant later.

They were *not* in Tyrill's prison cell.

Nor were they alone.

In the predawn darkness, it took Avall a moment to determine their actual location. Even then, he only truly believed when Lykkon proclaimed it aloud: "Oh Cold, cousins! We're on the Isle of The Eight!"

And so it was. They had arrived somewhere near the center of Priest-Clan's sacred isle in the middle of the Ri-Eron, where rose the various Fanes of The Eight. At the moment, in fact, they faced the Fane of Fate from before its Well. Indeed, they stood where he had stood almost a quarter ago when he had come here with Bingg seeking advice, and been shown the island in the lake for his pains, then gone home to discover that Strynn had already departed in search of Merryn.

So it was full circle, then—which could not be coincidence.

But these people—

Who were these folk who stood around, staring gape-faced and—not so much fearful as mightily surprised? He squinted in the gloom, trying to read colors or insignia, but the gloom washed most of both away. As best he could tell, there wasn't much to see, anyway: merely the dull colors that were clanless's lot. There were a goodly number of them, too: maybe two hundred.

And then he realized that what he had taken for a rising wind was in fact a low murmur of cautious wonder, even joy, that flowed from mouth to mouth. And in his shock at finding himself outside at all, when he had expected to confront Tyrill in her cell, it took an instant for their words to register. Yet when they did, they filled him with awe and wonder.

"Avall, Avall, Avall," they were saying. "The King has come again and Fate has sent him. The King! The King! The King has come to feed us. The King has come to call the lightning down on those who have ruined our land. Avall, Avall, Avall."

But in nowise so eloquently stated or well organized. Mostly it came as a rush of emotion that he actually felt as a physical force flashing through his veins. Which was reminder enough that he needed to release the triggers in the sword and shield and, as carefully as he could, ease the helm away from his face.

"Majesty," a man dared finally: sturdy, tall, and bare-armed, in clanless dull brown, yet handsome and well built for all that. And without more word, the man was on his knees. "Majesty, command us and, if you will, set us free."

Avall thought fast. He had no army at his back save Merryn

and Lykkon. Yet these people had seen what would surely to them have been a wonder, and he was not fool enough to doubt the force of faith. And as man after man and woman after woman knelt before him he realized two things together. One was that this was an extraordinarily large crowd to have assembled here at a time of night when the Isle of The Eight was supposed to be closed to supplicants—which in turn implied that either they were here without leave, or that those charged with enforcing the ban had abandoned that enforcement. The other thing was that these people were both ripe and eager to be led. And if he lacked his usual army, still these folk made up in fervor what they might lack in steel. Besides, he had the Lightning Sword against which no other blade could stand, and also the shield to ward off any harm.

And time was wasting, and he would lose the momentum of the moment if he did not act at once. Obviously it would be something akin to madness to attempt a jump to Tyrill's cell amid so volatile a situation; he must therefore contrive some other plan—before Priest-Clan got word that anything untoward was afoot.

"Quick," he demanded of the man who knelt before him. "Three things. First: What is your name?"

"Taravan."

"Second: The Lady Tyrill; she is to be executed today. Will that be in the Court of Rites?"

"Majesty, it will, and at dawn, and a curse on those who do such a thing, and forget the Ancient Laws by so doing."

"Finally: Will you be my man and follow me for this morning only? Or if not me, will you follow the Lightning Sword?"

"Ah, Majesty, we will follow."

"But we have no weapons," someone protested—someone young, by the sound of it.

"No," Lykkon replied, glancing around, "but the Fane of Law lies yonder, and the fence around that Fane is made of very real swords, one added there per year. If Fate has given us an army, surely Law will see that army armed."

"And what of Vorinn?" Merryn murmured, as Avall's makeshift militia began to rise.

"Perhaps he even now fulfills our errand, or that on which he came. Or perhaps he will arrive here in our wake. We have no time to wait, if we would lead these good folk to the Citadel."

"Well," Lykkon laughed roughly, "let's be at it, then."

Merryn stared aghast. "And here I thought *I* was a warrior."

And then, with a tide of two hundred hardy souls behind him, Avall syn Argen-a turned and strode away from one manifestation of Fate in order to face another.

CHAPTER XXXIV:

INVASIONS

(ERON: TIR-ERON—NEAR-AUTUMN:
DAY XVI—SHORTLY BEFORE DAWN)

~~~~~~~~~

Tyrill had been staring at the door for most of the night—ever since young Avall had come to her in what she increasingly believed had been a dream, promising a deliverance that still was not forthcoming. In spite of herself, she had almost gone to sleep after that…occurrence. Indeed, had once drifted off in truth, only to sit bolt upright in the light of the single candle they allowed her and whisper his name into the shadows: "Avall…Avall…Avall."

And with that it had all come tumbling back to her. It had to be him, *had* to be, for she knew that he commanded that which allowed him to speak across distance, though he had never spoken to her in such a manner. But he had come to her in the night—his mind to her mind, like clandestine lovers—and she had relayed her situation, and Ilfon's along with it, and he had promised her release.

It had been the most vivid dream she had ever experienced, too, and so she had risen and dressed, and made herself ready for anything—for Avall to appear out of a veil of smoke, she supposed.

But Avall had never come, and now dawnlight was creeping down that maze of mirrors, and in something less than a hand, as she reckoned it, they would come for her, and a hand after that—or sooner—she would be dead.

Not that being dead concerned her overmuch, for death would bring an end to what was effectively constant pain. But it would also mean leaving a great many things unfinished, and worst of all, it would mean leaving Eron a worse place than when she had entered it—and if there was one lesson she had learned at her mother's knee, it was to leave the world better for having been alive.

And so she sat and waited, and was only a little surprised when she heard booted feet approaching, heard the familiar tentative knock and that same nameless Ninth Face woman's voice warning her that she was about to enter.

She found Tyrill dressed in the set of clan regalia they had let her keep since her trial—let her keep, she supposed, so that she could wear it to her execution and so be more easily identified. So that she could drive home Priest-Clan's message that not even one as mighty as Tyrill san Argen-yr was exempt from Law.

Which was a travesty and a farce, since, as best she could tell, Law barely existed anymore. And so she composed herself to calm, and rose when her guard approached, gently took her hands, and bound them only with soft rope in lieu of chains, then stood aside for her to walk through the door and into the corridor beyond. She didn't know if these were the same four guards who had escorted her before, because they had drawn their hoods far forward over their faces and wore mouth-masks besides. One thing she did note, however: They had left the door open behind her. She wondered whether the candle would expire before she died or after.

This was it, then: She was going to meet her doom. Avall had not come. She had been a fool to believe that he would, a fool to think that her dream had been any more than a dream. And even if it were not, even if that *had* been Avall who had spoken to her, there were a thousand thousand things that could have forestalled his errand.

It was just as well it was early and these men around her blocking the view of the seemingly endless corridor before and behind, and that her lack of sleep was catching up with her, making her dull-headed. She yawned absently and heard one of them chuckle and say, "So eager to sleep now, Lady? When soon you will sleep forever?"

She ignored him. And then, quite suddenly, they had reached the foot of the first of several flights of steps that should take her up, then up again, to spit her out at last in the place where all Eronese traitors since time immemorial had died: a specially built platform in the midst of the Court of Rites, with all of Eron's nobility dressed in black, gathered around to watch and—more to the point—ratify.

But that was on Sundering Day at Sundeath, which was still several eights away. Not that those in power these days had any respect at all for ancient rites. Not anymore.

But surely they should be turning now! Surely there should be one more stair, and then she should step out into the watery light, and feel all those eyes upon her, and then mount those last few steps to where the swordsman stood, bare-chested, but with his face forever obscured beneath that terrible black hood.

Yet they did not turn, but continued on...and on...and on. Not so far as all that, in fact, yet it seemed an eternity. One thing was clear: they were not going to the Court of Rites—which meant that even if Avall did come, he would arrive at the wrong location.

So where were they going instead? And then they made one more turn and twisted up another stair and she knew.

Knew those eight facets and the tiers of seats within them and that famous blue faience dome overhead, with the windows beneath it still playing games with the morning light. Knew the dais and the Throne and the Stone. But did not

know more than a score of the faces that stared at her as the
guard marched her, yet again, to the Chair of the Accused.

The priest gate at the juncture of North Bridge and the
Riverwalk, where the causeway to the Isle of The Eight joined
the mainland, was a smoking ruin behind him, but Avall no
longer cared, as he strode along at the head of his ragtag army,
with Merryn at his side as grim-faced as he, and Lykkon on the
other, trying to look grim as well, but glancing back more often
than he gazed forward, and, like as not, grinning like a fool.

The gate had been a barrier, and those between had offered
resistance, and he no longer had the patience—or the time—to
suffer interference. He remembered shouting, "Leave now or
die" at the guard on duty. He did *not* remember if the guard
had in fact departed or had still been inside the gatehouse
when Avall had answered the rising eager madness in his
blood and called down the lightning on the structure. Merryn
had glared at him and Lykkon had gasped, but the crowd behind him—armed with identical Swords of Law "borrowed"
from Law's Fane—had cheered, applauded, and surged forward with so much eager glee that Avall did not recall passing
through the rubble.

Which had put him on the Riverwalk, with the sky to the
east pinkening alarmingly—which meant that he would have
to increase his pace. And so he did, running effortlessly over
the well-set stones, with Merryn beside him and Lykkon a little farther back and panting. Avall felt as though he could run
forever, and while his rational aspect informed him that all his
new strength was borrowed—a little from everyone around
him, who would all feel cold and attribute it to the nippy
morning air—once again, he had no time to be concerned for
such minutiae. After all, a King of necessity drew from all his
people, and The Eight knew that Avall had already paid them
back with interest for anything they now lent him in turn.

And so he jogged along ever faster, with his cloak billowing behind him like vast black wings until he discarded it and continued in just his surcoat, with the Lightning Sword now glittering in truth as it tasted the first raw rays of sunrise light.

Only a little farther; only another quarter shot, and he would reach the massive wall that fronted the Citadel and enclosed the Court of Rites. He wondered if they had word of his coming. He wondered if they would take his sudden approach as a signal to expedite Tyrill's execution. Things could still go badly wrong. And if they did—if he failed to overthrow Priest-Clan and the Ninth Face now, this morning—he feared that the mob behind him—which was increasing even as it marched, as more early risers caught the word and the mood and joined—would turn on him and rend him and his sister and his cousin to bits. Or else he would have to use the sword on them, and that he would never do.

Or would he? The sword told him that yes indeed he might, and that knowledge filled him with fear. But he put that fear to use as fuel for his anger and let it propel him along even faster.

The walls were beside him now, and the towers that flanked the doors loomed ahead. Normally those doors would be open, but it was no surprise that they were closed and barred today.

Which presented the first dilemma. If he hesitated for even a moment, he could easily be too late. But if he blasted his way through, Priest-Clan could take that as license to act in its own haste and execute Tyrill early.

He didn't really care. If they were going to kill her, why she was old enough to die anyway, and would probably welcome the relief. And if he found them there— Well, he could exact a great deal of revenge indeed before—cowards that they obviously were—the majority of Priest-Clan fled.

All of which was rank conjecture.

Or perhaps—the thought was barely a flicker—merely the sword's opinion.

But only for an instant, as Avall halted a dozen spans before the massive doors that were the first bulwark of the Citadel's defense, and raised the sword again.

"Brother, are you certain?" Merryn cried.

"Avall—do you think—?" From Lykkon.

He ignored them, though he heard Merryn murmur a fretful, "Lyk, I fear it's got hold of him, and when that happens— if he can't control it—the sword and he will both go mad."

Mad? He heard the word and laughed. What a stupid little word for such a marvelous, powerful feeling—for knowing he could do anything in the world—call down any power.

And why were these gates closed before him, anyway, when he was King and this the heart of his Sovereignty?

A blink, a furrowing of his brow in concentration, a feeling of the powers flowing into him and out of him and around him and of them ripping a hole in the Overworld and dragging its substance down and flinging it forth again—at the doors.

If not lightning, it might as well have been, for it arced from the sword and smashed into all that fabulously wrought wood and gilded bronze and blew it all to flinders.

"Tyrill, I am come!" Avall shouted recklessly, as, with an equally wild-eyed army at his back, he dashed forward and passed through the gates of the Citadel and entered the Court of Rites.

—Entered a court of silence, rather, where ranks of empty stone benches looked down on naught save a widening pool of ruddy morning light.

A glance showed the sun appearing.

Which sobered Avall enough for him to make a number of well-chosen guesses. And then the madness took him again and once more thrust him onward.

Vorinn couldn't breathe.

Water was all around him, water lapping at the gates of his nose and mouth, pressing relentlessly at his lungs, even as it reached out with a thousand tiny hands and found every fold and filament of his cloak and surcoat and began to drag him down.

Into what?

He had no way of knowing, for he had found himself in a place of endless dark. A dark without stars such as had shone overhead when he had begun this reckless, stupid venture that was now very like to kill him, Veen, and Tryffon, all three—and damn them for stupid, fools, too: to have put any trust in what had been made as the enemy's weapon. He could feel Zeff's sword hard in his hand, with Veen's hand and Tryffon's hands still wrapped around it, though Veen's was clearly slipping. And he could feel them crowding against him in a way he thought was odd, until a random kick connected with something so solid it could only be stone.

Which meant that he was in a real place again, and one that had real limitations, even if it was full of water.

And he did have a sword of power in his hands, and two good kinsmen trying to merge their strength of will with his.

But he could hold his breath no longer, and neither, surely, could they. His lungs were nigh on bursting and far, far too soon he would have no choice but to let water into his nose, and then his lungs would hurt for a little while, and then would come blissful nothing.

Except that he now knew that his soul would survive, and he could not stand to contemplate how that soul might feel: compelled to reproach its corporeal shell for one stupid failure—forever.

And *that* would be worse than dying absolute; he was as certain of that as he was certain of anything in all reality. He could not let it happen—not with two comrades likewise at risk. And if wishing with a magic sword in his hand got results, then he was more than willing to do some wishing.

He would try once more, and then—

Reflexes deeper than thought preempted him—enough that he began kicking his way upward with the sword above him, held now in both his hands. He could see nothing, but he felt the blade strike home against something solid. Something that rang like thick glass in whatever this place was.

And if there was something as hard as glass above him, perhaps there was air on the other side, and in any case, he could not hold his breath even one instant longer, and in that last moment of panic before he belched out his lone precious lungful of air, he stabbed upward and—somehow—called the lightning.

Light shattered the world above into a perfect circle, though a small one, and he felt himself driven down and down and down by the recoil. But there *was* light up there, and light meant air, and so, once again, he kicked upward. Veen had released her hold by then, but Veen was an ocean child and he knew her to be a strong swimmer. Tryffon—Tryffon was not young but Tryffon was strong and sturdy and had taught Vorinn himself to swim, and in any case, there was promise of air and for a very brief moment Vorinn didn't care. And so he let himself sink down until a different kind of darkness began to enfold him. And there in that peculiar cold dark, he began to hear tiny voices singing to him, telling him without words that for now they would keep him alive, but only for a moment, that if he would live, he would have to save himself *now* or perish.

And so he did. Folding his legs in the cold wet that surrounded him, he kicked away from that unseen bottom and drove himself upward again, with the sword held straight above him, cleaving that unseen way.

He felt himself brush past Veen and Tryffon—

—And enter open air. And keep on rising—propelled by his own massive push, or drawn by the sword, he never knew which.

Only that water was suddenly sluicing away from his head and shoulders, and he had found himself peering over a curb of stone. What kind, he neither knew nor cared; all that mattered was that he could breathe again, and so he hurled himself across that barrier. Or tried to, for barely had he begun when hands seized him by the shoulders and hoisted him up farther and faster than he had anticipated, so that before he knew it he was on his feet, blinking at a large crowd of earnest, eager, and somewhat awestruck faces that had gathered around what he realized abruptly was the Well of Fate on the Isle of the Eight.

"My friends," he tried to say—but only spat up water, so that it took two tries and far too much lung-splitting coughing to reach the words again. But they didn't matter anyway, because whoever had helped him out was now helping Veen and Tryffon over the ledge.

"The lightning has freed them," someone yelled. "And with them, the Lightning has freed the Well."

"Who is it?" someone else demanded.

"Tryffon of War," Vorinn heard Tryffon thunder behind him. "And Vorinn syn Ferr-een, and Veen san Ferr-lone."

"Fate has spoken indeed," someone else enthused. "First it gave us Avall, and now it has given us the bravest soldiers in his army."

"Avall?" Vorinn cried, reaching for the man nearest him. "Avall was here? You have seen Avall?"

"A quarter hand ago," someone else acknowledged. "A number of us were here and saw him appear much as you did, save that he did not come from out the Well, but appeared before it. Most of those who were here then went with him. Some of us remained to give thanks to The Eight. Some went to tell others of that first wonder."

"And now a second! We are saved."

Vorinn barely heard the short, round, serious-faced woman who had last addressed him. "I have come at Avall's command," Vorinn shouted. "Where has he gone?"

"To the Citadel," that woman replied. "And there is a mighty madness upon him. If you would find him, young Lord, go there."

Vorinn needed no further coaching, nor did Tryffon and Veen. Pausing only long enough to shed their sodden cloaks since they would obviously not be needing them now that stealth was no longer an option, they strode off in the wake of the mob that had preceded them.

But as they passed the smoking ruin of the priest gate, Vorinn found himself wondering if he was going to save Tyrill and Ilfon, or going to save Avall. He was halfway to the Citadel before he realized that every single person behind him was cheering and chanting his name. "Vorinn, Vorinn, Vorinn."

And that more people were pouring into the Riverwalk from either side, chanting that same thing.

If Tyrill had accused her captors of cowardice during her mockery of a trial, she condemned them for it thrice over now. How much could have changed, she wondered, to make them replace the ancient tradition of public execution with what was clearly going to be a far more private affair, with only the Council of Chiefs to witness, and not one soul from among the ranks of the clanless?

She supposed it was to drive home the notion of obedience to potentially recalcitrant chiefs so as to quell them farther into submission. *But at what risk? Were the Chiefs of Priest-Clan so fearful of the people as a whole that they dared not expose their more questionable acts to light of day? Were they indeed so fearful that they would risk defiling the sanctity of the Hall of Clans with High Clan blood?* And while she acknowledged that her blood was not quite innocent—equally innocent people had died by her hand, after all—it had been over a century since blood had been shed in this place, and that a fistfight between two Chiefs that had ended with bloody noses.

But what form would her death take now? She saw no sign of the headsman's block, never mind the headsman himself, though by the agitation evident in those still assembling on the floor, she suspected that this relocation had been a hasty decision.

A supposition confirmed a moment later when the door by

which she had entered opened again, to admit four sturdy guardsmen bearing between them the traditional oak block on which one stretched one's neck for execution. There was no straw to soak up the blood, however—but there was a many-folded thickness of cheap carpet in the arms of two more guardsmen. Tyrill watched with distant interest—or perhaps she was already easing into shock—as the rugs were placed in the open place before the dais from which she had herself, on countless occasions, addressed the Chiefs and the Priests and the King.

All that was needed was for the headsman himself to arrive—she hoped they were having trouble finding someone to agree to such a thing—and for the rising sun to send sign that the appointed time was upon them, and then...

And then...

Abruptly, Tyrill was crying. Not lavishly, but in spite of her iron desire never to show any sign of weakness in public, tears were leaking from her eyes.

She closed them. She had to. And she kept them closed as doors opened again, this time to admit—by the swish of their heavy robes—the Priests of...of The Nine, she supposed.

And then came another set of steps, heavier ones, as of a sturdily built man approaching. A very large man, indeed—to judge by the way his footsteps were echoing on all that inlaid marble.

Except...that wasn't one set of footsteps at all, she realized with a start. Somewhere beyond the Hall of Clans's sacred precincts, countless feet stomped and thudded, mingled increasingly with outraged shouts.

Tyrill opened her eyes at once, to see the Priests turn toward the Hall's main doors. She turned as well—as much as her bonds permitted—and saw the entire assembly likewise stand and stare.

But she saw something else, too: a file of blue-clad archers springing into view in the visitors' arcades—with every arrow fixed on a separate target among those Chiefs gathered on the floor.

Avall saw that there was a door ahead—*knew* that there was a door ahead—but that was all that mattered. The sword possessed him now, drawing him ever onward, and the only thing that restrained him at all was the fact that part of him still retained a real and tangible goal that was worth preserving. Otherwise— Well, he had a quarter's worth of anger and frustration pent up in him, a quarter's worth he had expected to discharge at Gem-Hold and been denied.

But discharge it he would—now, and diplomacy be damned. The gates to the Court of Rites were a ruin. The outer doors to the structure that housed the Hall of Clans at its core would be gone as well, had some of that multitude that flowed around him not dashed past him to wrench those doors wide open. He had been surprised that they had not been locked, but that surprise had lasted only for an instant; intent as he was on striding up the stairs, aiming at the darker chamber beyond, which led in turn to what had become the single, all-encompassing goal that consumed his life.

Shadows stretched long before him as he mounted up the wide slabs of pure white marble that comprised the final stair. And in that early light, the marble seemed to glow pink like flesh flayed free of skin and left to perish there. How many went with him, he had no idea. Only that Merryn and Lykkon were still present, though not at all pleased with him, and that Merryn had sought to yank the shield away—and got burned fingers for her trouble.

He hated that, too: Part of him did. But if they would only give him a chance—only a hundred breaths more, it would all be over. Since Tyrill was not in the Court of Rites, there was only one possible place she could be. He *knew,* and more to the point, the gems in his shield and helm and sword seemed to know in some uncanny way, beyond fear and doubt.

And then he reached the top of the stair and entered the building proper. He paused there briefly to let his eyes adjust to the relative gloom—and to see a number of Ninth Face guards dispersing down the corridor that encircled the Hall of Clans itself, while four more moved to block the entrance.

Their folly.

Avall had no patience for diplomacy. No time for more than the most minimal effort to save four lives. "Move now or die," he shouted. And with that he twitched the sword so that the whole length of the blade flashed fire—which made it easier to recognize.

One guard took his advice and dodged left and around one of the pillars that flanked the doors. One raised a crossbow, one a dagger. One hesitated.

All but the first one perished, as Avall flexed the sword a certain way—and sent power slamming into another splendid work of fine wood and well-wrought metal.

Miraculously, the doors withstood one blow—though those who had stood before them did not, as the fires of the Overworld burned their skin away—and a good portion of flesh along with it.

Avall snarled beneath his helm as he readied a second bolt and let it fly.

This time the portals gave way. The hinges on the one to the right broke free entirely, which left what remained of the other free to swing back against the wall of the span-long corridor that pierced the solid stone of the Hall of Clans's inner wall.

And with that second blow, Avall felt some of the madness that had possessed him dissipate. This was it. Tyrill was here, and most of his enemy. It would be easy enough: He would simply run in and—

Where was she, anyway?—as he felt the sudden weight of a

hundred pairs of eyes swivel toward him even as his own momentum carried him full into the chamber.

His gaze swept around the Hall. Time had slowed again, and that gave him ample opportunity to see that most of the assembled Chiefs had little claim to their titles. More to the point, it gave him time to note the nine Priests assembled upon the dais. And to see a small, frail, white-haired shape rise from a stone chair before all that multitude, less than a dozen spans away.

"Tyrill!" he shouted, and started forward, sword to ready, shield on guard.

"Avall! Lookout! No!"

—From Tyrill, Merryn, and Lykkon all together.

Too late—even with the gem driving his perceptions—Avall saw the archers in the gallery: the gallery that encircled the Hall on every side.

And he had blundered a third of the way down the aisle already.

He had just started to spin around to check behind him when the first arrow struck him—on the right side of his back, directly atop his shoulder blade.

He felt the impact before he felt the pain, and fortunately mail covered a double layer of leather there, which in turn covered a modicum of muscle and sturdy bone.

Yet for all that, it struck with sufficient force to set him stumbling forward when he wanted to retreat. Which opened his back to a clearer shot from another arrow, which found the lower curve of his left thigh. Thus impaled, he staggered on until his legs tangled in the shaft and sent him stumbling. He flailed wildly, which jiggled the arrow in his back. Pain became the world for an instant, and then redoubled as a third arrow found him a handspan to the left of the first and perilously near his spine. He heard the point crack against a rib. But what he felt even more than pain was a sudden numbness. He could no longer hold the sword—yet if he dropped it, everything would be over.

But there was still one mad thing he might do. Without thought—but with a prayer to whichever of The Eight might be observing to grant him aid—Avall flung the Lightning Sword down the aisle, watching it slide, hilt first, past countless aghast faces—

Until it was brought up short—perhaps it was Fate again—by the pile of rugs brought to soak up her blood, right at Tyrill's feet. The hilt, he saw, as the floor came up and struck him, was barely a span from the tips of her shoes.

Tyrill saw the flash of the sword as it slid toward her, and for the briefest moment feared that Avall had gone even farther down the road to madness than he appeared and had tried in some impossibly awkward way to kill her before Priest-Clan could.

Which was as stupid as it was preposterous.

And then suddenly that blade was lying stock-still within easy reach of her bound hands.

And the archers' attention was still focused, most of them, upon Avall.

It was rash; it was foolish; it was completely from reflex and utterly without reason. But it was also her single chance for life—or if not for life, for a death that would accomplish something worthwhile.

So it was that not even a breath passed her lips before she had flung herself forward onto her knees and was scrabbling for the hilt of that terrible, magical weapon: that weapon that Strynn had made and into which Avall had set one of those damnable, troublesome gems. She had avoided contact with them over the last few eights, but time for avoidance had ended.

Fingers still strong from eight decades of smithing grasped the hilt, even as shoulders that had swung many a hammer in her youth yanked upward. As she did, she felt something prick her palm and remembered the trigger and how one had to feed this sword blood in order for it to be in anywise extraordinary. She pressed down at once, securing her grip, then slid her other hand onto the hilt as well, since the presence of the bonds on her wrists effectively required it.

Power lashed out at her: a furious outpouring of energy that had as its vanguard a curious kind of questing, as though it sought to know who she was.

One who would serve this Kingdom, she raged back. *One who was there when you were made.*

And then she had no more time for thought, for the sword seized upon some instinct that lay latent far more deeply inside her than even the need for survival and yanked her hands aloft in defiance of her conscious will.

Which was how she remained when the first arrow thudded home in her breast. It nicked her heart, and she felt that trusty organ skip a beat and falter. But her senses had shifted now, so that she seemed to have complete control of her entire body, and more important, knowledge of how that body functioned. And she knew from what that knowledge told her that she was dying.

But if that were the case, then she had to make her death count in earnest. These folks around her—these so-called Priests—they had assailed her clan and her Kingdom and killed many people she had long known and loved. Worse, they had destroyed the order not only of her life, but of countless others. They had even—it seemed—destroyed Avall—and whatever else he was, he was a genius when it came to metal. And the wanton destruction of one as gifted as he was something that could not be endured—and certainly not twice in one generation.

That was the final trigger.

A twitch of her hand, a more subtle twitch of some part of her brain, and she thrust the sword into the Overworld and ripped out a portion of what she found there—and hurled it around the room.

Avall had called the Overworld lightning, but this was a

whip of the same unearthly force, and she lashed it, first of all, across the gallery where stood those damnable archers. She heard them cry out warning, heard them scream, heard them die. Heard some of their bows drop to the floor below, and heard the strange buzzing hiss as the fire from the sword ignited arrows already in flight.

More screams, and she heard feet pounding behind her and saw men and women rising and starting to flee—some of them—or rush forward to put an end to her.

And that could not be countenanced either. *She* had the sword. *She* held in her hand the most powerful weapon in that or any Kingdom. And if she lost it, it would fall into the hands of those who would use it to no good end.

So it was that she raised it one final time and pointed it at that marvel of blue faience mosaicked ceiling, and called down the lightning over and over. Eight times, she called it: one bolt for each of the piers that supported that splendid, airy dome.

So quickly did she move, however, that the dome still remained there unsupported for an impossible instant, as though considering whether it was subject to the laws of the world.

Then it began to fall.

It scraped and slid for the first few spans, but after that, it began to fragment at the edges. Yet it was still mostly intact when it slammed into the floor of the Hall of Clans, obliterating, so Tyrill intended, not only herself, but all nine Priests on the dais, and every sneaky, cowardly, upstart Chief in the Hall.

Tyrill felt herself knocked to the floor as the sword seemed to explode in her hand. And then she felt darkness reach out to enfold her. But she never felt the dome crash down atop her skull.

Relief. The first emotion that coursed through Avall when he saw Tyrill seize the Lightning Sword was relief. Yet hard on its heels came a sick feeling deep in his gut that Tyrill would not be able to control it, and more to the point, that he really had ruined things now, and delivered the ultimate weapon into the hands of the enemy.

And hard on the heels of *that* came the realization that he had lost control of the sword but still wore the rest of the regalia, which was therefore completely unbalanced. And finally, he remembered that he had been shot, not once, but many times, and that his back was a solid sheet of pain.

Which was when he finally stopped the skidding half roll that had sent him to hands and knees—and briefly chest and chin—from which he had recovered to knees again, only to come up short against the side of one of the pews where the Chiefs of Glass normally would have sat, where he collapsed once more.

He lay there winded, too far gone into shock to take more initiative, and felt pain wash over him in sharp red waves that threatened to become the world.

That position also gave him a prime vantage from which to see Tyrill wield the sword.

As to what followed— It was thunder, it was lightning, it was a whole summer storm let loose in one suddenly too-frail building. He knew when the archers died because he heard them screaming.

But when Tyrill aimed her blast at the dome— Well, that was *too* impossible. It was blasphemy: that an artist should damage another artist's masterwork. It was, in fact, an act of highest treason. But Tyrill had already determined to pay the price, he knew—and with a few deaths buy many, many lives.

And then the dome was falling. It took Avall a moment to realize that it represented an untold weight of stone and would surely crush him, but by that time, it was too late to rise and flee.

The only thing left to do was to raise the shield—and even that he did mostly from reflex.

It was the loudest noise Avall had ever heard, and the

strongest force he had ever felt. Though he was already sprawling upon the floor, the weight continued to push down, as though it would grind him into the marble.

And then it was over. His ears were ringing, he noted—which was not what he had expected. And then he realized that he really was alive, if totally filthy and totally awash with pain. He could see nothing at first, however, for the lightning had—for the nonce—burned away his vision. But then he discovered that he *could* make out dim shapes cut out against a duller light.

Shapes that moved. He tried to move as well, and felt something shift, then meet resistance, mostly against his left arm. Stone grated against stone; dust trickled down.

Sweat—or blood—slicked his hand and he released whatever he held—it proved to be the shield—and only then did he truly puzzle out what had just occurred.

Tyrill had brought down the dome, which should by rights have smashed him. But he had still born the shield at the time, and had raised it without thinking, and the power it possessed—which was to take whatever force was directed against it and fling it away to the Overworld—had still been in effect, and had taken even the force of the falling dome onto itself. And since that act also stripped away matter from whatever struck the shield, it had effectively made a hole in that portion of dome above him. Which, with the sturdy stone pews against which he had lain, had saved his life and limb.

Giddy with surprise, he tried to rise to a crouch, aware at some level that people were yelling, screaming, and crying out, but that most of those cries came from beyond what was now an open-air cylinder, not an enclosed hall. Yet the instant he moved, he was reminded of the arrows that pierced his flesh. Perhaps the gems would cure him, perhaps not, but neither would occur while those shafts still burrowed deep in his muscle and bone.

He had to get out, *had* to, and so he began to work his way free.

Which was when he discovered the pain in his right little finger—with so much else to torment him, he had almost missed it. He blinked through sweat and dusty blood and through the eye holes of a helm that had shifted askew. But what he finally saw through the clouds of stone dust still swirling around him made his heart skip in his breast and all his blood run cold.

His finger had been severed. A fragment of the fallen dome had clipped it neatly at the joint that wore the nail, pounding it completely flat and leaving it hanging by a thread of skin.

He was still staring stupidly at it when Merryn and Lykkon found him.

Only when he saw their faces and felt their arms slide around him to help him to his feet did he relinquish the helm at last. Merryn took it away solemnly, urging him across the shattered stones to where waited an army of earnest, confused faces above the nondescript colors the clanless wore. He tried to smile, but staggered, then collapsed entirely, and was totally unaware of anything but pain as Merryn and Lykkon laid him facedown in the corridor outside the shattered Hall.

He heard something about getting the arrows out, and something about the likelihood of there being a lot of blood, and something else about keeping the regalia free of blood, just in case, but also of keeping it close to hand.

And then someone—one of those nameless men who had followed him, he thought—was gripping the arrow in his calf and—not pulling, but pushing: driving it onward through his leg. The pain was epic, yet he endured. The arrow in his shoulder had evidently fallen out, while the one that had nicked a rib still jogged and poked, held in place by his mail. His unknown healer made short work of that as well, and pronounced him likely to live.

"Live," Avall echoed groggily. "Oh Eight, Merry—Lyk—*Is* it over? That in there? Did it fix things, or will I have to—?"

He reeled again as blackness hovered near, and only then

discovered that his churgeon was tying a bandage around his leg.

That accomplished, he let Merryn and Lykkon lead him to a seat beside the greater chaos that was the Hall. Dimly he was aware of a noise a-building: a rising chant of joy. It took him a moment to realize that they were chanting his name: "Avall! Avall! Long live King Avall!"

"I didn't do anything," Avall mumbled, even as he tried to determine what to do next, since standing did not seem to be an option. These people needed a King, and he had no Kingliness left to give them.

Yet even as he sat there debating, the chant began to fragment, as a new phalanx of commoners pressed their way into the vestibule. Avall blinked at them stupidly, noting flashes of red among the duller hues. Red...Warcraft crimson...The colors of War-Hold and Clan Ferr.

Ferr...

All at once he recognized them: the stocky, bearded man on the left, the solidly built woman on the right. And the tall, handsome man in the middle.

"Tryffon," he gasped, trying to grin. "Veen. And Vorinn...!"

Vorinn...

Something jogged in his memory at that. He started to rise, to take their hands, but as he slapped his right hand against his thigh, the severed finger joint made its absence known with a preposterous pulse of pain. But with that pain came realization: something he should have recalled earlier.

The King of Eron had to be physically perfect! And he, Avall syn Argen-a, was perfect no longer!

In spite of the pain that throbbed up his wrist, he grinned—and was still grinning, as he rose shakily to his feet and extended that hand before him so that Vorinn and Tryffon and Veen could see before all others. And then he raised that hand on high, with blood still running down his palm to vanish up his sleeve.

"Long live High King *Vorinn*," he shouted.

Tryffon syn Ferr-een, called Kingmaker, gazed at him like a fool—and then a grin likewise split his face. "Long live High King Vorinn!" he yelled, even louder than Avall.

And then that name once more—from Veen, and almost as quickly, from Merryn and Lykkon.

And finally, like a return of the storms Tyrill had unleashed, the chant took fire within the assembled multitude and went rumbling around the Hall.

"Long live High King Vorinn. And blessed be Once-High-King Avall."

It was to alternating chants of "Vorinn" and "Avall" that Avall finally succumbed to shock, blood loss, and pain and lapsed from consciousness, there in an out-of-the-way corner of what had once been Eron's Hall of Clans.

The first thing he heard when he recovered was "Vorinn, Vorinn, Vorinn..."

CHAPTER XXXV:

RELIEF AND RESOLUTION

(ERON: TIR-ERON—NEAR-AUTUMN: DAY XVI—MIDDAY)

~~~~~~

If someone had told Avall a day—or an eight—or a quarter—
earlier that he would be no more than a passive observer during the fall of the Ninth Face—and probably Priest-Clan along
with it—he would have laughed in their face. Fate didn't work
in his life that way. Fate had taken a fancy to him on the day of
his conception and had, in retrospect, gifted—or cursed—him
with a life that seemed doomed never to be ordinary. Of course
he hadn't thought of it that way at the time. His talents with
metal had seemed perfectly normal to him, as had his facility at
design. He had been born shortly before the seminal moment
of modern Eronese history in the agency of the plague, and
had been blessed with two of the most accomplished smiths in
generations as teachers and advisers. But, again, he knew no
alternative. He'd had a twin sister, so he had never been lonely;
and for brotherhood he'd had Rann, who was better than most
people's brothers-by-birth. Finally—

Where to begin on finally?

With that preposterous chain of events that had culminated
in his assignment to Gem-Hold and all that had precipitated,
perhaps? Certainly, any other person confronted with any of

those variables would have acted differently. Yet he, a very good goldsmith by his own reckoning, had somehow, through an equally odd set of circumstances, found himself on the throne of Eron—at another seminal moment in its history: two of them, in fact—and had, beyond all hope, survived to see his side ascendant.

The side that he chose to believe truly was the side favored by The Eight.

And now, suddenly, Fate seemed to be casting him aside.

Nor did he object even slightly.

Still, he had to go through the motions of being King a little longer.

Which was why he was sitting on a makeshift throne that had been set up in the Court of Rites in anticipation of an execution that had been capriciously relocated at the last possible moment. And *that* had to be Fate, too; for nothing of what had happened in the Hall of Clans there at the last could have occurred anywhere but where it had happened.

Even this seat had been Fated, he supposed: set up so that he could witness that in which he could not participate.

And curse his wounds for that, too; because the last thing he needed to be doing when more things needed to be done quickly and well in Tir-Eron than had ever been done before was sitting.

The victory was still imperiled, after all, maintained as it was by a few loyal and more-than-competent friends and an army of clanless folk, who had not existed as an army half a day gone by—some of whom had not even held swords that far back.

But they were at it now: enforcing his will, though it was Vorinn they—rightly—idolized, not him.

Vorinn, they liked because there was nothing *not* to like. Avall, they not so much liked as feared.

All because of the regalia. More precisely, all because of the Lightning Sword. Of course it was gone now: buried beneath the rubble of Sarnon's dome, and probably smashed past repair in the process. But that fact seemed of minor consequence to those who had seen what it could do, besides which, he still had the helm and the shield, one at his feet, one at his right hand.

For that matter, he still had a sword that could reasonably well pass for the Lightning Sword to those few who had not seen the two together. Why, it was even set with gems, though Zeff had put them there, not Avall himself, and that made all the difference. That sword was like him, he reckoned: basically well made but now tragically flawed past more than occasional—and risky—using.

So Avall simply remained where he was, wearing the first crown anyone could find in the Citadel, and robed in a reasonable simulacrum of the Cloak of Colors, watching folk scurry around the Court of Rites securing a Kingdom that was still, until Sundeath, legally his to rule.

He could wait that long, he supposed, but no longer. And then—

Better not to think about that now! He was still King and this was his Kingdom, and while he could not do much of anything until the wounds in his thigh and back healed—which he knew they would, and preternaturally rapidly—he could still oversee the swift and proper execution of his orders.

Actually they were mostly Vorinn's orders now—Vorinn, who had once again arrived expecting a fight and hadn't got one, and was even now overseeing what were still occasional, but very real battles, as Priest-Clan's secondary officers and chiefs mounted sporadic, if futile, resistance.

Vorinn's advice had been simple. A quarter of their combined forces had been dispatched to Priest-Hold to deny anyone entrance or exit until that person's loyalty could be confirmed. A quarter remained here at the Citadel, with one third of that number constituting a personal guard for Avall; another third, under Merryn, searching the Hall of Clans for residual rebels; and the remainder, under Tryffon himself, searching the Citadel for the same.

As for the rest of the clanless army: They had been dispatched down the Ri-Eron, to search each hold and hall as they came to it and depose any rebels they discovered, while summoning any clansmen with pretensions of being Chief to audience with Avall.

He wished he had the Sword of Air to ensure the truth of the oaths some of them were already swearing, but that was back at Ninth Hold. In the interim, he found that even the rumor (or threat, more often) of intervention from the Lightning Sword was generally more than sufficient to turn the tide of self-preservation in loyalty's direction.

He missed Rann, though—and Strynn, and the rest. But there was no going back to either of them—not yet.

And so, he sat, waited, hurt a very great deal, and bled less and less frequently from his wounds, while he drank more wine than was good for him, ate everything in sight, and tried to look Kingly while not moving his right hand more than required.

That had to be Fate, too: making the decision for him he still, in his heart, wasn't certain he could have made.

And so time passed, and finally those he had dispatched on various errands began to return with their reports.

Merryn was first to arrive. Breathless and dusty, yet obviously very pleased with herself, she came striding out of the Hall of Clans with a bounce in her step, a grin on her face, and two dozen Ninth Face archers and half that many Priests neatly chained together behind her, the whole under close escort by her clanless militia. A final word to the fellow she had appointed as her second, and she dashed up the steps to stand before Avall. Her cloak belled out behind her, and it took him a moment to realize that it was not the one she had worn earlier, but one of Warcraft crimson.

"There's a dead Priest back there in the Hall who claimed to be War's Craft-Chief," she announced airily. "He managed to escape from the Hall about the time the first arrow hit you—opportunistic little bastard, I must say. I, uh, convinced him to tell me where the rest of War-Hold's elite had got off to, and he said that those who hadn't died when the hold was torched had gone to rally Vorinn's brother in North Gorge—though he wasn't supposed to know that. They should be about two days march north of here—which means they can be here tomorrow night if we give them good reason. If you've got a spare herald and a spare horse, I'd suggest you make contacting them your first priority, since your army can't get here in less than two eights.

"That was one reason they hurried Tyrill's execution," Merryn continued. "She was the last person with any real power in the gorge that they could actually lay hands on. I think their initial intention was to treat her much as the Ninth Face treated some of their hostages—cut off a bit at a time—except that it wouldn't have worked in her case."

Avall scowled. "And you think you can trust this man? It sounds like he was trying to play both sides."

Merryn nodded. "He was. But I also think he was trying his best to look out for the clan with which he had been entrusted. He'd been Hold-Priest at War before the coup, and knew a lot of people there. He...wasn't happy with things as they were. In fact, I suspect the Ninth Face would soon have branded *him* a traitor."

"But you killed him?"

Merryn shook her head. "He asked for my knife and killed himself. That's why I think he was telling the truth. He knew—or thought he did—that he was a dead man regardless. His last words were 'people trusted me, and I've destroyed that trust, and I can't live without being trusted.'"

Avall gnawed his lips. "Not a bad way to die. Now, what about the Citadel?"

"I'm on my way there as soon as I finish here." She indicated the prisoners with her sword. "I thought we'd house these folks in the dungeons beneath the Court, since they're likely to be the highest-placed folks around, which means they're the biggest threat. Once things settle down I'd suggest they be put to work searching for bodies in the Hall. That way they'll be able to see the price of treason up close and stinking before they have their own trials."

Avall nodded sagely. "Well thought out, as I would expect. I'll trust you with it. Leave as many guards in the dungeons as you think you need, then divide the rest between Tryffon and Vorinn, unless some of them want to take a rest and let some of these folks who are guarding me take their place."

Merryn sketched a minimal salute and bounded away. Avall followed her with his eyes toward the slot in the Court where the stairs to the dungeons exited. She started down, then halted in place as she met two people coming up—slowly. One person Avall recognized instantly, one he did not. "Lyk," he said to no one. "And—"

Merryn and Lykkon spoke briefly, then two of the soldiers split off to support the figure with Lykkon.

But only when they were a dozen steps from the throne did Avall recognize that other man.

"Ilfon!" he cried. "Hail to you, Lord Chief of Lore!"

Ilfon smiled wanly, but looked pained and a little dazed as he let the two men help him to a seat two steps below Avall's makeshift throne. "Majesty," he began, "I fear I cannot properly stand and therefore cannot properly bow, but I greet you as well as I can, and thank you for the timeliness of your arrival."

"They hamstrung him!" Lykkon broke in furiously. "They were going to kill him at noon!"

"He's free now," Avall replied. "And I'm more grateful than I can say, though what good two cripples can do the Kingdom, I have no idea."

"Yours will heal," Lykkon grumbled. "His won't. And *I* have a score to settle on that account—when the time comes."

"When the time comes," Ilfon echoed. "And when the Law allows. For now—"

"Sit with me, if you will," Avall told him. "I know you must be eager to resume your duties and reclaim your hold, but I'm not sure that will be possible in the next little while. In the meantime, tell me what you will of what has transpired here— or rest; whichever pleases you."

"Both," Ilfon sighed. "But what would sweeten the telling of what is mostly a grim, sour tale would be a mug of wine— and perhaps a little imphor, to dull the pain..."

Avall refilled his goblet and passed it down to Ilfon with his own hand, while a self-appointed page bustled off to find another vessel. "I know where is some imphor," the man who had churgeoned him earlier, and who was still lurking solicitously nearby, offered.

"Get it," Avall commanded. "And see if you can locate a sedan chair, for later."

"My pleasure, Majesty," the man murmured, and departed at a run.

Half a hand passed, which Avall spent listening to Ilfon recount the events that had led to his capture. As the older man spoke, Avall was filled with a new appreciation of Tyrill. All his life he had thought of her simply as a hard old woman, given to arrogant rages and ruling her Hold with a tyranny that was all but legend—but which had also produced the best smiths since Eron was founded. Yet he had always taken her loyalty for granted—until he had actually seen it in action, first in the remaking of the shield that lay against his throne, and now, via Ilfon's report, in her final days as an underground assassin. It had also been she who had secured and coordinated the few messengers who had managed to get out, not only to the King, but also to the Chiefs of the other gorges. If anyone was responsible for the army now marching from North Gorge under Vorinn's brother, it was she.

"We will have to recover her body if we recover no others," Avall said flatly. "And frankly, I'm thinking we should leave the Hall exactly as it is: in ruins, as a reminder and a memorial. But I want Tyrill exhumed. I want to give her a proper burial."

"And you have to recover the Lightning Sword," Ilfon added with a smile. "No, don't worry. But it's true; otherwise, it's going to be too much temptation, and half a span of mortared stone above it won't deter anyone who's really power-hungry."

Avall frowned in agreement. "I know. And I hate it, and that's all going to be to do again. I—" He broke off, for Vorinn was approaching—on horseback, through the ruins of the Citadel's gates. (And fixing *those* would keep Smithcraft busy for a while, he reckoned—once they finished supplying enough chains to confine an entire clan.)

Vorinn rode to the foot of the wall around the seats, then dismounted easily. Like Merryn, he had found a cloak in his clan colors. Avall wondered if the story of its acquisition was as portentous as his sister's had been.

"Majesty," Vorinn began, after a bow even sketchier than Merryn's. "I am pleased to report that all halls and holds on North Bank as far as Stone are secure—which, I'm sure *you* will be pleased to know, includes Smith-Hold-Main and Argen-Hall-Prime. I am also—'honored' would be a more appropriate word than 'pleased'—to report that we have found Tyrill's body, and with it, the Lightning Sword, the latter of which I have with me now."

And with that, he reached to his scabbard and withdrew, indeed, that already-fabled weapon and extended it, hilt-first, to Avall.

Avall took it because he had to, but felt a keen reluctance to touch it.

"Where...?" he demanded, to distract himself.

"In her rooms in Argen-Hall," Vorinn replied. "In her own bed, as a matter of fact—with her bonds still on her and the sword still in her hands."

Avall felt his heart double thump, and found himself utterly at a loss for anything to say.

"I felt exactly the same way," Vorinn confided with a grim smile. "But I've had the whole ride here to compose myself—and to try to figure out what happened, and only one thing makes sense."

"That she got her final wish," Avall finished for him, nodding in realization. "She knew she was dying—from the arrow, if not from the dome—and like anyone would, she wanted to escape, and naturally the image in her head—the thing she wanted most—was to be in the place where she had always felt most secure. And I guess a dying wish is pretty powerful, because the sword jumped her there before the dome could—"

He broke off, unable to complete the sentence because the images that rode with the words were far too terrible.

"Just in time for her to arrange herself on her back, in her own bed, with the sword lying along her length and both hands gripping the hilt."

"I hope you remember it well, Vorinn," Avall whispered, "because that's the image I want to grace her tomb."

"It will be done as you have requested, never fear," Vorinn acknowledged. "When I am King."

"When you are King," Avall echoed. "And let me say again: *that* phrase has a marvelous sweet sound indeed."

Epilogue:
Dreams

~~~~~~~~

"Peace," Rann said softly. "It's one of those things you never appreciate until you don't have it, and then it becomes the most precious thing in the world, because without it there isn't time for any of the other important things in life."

"Like enjoying times like this," Avall murmured in reply. He leaned back in his rough-carved granite chair and allowed himself in a long, slow swallow from the cup of walnut liquor that was one of his true indulgences. And one he would miss...eventually. Which meant he should not take it for granted now—which prompted another lengthy draught.

Rann did not reply, comfortable as he was in the twilight that was weaving shadows across the water garden secreted atop the former Ninth Face citadel. A few stars glittered bravely in the purple sky behind them, but the sky Avall and his bond-brother faced was the fire-clouded sky of the west. The sun was sinking there, above the Spine, and the rays were painting the whole landscape ruddy gold. The pool a span from their feet looked like an ingot of molten metal. They had swum there earlier, while the air was still warm enough to allow such things. And though the water was warmed by the same hot springs that heated the hold, the autumn wind was too chill to permit lingering once the sun went down. Already night breezes were stirring the fur-trimmed robes Avall and Rann had donned at the end of that most practical of pleasures. Merryn had watched them silently—but she was often silent these days.

"—Like enjoying making," Rann continued eventually. "Like enjoying...love. Neither of those things ought ever to be hurried."

Merryn rose listlessly from where she had curled in a nest of cushions to the right. She paced the narrow pavement before Rann's and Avall's seats, then stopped, gazing east. "Peace," she mused. "It's hard to believe that what we've got right now doesn't extend everywhere. But it doesn't, not in Tir-Eron."

"Not like we have it here," Avall agreed. "But it's coming there too, merely at a slower pace. Yet every day something is better there than it was. One more stone is laid in the restoration of a building. One more person—one more *good* person— is confirmed in the Chieftainship of a clan. Someone who's been thought dead is found alive, or someone who's been missing is confirmed dead, and even that starts their survivors healing. It will be slow, but it will happen."

"And faster, once the Royal Army gets there, which should be any minute now."

Avall snorted amiably. "That used to be my army. And I don't miss it."

"It's still your army," Merryn retorted. "Until Sundeath."

"Until Sundeath," Avall conceded. "And that is going to be passing strange, let me tell you: to crown someone else King without rancor or remorse."

"It won't be the last strange thing you do in your life," Rann chuckled, helping himself to a drink of his own. "In fact, if I guess correctly, the strange things in your life are only beginning."

"*Our* life," Avall corrected. "Or so I assume." A troubled pause. "You are still coming, aren't you?"

Rann nodded. "West? Of course. The only question is whether I go now or in the spring. I've a few things I need to tie up here."

"Div may *come* here and tie you up and drag you back," Avall countered.

Rann regarded him seriously. "Do you really think we can do it? Build a new hold in the ring lake without the rest of the Kingdom knowing? Run our lives by our rules, without reference to useless rite and ritual?"

"We can if we're careful," Avall assured him. "If we choose the right people. We have a solid core now, but there will have to be others. There will have to be children, and Div can't give you any. And Myx and Riff and Bingg and Lykkon: All of them deserve mates, and they certainly won't get them in the Wild. Sure, the first two are betrothed, but that doesn't mean their consorts will follow them, their vows to that effect notwithstanding—or that we can trust those women not to reveal our secret, for that matter, which means we might ultimately lose two very good prospects. As for Lyk and Bingg: They deserve better than someone they've courted in haste."

"No one will have to stay," Rann reminded him. "That's what you said."

"Not unless they want to, and we'll have to make certain they do. And we'll... we'll have to stress that living there is not only an adventure but a privilege and a responsibility. Did I tell you that Mother may want to come?"

Rann raised a brow.

Avall smirked. "Actually, I think it's because we plan to take Averryn, and she doesn't want to be parted from him."

"At least she can get all the solitude she wants," Merryn snorted. "Not that I'm complaining, mind you. And, to be honest, there's very little remaining here for her."

Avall shifted in his seat. "There's another one who might want to go, though I'm not certain we dare take him."

"And who might that be?" Rann drawled after another lengthy draught.

"Ahfinn. And before you both come down on me, let me remind you that the man is an excellent administrator. More to the point, he knows more about the gems than anyone else who isn't one of us, so I'd be happier if he was where we could watch him."

"What about his trial?" Merryn demanded.

"We could give him a choice of death or exile—but that exile wouldn't be alone, and would have a very specific destination."

"Like a certain lake?"

"I'd *rather* have him where we can watch him," Avall repeated.

"*I'd* rather have him dead," Merryn snapped.

"At some point one needs to replace justice with mercy," Avall replied. "Besides, he may choose death anyway."

Rann stared at his goblet, which seemed to be absorbing the dying light. "The question is: Do we dare trust him around the regalia? Might we not be raising up another Zeff?"

"We won't *have* the regalia—nor the gems, except one to use for jumping."

Merryn froze in place and looked at him sharply. "You've decided, then?"

Avall nodded. "Vorinn and I talked about it all night before I jumped back here, and believe it or not, he agrees with me. We have to take all the gems and everything that bears one, regardless of who made it and when, away from Eron. Away from temptation, I should say. He thinks the threat of them will be enough to forestall further rebellion."

"So we're hiding them again?"

"You are—if you're willing. And a generation from now, they'll be legends—to most of the world."

"So shall we be," Rann sighed. "I wonder what that will be like?"

"Whatever it is," Avall replied with conviction, rising to face the glorious sky to the west, "it's bound to be exciting."

ABOUT THE AUTHOR

Tom Deitz grew up in Young Harris, Georgia, a tiny college town in the north Georgia mountains that—by heritage or landscape—have inspired the setting for the majority of his novels. He holds BA and MA degrees in English from the University of Georgia, where he also worked as a library assistant in the Hargrett Rare Books and Manuscript Library until quitting in 1988 to become a full-time writer. His interest in medieval literature, castles, and Celtic art led him to co-found the Athens, Georgia, chapter of the Society for Creative Anachronism, of which he is still a member. A fair-to-middlin' artist, Tom is also a frustrated architect and an automobile enthusiast (he has two non-running '62 Lincolns, every *Road & Track* since 1959 but two, and over 900 unbuilt model cars). He also hunts every now and then, dabbles in theater at the local junior college, and plays *toli* (a Southeastern Indian game related to lacrosse) when his pain threshold is especially high.

After twenty-five years in Athens, he has recently moved back to his hometown, the wisdom of which move remains to be seen. *Warautumn* is his nineteenth novel.